Aislinn's Shadow

The Kin Chronicles
Book One

A novel by:

Samantha Marshall

STARDUST
EMPIRE
PUBLISHING

Love a Free Book?

Learn to let go… or burn.

Dating Noah Acheson has always been gentle, predictable and above all, safe – but when Noah breaks the rules of their carefully crafted relationship, Deanna cuts him off, retreating to her private sanctuary deep in the Australian bush.

Stinging from Deanna's rejection, Noah returns from a brief stint fighting fires in New South Wales to face an infinitely more vicious fire front in Victoria. Though his broken heart still very much belongs to Deanna Schellponte, he's determined not to chase her – until the wind changes, turning the fires towards pack land, and Deanna is reported missing.

With fire raging all around, Noah races into the bush to find the woman he loves. To survive, Deanna and Noah must confront not only the fury of Mother Nature… but the ghost whose memory tore them apart.

Get your FREE copy here:

https://sliceofsammy.com/contact

Acknowledgements

For all those fighting their inner demons – be brave, we are with you. Together we are strong.

One

Driving out to the country was like entering another world. Aislinn Redding yawned and rubbed sleep out of her eyes as the car pulled to a stop beneath a stand of tall candlebarks. When she'd left the airport, her windows had been filled with the familiar hustle and bustle of the city but she'd been so exhausted from her long flight that sleep had claimed her immediately. Now, Aislinn shivered as she looked out at the dense bushland. She'd been only fourteen when her parents had moved with her to Ireland for her father's work. Twelve years later, the land she had cried for every night seemed completely alien.

The car door opened and she jumped at the sound. Footsteps crunched along the bare earth as the driver circled around to the back and Aislinn took advantage of the delay to calm her jangling nerves. When the door opened, she schooled her face into a polite smile.

"We're here," the driver announced, his face pulled into a welcoming grin.

"Thanks, Freddie." Aislinn undid her seatbelt and slid out of the car. Gone was the smog and the honking of impatient horns, replaced instead by a breeze laden with the scent of wattle and the carolling of magpies. Aislinn tipped her head back, squinting against the summer sun - hot, even here under cover of the trees - and drew a deep, steadying breath.

Freddie gave her a friendly clap on the shoulder. "Good to be home, hey?"

"It's been a long time." Aislinn forced another smile and turned to face the good natured driver. "The bush is a far cry from the windswept coasts of Ireland."

"I'll bet," Freddie chuckled. "Look, I know you're not in tip top shape at the minute but I can't take the car any further." He gestured over his shoulder at the impenetrable bush. "It's the rules."

"Don't worry; I know the way." At least, she hoped she did. Twelve years was a long time to try and remember a secret pathway through the bush.

Freddie popped the boot and started to haul out her luggage. Aislinn winced at the thought of carrying everything but her only other choice was to leave some of it behind - not an option when what little remained of her life was zipped up inside.

"Well, that's everything. I'd help you carry it if I could, but… human." Freddie thumped himself in the chest and grinned. "Pack land is way above my pay grade."

"It's fine, really." Aislinn returned his smile with a proper one of her own. "Thanks for the lift. It was good to see you again."

"You too. Good luck, Ash."

"Thanks." She shook Freddie's hand, then stood watching as he got into the car and drove back the way he'd come.

Alone at last, Aislinn eyed her designer luggage with apprehension. An overnight bag, two small suitcases and one larger case on wheels wouldn't normally provide a challenge but her injuries were still fresh and aching. She might heal fast but her father had sent her home faster. Safety had been the official line but she'd overheard his conversation with her mother. Compromised, he'd called her. And let's not forget that the Kin High Council had 'temporarily suspended' her contract of service until she could be proven healthy again - something the doctors had warned may never happen.

Tears blurred Aislinn's vision and she swiped them angrily away. She'd put her life on the line for her people and *this* was how they repaid her? Damn them all! Aislinn ground her teeth, pulling on her rage, using it to give her strength and resolve. She was *not* giving in, no matter what her father or the rest of the Kin High Council thought. Ignoring the pain in her chest, Aislinn swung the overnight bag over her shoulder, hooked one wrist through the pop out handle on the wheeled luggage and grabbed a suitcase in each hand. She was going home. She'd rebuild her life and prove to her family - and the Council - that she wasn't a liability to anyone.

Aislinn marched towards the bush, looking for the place that would mark the beginning of the trail. Moments later she found it; an old hollowed tree stump that had been burnt in a fire and scoured clean by years of wind and rain. Spindly undergrowth tugged on her luggage and for a moment Aislinn worried she'd leave a trail but the hardy plants swung back into place without as much as a bent leaf. Bolstered by the silent support of the bush, Aislinn tightened her grip on her bags and set off. Sometimes she saw a marker she remembered but for the most part she walked blindly, trusting her instincts to lead her on. After almost an hour's trekking she emerged into a sun-gilt clearing bordered by the rotten remains of an ancient wooden fence. Wildflowers dotted patchy tussocks of grass and in the centre of the space stood an old, burnt-out cottage. Aislinn grinned at the black and empty windows peering mournfully back at her. She'd made it.

The air was cooler here, with the tall trees reaching up to almost block the sun completely. Aislinn's body trembled with exhaustion and her skin was sheened with sweat, stinging against the many tiny scratches the bush had left on her face and hands. None of it mattered though, for an older woman had emerged from within the burnt cottage, her arms spread wide in welcome. Aislinn dropped her luggage and raced across the clearing to enfold her grandmother in a hug.

"Aislinn, sweet heart. Welcome." Twelve years had not changed Grandma Redding. Her blue eyes sparkled with life and greying red hair tumbled freely about her face. She wore a navy blue tank top over faded jeans and boots and her skin was tanned brown by many years spent in the sun.

"Oh Grandma, it's been so long!" Aislinn buried her face in her grandmother's hair to hide sudden tears. Grandma's scent rose all around her, familiar and comforting. Home. She was *home*.

"I only spoke to you on the phone last week, Aislinn," her grandmother laughed, pulling away to hold her at arm's length. "I think I'm getting better at those video calls, too."

"You are but it's still not the same as seeing you in person," Aislinn argued, a wide smile splitting her face.

"Indeed it isn't," Grandma smiled. "Now, let's get you home where you can rest, shall we? I'll call the boys to carry your luggage."

Before Aislinn could protest, Grandma Redding let out a loud whistle. Moments later a group of five men came rushing out of the burnt shack, their eyes alight with battle fever. When they saw Aislinn, they stopped, their mouths agape.

"Den Mother, what are you doing sneaking out of the cabin without us?" One man recovered quickly enough to step forward, his face familiar and yet grown enough that Aislinn struggled to place him. She swept his body with a quick, assessing gaze. 'Boys,' Grandma had said, but this specimen was most certainly full grown.

"I didn't sneak anywhere," Grandma snapped, thwacking the man on the bicep. "I am Den Mother and I go as I please. If *you* weren't paying attention when I left, that's not my problem, is it? Now where are your manners? Surely you remember Aislinn."

The man stepped closer, eyes narrowing as he reached Grandma's side. Aislinn searched his face, trying to put a name to this man whom she had obviously known as a boy. She looked beyond him to his companions but their faces were lost in shadow, no help to her memory at all. Unlike her Grandmother, the pack she'd left behind didn't have the security clearance - or the will - to speak with her via phone or internet during her time in Ireland, meaning that once familiar faces had evolved into total strangers.

The man before Aislinn had thick, golden-brown hair tumbling around his ears in a careless wave that spoke of more important things to do than look for a hairbrush. He was taller than she, about six three, with the sort of well-muscled frame earnt from a physical lifestyle. Jeans faded from use - ripped across one knee, no less - and an equally battered red t-shirt two sizes too small completed his look. Familiar… and yet not. Aislinn looked up just in time to see his nostrils curl.

"Something's wrong. She smells wrong." The man growled low in his throat, both hands clenching into fists. He took a half step in front of Grandma, his stance aggressive enough that Aislinn fell back a pace, adrenaline surging. It was then she looked into his eyes and knew him.

"Tobias Greenwood, you step back this instant!" Grandma Redding grabbed one muscular arm and dragged him aside.

"*Tobias?*" Aislinn whispered. The man before her looked nothing like the weedy young boy she'd been close to as a child - but there was no mistaking those eyes. Steely blue around the edges with golden starburst centres, they had haunted her dreams for many long years.

"I tell you, that can't be Ash. The scent is off," Tobias insisted, his voice still contorted by the low, rumbling growl in his chest.

"Aislinn is wounded and you haven't seen her for over a decade," Grandma Redding snapped. "Of course she'll smell different to you."

Tobias shook the older woman off and stalked up to Aislinn until he towered over her. She stood trembling, thrown by the strange behaviour of the man who'd once been a gentle, fun-loving boy. He bent down close and sniffed her hair, his proximity sending a tingle across her flesh and filling her nostrils with the smooth scent of butterscotch and cream. Aislinn's breath caught. It really *was* Tobias - she'd know that scent anywhere, even after all this time. She raised her eyes to his face, noting full cheekbones, sun bleached brows and a smooth, strong jaw. He may have been a weedy boy, but Tobias Greenwood had grown into one hell of a man.

And then he opened his mouth. "You say you're Aislinn Redding? Prove it."

"Tobias!" Grandma snapped.

"No, Grandma." Aislinn held up a placating hand. "It's okay. I know I smell different."

Tobias frowned, clearly surprised by her admission but Aislinn refused to be fazed. What was the use in denying it? She'd already been told her scent was polluted when the Kin doctors had examined her. There'd been pity in their eyes and voices as they'd explained what had happened and the ramifications of her new situation.

Compromised, her father's heartbroken voice mocked her.

Aislinn lifted her chin. "I'll provide whatever proof you need."

Tobias inspected her face for a long moment, his body close enough that a deep breath would have connected them. After a tense silence, he gestured at the men on the decking and they walked down to join him. Each one spread out until they flanked Tobias – with Grandma Redding behind them.

"I don't need your protection," Grandma growled, shoving through the line of men.

"Your protection is my job," Tobias answered, his tone implacable. Grandma merely sauntered past him until she stood beside Aislinn.

Her silent support – and Tobias' obvious disapproval – bolstered Aislinn's courage. "Let's get on with this," she snapped.

"Identify these men." Tobias gestured at the four men behind him. "If you're really Aislinn Redding, you'll know who they are."

A scent test? Aislinn choked back a laugh. If she really *was* an imposter, there were a dozen ways someone with her skills could fool her way through - but there was no sense pointing that out to Tobias and making him more suspicious than he already was. Instead, she simply glared at him and moved towards the group of men. He'd certainly changed, that sweet boy she'd left behind; but so had she. Whilst Aislinn had no desire to provoke a fight with her mind and body fractured, if Tobias thought she was going to be a pushover he was in for a nasty surprise.

The first man was tall, taller than Tobias, leanly built and watching her from a pair of sapphire blue eyes. His blonde hair was a mess of curls that hung almost to his shoulders and twelve years hadn't changed the rogue's grin he gave Aislinn when she stepped close enough to scent the sea breeze and limestone which clung to him like a second skin. "Zeke," she whispered, laying a hand on his chest.

"His full name," Tobias snapped. Aislinn narrowed her eyes a moment, refusing to look around.

"Ezekiel Smythe," she replied. Zeke said nothing but his eyes glimmered with approval as she stepped on to the next man.

Short and stocky, he had close-cropped black hair and muscles on his muscles. Green eyes narrowed as she stepped close and unlike Zeke, he stiffened when Aislinn leant close enough to inhale the smoke and pine scent of him. "You do smell funny," he murmured, his brow furrowed.

"So do you," she snapped, straightening. He blinked, the only indication of surprise. Aislinn flicked a glance at Tobias over her shoulder. "Jaxon Heliope-Flint."

She moved left again and came to a man who was her own height. His body had been shaped by life on the land but he wasn't overly muscular like Jaxon. His hair was a curious mix of mouse-brown and sandy blonde, cropped short and spiked out in all directions, and he smelt of almonds and sage. Deep brown eyes regarded her without welcome – but also without suspicion.

"Name," Tobias demanded.

"Are you going to be this rude all the time?" Aislinn whirled to face him, gritting her teeth against the curses bubbling in her throat.

"Name," Tobias repeated but his aggressive tone softened slightly.

"Rory Deepwater." She glanced at Rory and gave him a smile. The corner of his lip twitched in return.

Aislinn moved on to the last man, knowing his name before she even set eyes on him. Tobias had brought all their old friends. As children they'd roamed together, getting into all sorts of mischief every hour of the day and night. She'd once known all five of her boys as well as she'd known herself.

"Hello, Ash."

"Hello Dom." She looked into his face, struck anew by how classically handsome he was. As a boy he'd shown promise – full grown he was a pin-up for everything male. Tall but not too tall, cloaked in the scent of eucalyptus and rain. Perfectly tousled black hair, chiselled features and a sculpted figure, accented by strikingly pale blue eyes. He'd been gentle and kind in their youth and the laugh lines at the corners of his eyes showed that he'd retained that quality as an adult.

"He's watching you," Dominic whispered, his words no more than a breath, just enough for Aislinn alone to hear. "He missed you - we all did. My, how you've grown."

****

Tobias watched Aislinn lean into Dominic's chest, her head bowed so that he couldn't see her face. Dominic's lips moved but he was too far away to hear what was said. Tobias grunted, his hands clenching into fists as his gaze roved over Aislinn's body.

He had not been prepared. His memory had kept her safe, the lanky, laughing girl who'd tanned brown in the sun and incited him to all sorts of mischief – but that was not the person who stood before him now. She hadn't really grown any taller but she'd attained the full figure of a woman; slender and curved with swaying hips and heaving breasts that begged his attention. Her chocolate hair was tinted wine-red in the sun and blue-green eyes shone out of a face that was more beautiful than even his imagination had dared to dream. Aislinn had left the land a tomboy and returned a goddess.

She stepped closer to Dominic, her body melting into his as they embraced. Italian jeans hugged her legs and her black leather boots, whilst sturdy and practical, were also of expensive make. She wore a loose-knit long sleeve jumper in khaki that only served to augment the

7

depth of colour in her hair and Tobias wondered if it, too, carried a designer label. Whatever she did in Ireland, it clearly paid well - and no, he did not feel suddenly uncomfortable in his favourite old jeans and that t-shirt he probably should have thrown out years ago.

Dominic smoothed a broad hand over Aislinn's shoulders, continuing to whisper in her ear and eliciting a throaty laugh in response. Tobias bit down on a possessive growl. Mother Moon, she'd been here five minutes and he was already losing his mind.

"Do you believe now?" Grandma Redding whispered.

Tobias jumped. He'd been so caught up in the wonder of Aislinn Redding that he'd forgotten the older woman was even there - fool, fool, fool. He rolled his shoulders in what he hoped was a casual shrug. "I suppose I do. She still smells wrong."

"I know and it was unwise of you to mention it. She's been through more than you realise and my word should've been enough. I'm disappointed in you."

The words stung and Tobias felt the burn of shame in his cheeks. He'd known Ash was injured – he'd spoken to her father himself to arrange her homecoming. But she didn't smell of injuries, at least, not entirely. She smelled of… something else. He shook his head.

"Name," Tobias said, more to buy time than anything else. Aislinn knew who Dominic was and they both knew it. She turned her head, not quite relinquishing her physical contact with the handsome man in front of her. When her eyes met his, they were filled with the sort of challenge that set Tobias' more feral qualities howling in response.

"Dominic Schellponte," Aislinn answered, her voice husky. It had never sounded like *that* before, when she'd roamed with them as adolescents. Tobias rolled his shoulders again. It hadn't even sounded like that in his dreams. Oh yes, she was dangerous.

"Very well. You are indeed Aislinn Redding," he conceded. Grandma elbowed him in the ribs and Tobias coughed. "Welcome home."

Aislinn's answering smile was as heavily laden with sarcasm as her voice. "Gee, thanks, Tobias. It's great to see you, too."

Hah! He'd believed them close, once - closer than siblings - but the fact remained she'd been gone for twelve years and he'd heard not a thing from her, no phone calls or emails or even an old fashioned letter.

Tobias ground his teeth. He knew nothing about her now and he'd best remember that.

Grandma Redding clicked her tongue between her teeth and motioned to Aislinn's bags, still lying where she'd dropped them. "All right boys, let's collect Ash's things and go home."

Tobias narrowed his eyes as Dominic pressed a gentle kiss to Aislinn's temple before he moved off to do the Den Mother's bidding. She giggled and swatted at the other in response, sunlight rippling across the luscious waves of her hair and thumping him straight in the memory-heart.

"Jealous, Tobias?" Grandma mocked, her voice low.

"No," he grit out. The breeze changed direction, blowing Aislinn's scent straight to him - a scent that was hers and yet overlaid with something else. Tobias stiffened as at last he understood.

Grandma caught his arm in a vice grip. "Don't."

"Mother Moon, she's Marked," Tobias' breath came out in a rush, the shock so great he was unable to muster more than a whisper. Just as well, because if the other men had heard there would've been a massive uproar.

"Yes," Grandma's face was sad. "She is."

"We can't take her back! She's mated to another Kin." Tobias stepped away, his hands shaking. It was the way of all Kin to place their Marks upon their chosen mates – a Marking which altered their scent to display allegiance to a new pack. Marked. Aislinn, *his* Aislinn, belonged to another, and he to her. Tobias stared, tracing those curves and failing, again, to match them to the girl who laughed in his memory. No, he thought. Not his Aislinn at all - she was different, from the tips of those incredibly long eyelashes to the heels of her black leather boots. A stranger.

"Tobias." Grandma stepped in front of him, her face stern. "You will *not* speak of this. Aislinn has been through a very trying time and we're here to look after her. Your responsibility as an Alpha is to protect her, as is mine as a Den Mother."

Tobias shook his head. That was ridiculous - it went against everything his culture dictated. Aislinn was no longer a member of the Redding pack - she was mated to someone else and not only was her protection the absolute opposite of his responsibility, it was an affront to whoever she'd mated for him to even attempt it. In fact… "Who is it?" He ground out.

Now it was Grandma's turn to shake her head. "That story is Aislinn's to tell, not mine. Only a handful of people know."

"Her father and mother?"

"Yes, and myself. The doctors too but they're paid to keep quiet."

Tobias frowned. "Paid?"

"Enough. You *will* do this, Tobias. You may be Alpha whilst Andre is in Ireland, but I am your Den Mother. My word is law. Now take Aislinn home and protect her." Grandma's tone brooked no argument and her eyes flashed.

"Protect her from who, exactly?" He demanded. "Why does she need protecting in the first place?"

"That's classified - unless Ash wants to tell you herself, of course," Grandma added.

Tobias blinked at that. "*Classified*? What exactly does Aislinn *do* over in Ireland?"

Grandma raised an eyebrow, her face set in the hard lines of a woman used to having her orders obeyed without question. "Don't you think that's a question you should have asked the better part of ten years ago? Communication goes both ways, young man - and the answer, by the way, is also classified."

"Classified," Tobias repeated again, running one hand through his tangled hair. "Who is she, Joanne? Really?"

"Different than what you expected, but no less Aislinn than the girl who left." Grandma's voice was gentle but the reprimand was clear.

"Easy for you to say," Tobias growled. "You may be Den Mother but that doesn't mean I have to share your opinion. I'll take care of Aislinn, don't you worry about that - but she doesn't belong here." He turned on his heel and flinched.

Aislinn stood right behind him, her face crumpled with grief. She couldn't have been there more than a moment or he would've smelled her alien scent, but she'd clearly heard enough. Instinct had him raising a hand to comfort her, to apologise - then Tobias caught the glimmer of gold at her throat. A torc, sparkling with the touch of diamonds, custom-made to shift with the wearer when they changed forms.

Probably a gift from her mate, he thought. And as the new, improved, completely not-at-all his Aislinn stared up at him with tears glittering in her blue-green eyes, Tobias growled low in his throat and stalked off.

Two

"She doesn't belong here." Aislinn tossed and turned in her bed, unable to sleep. Tobias' words echoed over and over inside her mind, churning in her gut until she wondered if she might vomit. When he'd turned to face her, his expression had wrinkled in disgust. He *knew*. He'd worked out that she'd been Marked.

Aislinn sat up, rubbing at her aching head, and looked towards the drawn curtains. The faintest hint of stars were visible around the edges but a few magpies were carolling, so dawn had to be close. She was about to swing herself out of bed when a knock sounded at the door. "Yes?"

"It's Grandma."

Of course it was. Who else had she been expecting?

"Come in," she managed, shaking her head in an effort to clear the cobwebs.

The door opened and Grandma entered, carrying a laden tray. She took in Aislinn's huddled form and set the tray on the dresser, her face creased with concern. "Ash, sweetheart, are you all right?"

"No," she whispered, unable to help the words. A tear glistened in the corner of her eye. "I don't belong here. I should never have come."

"That arrogant fool," Grandma growled. She turned on the bedside lamp and settled herself on the bed. "Listen to me, Ash. Tobias doesn't know what happened. His reaction is natural for an -" she cut off.

"He's an Alpha, isn't he? That's why he reacted so strongly. He thinks I'm a threat."

"Yes," Grandma sighed. "I'm sorry. I should've told you earlier but the doctors advised against it - they thought it might frighten you away."

"As if I wouldn't work it out when I got here? That's ridiculous. I might have post-traumatic stress but I'm not made of glass." Aislinn chewed on the inside of her cheek. "Tobias is only twenty eight, right? That means he's smack in the middle of transition."

"Yes, though I don't think we'll see much out of him. The day he turned twenty five, he got up and he was just, well, you know. Alpha. All that extra charisma, the strength, the speed… and nobody was more surprised than Tobias. Everyone thought it'd be Jaxon," Grandma admitted, and Aislinn nodded in agreement. If she'd been a betting woman, she'd have put money on Jaxon, too. Grandma shrugged. "I had hopes of a strong one but it's been years and Tobias is yet to enter any sort of transitional phase."

"It's never too late," Aislinn reminded her. "Transitional energy does what it likes, as you well know."

"True, but I'd have thought we'd at least see *something* by now. Perhaps, if we're lucky, the shock of your homecoming will set him off."

"Yeah, that's totally what I need right now; Tobias hating me more than he already does. It'll do wonders for my mental state."

Grandma frowned. "Post-traumatic stress - is that what they're calling it?"

Aislinn nodded. "That's the closest thing the doctors could find to label me with. Do you think Tobias will turn on me?" It didn't matter their shared past - if Tobias deemed her a threat he could very well attack her, particularly when driven by the overload of instincts that an Alpha's transition evoked. "He might even try to kill me."

"Stop, Aislinn." Though gentle, Grandma's tone held no room for argument. "I told you, he's shown no signs of an active transition. Besides, he doesn't know what happened to you."

"Why didn't you tell him?" Aislinn asked, curiosity overcoming her self-loathing.

"It's not my story to tell."

Aislinn snorted. "I know the Council better than that, Grandma. It's classified, isn't it?"

Grandma sighed. "Yes - even I know only the bare bones of the story. The Kin High Council don't want word spreading, lest the people panic. However, if *you* decide to share your story with your packmates, they can't stop you." Her eyes dropped to Aislinn's chest, where a lacework of long slash marks were visible above the hemline of her top.

Aislinn raised her hands, cheeks flushing. The skin had sealed over but the wounds were still painful and red against her pale skin. She hadn't had time to buy long sleeved, high necked pyjamas to cover her injuries and had been forced to sleep in a tank top and underpants – something she'd done without a second thought before the incident.

"No, Ash. Don't be ashamed," Grandma murmured. She reached out and caressed Aislinn's bicep, her fingers trailing over a set of five red puncture marks. "These should have healed by now."

Aislinn swallowed heavily. "The doctors said they wouldn't get any better unless *he* healed them himself. His Mark stops my body finishing the job."

"Bastard," Grandma spat. "I will kill him."

"Grandma, he's not even in the country. He's not even in Ireland. He's not even Irish!"

"Wolfkin?" Grandma asked, her hands hovering over the slash marks.

"Bearkin," Aislinn choked out. Her body shook. She couldn't talk about it – she *couldn't*. Grandma leant away to grab the breakfast tray, settling it carefully onto Ash's lap. The scent of bacon and eggs made her stomach growl and distracted her – albeit momentarily – from the demons in her mind.

"Eat and get dressed," Grandma murmured. "Then we'll see about integrating you back into your birth pack."

"What? I can't go out like this," Aislinn protested. "I stink."

"Nothing a good shower won't fix, dear." Grandma patted her arm. "Now hurry along - I'll wait for you downstairs."

Aislinn sat silent as her grandmother left, her appetite gone as suddenly as it had appeared. How would the rest of the pack react when they realised she wore the scent of a bear? A race notorious for their hostility towards the rest of the world, who'd caused a war ending in their exile almost two centuries ago. A race of Kin who hunted, tortured and terrorised for fun. Aislinn clenched her shaking hands in the sheets. If anyone found out – if *Tobias* found out! He was an Alpha now. *The* Alpha, whilst her father was away in Ireland. If he found out she was Marked by a bear he could very well throw her out. Or kill her.

Maybe you'd even let him, a tiny, inner voice mocked. The bacon and eggs stared up from the tray and for a moment, Aislinn couldn't breathe. Her vision swam and the walls crawled, the wallpaper turning from pale pink to soft green, the ambient noise dropping away until all she could hear was the insistent grunting and growling of bearkin - and her own screaming. *No.* Sharp pain cleared her vision and Aislinn looked down to see the tines of the fork buried in her thigh. Well, that was one way to do it. And who'd notice a few more puncture marks, anyway?

Aislinn yanked the fork free, wiped it on her sheets and speared a piece of bacon. She was a warrior. She wasn't going to just lie down and die. And if Tobias Greenwood's hormones decided to turn on her, she'd simply show him what she was made of and make a speedy exit before he had time to recover. Aislinn chewed mechanically, barely tasting the bacon as she planned her potential escape. Damn them all. Every last one.

****

Tobias woke after a restless night filled with unusual dreams. A thousand women had worn Aislinn's face, but when he got close they were all masks and the real Ash was nowhere to be seen. He showered away his cold sweat and went about his morning chores with all the life of a machine, barely noticing the soggy cereal he forced down his gullet. Dumping the empty bowl in the sink, he stumped out into the early morning light and squinted resentfully at the rising sun, wondering whether he could get away with going back to bed and forgetting the day entirely.

Zeke unfolded his ridiculously tall frame from the wooden bench beside Tobias' front door and gave him a critical once over. "Man, you look like shit."

"Good morning to you too, asshole," Tobias grumbled.

"Still cranky about Ash?" Zeke fell into step as Tobias made his way out of the waist-high gate at the front of his yard.

"No."

"Bullshit." Zeke's brows waggled suggestively. "You been thinking about her all night?"

Mother moon, yes. In complete contrast to his nightmares, Tobias had spent his waking moments imagining running his hands over her curves, cupping her full breasts, making her moan – "No. I haven't given her a single thought."

"Oh man." Zeke shook his head. "You still got it bad for her, don't you?"

"I never 'had it' for her to begin with," Tobias protested as they crossed the common lawn.

"Riiiiight. That's why you spent weeks mourning after she left."

"I didn't."

Zeke slapped him on the shoulder. "I found the tree where you carved her name, dude."

"Oh."

"I took the liberty of erasing the evidence, just in case it ruined your macho Alpha image."

"Um, thanks." He'd always wondered what had happened to that tree.

"I gotta admit though, she's way hot now," Zeke continued. "It was all I could do to stop from burying my face in that luscious hair of hers and Dom looked ready to just carry her away. I know she smells odd but hot damn, if she so much as crooks her finger I'll -" he cut off with a yelp as Tobias threw him onto the ground.

"You won't even *think* about her," he growled. His teeth had lengthened to fangs and fur rippled up his arms as he prepared to shift.

Zeke merely grinned. "Oh man, I got you that time. You *do* have it bad."

"No, I don't." *Liar.*

"Then why the macho show?"

"Tobias?" Jaxon jogged up, green eyes widening as he took in the scene before him. "Is everything okay?"

"Fine. Everything's fine." Tobias got to his feet, hauling Zeke up with him. *Idiot,* he scolded himself. *She's mated. To someone else.*

"Just a morning wrestling match," Zeke said, punching Tobias in the arm.

Jaxon narrowed his eyes. "With a little shifting thrown in?"

"I got carried away."

"Right. Well, I'm finished my guard rounds and I'm going to catch some sleep." Jaxon yawned and stretched his neck. "Rory's taken over."

"Sleep well." Tobias watched as the other man loped off, then continued on his way.

"Are you sure this extra security is necessary?" Zeke asked, scuffing the grass with his bare feet as they went. "We *do* live in a community full of wolves - in case you forgot."

"Andre told me to beef up security anyway." Tobias had wondered why, at the time. Now it made sense – if Ash was mated to another Kin, there'd be trouble if he came looking for her.

"So where are we off to?"

"We're meeting Dom at Grandma Redding's. She wants to re-introduce Ash to the pack, and we're providing escort." Tobias sped up to forestall any comments Zeke might have about an Alpha and his second escorting the women around a community which should be completely friendly.

He was almost across the common lawn now and Grandma Redding's house loomed ahead. All the pack's houses faced the large lawn area in a rough circle, with farms and an orchard set behind them on one side and a large freshwater lake on the other. The bushland beyond provided good, natural cover and Redding Pack territory was edged on one side by cliffs and the other by a dirt road that led into Gerup, the nearest Kin township. There was a contingent of shared cars stashed in a garage near the road in case anyone wanted to go into town - and indeed, some of the pack members lived or worked in town - but for the most part, the Redding pack was content to keep to themselves.

It was a simple life in the pack. Wasn't it? Tobias shivered as he approached Grandma Redding's house. If it was so simple, why had Andre, the pack's senior Alpha, left for Ireland twelve years ago with his family and never returned? Tobias' own father, Rupert Greenwood, was Andre's second. He'd taken his wife and followed four years later, leaving his son to be raised by the pack - something Tobias had never questioned until now. Why had Andre taken Aislinn with him, but Rupert had left Tobias behind? What had happened to Ash to have her sent back? Why was she Marked by another Kin but kept hidden away in the Australian bush? Had her relationship somehow endangered Andre's position as Canis representative on the Kin High Council?

Too many questions. Tobias shook his head. His job was to protect the pack, no more and no less and right now, the only question he needed to consider was how Aislinn fit into that scenario. Andre obviously assumed Tobias would step in if Aislinn's mate came for her; the only problem being that his little band of four – five, if he included himself – were the only warriors on hand. All the pack could fight if need be, being wolves and all, but if something went *really* wrong, there wouldn't be enough skill on hand to do things properly. Tobias chewed his lip again, wishing he'd thought around the shock of Aislinn's imminent arrival to ask Andre - or even better, his father - some intelligent questions.

"Hey, guys." Dominic appeared from behind Grandma Redding's house, inclining his head as he approached. "I was just doing the rounds."

"Everything okay?" Zeke asked.

"Yes. The Den Mother and Aislinn are inside." Dominic's eyes lit up as he said Aislinn's name and Tobias growled low in his throat.

"What's wrong?" Dominic tilted his head at Tobias. "You thinking about claiming her?"

"Solaeden save us, Dom," Zeke laughed. "She's not a hunting trophy!"

Dominic blinked, his pale blue eyes almost luminous in the early morning. "Of course not. I just don't want to step on anyone's toes when I ask her to dinner."

"You want my permission to court Ash?" Tobias demanded, incredulity stealing his anger.

"Why not?" Dominic drew in a deep breath that whistled between his teeth. "She was always cute, but she blossomed into something spectacular whilst she was away."

Tobias snorted, torn between possessive aggression and outright amusement. For a long moment, he debated telling them she was Marked, then decided it would be far more interesting to let Ash handle the situation herself. If she wasn't going to be upfront about her mate, then neither was he - at least, not until he found out more about what was going on. "I think we should let Ash settle in, but after that, sure. Why not?"

Dominic opened his mouth to speak but at that moment the front door opened and Grandma Redding sauntered down the steps. She wore her customary jeans and tank top, this time in a dark grey that set off her red hair. Her hips swayed as she descended the steps from the porch and Tobias wondered, not for the first time, why she hadn't remated after her husband had died.

"Aislinn's on her way," Grandma said in a low voice. She levelled her gaze at Tobias. "I expect you all to be polite."

"Yes, Den Mother," they murmured in unison.

The door opened again and Aislinn stepped out. Tobias' breath caught in his throat. Yesterday, she'd been sweaty and discomfited; today she was glorious. Tight, dark jeans rode low on her hips, hugging her butt and thighs before belling out over high-heeled black boots. She wore a knitted black jumper which clung to every curve and hollow, accented by the same golden torc she'd worn the day before. Thick chocolate-red hair tumbled about her face, down her back and spilled over her breasts in a way that made Tobias want to sink his hands and face into the soft waves. He cleared his throat and purposefully did not look at either Grandma or Aislinn. That left Zeke, who was grinning at him like an idiot, and Dominic, who studied him with calm calculation.

"Morning, guys." Aislinn stopped in front of them and dished out a smile that made Tobias' knees weak. Mother Moon, ten seconds and he was already in trouble - but she'd affected him that way since they were children and had been just as oblivious to it then as she was now. Tobias knew he should respond to her greeting but he didn't trust his mouth, so he bit his tongue until he tasted blood instead.

"Morning, Aislinn. You look lovely today." Dominic enfolded her in a tight hug, his voice wrapped in velvet.

"Thanks, Dom." Aislinn melted in the other's arms and once again Tobias was forced to watch with clenched fists while Dominic pressed a friendly kiss to her temple. "Please call me Ash, like you used to. I know it's been a long time but I'm still the same person." She drew back enough to look over at Tobias and he knew the words were intended specifically for him.

"Ash." Dominic savoured the nickname like it were a fine wine and Aislinn, still in the circle of his arms, beamed up at him. "Of course." The other wolf took a lock of her hair between his fingers and Tobias felt his hackles rise, a warning growl rumbling in the depths of his chest.

"Aren't you hot, babe?" Zeke said, too loudly. He stomped on Tobias' foot as he moved to extricate Aislinn from Dominic's embrace, lifting one of her arms for emphasis. "It's the middle of summer and you're wearing a jumper!"

"Oh." Aislinn looked thrown for a moment. "I – I don't have any summer clothes with me. I had to travel light and it's winter in Ireland. I didn't plan ahead very well."

Tobias sniffed the air as she spoke. She was lying. Why would she lie about her clothes? "Grandma could have lent you something," he said with a frown.

"Oh," she said again, panic flitting momentarily across her features. "I don't think we're the same size. It's no biggie – I'll get something in town in a few days."

That at least smelt true, so Tobias let it go. He glanced at Grandma Redding, surprised when she said nothing. She was more than close enough to scent the lie and had a reputation for enforcing the truth without care for the cost. Why didn't she say anything?

"Let's get moving, before it gets too hot. This afternoon I thought Ash might like to go with you boys to the watering hole, or the den. To relax like old times," Grandma said.

"If she likes," Tobias managed, trying to imagine what Ash would look like in a swimsuit and if he could handle his packmates ogling her. Mated, he reminded himself, his eyes moving to that golden torc. Marked and mated.

"I don't know about swimming," Aislinn gasped, one hand to her mouth. Everyone turned to stare at her and Tobias' eyes narrowed. Of course. She wouldn't want anyone to see her Mark, would she?

"You used to love swimming," Tobias said, his tone crisp.

Aislinn blushed. "I – I think the den would be a better start. I haven't seen you all in so long. We have twelve years to catch up on." She smiled up at Zeke and Dominic but her expression faltered when she met Tobias' stern gaze.

"The den sounds fantastic." Dominic swept in, sliding his arm around Aislinn's shoulders and guiding her away. "And it'll be much cooler than the house. We'll take you as soon as this is over."

"Thank you," Aislinn sounded so genuinely grateful that Tobias felt a stab of shame.

"I told you to behave," Grandma Redding snapped, her eyes flashing.

"I'm trying. She smells wrong," Tobias growled. He knew Zeke was listening but he'd made no secret of the fact that she smelled different yesterday. "It's a little hard to adjust."

"You're going to be more sensitive to her because you're transitioning." Grandma Redding's face softened as she looked up at him. "You need to give her a chance."

"I'll try." Tobias watched Aislinn walking with Dominic and wondered if he really could trust her, knowing she was Marked by another.

****

Aislinn could feel Tobias' piercing gaze on her as she walked. She snuggled closer to Dominic, the weight of his arm across her shoulders a welcome comfort. He, at least, was being friendly.

Grandma's first port of call was Jaxon's mother, Sarah Heliope-Flint. The other woman answered the door covered in flour and the youngest two of her eight children, beckoning them inside with a cheerful laugh.

"Sit down, sit down," Sarah gushed, transferring the baby to her hip and disentangling a blond wolf pup from around her neck. "Juliet, baby, you need to put some clothes on for Mama, please."

The golden-furred wolf shimmered into an enchanting little girl who promptly stamped her foot. "Not a baby!"

"Oh, sorry, princess," Sarah said absently, already shuffling pots on the stove to make room for an old-fashioned kettle. "I keep forgetting how big you are. Will you put some clothes on for me, please, my big girl?"

"Yes, Mama." Juliet giggled and ran from the room.

Dominic pulled out a chair and beckoned Aislinn into it, taking the one on her left while Sarah and Grandma chatted over chipped crockery. Tobias looked like he was about to sit down himself, when three dark shadows came flying out of the next room and launched themselves at him.

"Tobias! Tobias!"

Ash stifled a laugh as a stunned looking Tobias staggered beneath the weight of three young boys, ranging in age between six and ten years old. Their black hair and green eyes made them the spitting image of Jaxon - but for their cheerful natures, because Jaxon had always been quiet at best and surly at worst.

"Eli, Rex and Achilles! Get down this instant! You'll break Tobias' arms off," Sarah scolded, plunking a plate of fresh scones in the centre of the table. She smiled over at Ash. "I swear they get more energetic every day."

"They're gorgeous," Aislinn answered, chuckling as Tobias wrestled all three onto the carpet and promptly began romping with them. She was unable to look away from the joy in his face, the flex of his muscles beneath another t-shirt that was far too small - until Zeke sat in the chair on her other side and pointedly handed her a jam laden scone. Ash smiled and accepted, looking back up at Sarah. "Where's Brian?"

"Down with his precious potatoes." Sarah sighed, waving a hand in the direction of the farm. "Honestly, that man never takes a moment for himself."

"Judging from your ever expanding litter of pups, I doubt that," Grandma chuckled, her eyes dropping to Sarah's apron-clad belly.

"Another?" Ash gasped, noting the way Sarah blushed. "Oh, Sarah, congratulations!"

"You'd think we don't own a television," Sarah laughed, patting her tiny baby belly. "No, Bella, not Mama's hair," she added, and reached up to disentangle the almost-toddler's fingers from her messy bun.

"Jaxon must be excited," Ash ventured. She'd been familiar with two of Jaxon's younger siblings and the one older before she'd left for Ireland, but the rest were entirely new to her.

Sarah snorted. "Oh, you know Jaxon, Ash. He wouldn't be excited by a giant plate of bacon all to himself."

"Bacon?" Three young male faces appeared very suddenly at the table. "There's *bacon*?"

"No, my sweets, no bacon." Sarah made shooing gestures at her brood but they remained, the eldest staring up at Aislinn with Jaxon's intense green eyes.

"Hello," Aislinn said, smiling. "Which Heliope-Flint are you?"

"Achilles," he announced, puffing out his chest. "I'm almost eleven."

"Goodness me," Aislinn laughed, reaching out to ruffle his hair. "Almost a man."

"I'm going to be an Alpha like Tobias when I'm grown," Achilles said, tilting his head so that she could pet his hair better. "You're pretty. Want to be my mate?"

Aislinn froze, her heart thumping unevenly. The cozy kitchen darkened and warped, the smiling faces of the pack turning sinister. In the centre of it all stood Achilles, face open and green eyes glittering with innocent youth. She forced herself to swallow and said shakily; "That's a lovely offer, Achilles, but I think you'll be far too popular for someone like me once you're grown."

Achilles turned into her palm and bit the inside of her wrist affectionately. "Okay. Come on, Rex, Eli - let's go climb that tree out the front."

"Yeah! Yeah!" The younger two scooted after their older brother and moments later the front door slammed shut.

"Scoundrels," Sarah laughed, plopping into a seat at the other end of the table. "Always getting into mischief."

"Like their father." Grandma Redding set a teapot down by the scones and Aislinn gratefully wrapped both hands around the mug she was offered. When she dared look up, she found Tobias watching her with predatory intent from his position against the door jamb. What did he suspect?

Making a concerted effort to calm herself, Aislinn looked up at Sarah and smiled. "It's so good to see you again, Sarah. I honestly worried I'd never get back here once I got to Ireland." That much, at least, was true.

Sarah shivered. "I honestly don't know how you handled the cold."

"It's not so bad once you get used to it," Aislinn admitted, taking a sip of her tea - a sharp, aromatic brew that immediately bought back memories of her childhood. "The snow has a certain charm."

"We get snow here sometimes," said Dominic, pointing towards the nearby mountains. "On the really cold days."

"Last August we had some," Sarah nodded in agreement. "Tobias organised a snowman building contest for the kids. They thought it was a hoot."

"A snowman building contest?" Aislinn flicked another look up at Tobias and offered him a smile.

He blinked and, with some effort, quirked the corner of his lip. "Jax told me that if we didn't do something to get them out of the house, Sarah might've lost her mind. It was the best I could do on short notice."

So. That sweet natured boy she'd known *had* survived. Aislinn munched a scone while the conversation flowed around her. How much of Tobias' behaviour was an instinctive reaction to her scent bought on by his supposedly non-existent transition? Kin were half animal as it was but those who grew into Alphas or Den Mothers had a far greater dose of wild energy. For the most part that meant speed, strength and agility beyond that of their peers - and the ability to scent lies, which she already knew Tobias could do after his reaction to her clothing story earlier that morning. The stronger the Alpha, the more unique his powers, with no way to know exactly what they were until transition decided to rear it's hormonal head.

Aislinn rolled a blackberry across her tongue as she thought. Grandma had said that so far, Tobias' transition had been easy, which meant he was either going to be fairly weak or his body hadn't seen fit to unleash itself yet. For males, transition happened anywhere between the ages of twenty-five and thirty and often dogged them for a great deal of that time. Women, on the other hand, came into their powers much younger and far more suddenly - after a good week in bed sleeping off what seemed to be a never-ending migraine, they woke with a terrifying array of new senses and abilities that needed sorting out all at once. The only bonus was that it was all over and done with quickly, whereas the men often needed older Alphas or Den Mothers around to provide them guidance and support until their powers had settled. In the worst case scenarios they were assigned a damper, a Kin with the rare ability to calm those hormonal surges, lest they cause irreparable damage to themselves or those they cared about.

"Ash?" Zeke's laughing tone grabbed her attention and Aislinn wondered how many times she'd been addressed already.

"Sorry," she blinked sheepishly. "Lost in my own thoughts."

"Homesick for Ireland?" Sarah smiled. "You must have left some loved ones behind - aside from your mother and father, of course."

Yes, but she wouldn't have been able to stay within those green walls another minute longer, no matter what the Council and their army of doctors had decreed. Aislinn suppressed a shiver and said; "A couple."

A low, rumbling growl punctuated her words and Aislinn looked up in time to see Tobias storm to the front door, yank it open and disappear outside, slamming the wood so hard behind him that the pictures swayed on the walls.

"Oh!" Sarah's hand flew to her mouth in surprise, giant blue eyes rounded in shock. "Is he alright?"

"He didn't sleep well, little mother." Zeke reached across the table to pat Sarah's hand. "Tobias has a lot on his mind right now."

"Of course, of course. We do put such a lot of pressure on him, the poor dear." Sarah shook her head. "It can't be easy to have taken over the Alpha duties so young."

Aislinn felt her stomach knot as she met Zeke's sapphire gaze. She was grateful for his support but they both knew that wasn't why Tobias had stormed out. It was just lucky that the Redding pack's isolation - and the bearkin's long exile - meant they were unlikely to recognise the acidic taint marring her scent belonged to the ursine branch of Kin. Ash doubted that even the sweet natured Sarah Heliope-Flint would welcome her with open arms if she knew the truth.

Grandma clicked her tongue against her teeth and looked up at the clock. "Sorry to love and leave, Sarah, but we really must be going. I'd like to swing past Jem's place before lunch."

"Of course! Do come back soon, Ash, won't you? It's so lovely to see you again," Sarah gushed, enfolding Aislinn in a one-armed hug that smelled of apple crumble.

"And you." Aislinn smiled, hoped it didn't tremble. "Thanks for having me on short notice."

"Any time. Welcome home," Sarah beamed, waving as Zeke strode to open the door. Aislinn waved back and ducked outside.

****

Joanne was going to have his hide, Tobias thought, pushing off the tree where Achilles and his younger brothers were climbing. Indeed, as Grandma Redding exited the Heliope-Flint home, her steely eyes were already glaring his way. What else should he have done, though? Watching Aislinn mourn the loss of a life - and a man who was definitely *not* him - in Ireland had set fur crawling all over his arms and shoulders. His eyes strayed again to the golden torc around her neck and he had the sudden and irrational urge to rip it off.

Instead, he stepped up to Grandma Redding, almost hoping for the sharp side of her tongue. She simply looked him up and down and said, "Jem's place."

Jemima and Frank Smythe lived two doors over in a small, elegantly decorated cottage at complete odds with the chaotic coziness of Sarah's kitchen. When Zeke's younger sister opened the immaculately painted blue front door, it was the scent of eucalyptus and lemon that permeated the air rather than baking pie and coffee.

"Tobias!" Sienna Smythe was a few years younger than he, willowy and attractive with well-manicured nails, winged eyeliner and carefully set blonde curls. She smiled in welcome, stepping back from the door in a neatly pressed mauve sundress that set off her sapphire eyes, the female equivalent of her brother's. "What an unexpected surprise."

"Hello, Sienna." Tobias smiled down at the woman he'd always viewed as the sister he never had. "Sorry to intrude. Were you heading to work?"

"Mmmm," she nodded, stepping back to usher him through the door. "I wasn't rostered on today but Lillie called in sick and - *Aislinn*? Lady Lunaida, it is you!" And in complete contrast to her perfect grooming, Sienna shoved Tobias aside and leapt into Ash's arms.

Aislinn went white and staggered backwards until both women collapsed against Dominic, who held them upright with a bemused look on his face. Before Tobias knew what he was doing, he'd wrapped an arm around Sienna's waist and yanked her away.

"Are you alright?" He demanded, holding Sienna tight against him whilst he bent to peer into Aislinn's face.

"Fine." Ash sagged against Dominic for a second longer and then struggled upright. "Sorry, Sens. You took me by surprise."

"Ash is injured." Tobias looked down at the petite woman in his arms, her sapphire eyes wide with confusion. "Go gently on her, sugar plum."

"Oh! Sorry, Ash, I didn't know. I was just so happy to see you after all this time. Where have you *been*?" Sienna thumped Tobias in the chest. "Let me go, you giant hunk of meat. I'm not going to crush her again, I promise."

"Gentle hugs," Tobias warned, tightening his grip when she wriggled against him.

"I promise!" Sienna squealed in delight as he prodded her in the ribs for good measure, then ever-so-carefully enfolded Aislinn in a soft embrace. "Welcome home, Ash."

"Thanks, Sens." Aislinn returned the embrace but her brow was furrowed. "How come you're still so tiny? Zeke's got to be at least seven feet."

"Genetics," Zeke said, strolling up with Grandma Redding. "And, for the record, I'm only six eight. Not my fault if y'all are short asses."

"Do *not* let Mother hear you saying y'all," Sienna hissed, releasing Aislinn to elbow her older brother sharply in the ribs. "You know how she feels about being proper."

"Sure, Sens." Zeke rolled his eyes. "Aren't you late for work by now?"

"Huh?" Sienna looked at her watch and cursed. "Okay but when I come back, Ash and I are having wine and popcorn together on your couch."

Zeke had the grace to look indignant. "*My* couch?"

"Of course. You know Mother would never let us eat popcorn on hers," Sienna snorted, skipping up the steps to unhook her purse from the rack by the door. "Unless Tobias will let us use his place, of course."

"Er," Tobias said, blinking in surprise. Aislinn, in his house? On his couch? He couldn't think of a worse kind of torture.

"Good! Thanks, babe." Sienna whirled up to him, throwing both arms around his neck and planting a kiss on his cheek. "You're the best."

"Get off him, you spineless suck job," Zeke laughed, and promptly received the same treatment.

"Wouldn't want you to be jealous, big brother. Bye, Dominic, Den Mother. See you later, Ash!" Sienna waved and then jogged away in the direction of the shared garage.

"Bye." Aislinn managed a wave but Sienna was well and truly gone.

Tobias took a step back as, without the toffee apple scent of Sienna Smythe to cover it up, Aislinn's altered scent hit him full force. He felt fangs sprout in his mouth and turned away, clenching his fists until his nails bit into his palms. *Relax, dammit. Relax!*

"So, Sens is still the same," Zeke was saying, leading the way up the front steps of his mother's house. "I didn't realise she'd be here or I'd have warned you."

"You don't live here now?" Aislinn's voice followed him up the steps and in through the door, giving Tobias a precious few moments to retract his teeth.

"Oh no, little sister-wolf," Zeke laughed. "I moved out as soon as Mother realised I might be bringing home booze, or girls, or both simultaneously."

"And how often is that a problem, Ezekiel Smythe?" Aislinn teased.

"I'll have you know I'm the very model of a gentleman, my dear," Zeke returned, straightening his back and offering Aislinn his arm. Laughing, she took it and Zeke winked, bending to murmur in her ear as they ventured further inside.

Grandma Redding appeared silently by Tobias' elbow. "Got it handled?"

"Yeah," he nodded. Trust Grandma to notice. "I'm trying, Joanne. I really am."

"I can see that. I'll admit, I didn't think you'd have this much trouble." Grandma frowned. "Are you sure you're up to this?"

What other choice did he have? Tobias sighed, staring up at Jemima Smythe's picture-perfect hanging flowers. "Yeah. It'll settle down eventually."

"If you say so." Grandma's voice carried a scepticism that cut him to the bone. "Tell me if you can't handle it, Tobias. I don't need you and Aislinn killing each other."

"Unlikely." Tobias snorted at the thought. She was tiny and, if reports were to be believed, injured. He'd tear her to pieces before she'd even blinked - and then he'd have to explain it to her father. "Come on, we better catch up before Jemima thinks we're being rude."

Three

Aislinn followed Zeke through his mother's house without really seeing any of it. She got the impression of open windows and expensive wall art and managed, somehow, to reply to Zeke's casual banter but all she could think of was one Sienna Ellyse Smythe.

More particularly, the way Sienna had beamed up at Tobias while he'd held her close, tickling her ribs the way he'd done with Aislinn when they were children. And *Sienna*, of all people! Ash remembered a chubby faced girl child who was more interested in dolls than people and dreamt of one day being a fashion designer. Tobias had tolerated her in the way that all younger siblings are tolerated, and though Sienna and Ash had gotten along well, the four year age difference between Sienna and the boys meant they may as well have lived in separate universes.

Aislinn frowned. What had happened since she'd left to bring Sienna so closely into the fold? Or did Tobias tickle and squeeze everyone these days? Aislinn dismissed that thought immediately. No, that didn't match up to anything she knew about Tobias Greenwood - even if he *had* developed that mystical charisma that seemed to haunt Alpha males, he'd never been casual in his affections. She flicked a glance down the long hallway, where Tobias was holding the door open for Grandma Redding. The sun burnished his golden-brown hair with copper and gilded every single muscle on his considerably toned body. In that moment, with his face turned away and his body matured into that of a man, he could have been a stranger.

"Ash? Gorgeous, you okay?" It was Zeke, his voice quiet at her elbow.

Aislinn turned to find Dominic and Zeke both watching her, one with an easy smile and the other with gentle concern. It would've been easy enough to lie but she'd no wish to build her new life on a mountain of deceit, so Aislinn simply said; "I was just thinking how twelve years makes such a difference. It's like I don't know any of you at all."

Zeke's sapphire eyes flicked down the hall and back again. "Once Rupe and Steph left, Tobias had nobody. He pretty much lived here or, when we were feeling brave, I'd go stay at his place. Sometimes Sienna came with us. He's part of this family now, too."

"Why didn't they take him with them?" Ash murmured, feeling the burn of shame on her cheeks. If Tobias and Sienna were basically siblings then it was no wonder they were so close.

"I don't know." Zeke backed the rest of the way down the hall to a pair of double French doors. "Did you ever ask?"

"Of course," Aislinn nodded. "When Rupert and Stephanie arrived in Ireland without Tobias, I was so angry I tried tearing Rupert's head off."

Dominic stared at her, aghast, but Zeke chuckled. "That sounds like you."

"They never really answered, not in detail," Aislinn recalled. "Just said he didn't want to come."

Now why had she said *that* out loud? It was one thing to be honest where she could, but another entirely to march out all her embarrassing teenage secrets in front of people she hadn't seen in over a decade. Aislinn was saved from Zeke's reply by the arrival of Tobias and Grandma Redding, who promptly shoved everyone aside so she could rap smartly on the French doors.

"Busy," a male voice grunted.

"Frank Smythe, don't you dare 'busy' me," Grandma said loudly. "Open the door this instant, young man, or I shall open it for you."

A fraction of a second later, the doors were flung dramatically open and a taller, older version of Zeke stood blinking in the doorway. Frank Smythe had made an attempt to settle his golden curls into some semblance of respectability, but whatever he'd been doing had his face and clothes covered in grease and errant ringlets poking out in all directions.

Zeke coughed delicately. "Dad… are those car parts on Mother's carpet?"

"I got an email from Max saying the four wheeler's done a head gasket and he was worried we'd need a new one but I volunteered to take a look and - holy shit, there's car parts on your mother's carpet," Frank said, staring down at the mess of blackened metal as though seeing it for the first time.

"Come on," Tobias said, his tone suddenly crisp with the edge of leadership. The males sprang into action and in a matter of minutes, the offending parts were outside and Zeke and Tobias had disappeared further into the house in search of cleaning products.

"Sorry about that, Joanne," Frank said, leading the way into the kitchen. He made to lean on the bench, noticed his shirt was black with grease and promptly stripped it off, revealing a lean chest sprinkled with blonde hair. "Bloody grease gets everywhere," he muttered, kicking the bin open and dropping his shirt inside.

Grandma exhaled through gritted teeth. "Frank, surely you remember Aislinn?"

"Aislinn?" Frank turned away from the fridge, now carrying a jug of water with lemon slices in it and a set of matching crystal tumblers. "Shit a brick, I didn't recognise you at all!"

"Hi, Frank. Good to -" Aislinn cut off as, for the second time in ten minutes, someone drew her into a bone crushing hug. The walls instantly bent inwards and there was only darkness, heavy breathing and the scent of male sweat. A hard, masculine form pressed up against hers, holding her down against the desk. Paper whispered as her notes scattered, the sound unnaturally loud. Aislinn struggled but she couldn't get free, couldn't breathe, couldn't move. Somewhere, someone was laughing, reaching for her and though she tried to run she was frozen, shackled in place by great, creeping bands of iron that caged her chest and squeezed mercilessly.

"Ash? Ash, babe, come back to me. Come on, Ash. *Ash.*" Strong arms, supporting but not caging. Warm sun on her face and the breeze, heavily laden with the scents of an Australian summer, filling her lungs with the scent of freedom. "Ash," said the voice again. Aislinn frowned, swimming through the nightmare and up, up, up. Tobias? She opened her eyes and squinted in the sudden light.

"Zeke," she managed, blinking back tears. "Where are we? What happened?"

"You're outside, baby girl. You collapsed but I've got you," he murmured, brushing her hair back from her face. "I've got you."

Aislinn stiffened at the tender touch and Zeke removed his fingers from her brow, humming a tuneless yet comforting nothing under his breath as he rocked her gently against his chest. They were sitting in his mother's front yard, Zeke with his legs crossed and Aislinn draped casually over his knees, one of his arms behind her head in a supportive but not at all possessive manner. She could see the trees, the sky, the open expanse of the bush and knew that if she rolled to her feet and bolted, Zeke would make no move to stop her.

"Sorry," Aislinn murmured. Her voice was little more than a zephyr but she knew Zeke heard it from the way his chest rumbled with an affectionate growl.

"Don't you ever say that to me, little sister-wolf," he replied. "Dad jumped on you like a lunatic and you went completely white. Dominic caught you as you swooned and fell. It was very romantic."

"Hah." Aislinn looked into those sapphire eyes. "Very funny."

Zeke's lip twitched. "I try. Tobias tore Dad off you like there was no tomorrow, Grandma was shouting and Dominic looked like a deer in the headlights. You were turning blue so I thought maybe the sun and the air might help."

Aislinn turned her head toward the common lawn and sighed. Her skin was caked with dried sweat and she could smell the acrid scent of bearkin, clinging to her like a second skin. How could Zeke stand to be so close to her? It was awful and there was no telling if she'd ever be clean again. After the incident, she'd scrubbed and scrubbed and scrubbed in the shower but even when she bled the scent remained. The scent of *him*. Now, here in another country, those nightmares still sought her out when she least expected it, turning even the simplest things into a complete farce.

For the first time since she'd woken in the hospital, Aislinn felt the itching across her flesh that preceded a shift. Surprised, she stifled it. She'd been unwilling and unable to call her alternate forms for weeks, despite wanting nothing more than to forget her problems and run on her four lupine legs as far and as fast as she could. Why was it returning now? Was that a good sign? Or would she try to call the wolf only to discover that she was somehow tainted by bearkin?

Twin gods, what if she shifted into a *bear*? Aislinn gasped at the thought, trembling in sudden fear. If anyone saw her change into a bear, she'd be killed for sure. It was a rare occurrence to have DNA altered by a Marking but if the bearkin was powerful enough, he could do it. The doctors had done a lot of tests and they'd all come back with wolfkin DNA but what if the change set in later? Aislinn shuddered.

"Ash? Babe?" Zeke's fingers squeezed her shoulder, ever so slightly.

"I'm fine," she replied, aware her voice was thready and breathless. "Just a panic attack. It'll pass. Thanks for bringing me outside."

"A panic attack," Zeke repeated, his tone considering. "They can make you faint?"

"Yeah," Aislinn answered, offering a weak smile. "I guess I freaked out when Frank jumped on me like that." It was the truth but by Lunaida it made her look like a useless weakling.

Zeke, however, merely nodded, his face creased in gentle concern. "I get that. I'll warn the others."

"Thanks." Aislinn choked down a bitter laugh. If Zeke knew what she'd been like before the incident, he wouldn't be looking so understanding - he'd be wondering what on earth was wrong with her.

She longed suddenly for Flynn. He'd understand; they'd shared too much together, fought too many demons side by side for anything else. But Flynn was back in Ireland, pulling double duty to fill the vacancy she'd left in the team - part necessity and part punishment after he'd torn up her hospital room in a fit of rage. After that, Flynn had been forbidden from visiting again and Aislinn had been shipped back to the pack without an opportunity to as much as wave goodbye. For safety reasons, of course, her father had explained - all the while completely unaware that she'd heard him label her as 'compromised' only hours earlier.

Rage swamped Aislinn's body and she rolled out of Zeke's lap, struggling to her feet. Damn her father. Damn the Council, and the doctors, and everyone else who'd tried to throw her a pity party before they gave up and schlepped her back 'home.' She was *not* going down without a fight. Not today, not tomorrow - not ever.

"Feeling better?" Zeke unfolded from the grass, his face pulled into a wry grin.

"Much. Thank you." Aislinn nodded - then flicked a glance back at the house. "That said, I'm not sure I can go back in there. Sorry."

"No need to tempt fate," Zeke replied, shrugging. "I can hear the others coming anyway. Tobias stomps those floorboards like a fairy elephant - drives Ma insane."

True to his word, a second later the front door swung open and Tobias preceded Dominic and Grandma Redding outside. Frank Smythe hovered in the doorway, his face pinched with worry and his chest now covered with a clean shirt. "Sorry, Ash," he called.

"It's fine, Frank. Not your fault." Aislinn managed a little wave and was glad when Frank nodded and stepped back inside the house.

Grandma lingered in the doorway to say her farewells and Aislinn braced herself for questions as Tobias and Dominic approached. The former said nothing, his jaw working in a way that told Aislinn he'd never managed to break the habit of grinding his teeth. Dominic, however, paused in front of her and ran worried eyes over her body. "Are you okay? You gave me a fright."

"Fine, thanks."

Tobias snorted. "Really? I can smell your fear."

"Thanks, asshole," Aislinn snapped. "Is this how you treat all the pack members, or have you saved this particular brand of nasty just for me?"

"I was only stating the truth," Tobias objected, blinking in surprise.

"Bullshit." Aislinn stepped forward, shaking off Dominic's placating hand. "It wouldn't kill you to be nice for once. For your information, I had a panic attack. Does that satisfy your curiosity, or would you like to tell everyone for the millionth time that I smell bad?"

"I -" Tobias broke off as she poked him in the chest.

"Forget it. Whatever you were going to say, forget it. I'm going home." She turned on her heel and stalked off, flipping the bird over her shoulder.

Once upon a time, she'd trusted Tobias. They'd been closer than siblings, better than friends. Inseparable, to the point where both sets of parents had given up trying to enforce individual lives and starting calling everything 'theirs' instead of 'his' and 'yours'. And though the long, empty years of silence between them had cut her to the core, Tobias had still been among the people Aislinn had most looked forward to seeing when she returned. Yet here he was, treating her like something odious he found on the bottom of his shoe. Aislinn snorted. Of course he thought she was odious! After all, she stank and he wasn't about to let her forget it.

She doesn't belong here. His cruel words from the previous day swirled around in her head and pricked her eyes with angry tears. How dare he? He had no idea what she'd been through. Tobias Greenwood might be Alpha while Andre was away but that gave him no right to judge her.

"Ash? Aislinn!" A male voice was calling her and she hesitated, willing it to be Tobias - not this new Tobias, but the Tobias she'd romped and laughed with as a child. It was Dominic, though, who leapt in front of her with his arms spread wide.

"What?" Aislinn took a deep breath and tried to sound civil. "What is it?"

"Don't leave," Dominic implored. "Tobias has gone home. Why don't you let Zeke and I escort you down to the watering hole?"

"I don't want to swim," Aislinn growled, using her anger to mask the sudden flash of panic. If she undressed they would *see*. That could not be allowed to happen, no matter how hot and awful she felt.

"No, I know. I thought you might like to relax in the shade and dip your feet in the water. Then when you feel better, we can go to the den and meet up with everyone else." Dominic's open face was creased with concern, pale blue eyes all but begging.

Aislinn hesitated. She should say no. She should just go home with Grandma and forget everything for the day. She glanced over her shoulder only to see Grandma Redding walking off with Tobias. Great. If she went home now, she'd just be sulking by herself in the hot, gloomy old homestead. As if she felt the weight of eyes on her, Grandma Redding looked over at Aislinn and nodded. What the hell did that mean? Was it encouragement? Understanding? Pity?

Aislinn turned back to Dominic and forced herself to smile. "I'd love to come to the waterhole. Dipping my feet in sounds heavenly."

"Great!" Dominic grinned and offered his arm the same way Zeke had done earlier. Aislinn hooked her elbow through his and together the three of them made their way across the common lawn, threading between the houses and down towards the bush.

"The waterhole is just the same as always," Zeke said, hands thrust casually into his pockets. "You'll love it, Ash."

"I always did," Aislinn smiled in response and for a moment, the twelve years separating them seemed to disappear. "You boys used to race down there like idiots and throw yourselves in without a care for your mother's grey hairs."

"We still do," Dominic laughed, the sound hearty and warm, and poked Zeke in the arm. "Race you?"

"I'd hardy call it a race where you're concerned." Zeke's face broke into a roguish grin and he grabbed the hem of his t-shirt. "Last time we raced I beat you by miles."

"Oh? Watch this, then." Dominic flicked a look at Aislinn from beneath his eyelashes and before she knew it, both boys had stripped down to their underwear and were sprinting across the bare earth ahead of her.

Aislinn followed slowly, watching their muscled bodies gleam in the sun and listening with half an ear to the wild, ridiculous taunts they spouted as they ran. The path she was on sloped downhill, winding back on itself and into a copse of tall paperbarks that provided ample shelter from the blistering summer sun. Ahead, a stand of gums marked a fork in the road; the main path curved left and continued down to the freshwater lake but a smaller track went forwards, through a tunnel in the scrub. Aislinn knew that beyond it, great heaps of rock surrounded a pool of deep, clear water which was the starting point for one of the streams that fed into the lake below. She could hear Zeke and Dominic yelling and laughing and couldn't help smiling herself as she ducked her head to enter the scrub tunnel.

Back before her trip to Ireland she'd been innocent and carefree, romping in the bush with her little band of youths. They'd shifted and laughed and run all day, so busy exploring the pack's land and making mischief for their elders that it never occurred to them there might be an outside world. A cruel, cold place which swallowed you down, chewed you up and spat you back out, broken and stinking of bear.

Stop it. Aislinn paused before the final bend of the tunnel to massage her aching temples. It would do no good to focus on the bad times and she certainly didn't need another panic attack so soon after the last. When she was sure her composure had returned, Aislinn squared her shoulders and stepped out into the dappled sunlight.

The watering hole was a beautiful place, green moss clinging to rocks which in turn held back the dense scrub of the bush. One edge of the waterhole looked out over the lake, barely visible between the tall, peeling trunks of the gums. Opposite, the hill they'd just descended jutted up into the air, high enough to shelter swimmers from prying eyes above. Zeke was swimming strongly within the clear pool while

Dominic stood poised on the edge, water glistening on his muscular body. He grinned at Aislinn, gathered himself and dived into the water with the grace of a sea lion.

Aislinn shook her head in amusement as she made her way slowly to a pile of rocks on her left. Though shaded by the nearby trees, they still held the warmth of the sun and it wasn't long before she eagerly removed her boots and peeled off her socks.

"Nice, isn't it?" Dominic swam up close, crossing his arms over a rock half submerged in the water. "You look better already."

"Thanks." Aislinn gave him a little smile. "Zeke's right - it hasn't changed at all."

Dominic opened his mouth to say more but Zeke burst out of the water behind him, wrapped his arms around Dominic and dunked him under the surface. The tall, blonde rogue looked up and met her eye. "You need anything, gorgeous, you let me know, okay?" Then he was gone, following Dominic under the water in a twisting game of tag.

A soft smile tugged at Aislinn's lips and she tipped her head back, enjoying the feeling of the sun on her face even as it soaked into the black fabric of her jumper and threatened to turn her body into a furnace. She kicked her feet idly, considering her next move. If the pack accepted her, then maybe she really *could* rebuild a life here. Blend back in, pick up where she left off and leave the monsters firmly locked in the closet. Aislinn laughed at that particular piece of fancy. No, she'd left here a child and returned an adult; picking up where she left off would be impossible. She needed to utilise her knowledge of her packmates to help her start over, armed with twelve years' worth of life experience and the understanding that they were now *all* mature adults. Or, in the case of one Tobias Greenwood, adults under the constant threat of chaotic energies well out of his control.

Zeke and Dom surfaced at the other end of the pool, engaged in mock battle. Aislinn cocked her head as she watched them playing, noting their fine bodies. Not a single one of her boys had grown up unattractive, though it still remained to be seen whether Jaxon or Rory were able to cope with her altered scent. For a moment, Aislinn allowed herself the luxury of picturing a life with the pack of her youth. She had no skills to offer that would be pertinent to pack life so she'd have to go back to school but it was possible. Perhaps one day she might even meet someone who was able to look past the panic attacks and the stench and see the lonely woman underneath.

Slow down, Aislinn, she told herself. *One step at a time. Besides, who are you going to settle down with, anyway?* She tried picturing herself with Zeke and immediately dismissed the idea. He'd been like a brother to her as a child and those feelings had not changed. Still, the fantasy amused her and cut down on the pain of missing Flynn, so Aislinn turned her eyes to Dominic. He'd been handsome and charming as a boy and those qualities were more than tripled now, but - well, he was boy next door nice. Past experience said she needed a man who could ignite her, someone who made her skin tingle and her fingers itch to touch. Dominic was certainly gorgeous but there hadn't been a spark between them so far and Aislinn knew in her heart of hearts that there never would be. He was sweet and inherently gentle and she'd crush him in five seconds flat. She wasn't into assholes, but she *did* need someone strong enough to argue with her, to challenge her, to treat her as an equal rather than putting her on a pedestal, or worse, coddling her as if she were spun from gossamer.

What about Tobias? whispered a little voice inside her head.

Tobias! Aislinn snatched a pebble from the ground and tossed it into the pool. The weedy, earnest boy she'd once known had complemented her perfectly; just rational and stubborn enough to make her stop and think before doing something truly stupid, not afraid to call things as he saw them and never failing to jump feet first into whatever ridiculous scheme she cooked up with that lopsided smile she'd adored. Now? He'd made no secret of the fact that he distrusted her and it was clear her altered scent offended his Alpha nature. She may have cried for him in the past, but the fact remained that he'd made no attempt to contact her since she left Australia twelve years previously. Aislinn had thought, at first, that he'd grown into something hard and unfeeling but the sweet, gentle side he'd shown Sienna earlier said otherwise. If Tobias really was the same person she'd left behind, then he hadn't bothered with her for a reason. Although really, she shouldn't be surprised - Rupert had told her himself, upon his arrival to Ireland, that Tobias hadn't wanted to come. That he'd outgrown her and moved on with his life and so should she.

"You look sad."

Aislinn blinked as Dominic dropped down onto the rock beside her. She'd been so lost in thought she'd not even noticed his approach - Flynn would kill her if he knew, and rightly so! What a rookie mistake. She was just lucky it was only the very delicious, dripping wet Dominic and not someone more dangerous. Realising the wolfkin in question was still waiting for an answer, Aislinn shrugged. "Not sad, not really. Just thinking."

Dominic shook his head, spraying her with water and grinning when Aislinn squeaked a protest. "Maybe you need to think less and enjoy more."

"Sometimes that's easier said than done," she answered, crinkling her nose as icy droplets trickled under the neckline of her jumper.

"Share your thoughts with me, then," Dominic invited, setting his palms against the rock and leaning forward. "A problem shared is a problem halved, yeah?"

"All right." Aislinn reclined on her elbows, eyeing the water that dribbled down the column of Dominic's spine. "I was thinking - again - about how different we all are. The same, but different. And wondering how I fit in, or if, maybe, I don't."

"Of course you do." Dominic's answer was as quick as it was valiant. "You're one of us."

"Thanks, Dom, but honestly, we don't know each other any more. Twelve years is a long time apart and all we really know is who we *used* to be. Things change. People change. You grew these, for a start." Aislinn poked his muscular bicep and was rewarded with a blush.

"Oi, you two, no canoodling." Zeke erupted out of the water in front of them, flopping onto the rock on Aislinn's other side. "Not unless there's room for one more."

"Canoodling?" Dominic looked equal parts amused and embarrassed and Aislinn couldn't help the laugh that bubbled out of her, clear and true.

"What?" Zeke asked, his grin widening. "You got a problem with canoodling?"

"I'm willing to bet actual money that neither of you even know *how* to canoodle," Ash guffawed, wiping a tear of mirth from her eye.

"Oh, I'm sorry, Ms. Woman of the World," Zeke scoffed, his eyes twinkling with challenge. "Are we too much the country boys for you?"

"Definitely," Aislinn chuckled, reaching out to bop him on the nose. "But don't worry, sweet little bumpkin, there are some girls who really go for that. Just don't start wearing flannel shirts or I might have to disown you."

Zeke roared with laughter and for a long moment, Ash missed the joke - until she saw Dominic looking injured. "What's wrong with a flannel shirt?" He demanded.

Ash sniggered, sitting upright long enough to give him a playful shove. "Nothing, as long as you take it off - so I can set it on fire."

"Careful, you'll hurt his feelings," Zeke quipped, then howled with laughter again as Dominic reached over Aislinn to shove him into the water.

"I'm not afraid to have feelings," Dominic announced, puffing out his chest. "It's sexy to have feelings."

"Tell that to your flannel," Aislinn returned.

"That's it! You're going in too," Dominic growled playfully - and before Aislinn had a chance to protest, he bundled her into his arms and rolled them both into the waterhole.

The clear water closed over Aislinn's head, the chill biting into her injuries and forcing the breath from her lungs. Dominic's body was warm and supportive but her clothes were heavy and dragged at her flesh, clinging to all the nooks and crannies. She should be able to swim like this. She should be able to move her arms and legs - but instead, it felt as though she were filled with lead, unable to do more than hang limp in Dominic's embrace.

They surfaced quite suddenly, Aislinn's breath coming in great gasps. Iron bands had fastened around her torso and were squeezing tight, digging into the areas where the most pain could be caused. Ash's hair hung over her face and her head sagged against Dominic's shoulder, his beacon of warmth the only thing keeping her anchored to a world of cold and dark.

"Ash?" Dominic's voice was full of confusion. She tried to answer but her throat was closed over, slave to a thousand screams she couldn't voice. Cold. She was so cold.

"Dom, what are you doing?" Zeke. Oh Zeke. She'd never been so glad to hear his voice. "Why is Ash in the water?"

"We were all kidding around," Dominic sounded confused by the rage in his friend's tone. "I didn't think-"

"She's injured, you fucking idiot!" Someone pushed her hair out of her face and Zeke peered down at her, his eyes filled with concern. "Look at her, she's white as a sheet and her lips are blue."

"I'm sorry, Zeke, I didn't mean to-"

"You're useless. Give her to me." Zeke wrenched her free of Dominic's embrace and cradled her in his arms like a child.

Aislinn wasn't sure how they made it to the edge of the waterhole but they did and moments later Zeke was sitting down in the sun with her in his lap, the heat of his body helping to ease the pain and the cold.

"She seemed fine before," Dominic began, water sheeting off him as he got out of the pool. "I was just playing."

"That doesn't mean you have to throw her in, you flea-bitten lunatic! Go to the den and start the fire. Get blankets, lots of blankets. Come back to me when you're done. And dressed," Zeke added, his tone firm with command. Dominic didn't even bother arguing - he turned and raced away.

"Y-you're a second," Aislinn managed.

"Someone has to watch Tobias' stupid ass. You surprised?" Zeke smiled, pulling her closer to his chest with one hand and using the other to wring water out of her hair.

"T-thanks."

"Shh. Sorry about Dom, babe. I thought I was watching him." Zeke shook his head. "He always goes to pieces when he sees a pretty face."

"'S'okay," Aislinn managed. Her chest ached with every breath and tears pricked at her eyes but at least she *was* breathing. She hadn't felt this awful since she'd been in hospital weeks ago.

"Tobias told me to take care of you," Zeke grumbled, almost to himself. "Fat lot of good I'm doing."

"T-tobias?" Aislinn tried to sit up, looking around in alarm.

"Hey, relax, babe. He's not here. Grandma took him away for an uber tongue-lashing." Zeke sighed. "I don't know why he's being such a feral - Lunaida knows he's pined for you every day since you left."

Aislinn frowned, the effect ruined by her body's traitorous shaking. "He has?"

"Yup."

"I suppose it's fairly slim pickings around here," Aislinn managed. Her throat closed over and a paroxysm of coughing wracked her body.

Zeke held her while she choked, stroking her arm and humming tunelessly. When at last the coughing subsided, he said; "It's not as bad as you'd think but you're missing the point. You can't see yourself the way we do."

"What do you mean?"

Zeke's gaze flickered with heat, raking the length of Aislinn's body with such sensuality that she gasped. His hands tightened as he leant down and breathed deep of her scent. "You're not meant for me but I'd have to be dead not to notice you, little sister-wolf. You left here a kitten and returned a wildcat." He nipped her jaw to illustrate his point.

Aislinn gaped as Zeke pulled back, her pain momentarily forgotten. He blinked again and suddenly the rogue was back, friendly and laughing the way she was used to.

"I-I…" she trailed off, too confused and tired for words. They thought she was *attractive*? What was *wrong* with them?

"Ready," Dominic's voice preceded him into the clearing, derailing Aislinn's train of thought. The wolfkin was still wet but he'd pulled on a pair of shorts somewhere during his travels.

"I should hope so." Zeke's voice carried a steely edge as he stood, still cradling Aislinn to his chest. She was surprised when Dominic flinched, stepping back to bow his head in submission as the taller man stalked past.

"Zeke," Aislinn began. She stopped, her teeth chattering. What had she been going to say?

"Hold on, gorgeous." Zeke's arms tightened again but this time, it was for comfort.

Aislinn felt the pull of intense motion and knew he'd accelerated to super speed, one of the benefits of being Kin. Scenery passed by in a blur and within moments she was within a cave. Zeke deposited her gently in a nest of furs and piled blankets on top. When he stepped back, Aislinn saw she was close enough to the fire pit that a stray spark would set her alight. She tried to smile but her muscles refused to obey.

"When you're warmer, we'll get you some dry clothes." Zeke appeared in her line of sight with a mug. "Here."

Aislinn took a dutiful sip and then coughed wildly as her throat burned. "Whiskey?"

Zeke grinned. "Rum," he answered. "I'd prefer whiskey myself, but Tobias likes this junk better."

"You even *drink* what he tells you to?" Aislinn spluttered, choking down another mouthful. It was awful but it warmed her insides and fought back the terrible cold.

"No, we all have our preferences but Tobias is the only one who drinks rum. Which is why it's the only thing we have left," Zeke added.

"Why?"

Zeke hitched one shoulder in a lopsided shrug. "He doesn't drink much."

"Too serious," Aislinn answered, obediently finishing the last of the rum.

"True! Oh babe, I've missed you," Zeke chuckled, moving out of her sight. When he returned, he'd towelled himself dry and wore faded denim shorts and a ripped t-shirt featuring an ancient rock band.

"Ash? Zeke?" Dominic's voice was filled with trepidation. Aislinn looked up to see him silhouetted in the doorway. Zeke marched over and whispered something in his ear; Dominic paled and nodded, then disappeared again.

"What did you say?"

"I told him to get dry and properly dressed before I chopped his dick off," Zeke growled. "I also said he's going to be the one to tell Tobias what happened."

Biting her lip, Aislinn flicked him a desperate look. "I really don't think this is a Tobias-worthy incident. It's just another thing for him to be pissed about where I'm concerned."

"If only it were that simple, babe." Zeke sighed and crouched down beside her head. "We're all still friends but you were right before; some things *have* changed. You can't see right now but behind you is a passage leading further into the mountain to another cave."

"The one with the quartz in the walls. We used to dry our wet clothes in there," Aislinn recalled.

Zeke nodded. "That's the one. Nowadays it's the training room. We practice every day. Twice a day, sometimes. I'm sworn to Tobias but the others haven't made a choice yet and let's face it; sooner or later, something's going to happen that's going to either cement us into a single pack or divide us for good."

Aislinn stared at the flickering fire, the words 'something's going to happen,' ringing in her ears with all the finality of a death knell. "Who taught you to fight?"

"Rupert." Zeke poked at the fire with a stick. "Before he left."

Aislinn sucked in a breath. Tobias' father was one of the fiercest fighters she'd ever seen and was an invaluable asset to Andre in Ireland - yet despite that, he'd spent four years in Australia turning five boys into warriors before they were even men?

"Why?"

"Who knows? He was a tough master. Fair but tough. Beat us black and blue every damned day," Zeke laughed. "Lucky we heal so fast."

"Yeah," Aislinn grunted, thinking of her own injuries. "Lucky."

They both fell silent and presently Aislinn felt sleep creeping up on her. She tried to fight it, opening her mouth to ask Zeke to take her home but no noise came out. Moments later, everything went black.

****

Tobias walked away from Grandma Redding with his ears ringing. She'd taken him to the far side of the pack's orchard before letting loose with her temper. She'd railed about being nice and making friends and helping Aislinn heal and settle in but each and every time she'd found a way to come back to protection - all without divulging any information about Aislinn's Irish adventure. How was Tobias supposed to protect her, when he didn't know what to protect her *from*? He shook his head. Aislinn didn't belong to the pack any more; Marking and mating was a process of exchange, a marriage not only of hearts but souls. If she'd picked someone else - as her glittering golden torc proved - she wasn't his responsibility. And yet…

Tobias growled low in his throat. The wolfkin in him knew she was dangerous but the man in him wanted to hold her close and form those curves in his hands. The war inside him had started the moment he'd caught her alien scent. In only a day and a half, he was ready to rip himself – and anyone else stupid enough to get involved – into tiny little pieces. He thought of Dominic and clenched his fists. The handsome wolfkin had made no secret of the fact that he wanted Aislinn. What claim did Tobias have to her? What claim did *any* of them have to her?

None. She belonged to someone else.

Tobias wanted to howl his frustration and rage. He could've called his wolf form and run for miles but that would have been in direct opposition to Grandma Redding's parting orders.

"Don't let her out of your sight." The words rang in his mind and he grunted. Oh yeah, smart. Put her in the care of the man who couldn't decide whether to rip off her clothes or her head. Or both. Neither of which he was actually entitled to do - not that it mattered to his warring instincts.

"Shit," Tobias whispered, running a hand through his hair. If this was transition, no wonder the Kin High Council made such a huge fuss over it. He could barely think for the thumping drums in his head, the shoving tides of sensation and emotion - all of it triggered by one Aislinn Jaide Redding. Tobias sighed. There was simply nothing for it; no matter who Ash belonged to or what mysterious past she carried, he'd sworn to look after her and he would uphold that oath until it killed him. Which, given the current level of chaos raging inside his body, was extremely likely.

He made his way back towards the common lawn slowly, taking advantage of the time to resume his normal level of composure. Despite the war raging inside him, he *had* missed Aislinn and perhaps taking the opportunity to get to know her better would help them both. In fact - pulling his phone from his pocket, Tobias typed a message to Sienna and sent it off. That would do nicely.

He looked up to see Dominic come rushing barefoot out his front door, his hair wet and unkempt, his clothes uncharacteristically rumpled. "Dom!"

"Tobias." Dominic ran a hand through sodden hair and grimaced. "I was about to come looking for you."

"What's up?"

"Well, we took Ash to the watering hole as planned," Dominic said slowly. "She didn't want to swim so she just sat on the edge."

"Yeah, she said that this morning," Tobias waved a negligent hand. "Get to the point, man."

"We were mucking around and I tackled her into the water and she had another attack." Dominic flinched away from Tobias as though expecting a blow. "She turned white and blue and couldn't breathe... Zeke took her to the den to try and recover but she looked bad."

Fear slammed through Tobias and he swung in the direction of the den. "You forgot she was injured?"

"She's a wolfkin!" Dominic sounded desperate. "Any injuries she sustained in Ireland should be healed by now."

"Yeah. I know." Tobias flung himself forward as fast as he could, his preternatural speed augmented further by his Alpha energy. Bushland blurred and in moments he was skidding to a halt in the middle of the den. Zeke was there, on his feet and tensed for battle but he stepped aside as soon as he saw Tobias. Aislinn slept on a pile of furs, covered by so many blankets that only her face was visible. Despite the fire, the blankets and the oppressive heat of the day, she was pale and shivering.

"What happened?" Tobias moved around the firepit and crouched down beside her. "Another panic attack?"

"I guess so; Dominic threw her into the water and her body went nuts. It happened in less than a second."

"Was it really that cold?" He leant closer and sniffed. Odd. The other male's scent was incredibly strong – so strong he could barely smell Aislinn underneath.

"No, man, that's what's weird. It was chilly but nothing a wolfkin shouldn't be able to handle. Dom was an idiot though, pulling her under even after she said she didn't want to get wet." Zeke poured a finger's worth of rum and offered it.

Tobias raised an eyebrow, then took the glass and swallowed the lot. "Maybe I should check her over and see if I can find anything."

"I thought of that too but she's still freezing – touch her and see."

Tobias laid a hand against her forehead, surprised to see his fingers trembling. Aislinn felt as cold and lifeless as a block of ice. Frowning, he shook his head and sniffed her again. Why was the other Kin's scent stronger now? Surely he hadn't been here? No, that was impossible. Whoever she'd exchanged Marks with had to be in Ireland, at the very least - and even if he *was* in Australia, nobody was getting into the den without Zeke noticing. Holding his breath against the overwhelming scent, Tobias ran gentle fingers down her cheek. Asleep, she looked far more like the Aislinn he remembered. She turned her face into his hand and sighed, her body visibly relaxing as though even in her sleep, she'd recognised him. Tobias felt a stab of shame. He'd been such an asshole to her in the short time she'd been here and no matter what or who she smelt like, Ash didn't deserve that - from anyone, let alone a man who'd once known her better than he'd known himself.

"Is she all right?" Dominic's voice preceded him into the cave.

"You are such an idiot," Tobias growled low in his throat as he stood and turned to face the other wolfkin.

Dominic flinched, hesitating in the cave's opening. "I didn't know," he insisted, hands raised in a placating gesture.

"Dude, you knew," Zeke said, frowning. "You weren't thinking with the right brain."

"You pulled her into the water to make a move on her?" Tobias frowned. *That* made a difference to how lenient he was going to be.

"Of course not!" Dominic was aghast. "I wouldn't do something like that - yeah, I messed up but I'd never force someone. Come on, Tobias," he added, his face desperate.

"Fine, but you owe her an apology when she wakes up."

"Who's apologising?" Jaxon strode in and propped to a halt when he saw Aislinn. "What's she doing here? She's stinking out the den."

"Aislinn's injured and it's our job to protect her," Tobias answered.

"She doesn't belong here, Tobias. You said it yourself." Jaxon stared down at Aislinn, his nose wrinkling in disgust. "Don't tell me you've flipped overnight."

Tobias pressed his lips together in a thin line. "No," he allowed eventually. "I haven't flipped overnight. But she was one of us, once."

Jaxon tilted his head to one side, considering. "I'm not sworn to you, you know. Technically I don't have to do what you're asking."

Zeke's jaw dropped and Dominic gasped but in true Jaxon style, he didn't so much as flicker an eyelash. Tobias rolled his shoulders, considering his response very carefully.

"You're right, Jax; you're not sworn to me. But you are, until you decide otherwise, attached to the Redding pack as a whole and the Den Mother commanded us to watch over Ash." Tobias felt like a hypocrite but as he expected, mere mention of Grandma Redding caused Jaxon to subside with little more than a grunt. Joanne Redding was someone they'd been taught to respect from their cradles and her word as Den Mother was never questioned.

"Evening, guys." Rory strolled in, his brow damp with sweat.

"How'd the patrol go? Any news?" Zeke asked, his tone filled with a sort of panic that Tobias completely understood. Any topic was better than the potential schism of a friendship that had lasted, so far, for their entire lives.

"Nah. There's nobody out there." Rory waved a dismissive hand in the direction of the outside world.

"That's because Aislinn's stink chased them off," Jaxon groused, jabbing a thick finger in the direction of the fire.

"She's here? What the hell have I spent all afternoon running around for?" Rory stomped over to Aislinn and looked down at her. "Mother Moon, she looks like shit."

"Which is why you spent all afternoon running around," Tobias growled. Rory glanced at him out of the corner of his eye and shrugged a shoulder.

"Sun's setting," Jaxon announced. "Someone come spar with me. I can't stay in here with stinky Ash."

Tobias watched as Jaxon, Rory and Dominic slipped into the passage to the back cave. As soon as they were out of sight, he heaved a massive sigh and dropped his head into his hands.

"It went better than I thought, bro." Zeke slapped Tobias on the back.

"Jaxon can't stand her. Rory's neutral and I'm pretty sure Dominic wants her in his bed. How is that good? Next thing you'll tell me you don't like her, either," Tobias grumbled.

"Eh, she's the same old Ash to me. Enhanced but still Ash underneath." Zeke cupped some imaginary boobs when he said 'enhanced' and Tobias snorted a laugh. "You knew her better than any of us, though. What do you think? And I'm asking *Tobias*, not Tobias' angry transitional powers of doom."

"She's quieter."

"You think? The first ten minutes she was here, you told her she stank. That's bad form even for you, dude."

"I know. Solaeden save me, I know." Tobias buried both hands in his hair and tugged. "She deserves better than that."

"Too damned right she does." Zeke knocked back another glass of rum and winced. "I hate this stuff."

"I'm taking Ash into town tomorrow to pick up some more clothes," Tobias said, nodding at the almost empty bottle. "I'll buy more whiskey for you while I'm there."

"I didn't know Ash was planning to go to town tomorrow," Zeke frowned.

"She isn't. I figure I owe her for being a jerk, so I sent Sens a text before I came down to the den - she's going to meet us at the boutique in the morning."

Zeke raised an eyebrow. "On a Sunday?"

"Yup." Tobias yanked his phone from his pocket and dropped it onto the scarred old table that had been in the den since they'd first claimed it. "Sens spoke to Ysera and got permission to open up specially, just for us."

"Smooth way of apologising, dude." Zeke thumped his glass down on the table beside Tobias' phone and nodded. "I like it. Chicks dig stuff - well, Sienna does, anyway."

"Yeah." Tobias' stomach churned with guilt as he stared at the table. Aislinn had helped him sneak it out of his father's house in the middle of the night and they'd giggled and shushed each other all the way to the cave. It was the first piece of furniture that had ever graced the den. "I guess I don't really know what she likes any more; but she did say she wanted to get some clothes."

Zeke sucked on his teeth for a moment, sapphire eyes narrowed as he watched Aislinn sleep. "You want me to tag along?"

"What?"

"To town. So you're not on your own with her."

"I don't -" he stopped, frowned. "Are you asking for my sake or hers?"

His second raised a golden brow. "You really want a straight answer to that?"

"Indulge me."

"Let's say both, then, eh?"

Tobias blew out between his teeth. "I dunno. Maybe."

"Think about it and text me later, yeah? I'm on the last patrol of the night, so I'll be around." Zeke tugged him in the direction of the back cave. Come on, bro. Let's get out the back and romp with the others."

"We shouldn't leave Aislinn," Tobias murmured.

"Let her sleep. Nobody's getting into the den without us knowing about it and Dominic needs a thumping."

"He does?"

"He was hitting on your woman," Zeke reminded.

"She's not my woman," Tobias growled, his hands clenching into fists.

"Yeah, man, sure; whatever you say. Come on," Zeke waved an arm and Tobias followed him reluctantly into the back cavern.

Four

Aislinn woke to the rhythmic sound of wood thudding against wood. Smoke tickled her nostrils and she smiled, wondering if Flynn had remembered to put the kettle on before he hit the training mat. Probably not - once Kaira arrived, he'd be in a world of trouble and she'd probably have to separate them. Again. Aislinn sighed, turning her face further into the soft furs beneath her, savouring the lingering scent of Tobias.

Tobias?

Blankets fell to the floor in a heap as Aislinn sat up, staring wildly around her. A fire still blazed in the firepit, smoke billowing up and out of the natural vent-hole in the ceiling. Familiar pitted, wonky furniture dotted the area and Aislinn blinked rapidly as she realised she wasn't in Ireland at all, but alone in the den in the middle of the Australian bush.

Her heart thundered in her chest and she raised trembling hands to push her hair away from her face, once again catching the lingering scent of Tobias. Aislinn frowned. She'd been lost in a cold, dark nothing and dreamt of Tobias' hand on her face, his voice giving her an anchor to cling to. Had he, in fact, been close enough that it wasn't a dream at all?

Aislinn rolled off the pile of furs and gained her feet. It was dark outside, the last fading rays of sunset no more than a hint of pink on the horizon. Had she really slept most of the day away? She tugged at her rumpled clothing, doing her best to neaten it and grimacing as she discovered everything was still damp. The day had been hot enough to dry her out, but apparently the million blankets Zeke had piled on top of her had also conserved the moisture bestowed upon her by the lake.

Her stomach rumbled and Aislinn drifted over to one of the den's mismatched side tables, where someone had left a plate of sandwiches and a hastily scrawled note that said 'For Ash.' Oh, Zeke. Sweet, gentle Zeke. Two minutes later the sandwiches were gone and Aislinn stretched experimentally, relieved to find the iron bands of cold that had incapacitated her earlier were well and truly gone. Her body ached all over but it was the same ache she'd endured for a month now – a dull, overall throbbing accompanied by sharp stabs and pulls when she moved.

"Ash?"

Dominic. Great - she could've really used a few more minutes to collect herself before having to speak to anyone. Aislinn took a deep breath and turned her head. Dominic was standing half in the tunnel entrance, his broad shoulders drooping and a thick purple bruise covering one side of his face.

"What happened?" Aislinn demanded, discomfort forgotten as she crossed the room. "Who did that? Hold still, dammit."

Dominic froze in the act of pulling away and Aislinn grabbed his jaw for good measure, tugging imperiously until he bent to her level. She traced the swelling with her free hand, frowning at what was very obviously a reprimand. "It's fine," Dominic said softly, one of his hands covering her own. "I deserved it for tumbling you into the water."

"I'll be the judge of that," Aislinn growled. "Now *who did it*?"

"Tobias, of course."

Of course. Aislinn narrowed her eyes, well aware of the growl thrumming in her chest as she leant closer to examine the wound. A spectacular bruise but only light grazing and with a Kin's accelerated healing, Dominic would be back to normal in no time. "Tobias is an ass. Also, you need to keep your guard up."

Pale blue eyes went wide. "What?"

"Staves, right?" Aislinn twisted the other man's jaw so the fire illuminated the bruise better. "He hit you from above."

"Yeah, he did. I'm not as good with a staff as Tobias," Dominic admitted. He swallowed, his throat working beneath Aislinn's fingers. "I'm sorry, Ash. I didn't mean to hurt you."

"I know." All at once, Aislinn realised they were close enough to share breath. She patted his cheek and stepped back, offering a smile. "It was an accident, right? And I'm fine. No harm done."

"I'd hardly call sleeping most of the day away 'fine,'" said Tobias.

Aislinn jumped, whirling to find him leaning nonchalantly against the tunnel entrance, cradling a staff with one arm. Good grief, she *was* losing her touch. Twice now in the same day someone had crept up on her and she hadn't noticed - twice now she could be dead. Gathering scattered wits, she frowned up at Tobias and said; "The panic attacks sap my energy. I didn't plan on a nap, it just happened."

Tobias swept an assessing gaze over Aislinn's body. "Fair enough. Are you feeling better?"

What? Aislinn glanced at Dominic, who looked just as surprised to hear Tobias being nice. Still waiting for the catch, she cleared her throat and said; "Yeah, thanks. I am."

"Good." Tobias tilted his head to one side, the golden starbursts in his eyes blazing as he assessed her again. "You look much better."

Aislinn barked a sharp laugh at that, unable to stop the self-conscious hand that tugged on her matted hair. "I doubt that."

Tobias opened his mouth to reply but stopped as tinny music filled the cave. "Damn." He strode to the den's well-dented table and snatched a mobile phone off the surface. "It's Andre."

Mere mention of Aislinn's father – the main Alpha of the pack – bought all the boys running from the other cave. They skidded to a halt in various stages of disarray as Tobias flipped the phone open and pressed it to his ear.

"Tobias," he said. Aislinn strained to listen but though she could hear her father's voice, she was unable to make out the words. "Yeah, she's here. No, no trouble."

Aislinn blinked. Tobias' tone was easy, almost laughing but there was no mistaking the scent of deceit curling around him as he spoke - which, on the other end of the phone, her father had no chance of catching. She watched Tobias nodding and uh-huhing, the way he propped one hip against the table, causing his t-shirt to ride up - did the man not own a single thing that actually fitted him? - revealing a healthy length of tanned brown skin that had Aislinn swallowing an appreciative hum. It was only when he moved, cutting off that tantalising view, that Aislinn realised he'd hung the phone up.

"He didn't want to talk to me?" She frowned up at Tobias, who was watching her with an odd expression on his face.

"Sorry, Ash," he murmured.

Well then. Aislinn stared into the fire, clenching her teeth against the hurt. Her father had known she was here - Tobias had said as much - and he'd chosen not to speak with her. "What did he say, then?"

"Nothing much," Tobias answered, frustration riding high in his tone. "Have we been keeping up regular patrols. Have we seen anything unusual. Have we been escorting you everywhere. Have we been wagging our fucking tails and begging for treats on demand."

"Well you've definitely failed at the last one," Aislinn snorted, unable to stop the smile tugging at her lips.

"What I don't understand," Tobias growled, glowering down at his phone, "is why?"

"*She* can tell us," Jaxon snarled, tossing a fresh log on the fire and sending up sparks. "Can't you?"

Aislinn raised an eyebrow at the challenge glittering in Jaxon's green eyes, refusing to be cowed. "The strength of the wolf is the pack, and the strength of the pack is the wolf. Surely you know that by now, Jax."

"Don't call me that." Jaxon growled low in his throat and stalked towards her, one arm outstretched as if he meant to grab Aislinn by the scruff of the neck and shake the answer out of her. "You don't belong to the pack. You don't get to call me that."

Adrenaline surged and with it, the urge to shift. Fight, or flight? Aislinn had no wish to hurt Jaxon and drive an even bigger wedge through the pack, so she accepted the wolfkin energy and tugged on her wolf form in the same way she might shrug on a favourite coat. Damp clothes fell to the floor as she leapt away, relieved to find she still *was* a wolf and not a bear the way her nightmares had insisted.

"Ash, wait!"

She paused at the cave door. It should have been Tobias, calling her back to apologise and set things right but, as so many times since she'd arrived, it was Zeke. With a threatening growl and a shake of her russet fur, Aislinn bounded away into the night.

****

Tobias stared down at the pile of neatly folded clothes on his bed and grimaced. He'd washed Ash's clothes and dried them, but her altered scent was still so strong that he'd ended up stuffing them into a bag and stashing it under the bed in the spare room. Then he'd felt guilty, so he'd dragged the bag out and put it down in the lounge. Then he'd been curious, so he'd pulled the clothes out and tried to work out, if not who, then *what* sort of male Aislinn had chosen to mate with. Most Alphas and Den Mothers had sensitive enough noses to differentiate between species by scent alone and Tobias was no exception, but he was also limited to the Kin he'd met in his travels - and the scent mingling with Aislinn's didn't match any of those. After a good half hour of sniffing her clothes and driving himself crazy, Tobias had decided to make a sandwich but the next thing he knew, he'd woken up in the bathtub in his wolf form with the bathmat shredded into pieces around him.

Not a good sign.

After regaining his normal body and heading to his room for new clothes - he'd torn apart whatever he'd been wearing earlier - Tobias had discovered Aislinn's clothes stuffed underneath his pillow.

Even less of a good sign.

Shit a brick, what was he going to do? Tobias ran a hand through sweat-damp hair and growled low in his throat. Last night, she'd fired up at Jax and it had been all he could do not to leap across the room and either tear Jaxon's throat out or pin Aislinn to the ground and demand answers to his questions. Because, for all Jax had overstepped his mark, Aislinn's ambiguous response had proven beyond doubt that she knew *exactly* what was going on. But instead of taking charge like he was supposed to, he'd stood like a statue while she fled, Zeke called after her and Jaxon charged out into the night like a tiger with a thorn in his paw.

Tobias picked up Aislinn's black jumper and kneaded the soft fabric with his hands. Interestingly enough, not only had Jaxon been unable to catch Ash after she fled, he'd admitted later he hadn't found a single sign to show where she'd gone - as though she'd managed to completely disappear. Tobias had assigned Jaxon double patrol duties for his bad attitude and then walked home via Grandma Redding's where, as he'd half expected, Aislinn's bedroom window had been dark and the bedcovers pristine.

What *was* that scent? Tobias blinked, realising he was rubbing his face on her clothes again, and dropped the jumper back on the bed. At this rate he'd need to wash everything a second time, or Aislinn would realise he'd been rolling on her clothes like a pubescent boy with a movie poster and an odd sock.

First thing's first, Tobias. You promised to take her to town and maybe, if you play your cards right, she'll let something slip. He nodded, padding down the stairs and heading for the door. When he'd knocked on Grandma's door last night he'd mentioned picking Ash up at ten so they could go into town for shopping and lunch, which meant he had to get a move on or he'd be late. Tobias grabbed his phone and wallet off the bench, made to shove them in his pockets, and - still naked.

Clothes. Right.

Drawing on his preternatural speed, Tobias raced back upstairs, yanked a pair of denim shorts and a loose black tank out of the drawer and tugged them on. Good enough. This time, his phone and wallet slid easily into his pocket and in minutes, Tobias was knocking politely on Grandma Redding's door.

Grandma pulled open the door so fast Tobias had the distinct impression she'd been waiting for him. She looked him over, grunted, and said; "Who are you taking with you?"

"Zeke."

"Didn't he do the last round of the night?" Grandma frowned, looking at her watch. "Wouldn't Dominic be a better choice?"

Yeah, but Dominic and Aislinn had been all-but nose to nose by the fire last night and every time Tobias thought about the tender way she'd probed his bruised cheek, he wanted to murder someone. Or set something on fire. Or murder someone and *then* set them on fire. He'd settled instead for asking a very tired Zeke to make good on his offer of backup - and Zeke, bless him, hadn't even blinked before agreeing.

"I need Zeke; Sens always flirts with Dominic and I won't get any help out of her while she's giggly."

Grandma snorted. "Foolish girl. Pity the man who ends up with her - she's flightier than a flock of seagulls outside a fish and chip shop."

"She's not like that at all," Tobias defended Sienna on instinct. "She's just not like you, Joanne. Cut her some slack."

"Humph." Grandma Redding rolled her eyes. "I suppose I wouldn't know; I'm not the one who keeps inviting her to sleep over at my house, now, am I?"

Sienna kept inviting herself, but there was no use explaining that to Grandma Redding. Zeke and Sienna spent as much time sleeping at Tobias' house as he spent sleeping at theirs, the habit so deeply entrenched that nobody blinked if they came home and found an extra body in the spare bedroom.

So Tobias said; "As long as she's sleeping somewhere, Grandma," and left it at that.

"Indeed. Ah, Aislinn my dear, there you are. Did you sleep well?" Grandma ushered Aislinn out onto the porch.

"Well enough," Aislinn answered with a shrug. "Hey, Tobias."

"Hey," he managed.

She was trying to kill him, Tobias decided, backing down the stairs and leading the way to the communal garage. She was really, honestly trying to kill him. He slid a glance at Aislinn out of the corner of his eye - skinny jeans so tight they might as well have been painted on, a clinging, three-quarter sleeve top in deep violet and a motherfucking *corset* in black brocade which thrust her breasts up like some sort of proverbial feast. Thick red-brown waves of hair tumbled over her shoulders and down her back, accented with a single gold clip at one temple which matched the torc around her neck and the gold buckles on her ballet flats.

Tobias swallowed, forcing himself to focus on the golden torc which had haunted him since she arrived. It hadn't fallen off when she shifted last night, confirming his suspicion that it was one of those new, *very* expensive necklaces that adapted during a shift so it could be worn at all times. And, now that he was getting a better look at it, the thing bulged in a way that told Tobias it was also a locket.

It was only when they reached the car, already idling, that Tobias realised they'd walked the entire ten minutes without him saying a word.

"Zeke!" Aislinn rushed into the arms of the man leaning against the driver's door, her tone so relieved that Tobias felt his cheeks flush with embarrassment.

Way to go, Tobias - so busy ogling the woman you forgot to be polite.

"Morning, gorgeous. Look at you," Zeke hummed appreciatively, plucking at Aislinn's violet sleeve. "Much as I love the wrapping, aren't you melting? It's going to be a scorcher today."

Zeke, like Tobias, was dressed in shorts and a tank, the neckline of which Aislinn tugged on playfully. "I told you, numb nuts, I didn't pack any summer things. Remember?"

"Not at all," Zeke replied breezily. "I was too busy being distracted by all your curves."

"Stop it, you beast!" Aislinn laughed, shoving him square in the chest. She paused, fingers splayed across Zeke's sternum in a way that made Tobias' hackles rise, and leant forward to peer into his face. "Have you slept since doing the rounds?"

"Sure," Zeke answered, and blinked as Aislinn swatted his shoulder. "Okay, fine, no - but I've only been up since four. It's not so bad."

"You should be home in bed," Aislinn growled, flicking a black look at Tobias over her shoulder.

"And miss the chance to drive your lusciousness into Gerup? No way." Zeke shook his head, flicking a finger against her chin. "Now come on, or we'll be late and Sienna will be pissed."

Aislinn chuckled at that and opened the door, sliding into the back seat. After a moment's hesitation, Tobias moved to follow her, passing Zeke on his way around to the other side. "I'm going to regret this, aren't I?" He muttered.

"Just close your trap and we'll be fine," Zeke replied, his voice soft enough that Aislinn, inside the car, wouldn't be able to hear him. "Oh and wipe your chin, dude. You're drooling."

"Fuck you," Tobias growled, yanking the door open while Zeke laughed uproariously.

"You don't have to sit with me," Aislinn gasped as he slid into the back next to her.

"You don't want me to?" Tobias asked, freezing half way to his seat belt.

"No, it's not that, it's just…" she hesitated, her blue-green eyes haunted. "The smell."

The smell.

The moment Aislinn said it, Tobias was swamped with her altered scent. He held his breath until the red fog clouding his vision cleared, then exhaled in a gust and forced a smile. "I can handle it."

Aislinn closed her eyes, the woman who'd been joking with Zeke only moments earlier replaced by a ghost. "If you're sure."

"Ash," he began, his voice soft. She opened her eyes and in that moment, Tobias thought he'd never seen another person look so terribly mournful. He opened his mouth to say - what, he had no idea - but then Zeke flopped into the front seat, slamming the door behind him.

Aislinn immediately retreated, lowering the window on her side of the car and all-but sticking her head out. It was at that moment Tobias realised he was holding his breath again, and forced himself to let it out. Dammit, he hadn't thought this through. But Aislinn clearly had, or why else would she have rolled down the window? He looked up to find Zeke watching him in the rear view mirror, something akin to pity on his face. A moment later music blasted through the car, loud and obnoxious and for once in his life Tobias was glad that he couldn't hear anything else.

****

Aislinn stared up at the sign above Ysera's Boutique with despair heavy on her heart. How was she possibly going to get out of this one? She should've said no when Grandma told her Tobias' suggestion - but as Grandma pointed out, she *had* promised to go into town for some more clothes.

"One of the advantages of being a designer is I can come in whenever I want," Sienna was saying as she unlocked the door. "Talk about VIP service, right? It'll be just us." She frowned over Aislinn's shoulder. "And them, of course."

"Don't worry about us, little sister wolf," Zeke grinned. "We've got no interest in your lady things. Ysera still has that kitchenette upstairs, yeah? We'll just make coffee and wait."

"It's the no interest part that's the problem, bean pole," Sienna argued, yanking the door open and ushering them all inside. "How's a girl supposed to know what's sexy when you're busy staring at Arabica beans?"

"Baby girl, you do *not* want me telling you what I think is sexy," Zeke laughed, flipping on the lights and then the air conditioner. "I'm your brother. That shit is just weird."

"Tobias should be telling us," Sienna said, her tone suddenly dripping with honey. "Don't you think, Tobias?"

Tobias looked up from his position at the base of the stairs, eyes wider than a deer caught in headlights. "What?"

"Were you even listening?" Sienna propped both hands on her hips, silver bangles jingling merrily in the silence. She wore a stunning white sundress covered in deep pink spots, with a vivid pink ribbon around the waist that matched her lipstick. Teamed with pink heels and immaculate victory rolls, she was every bit the retro pin-up. "I said, don't you think you should be telling us if we're sexy or not?"

"Er," Tobias blushed, glancing at Aislinn and then away again. "You're alright, I guess."

"*What*?" Sienna stomped her foot and shook her ringlets. "Tobias Greenwood, you're a disgrace. Go upstairs and make me a latte before I geld you!"

The moment a flustered Tobias and a laughing Zeke did as they were told, Sienna turned to Aislinn and winked. "Perfect. I thought we'd never get rid of them."

"Yeah," Aislinn managed. "Men, huh."

"Tell me about it," Sienna rolled her eyes, grabbing Aislinn's hand and dragging her into the racks of clothing. "I've been trying to get Tobias to loosen up for years."

"Oh? Are you two -"

"Shhhhhh," Sienna all-but tackled Aislinn into a stand of dresses, her eyes wide. "No, no, no. Tobias has no idea."

Ah. So she hadn't been imagining it. "How long have you been in love with him?"

"Too bloody long," Sienna growled. "I even flirt with Dominic like a lunatic in the hopes he'll notice but he doesn't even bat an eyelash. I'm just his little sister and I likely always will be."

"Oh, Sens." On impulse, Aislinn folded Sienna into a gentle hug. "I'm sorry. Men are so stupid sometimes."

"Lunaida knows I'm not supposed to be telling *you* this," Sienna sniffed, nevertheless melting into Aislinn's embrace.

"Why not?" Aislinn drew back long enough to tuck a stray strand of hair behind the other woman's ear.

Sienna looked up at her in genuine amazement for a long moment, then snorted. "If you don't know, then I am *not* telling you."

"What?"

"Nope! Uh uh," she shook her head, eyes glistening with mischief as well as tears. "Some things a girl's gotta find out for herself, Ash - but thanks for being kind to me."

"Of course," Aislinn said, her brow furrowing in confusion. "We're friends, aren't we? I mean, we used to be."

"Friends," Sienna repeated. "Yeah. I like that idea."

"Good," Aislinn said, still not quite sure what she'd missed. "Now, about the clothes. I have a problem…" she trailed off and bit her lip. "I need to keep covered up."

"In the middle of summer?" Sienna frowned. "Zeke said you were only wearing that because you didn't have any other clothes."

"True," Aislinn admitted. "But…"

Shit. She was going to have to do it. Either start her new life out on a lie, or take a risk and trust Sienna Smythe. With trembling hands, Aislinn reached for the neckline of her violet top and gently tugged it down to reveal the leading edges of her scars.

"Oh," both hands flew to Sienna's mouth, her sapphire eyes like saucers as she stared at the angry red slashes. "*Oh.*"

"Shhh," Aislinn whispered, letting the fabric go and clutching desperately at Sienna's hands. "One secret for another, yeah? Please."

"They don't know?"

"I can't tell them." Aislinn shook her head and now it was her turn to tear up. "I want to but I can't. I can't even think about it."

"Okay. Of course. Do they hurt?"

Aislinn nodded glumly. "Yeah."

"And… everywhere?"

"Yeah," she nodded again. "Pretty much."

"Mother Moon, Ash," Sienna shook her head, hands trembling. "You're so *brave.*"

"Brave?" Aislinn echoed, surprised. "You don't know -"

"It doesn't matter," Sienna cut her off smoothly. "I don't need to know. Anyone who can walk and talk and smile and laugh and carry that sort of pain is brave. You don't work in admin in Ireland, do you?"

"No," Aislinn answered quietly. "I don't."

"Oh, those boys are *so* wrong about you," Sienna muttered, snorting a sudden laugh. "Oh, my goodness! If only they knew."

Despite the entire ridiculous situation, Aislinn found herself giggling too and before long they were both laughing hysterically, collapsed against a shelf full of old winter stock, tears of mirth rolling down their cheeks.

"Are you two okay?" Tobias' head poked around the corner, his face contorting with astonishment. "What on earth are you doing?"

"Get out," Sienna wheezed, gathering herself long enough to point at the stairs behind him. "We're busy, Tobias!"

With a parting look that said he highly doubted their level of busy, Tobias disappeared and Sienna promptly collapsed into a fresh round of giggles. "Okay," she said at last, drying her eyes. "Let's do this."

Aislinn blinked in surprise. "Do what?"

"Build you a new wardrobe, of course." Sienna winked. "I'm a fashion designer, girlfriend - don't you think you're getting away that easily. Now come on, I've got tonnes of ideas."

****

The more Tobias thought about it, the more he was sure he'd regret inviting Sienna to spend more time with Aislinn. After six cups of coffee and who knows how long listening to their whispering and giggling, he and Zeke had been seconded to take them to Gerup's one and only restaurant for lunch - so that Sienna could, in her own words, show off Aislinn's 'transformation.'

They were both trying to kill him.

He'd thought the jeans and corset were bad - he really had no idea. Tobias looked up from his glass of iced water to where Aislinn stood with Sienna by the bar. She wore a floor length dress of cornflower blue lace, fitted across the bodice with a modest neckline and capped sleeves. The skirts flowed down from her waist, dotted here and there with dusky roses, swirling when she moved and clinging to her hips when she stood still. The ever-present gold torc gleamed against the dress, a match to the same gold hairpin Ash had worn earlier - only now Sienna had coiled a length of Aislinn's hair into an elaborate looking bundle that somehow resembled the exact roses on her dress. The entire effect was summery, soft, feminine - sexy.

"You're growling," Zeke said conversationally, stirring his glass of water with a casual finger. "Put a lid on it, dude."

Tobias bit down on his tongue until he tasted blood. From here, without the stench of whoever else Ash had chosen to mate with, he was free to imagine what his life might've been like if he'd been smart enough to get there first. "Why didn't she ever try and call?"

"It's a big world out there." Zeke shrugged. "Maybe you're eternally friend zoned."

"Ouch." Tobias punched Zeke in the shoulder and got a grin in return. "Some second you are."

"My job is to tell you the truth, not kiss your puckered ring hole," Zeke answered, flipping the menu open and scanning the contents. "Why'd Sienna have to pick this place? Closest thing I can get to a steak here is salmon."

"It's run by a bunnykin," Tobias answered absently, watching Aislinn laugh in response to something Sienna said. "You're lucky the entire menu isn't carrots."

"You're a carrot," Zeke muttered. "Why don't you just tell her?"

"Tell her what?" Tobias blinked, turning to see Zeke regarding him with both brows raised.

"Dude, come *on*. The entire restaurant could be naked and breathing fire and you'd still be staring at Ash."

Tobias flushed and decided to adjust his table setting. "I wasn't."

Zeke snorted. "What, you were staring at Sienna? Don't make me laugh."

"Maybe I was. Sens is pretty."

"So is chocolate cake. Doesn't mean you want to stick your -"

"Can I take your order?" A waitress bustled up, pen and paper in one hand.

"Sure." Tobias rattled off a couple of items while Zeke coughed and spluttered into his water and then sheepishly placed an order of his own. "Those two ladies are with us, too," Tobias added when the waitress made to leave.

"Not a problem, I'll stop by before I head to the kitchens." She smiled and whirled away.

Tobias raised an eyebrow at Zeke, who was mopping his face with a napkin. "You were saying?"

"I hate you," Zeke grumbled.

Tobias' grin was arrested by the acrid stench of what's-his-name, and he barely managed to school his expression as Aislinn plunked into the chair next to him.

"You guys order?" She asked.

"Sure did. Where's Sienna?" Zeke's brow furrowed slightly as he looked around. "Not trying to stuff more crap in the boot of the car, I hope."

Aislinn raised an eyebrow. "So suspicious! She saw someone she knew and went to say hi."

"You two seem to be getting along well," Tobias noted, hoping it sounded casual rather than interrogative.

The ghost of a smile drifted across Aislinn's features. "Sisters in arms, I guess." She looked up at Tobias from under her lashes. "Apparently we're having wine and popcorn night at your house next week."

"My house!" Tobias protested. "I thought Sens was only kidding when she said that."

"Apparently not."

Tobias groaned, burying his head in his hands. "Great."

"You got something against wine and popcorn?"

"No, but-" He couldn't handle Aislinn's clothes under his roof - what was he going to do if she was there in person?

"You still have that old quilt?" Aislinn asked, tilting her head to one side. "With the fluffy edges?"

"Of course he does." Zeke snorted over the top of Tobias' hesitation. "Let me guess - it was your favourite."

Aislinn nodded, eyes twinkling in memory. "We used to sneak under the quilt in the middle of the night and tell each other ghost stories. Remember?"

"I guess," Tobias murmured, kicking Zeke under the table in silent warning. His second might not have known the relevance of the quilt - but he knew without a doubt that Tobias slept underneath it every night, a fact that Aislinn absolutely did *not* need to find out.

"Oh come on," Aislinn flicked the back of his wrist, giggling. "We'd curl up underneath it in wolf form and your mum would find us in the morning. And it had to be that quilt, because -"

"The fluffy edges were tickly, like feathers," Tobias finished softly.

"You *do* remember!"

"I'm surprised you do," he said, unable to stop the words tumbling out.

Aislinn frowned but at that moment, the waitress appeared with their meals. Sienna slipped into her chair with a glass of wine each for her and Aislinn and just like that, the topic changed.

Tobias looked down at his lunch - eggs benedict on top of hash browns with thick lashings of hollandaise and extra crispy bacon - and broke open the poached egg without really seeing it. Why had she bought all that up? To taunt him? Those days were precious, gilt with the promise of forever and now Aislinn had tainted them with her strange, altered scent. He glanced at Zeke, only to catch Aislinn playing with her golden torc out of the corner of his eye. Red fog clouded Tobias' vision and he clenched his fist around his fork until the silverware dug painfully into his palms. Not now. He would absolutely *not* lose his mind in the middle of the restaurant.

Sienna said something and started giggling and it took a moment for Tobias to realise she was looking at him, her sapphire eyes bright with mischief.

"What?" He said, trying to blink through the drums beating inside his head.

"You two," Sienna motioned between himself and Ash. "So alike."

Tobias frowned, still confused - until he looked down and realised that, sight unseen, he and Aislinn had ordered the exact same meal, right down to the extra crispy bacon and double hollandaise. "Hah," Tobias said, dredging his voice up from heaven knew where. "Imagine that."

There must have been something in his tone because Aislinn flinched and Zeke shook his head in silent warning. Tobias squeezed his eyes shut, the thumping in his brain even worse than before. Get a grip. Get a grip. Get a *grip*. He took a deep, steadying breath - and got a lungful of Aislinn's altered scent. Rather than howl the place to bits, Tobias lent to his left, where Sienna was sitting, and buried his face in her hair. It was completely and utterly inappropriate on a whole number of levels but he decided, in that desperate moment, that it was sure as hell better than heaving the table halfway across the restaurant like his instincts demanded.

"Tobias?" Sienna's squeak was half astonishment, half embarrassment.

"Sorry, couldn't help it," Tobias admitted, while they all stared at him with mouths open. He groped for something to say and settled on; "You smell nice today, Sens."

Sienna Smythe blushed an attractive shade of pink that covered almost every available inch of bare flesh. "Thank you."

The meal finished quite quickly after that and Tobias was more than glad when Sienna said she'd take care of the bill and meet them outside. Aislinn went to the ladies' room, leaving Zeke and Tobias to head to the car alone.

"Have you gone nuts?" Zeke hissed as he yanked the driver's door open. "What were you thinking?"

"I had to do something," Tobias growled, running one hand through his hair. "My instincts were trying to tear me apart."

Zeke paused, his ire momentarily forgotten. "The smell?"

"Yeah." Tobias nodded. "Hit me out of nowhere."

Zeke frowned, worrying his lower lip between his teeth. "Not cool, dude. Maybe you should ride in the front with me on the way back - I promised Sienna a lift, so she can sit with Ash."

"Maybe that's a good idea." Tobias ran a hand over his face. "Sens is going to be *so* pissed at me."

"What, for sniffing her like a lover? No, I don't imagine that would bother her at all," Zeke drawled.

"You know sarcasm is the lowest form of wit, right?" Tobias muttered, still safe behind his palm.

"Considering you basically just claimed my sister in the middle of that fucking restaurant, you can deal with it," Zeke snapped.

Tobias froze. "You don't think she thought -"

"Dude, *I* didn't know what to think." Zeke shook his head. "Look, they're coming. For Solaeden's sake shut your mouth and try to be polite on the drive home, okay?"

Tobias dropped his hands as Aislinn and Sienna arrived, the former silent and the latter bubbling with laughter. She skipped straight up to Zeke and handed him a plastic take-away container. "This is for you, big brother. From one of the waitresses inside."

"Me?" Zeke accepted the container, looking confused. "What is it?"

"A slice of chocolate cake," Sienna answered. "She said you'd understand."

Now it was Zeke's turn to blush and even through his personal confusion, Tobias chuckled. "Looks like you got yourself an admirer."

"Shut up," Zeke muttered, opening the car and shoving the cake inside. "Can we please just go home?"

Sienna pouted. "But what about ice cream?"

"Sorry Sens, I'm beat," Aislinn demurred, her face drawn and pale. "I'd really like to just head home."

Zeke dashed to Aislinn's side, yanking the door open. "You okay, babe? You're not going to faint on me again, are you? Because that waitress might be disappointed if I have to sweep you off your feet while she's looking."

Aislinn summoned the ghost of a smile. "I think I'll be fine. I just really want to go home."

Were those tears in her voice? Tobias blinked and turned for a closer look but it was too late; Ash had swung herself into the car, arranging her skirts on the seat, with her head bowed enough that her hair covered her face.

Zeke prodded Tobias and he tugged open the passenger door, sliding into the seat while Sienna got in the back. As the car pulled away from the kerb, Tobias' pocket buzzed. He wriggled in the chair until he could lever his phone out, scrolling through the message with a furrowed brow. "Ash, who drove you from the airport?"

"Pardon?"

Tobias twisted to look into the back, where Aislinn's pale face stared back at him. Her altered scent punched him right in the gut and he swallowed around it. Why did it seem so strong all of a sudden? "I said, who drove you in from the airport?"

"Freddie," she answered, tilting her head to the side. "Why?"

"I thought so. I just got a message from Grandma Redding; apparently Freddie didn't turn up for work yesterday afternoon. They're trying to track his movements, work out where he might be." Tobias twisted back to the front, frowning down at his phone. "Did he say where he was headed after you?"

"No," Aislinn replied softly. "I know he has a Kin girlfriend somewhere around here, though - that's why he gets so many Pack contracts."

"Hmmm. Okay, I'll let Grandma know - maybe he's with her."

"I hope so," Aislinn's murmur was so soft that Tobias almost wasn't sure he heard it. "I really, really hope so."

Five

Carolling magpies roused Aislinn and she sat up, scrubbing her face and blinking groggily at the digital clock on the desk beside her. 6am. Better than 2am, she supposed, which is when she'd originally sat at the tiny desk in her room. She stared down at the rumpled pages of her diary and grimaced. Drool had blurred some of the words but her angsty, nightmare-driven entry was more than legible - and not something she really wanted to look at in the harsh light of day.

Aislinn slammed the book shut and returned it to the hidden compartment in the bottom of her wheeled luggage, along with the other important things she'd packed. A hidden compartment in a suitcase might not be the most inventive hiding place in the world but it would stop casual passers-by from reading things she'd rather not be read. With her thoughts out of her head and safely locked away, Aislinn stood and stretched. Her body was tired from the previous day's exertions but in no more pain than usual, so she indulged in a little early morning tai chi before padding across to the bathroom to shower.

Half an hour later, dressed in loose cotton harem pants and a flowing top in layers of pastel gauze, Aislinn braided her hair over one shoulder and stepped out into the morning sunlight. The sun was up and the promise of another hot day hung heavy in the air but for now, the houses were still sleepy and shadowed, the common lawn quiet and peaceful.

"Aislinn? That you?" A drawling male voice preceded a silver-haired man around the corner of one of the houses.

"Bill? Bill Deepwater?" Laughing in delight, Aislinn hugged Rory's grandfather and stepped back. "Lunaida's blessing, you're still alive."

"Last I checked." Bill's laugh was deep and solid, like the rest of him. Barely topping five feet and with wrinkles on his wrinkles, Bill

Deepwater had been a part of the Redding Pack for as long as Aislinn could remember. With rich brown eyes and wispy white hair combed neatly to one side, the older wolfkin had an uncanny knack for fixing things and was often found 'pottering' in the shed attached to the cottage he shared with Rory. Now, his work-rough hands took hold of Aislinn's elbows and squeezed gently. "Haven't you bloomed into a pretty flower, now? Reminds me of your grandmama."

"Stop it," Aislinn chuckled, reaching out to straighten the handkerchief poking out of Bill's shirt pocket. "Someone might think you've got designs on my grandmother, talking like that."

"Maybe I do." Bill winked and they shared a laugh. "The boys've been taking care of you now, I hope?"

"Maybe I'm taking care of them."

"You always did." Bill nodded sagely. "About time, too. The bush been mighty restless of late."

"Restless?"

"Mmmm, the scranimals are scamperin' and the trees are whisperin'. I'll bet your Tobias can feel it, too." Bill nodded again. "Alphas always can."

Aislinn paused at that. She'd felt uncannily restless all night but had put it down to the debacle at the restaurant the day before, when Tobias had pretty much propositioned Sienna in the middle of lunch. Okay, maybe propositioned was a *little* too strong - but the way he'd drawn her scent in, as though it were some sort of life saving tonic - that sort of behaviour was usually reserved for lovers and mates.

Which was totally fine, Aislinn told herself for the thousandth time. Tobias Greenwood could bed whoever he wanted - and considering Sienna's feelings were painted all over her face, maybe it was about time.

"You alright, lass? You're looking a bit grim, there."

"Oh," Aislinn blinked, realising she'd been staring off into space while her companion patiently waited for a response. "Sorry, Bill. Got a lot on my mind." And then, because she'd learnt from Flynn never to wash off the instincts of the sensitives, she said; "Where does the bush call you most?"

Bill pointed, his wizened face solemn. "Westerly."

"There's a foxkin earth out that way, isn't there?" Aislinn frowned, dredging at her memory. "Or there used to be."

"They're still there. Fickle lot, spend a lot of time with the nearby humans." Bill shrugged, as though there were no accounting for taste.

"Humans aren't so bad, Bill. Just different."

"I hear you, little one - but I prefer the furries myself." Bill winked and then patted her on the arm in a fatherly manner. "'Cept the bears, of course. Exiling them was the best thing we ever did. My gramma was alive during the wars and let me tell you, she saw things nobody ever should. You know they *eat* people? Even Kin."

"Yeah," Aislinn said, shivering. "I know."

"Well, I best be off. Good to see you, lass." Bill waved and then loped away, surprisingly spry given his advanced age.

West, huh? Aislinn walked into the cover of the bush and undressed, rolling her clothes together into a bundle she could easily carry in her teeth. She shifted into wolf form and snatched the roll of clothing off the ground, jogging steadily westward. Her wounds ached less in this body, as though having fur to cover the scars somehow lessened their impact. Aislinn broke into a run, enjoying the feel of the solid earth beneath her paws and the rhythmic thump of her heart in the early morning. A week ago this had been impossible - not just the shifting but exercise of any sort. Maybe returning to the bush *was* a good idea, in spite of Andre's desire to simply send his stinky daughter somewhere else.

Before long, she heard the sound of more running paws and the crackle of a body pushing through bracken. Having made no attempt to disguise her own movements, Aislinn slowed and eventually drew to a halt in the shelter of some eucalypts.

A black-furred wolf emerged from the trees and Aislinn didn't need the pale blue eyes to tell her it was Dominic. They circled each other for a moment, exchanging a quick nose rub before Aislinn ducked behind the shelter of a thick bush and resumed her human body, hastily tugging her clothing on. When she stepped back out, Dominic was human but naked, one hand propped on his hip and his sleek black eyebrows arched.

"You carry clothes with you?" He queried, puzzled. Since clothing was impossible to shift, nudity was a fact of Kin life and as a general rule, those who spent a lot of time moving between forms were comfortable with that. Anything else simply wasn't practical.

"Not normally." Aislinn forced a smile on her face. "I couldn't be bothered going home to strip but I didn't want to leave them behind, either." She waved a hand down at herself and shrugged. "Wearing my clothes seems easier than carrying them."

"Fair enough." Dominic smiled, then hesitated. "Nothing wrong, I hope?"

"Just out for a run. You on patrol?"

"Yeah, almost done though." He swept a hand out towards the bush. "Walk with me?"

Since he was pointing in the direction she'd already been going, Aislinn nodded. "Sure."

"I hope I didn't startle you earlier," he said as they set off.

Aislinn snorted, skipping neatly over a thorny bush, and cut a look at Dominic out of the corner of her eye. "Not likely; I smelt you coming a mile away. Probably shouldn't wear aftershave whilst you're out on patrol."

He winced. "I overslept and didn't have time to shower. Tobias is running us ragged with all this border crap - we're out in the middle of nowhere. Why bother?"

"It doesn't hurt to be prepared for anything," Aislinn said, suppressing a stab of guilt. "Besides, if you weren't out patrolling, you'd never have run into me, right?"

"There is that." Dominic chuckled, the sound very male and throaty. "I haven't been lucky enough to have you all to myself yet."

"Dominic Schellponte, are you flirting with me?" Aislinn teased - and was surprised when he rewarded her with a brilliant, breath-catching smile.

"Maybe I am," he answered. "Would that be all right, Ms. Redding?"

Holy shit, he *was* flirting with her. What now? Aislinn opened her mouth to tell him it was a terrible idea - and had a sudden and vivid memory of Tobias burying his face in Sienna's hair. "Yeah," she found herself saying. "I think I can handle that."

Dominic's growl was almost a purr and it set the hairs on Aislinn's arms on end. "Excellent."

"How's your face?" She asked, more to fill the silence than anything else. He should be well and truly healed by now and they both knew it.

"Fine," Dominic answered, waving a dismissive hand. "But I'm interested in what you said about my guard. Are you familiar with staves?"

Aislinn grinned. "A little." They were her favourite, but there was no need to tell Dominic that. "You need a lesson?"

He looked inordinately pleased at the suggestion. "Maybe I do."

"All right." Aislinn bent down and swept up a long, thin tree branch from the ground, tossing it at the startled male. "On guard."

"Now?" Dominic asked, fumbling to catch the branch as it thumped him in the chest.

"Why not?" Aislinn scooped up a second branch - a little too long for her - and snapped it over one knee with a practised movement. "I promise not to hurt you."

As she'd expected, Dominic's surprise disappeared. "Oh, really? And what if I hurt *you*?"

Unlikely. "Then you'll have to kiss it better," she teased. Dominic blinked, his jaw dropping - and Aislinn smacked him in the ribs with her staff.

"Hey!"

"Guard up, honey," Aislinn drawled, mimicking Flynn. "Next one won't be so gentle."

Dominic said nothing, continuing to stare - but he parried her next strike. Aislinn moved carefully, using the environment to her advantage so that he didn't notice the weakness of her body, throwing out a few probing strikes whenever she came within range.

"You're lagging on the left," she said. "That's how Tobias got in. A feint down here -" and she illustrated her point, drawing Dominic's weapon down, "and it leaves you wide open here." Aislinn reversed the staff, stopping millimetres from the exact place Tobias had struck the day before.

Dominic froze, almost cross-eyed as he stared at the branch. "How did you do that?"

"Like this." She demonstrated again. "You try."

Goggling as though he'd never seen her before, Dominic nevertheless mimicked her movements. Aislinn sidestepped the feint and swept her staff up to block the incoming blow, sliding it down the length of the branch and slipping inside Dominic's guard to jam the butt of her branch against his jaw. "And that's how you defend against it."

"Shit," Dominic managed, jerking half a step back. He rubbed at his throat, but there wasn't a single mark. "Huh. You didn't actually hit me?"

"Of course not. Wouldn't want you to have to explain a second bruise," Aislinn winked, pointing to the ribs she'd struck earlier. "I know how to be gentle."

Dominic stared down at the staff in his hand, then back up at Aislinn, his pale eyes wild with sudden fire. "Show me again."

She did, alternating attack and defence until Dominic was proficient at both and called a halt, his chest heaving. Aislinn dropped her branch on the ground and wiped at the sweat on her forehead. "Man, I'm so out of shape."

"Out of shape?" Dominic repeated, laughing. "Are you nuts?"

"Most likely." Aislinn shrugged, grinning. "Still, I stand by - wait, someone's coming."

Half a second later a mousy brown wolf loped out of the bush and unfolded into Rory. "Tobias needs you," he said without preamble.

"Which one of us?" Dominic asked, dropping his branch on the ground.

"You, but he also asked me to track down Ash so I guess that's two birds and all." Rory nodded a greeting at Aislinn. "Grandma Redding got a call from the Melbourne embassy, with the address for Freddie's girl. She's a foxkin, lives out west."

West. Aislinn's heart leapt into her mouth and she stepped forward. "Let's go."

"What? No." Rory held up both hands, shaking his head. "Jax and I are due on patrol. Tobias said you were to go back to Grandma's and Dom was to meet him at the garage."

"*Go back to Grandma's?*" Aislinn repeated.

"Where you'll be safe," Rory said slowly, as though speaking to someone hard of hearing.

"I don't think so," Aislinn snorted. "If we're looking for Freddie, I'm going too."

"Tobias said-"

"Tobias can stick his head up his own ass for all I care," Aislinn growled. She dredged deep inside herself, marshalling energies that had been allowed to sleep for over a month, and looked Rory square in the eye. "I'm going."

"Okay," Rory nodded, taking a step backwards, and glanced at Dominic. "Look out for her."

Aislinn swung her blazing gaze to Dominic - only to find him grinning. "Somehow," he said, "I think she's going to be looking after me. Come on, Ash. Time to watch Tobias stick his head up his own ass."

****

Tobias looked at his watch for the fifth time in as many minutes. Where the hell was Dominic? He should've been well back from his patrol by now. Bracken snapped and rustled to the left and he straightened, motioning Zeke to start the car. About time.

Dominic came loping out of the bush in wolf form, a slender, russet-brown wolf by his side. Who the - was that *Aislinn*? Yes, his nose confirmed, it was. He'd seen her wolf form briefly in the den two nights before but it'd been little more than a glimpse in poor light. Now, it was easy to see her wolf body had matured as well as her human one. Strong, sleek, well-muscled, with almost too-big ears and those deep blue-green eyes that could never be mistaken for anyone else's.

"What are you doing here?" He growled, his voice a confusing muddle of half-shifted yipping. Tobias blinked, looking down to see fur rippling across his forearms. What the hell?

In the few moments it took for him to reverse his almost shift, Aislinn had slipped into the bush, resumed her human form and emerged fully dressed. She was barefoot, with blue cotton pants that tapered in at the ankle and wore a multi-layered top that whispered as she moved. Her thick, red-tinted brown hair draped across one shoulder in a lazy braid and Tobias had to clench his teeth against the urge to grab hold of it and shake her - an urge that only intensified when he set eyes on that damned golden torc around her neck.

"I thought you could use some backup." Aislinn shrugged and, without bothering to wait for his opinion, opened the passenger door and slid in next to Zeke.

Tobias, unsure whether to be astonished or apoplectic, turned to Dominic. "What the fuck, Dom?"

"Don't look at me," Dominic answered, yanking on the shorts and t-shirt that had been brought along for him to wear. "Rory told her to go back to Grandma's and she strong-armed him."

"And you had nothing to add?"

Dominic shrugged. "You heard her - she said we could use the backup. I couldn't really argue."

"*Backup*?" Tobias repeated. "Fuck's sakes, we're going to visit a fox and a human. They're probably sipping iced tea and watching movies."

"Well in that case, no harm her coming along, is there?" Dominic said, running a hand through his hair and heading for the back door of the car. "You're the one who said we have to accept her back into the pack. Don't be a dick."

Red fog descended over Tobias' vision and he turned his face up to the sky, nails digging into his palms until the urge to gut his friend passed. When he looked back down again, blood trickled from the inside of his clenched fists and though his fingers were definitely human, the puncture wounds in his palms belonged to claws.

Not a good sign.

Hastily wiping his hands on one of the rags that were always lying around the garage, Tobias yanked open the door and slid into the backseat beside Dominic.

"Here we go," Zeke said cheerfully, gunning the engine and putting the car in gear. "Next stop, Freddie-ville."

"How long by car?" Aislinn asked, slouching down in the seat and propping her feet on the dash.

"Couple hours." Zeke waved one hand in a give-or-take motion. "Why? Bored already?"

"No," Aislinn snorted. "Just wondering whether it's worth putting some music on. Dom, have you got your phone?"

"No, it's back at the house," Dominic mourned.

"Just as well," Zeke chuckled. "I don't think I could handle two hours of crooning jazz."

"*Really*?" Aislinn twisted in her seat to stare back at Dominic. "Tell me he's kidding."

"What's wrong with a little jazz?"

"Mother Moon, I'm not even going to answer that. Tobias, have you got your phone?"

Tobias froze as those blue-green eyes pinned him. Yeah, give Aislinn his phone so she could see that his background screen was a picture of the two of them lounging down at the watering hole the day before she left for Ireland? Sure. Great idea.

"Here, babe, use mine." Zeke rummaged in the console and tossed his phone to Aislinn. "No picking on my metal collection though, yeah?"

"Good grief," Aislinn muttered, tapping away at the screen. "You can tell a lot about a man from his choice of music, you know - and you two have both just been pidgeon holed."

"Oh, because you're so high and mighty," Zeke scoffed. "What do you listen to, eh? Pretty little pop stars?"

"You'll have to wait and see," Aislinn smirked. "Or listen, as the case may be. Here we go - these guys are my favourite."

Moments later, the sounds of alternative rock filled the car and Aislinn, Zeke's phone safe in her lap, leant her head back against the seat and closed her eyes, singing along. Tobias watched her throat moving, watched her lips form the words - though the sheer volume of the music made it impossible to hear her actual voice - and felt his heart constrict. When he looked up, it was to find Zeke watching him in the mirror, his second's face a mask of astonishment.

Because Aislinn was playing Tobias' favourite band.

****

When Zeke finally drew the car to a stop beneath the shade of an enormous oak tree, Aislinn was the first to leap out, stretching her legs. The ride had been fine, really - if you didn't count the itching between her shoulders whenever Tobias stared at her. He probably hated her taste in music, Aislinn thought, screwing up her face while she waited for the men to join her. Whatever. Anything was better than having to finish the argument he'd been ready to start when she'd loped out of the bush at Dominic's side.

"There's Freddie's car," Zeke said, strolling up beside her and pointing. "At least, those are the plates Grandma gave us."

"That's the car," Aislinn confirmed, nodding. "Weird to think I only sat in it a few days ago."

"Four," Tobias said absently, shaking his leg as if to ease a cramp.

"Four what?"

"Four days," he answered, flicking her a look from underneath his lashes. "Since you came back."

Not quite sure if he meant it as a good or a bad thing, Aislinn turned to study the house in front of them. Freddie's girlfriend Macy had a cozy little two-story nestled amongst close-growing oaks very similar to the one Aislinn stood beside. The weatherboards had been freshly painted a bluish shade of grey, with white doors and window accents. Flowers bobbed gently in their window boxes and thick, dark green grass spread across a lawn broken only by acorns and smooth white stepping stones.

"I feel like I'm walking into Little Red Riding Hood," Dominic mused, turning in place. "Or maybe Hansel and Gretel?"

"Not enough candy," Aislinn murmured, crossing the lawn and ascending the few steps to the front porch. She knocked, waited. Knocked again. Waited again. "Hmmmm."

"Maybe they're not here?" Zeke suggested.

"Both their cars are," Aislinn answered, craning her head to try and see through the lace-covered windows. "They have to be."

"I'll check the back," Tobias announced. "Come on, Dom."

Aislinn waited until they were out of sight and then looked up at Zeke. "Care to make a bet?"

"On what?"

"On this." She bent down and flipped over the welcome mat to reveal a shiny silver key underneath. "People are so predictable."

"Wait, Ash, you can't just break in," Zeke protested.

"I'm not," she replied, slipping the key into the lock and turning it. "I've got a key."

The inside of the house was as quaintly furnished as the exterior, with thick rugs, plush pillows and more shabby chic furniture than Aislinn could take in at any one moment. She padded over to the kitchen, leaving Zeke to close the door behind them, and drew in a long, slow breath. Something… what was that scent?

"Hello?" Zeke called, his voice echoing up through the house. "Macy? Freddie?"

"What are you doing?" Aislinn hissed, one hand over her thumping heart. "You scared me half to death."

"What if they're busy upstairs? You know," Zeke wriggled his hips.

"Then you'd hear them," Aislinn pointed out, tapping her ear for emphasis. "You do have super hearing, right?"

"Of course. It's just…" Zeke frowned and bit his lip.

"Yeah," Aislinn answered. "I know. Something feels off."

The fruit in the fruit bowl was still fresh and the milk, when she checked in the fridge, was still in date. Tobias and Dominic entered just as she made her way towards the stairs - and froze.

"Everything looks fine around the back," Tobias was saying. "Shoes on the shoe rack and all that regular stuff."

"Blood," Aislinn whispered. The men went silent and, without bothering to look behind her, she padded up the stairs. A floorboard creaked and she held up a cautionary hand, glaring back at Tobias, who had a foot on the bottom step. "If you can't come quietly, then stay put."

He blinked, taken aback by the command but Aislinn didn't have time to explain herself. She tiptoed to the top of the stairs and slid into the shadows, drawing them about her shoulders like a cloak until her body dissolved and was no more than a suggestion of movement within the gloom. The small sitting room at the top of the stairs gave way to a hall in one direction and a set of double doors in the other, presumably leading to the master bedroom. One of the doors was slightly ajar and it was from within that Aislinn scented the coppery tang of blood.

The shadows took her inside, no more than a zephyr in the stifling summer air. It was indeed the master bedroom, curtains thrown wide to look out on a small balcony containing a white wrought iron table and chairs. Sitting in the centre of the table, glassy eyes staring in through the open windows, was Freddie's head. His body remained tied to the chair alongside, where he'd been forced to sit and presumably watch the systematic dismemberment of Macy, whose body parts were strewn around a bedroom streaked with blood and gore. It had been pretty once, in shades of pale blue and grey with hints of white - now, shredded clothing and smashed furniture served as the centrepiece for Macy's matted hair, broken bones and flaccid flesh.

Aislinn swept through the ensuite and the remaining rooms on the upstairs floor but there was no sign anyone else had been there save for the carnage in the bedroom. She materialised at the top of the stairs, staring down at the three confused men below. "I've found them."

There must have been something in her tone, for they were only moments behind Ash as she trudged back into the master bedroom, weaving her way across the blood spattered carpet towards the balcony doors.

"Holy shit," Tobias breathed and a moment later, someone gagged.

"Vomit in the hall," Aislinn commanded, not even bothering to turn, "or you'll ruin the evidence."

Such as it was.

"Where are you going?" Tobias appeared beside her just as she laid a hand on the blood-slicked handle.

Aislinn looked up at his white face. "Outside."

"He's dead."

"Yeah, but he might still have something to tell us." Without waiting for his response, Aislinn tugged the door open and stepped out into the fresh air, breathing deep regardless of the heat.

Freddie's head was, apart from being severed from his body, relatively unharmed. The acrid scent of fear clung to the human's clothing, strong enough that she guessed the attack had been fairly recent. His hair was caked with blood - probably from whoever's hand had placed him on the table. Aislinn stood and stared at the body, chewing her lower lip.

"What are you even searching for?" Tobias asked finally. She glanced sideways to see he was now a pale shade of green.

"Clues."

"To what? He's dead," Tobias repeated.

"First dead body?" Aislinn asked. He nodded. "Right. So, look at his wrists. See how they're grazed and bloodied? He struggled. And his clothes are torn - so he didn't go into that chair without a fight. Here," she splayed her hand to mimic a big, swiping paw, and held it over Freddie's sternum. "Those slash marks are what took his head off."

"Who the hell has claws that big?"

Ah. Well. Aislinn sighed. "Bears."

"Bears?" Tobias stared down at Freddie and then, very slowly, looked up at Aislinn. "They made him watch while they killed his girlfriend."

"Yeah. Meaning he was the target and Macy was simply leverage."

"For what?"

Aislinn's stomach turned very, very cold. "If I had to guess, I'd say information." And she swept back inside the bedroom before he had an opportunity to say anything more.

Zeke was crouched over the remains of an arm, his brow furrowed. "These… look like teeth marks."

"They are," Aislinn said. "Her arms were gnawed off."

"Fuck." Zeke covered his mouth with the back of one wrist and stood up quickly. "Why?"

"Because they were using their claws to hold her still." Aislinn's voice was steady but her body was shaking; it was too much too soon. She made a supreme effort and pulled herself together. "Where's Dom?"

"Here." His hoarse voice sounded from the doorway, where he sagged against the frame. "Sorry. I've never seen anything like this before."

"It's all right," Aislinn soothed. "It's pretty gross."

"What do we do now?" Zeke looked towards the balcony and frowned. "Tobias? What's wrong?"

The Alpha didn't answer and, feeling the burning weight of his gaze, Aislinn turned. Tobias stood with his hands by his sides, fingers clenching and unclenching. His blue eyes were flat, the golden starburst centres dull and his pupils so tiny they were almost non-existent. He was fixed on Aislinn and as she watched, his head lolled to one side like a doll's, lips curling back from his teeth. Sharp, pointed teeth.

"*You,*" he snarled, fur rippling up his arms in waves. "You did this. Didn't you?"

"Dude, come on. Get a -" Zeke broke off as Aislinn flung up a cautionary hand.

"Don't," she whispered. "He can't hear you."

"He can't?"

"No." Aislinn sighed. If it wasn't one thing, it was another - she hadn't been sure her shadow powers were going to work until she tried them and now, Tobias' first proper transitional rage meant she was going to have to further plumb the depths of her own energy. An energy she wasn't sure was going to answer, because it had been buried during the incident and remained dormant since.

"Ash?" Zeke's voice was full of uncertainty.

"Whatever you do, Zeke, don't move - and when this is over, remember to call Andre and report Freddie's murder."

"Aislinn Jaide Redding," Tobias growled, his voice hitching at the last. "I waited for you. I *waited*."

"Here I am, Tobias," said Aislinn quietly, deliberately stepping between Tobias and his pack mates. "Here I am."

His lip curled again and his hands - claws, now - clenched. "You stink."

"I know."

"You're the reason Freddie's dead."

"Yes."

Zeke and Dominic both gasped but Aislinn didn't have the time to spare for them. She'd have one chance at this, just one - and for all their sakes, she couldn't afford to mess it up.

Tobias took a slow, lurching step forward, a growl rumbling in his chest. "Tell me, did you sleep with Freddie too? Or is it just bears that turn you on?"

"You don't know what you're talking about," Aislinn said slowly, but Tobias cut her off with a snarl.

"I can smell it. I can smell *him*." Quick as lightning Tobias moved, wrapping clawed fingers around Aislinn's torc and dragging her so close they shared breath. "I can smell him all over Freddie, and all over you. *Inside of you*."

Zeke took half a step forward. "Tobias, stop! Ash didn't -"

"Don't," Aislinn warned, gritting her teeth as the torc cut into her throat. "He can't hear you, Zeke. He's trapped in a transitional rage. For the love of all you hold dear, stand still."

Tobias stared down at her, blue light flickering in the depths of his eyes. Slowly, so slowly, he used the torc to lift her off the ground, bringing them to eye level. His voice, when he spoke, was marred by the feral energy that was slowly but steadily overwhelming him. "After all these years, after everything, you dare to come here wearing the Mark of a *bear*?"

"I can explain," Aislinn gasped. Her best chance was to wait until the transitional episode peaked, then step in. It shouldn't be long now - except the torc was cutting off her air and spots were dancing in front of her vision.

"Mother Moon," Zeke whispered behind her, and Aislinn felt tears sting her eyes. He'd figured it out. "Oh, shit."

"Tobias, I know you're in there," Aislinn whispered, straining against the pain in her throat. "You can hear me; I know you can. You don't have to do this. Don't make *me* do this."

"Enough!" Tobias roared, the sound more animal than man, his rage a physical force. Fur swept up his body and across his neck and as his snout began to elongate, his voice thundered through the room and shattered Aislinn's heart into a thousand tiny pieces. "You *slut!*"

Pure, feral energy crackled through Tobias and he leant towards her, jaws gaping wide. Aislinn stared into his blue and yellow eyes, watching the rage build to catastrophic proportions - and kneed Tobias Greenwood square in the balls. He howled, releasing the torc and dropping to the floor. Aislinn caught herself with one hand on his shoulder, pressing the other palm to the middle of his forehead and summoning the cool, deep pool of shadows within her. It clashed with Tobias' energy and they grappled, a silent moment that seemed to last forever but was truly only a second. He was strong. Holy shit, he was strong - almost as strong as Flynn.

But she was stronger, and more experienced.

Weaving the shadows into a net, Aislinn shoved down on Tobias' head, catching the wild Alpha energy as it exploded outwards. He roared, writhing on the floor, a curious mix of man and wolf and fur and fury but Aislinn didn't relent. Down, down, down she pushed, stuffing the energy back in, wrapping it in her cooling, calming shadows and, when Tobias' spirit was firmly back inside of his body, she commanded it to sleep.

Tobias stared up at her and for a single, fractured moment, his eyes were clear - and then his lids drifted down and he slumped, unconscious, to the floor.

Silence fell, save for the ragged sound of Aislinn's breathing. She now knew with certainty that all her abilities had recovered from the incident, but at what cost? Tears streamed down her face and she looked up at Zeke without really seeing him. "He'll wake up in a minute," she said, her voice hoarse. "He'll be fine."

"Ash -" Zeke began, and then stopped. After all, what could he say?

Aislinn turned and ran. The balcony door was still open and in moments she'd vaulted over the balcony, calling the shadows as she fell and melting into them moments before she would've hit the ground. Behind her, Zeke swore and she heard the crash of furniture but by then she was in the trees, summoning her inner wolf. Fur sprouted, claws grew, teeth lengthened and in a bone-grinding heartbeat she was pounding across the bare earth on all fours. Instinct took her towards pack land but after a few seconds she swung in the opposite direction. Her grandmother had suffered enough. Freddie had suffered, Macy had suffered. Her father, her mother – she would not be a burden to her family any longer.

Freddie was dead. Aislinn ran on, the shadowed landscape blurring as she increased to super speed. Solaeden save her, Freddie was dead. How had the bears found her? How had they managed to follow her home?

A howl went up behind her and all thoughts of Freddie fled. Tobias. It was testament to the strength of the power now flowing through his veins that he'd woken so quickly. He'd be an Alpha to be reckoned with, once he mastered the energy which had erupted so suddenly.

Slut. The word rang in her head and Aislinn bit her lupine tongue to prevent the mournful howl that was building in her throat. When transitional energy got out of hand the Alpha in question often said and did things they didn't remember later, things that weren't real - but that didn't make them any less painful for the victim.

The oak trees ended suddenly and she shot across a small field and into proper bushland. Summer's heat pressed down from all angles yet Aislinn felt a curious sense of freedom as she fled. She knew this country, even after twelve years away. It seemed to welcome her with open arms, each tree bending out of her way, every shrub caressing her coat with encouragement as she passed by. Tobias would likely try and follow but he didn't know her anymore. She might've arrived home damaged but Aislinn had trained to be a warrior and she was better than anyone, even Flynn. And if the bears were truly hunting her, then the best way to protect everyone was to be as far away as possible.

She raced along, over boulders and through scrub tunnels, crossing creeks wherever possible to confuse her scent. When she sensed Tobias' howling pursuit getting further away, she slackened speed and began to plan. If the bears had been at Freddie's, they'd expect someone from the pack to check on him sooner or later. They might even be watching the roads, waiting for Aislinn to take the bait. Which meant that she had to lose not only her friends, but the bears too.

Aislinn cut towards Melbourne, leaving as obvious a trail as she dared. Neither Tobias or the bears could be allowed to realise they were being tricked until it was too late. She picked up speed again, eking every last iota of strength from her muscles as she ran. She was smaller. Lighter. *Faster.* Another scrub tunnel loomed and Aislinn swung inside. It was bisected at one end by a shallow, wide creek; she crossed, taking care to spend a moment rubbing against the tunnel's edge on the other side, then slipped into the water and quietly padded upstream at a right angle.

Now, for a few minutes, she must be silent. Any pursuers that managed to follow her this far must be made to believe she'd gone further into the tunnel and back towards Melbourne. Aislinn followed the stream as far as she was able then jumped lightly up a heap of bare rocks, finding herself in a small, rocky gully. Good. She slipped carefully between the boulders, pulling the shadows tightly around her, silent and invisible.

A soak of water dribbled out between two rocks and Aislinn paused for a few minutes' rest, lapping carefully at the little spring. Should she wait until dark, or keep on and hope the ground cover stayed thick enough to shelter her from pursuing eyes? No, she was still too close to foxkin territory to stop. It'd be better to run as long as she was able.

But where should she go? The gully continued south and if Aislinn's memory served her correctly, she'd pass the edge of Redding Pack land and end up in the middle of nowhere. If she cut back east, she'd skirt the edges of both fox and wolf territory, eventually arriving in a Kin town called Kilpenny. It was far enough away from pack land to be an unlikely choice and was in the opposite direction to Melbourne, so neither of her pursuers should think to look there first - and by the time they did, she'd be gone.

Aislinn began jogging further up the gully, letting it twist and turn her as it would. It'd been more than a month since she'd exercised so thoroughly and even in wolf form, her body ached unmercifully. Coming at last to the end of the gully, she groaned to see it had become almost sheer-sided cliffs. The sun beat down overhead, casting very little shadow and negating her ability to dissolve in the darkness. She couldn't afford to waste time backtracking, so she gathered her remaining strength and sprang upwards, clinging to precarious claw-holds as well as any mountain goat. After a few minutes' desperate scrabbling she rounded a tiny switchback, forced her way between some thick shrubs and was out on the plateau above pack land.

Scrub and gnarled, wind-blown trees dotted the edge of the plateau but not far in, tall gums rose in a forest which would easily hide her. Aislinn was further north than she'd first anticipated but that would work in her advantage; it would be longer before anyone thought to broaden their search quite so far. She turned her nose east and set off at a steady, ground eating lope. Sweat trickled down her skin, matting her fur and making her acrid scent even easier to follow but there was nothing she could do. Except, of course, to hope she was far enough away from the creek that nobody would notice the stench before the wind and the sun erased it.

Hours passed. Aislinn's legs felt like jelly but she pushed on, worried now that if she arrived at Kilpenny too late in the evening, she'd be forced to spend the night outdoors - not an issue for a wolf, but certainly making her scent easier to track.

The sun was just above the horizon when Aislinn entered the outskirts of Kilpenny from the opposite direction to that with which she was familiar. The town was frequented by the horsekin who were local to this part of the country and other Kin who lived nearby. As a general rule the horses didn't love having wolfkin close, but many decades ago Andre had rescued three young horsekin from a human brumby drive. He'd gone on to become pack Alpha and one of the stallions he'd rescued had gone on to lead the horsekin herd. A truce had sprung up between them – uneasy but a truce nonetheless. Andre had once shown Aislinn a secret shifting place in Kilpenny and most importantly of all, Tobias had not been with them.

Aislinn padded around the edge of town until she came to the hanging teatree from her memory. Careful not to disturb the earth around it, she stepped from one tussock of grass to another, pushing slowly into the centre. Beneath the hanging boughs was a small clearing; cool, silent and completely hidden from the outside world. It was empty and Aislinn heaved a sigh of relief.

Her body shimmered and stretched and once more she was human. And naked. Padding quickly to the base of the teatree, Aislinn dug her fingers under one of the roots and pulled with superhuman strength. A trapdoor made of woven branches and solid earth lifted up, revealing several sealed plastic bags of cheap clothing. She took out one of the bags, relieved to find a long-sleeved burgundy t-shirt and a pair of black tracksuit pants. They were both two sizes too big but the pants fastened with a drawstring and the t-shirt covered her scarring. There was every chance they wouldn't be missed, considering it was summer, so Aislinn felt less guilty about borrowing them.

Further rummaging revealed an old pair of runners that were clearly second-hand and smelt of horse. Pleased to have something that would help dilute her scent, Aislinn crammed her feet inside. They were a size too small but nothing she couldn't fix by curling her toes up a little. She wished for a hair tie but found instead a broad-brimmed hat, the type often favoured by stockmen. Her mouth curled up at the irony. A horsekin who wanted to look like a stockman?

Aislinn shoved the hat on her head. It was big enough that she could push her hair up inside, keeping it off her face and hidden from view. Stuffing the empty bags back into the cavity, she replaced the trap door and brushed over the disturbed earth with one of the teatree's many hanging fronds. Just as she prepared to step outside, great bands of iron seized her chest, forcing her to her knees.

Not now. She fought for breath, clasping at her throat. In all the fuss and fury, her post traumatic stress and the panic attacks which went with it had seemed another world away. Now, reality came crashing back in, but it was far too dangerous to succumb to her inner demons here. For the first time since the incident Aislinn fought the pain, willing the iron away. Her altered scent rose around her, filling the tiny clearing with a bitter combination of wolf and bear. Grey fog blurred her vision and Aislinn swayed. *No. Don't give in.* She closed her eyes and thought of her mother. Her grandmother. Tobias.

The iron bands faded as though they'd never been, leaving Aislinn gasping and blinking alone in the middle of the teatree. What was going on? Normally the attacks lingered, but this - it had cut off as though someone had flicked off a light. Shaking her head to clear it, Aislinn pushed to her feet. There was no time to think about it now; if a horsekin discovered her in their secret place, she'd have another fight on her hands and she was already exhausted. Horsekin might be prey animals, but their hooves were more than sharp enough to cleave flesh and their teeth were definitely strong enough to rip with. No, she had no wish to fight a horse.

Aislinn pushed the panic attack out of her mind and ducked through the hanging teatree fronds, stepping out into the last of the afternoon sunlight. She scurried between and behind buildings, peeking out onto the streets to check it was safe before crossing to the other side. Most of the town was indoors, likely due to the heat, but she nevertheless kept her head down, trusting the wide brim of the hat to shield her face.

Kilpenny's main street boasted a handful of shops and restaurants, a public toilet and two inns. One had been converted into a motel and Aislinn could see cars parked out the front of some of the little self-contained rooms. The other was a more traditional establishment with a restaurant and bar downstairs and rooms in the upper two stories. Aislinn noticed a tiny mark in the corner of the sign, something that all Kin would recognise as the symbol for neutral territory.

She took a few steps towards the *Wild Brumby* and then hesitated. If she went to a Kin friendly hotel and Tobias happened to enter the town searching, it'd be the first place he'd check. Aislinn rolled her lower lip between her teeth, looking down towards the motel. At least at the inn she'd have her identity protected – after all, it was a neutral establishment and that meant the owners would go to great pains to keep it so. The motel offered no such security.

Aislinn squared her shoulders and crossed to the *Wild Brumby*. The door swung in easily, revealing a large, well-appointed dining room and bar. A reception desk nestled in the curve of a spiral staircase, dark wood against burgundy carpet.

"Good morning." The woman behind the desk looked up with a friendly smile. "Welcome to the Wild Brumby Inn."

"Hello." Aislinn smiled back, scenting the air as delicately as she could.

"May I help you?"

Aislinn breathed a tiny sigh of relief. She was human. "I'd like a room please."

"Of course." Red-painted nails hovered over two different guest books, one green and one blue. The one marked for the third floor was clearly marked with the neutral Kin symbol. "Which floor were you after?"

"Third floor please," Aislinn smiled. The woman nodded and opened the book.

"I'll need a name and a species," she said, her pen poised above the page.

"Lynne Auburn. Sheepkin," Aislinn supplied.

"How long do you plan to stay?"

"Just the night." Aislinn reached to her pockets and then froze. She wasn't in her own clothes, with her handbag and purse on hand. She was wearing borrowed tracksuit pants from the horses' stash and had no money.

"All right." The woman opened a drawer in her desk and pulled out a set of keys. She wrapped them in a piece of paper and slipped the two items into an envelope. "Listen close now. There's a separate set of stairs that go down to the old servant's entrance from the third floor landing. That's in case you need to come and go on all fours. The form in the envelope is for you to fill out your payment details. I'm not authorised to take Kin payments but Jenna will come up once she starts work later. Fill out the form and leave it in the lockbox outside your door. The room key opens the box and she has the master, so the info is safe. If it's not there when she comes around, she'll call her boys. I'd suggest filling out your form. Any breakages must be paid for, anything missing from the room after you leave will be charged to the account on your form. No humans are allowed onto the third floor, even when accompanied by Kin. I'm Sarah – pick up the phone and dial zero for this desk. Any questions?" Sarah smiled, holding the envelope out towards Aislinn.

Aislinn struggled to sift through the information Sarah had unloaded. "Er... no, I don't think so."

"Great. Just take the stairs to your right." Sarah waved a hand at the spiral staircase and then turned her eyes back to her computer screen. "Enjoy your stay."

"Um. Thanks." Aislinn smiled, turned and trudged up the stairs.

Four flights later, she stepped onto a landing carpeted in forest green. A young man lounged on a chair beside the only door, a cowboy hat pulled low over his face. He sat up as she approached, regarding her out of eyes that were an unusual shade of olive. After inspecting the room number on her key and sniffing loudly, he opened the door and ushered her through.

Aislinn located her room and fumbled the key into the lock. Once inside, she bolted the door and leant against it with a sigh of relief. The room was simple; a bed, a desk and chair, a bar fridge and a small bathroom off to one side. The dark green curtains bordering the room's single window were open and she crossed the room to twitch them shut.

Biting her lip, Aislinn picked up the pen on the desk and contemplated the payment form. After a few minutes' thought, she filled out the information for her father's account and slipped the sheet of paper into the secure box outside her door. The only two accounts she knew off the top of her head were her own, or Andre's. Surely Tobias' first query would be about Aislinn, not her father. They shared a surname, obviously, but all she needed was to buy time until dawn.

Taking a breath and attempting to calm her racing heart, Aislinn grabbed the chocolate chip biscuits off the bedside table and sat on the bed to eat. Once the biscuits were no more than crumbs and memory, she took off her hat and shoes and curled up on the bed - but as soon as her head hit the pillow, her breath caught in her throat. No. She wouldn't cry, not now. She had to plan her next move, figure out where to run and how to avoid not only the bearkin who'd tortured Freddie and Macy, but her family and friends.

Tobias' face rose in her mind, not smiling and laughing as it was in her childhood memory, but as Aislinn had last seen it - dull eyed and filled with loathing. *Slut.* Tears leaked out the corners of her eyes and she squeezed the lids tight. No, dammit! *Slut.* Aislinn curled up into a ball and pulled the bedding over her tired body. *Slut.* She grabbed a second pillow and hugged it to her chest, where an ache had started to build. *Slut.* It was difficult to get air. She tried to sit up but all of a sudden her chest was seized in bands of ice. *Slut.* Each breath stuck in her throat and her heart struggled to pump past the pain in her lungs. *Slut.* Aislinn opened her eyes, seeking salvation in the ceiling but the agony was so intense she only saw stars. Her chest was wrapped in frozen iron but her wounds burned with a fire akin to acid. *Slut.*

Unable to breathe, to see, or to move, her body labouring under a strain the likes of which she'd never known, Aislinn wondered if she was going to die. The thought cut through her panic like a knife, bringing clarity and a sharp spike of temper. No. It couldn't end like this. She wouldn't *let* it end like this. Lots of people suffered panic attacks, or dealt with post-traumatic stress disorder; she merely had to find her own way to do the same. Never mind that each attack seemed worse than the last - if she focussed, she could do it. After all, she'd done it before, hadn't she? All it took was determination, and thoughts of her family. No, not her family. Thoughts of Tobias.

Tobias. The moment his name rang inside her skull, Aislinn reached for every memory she had, filling her heart and mind with his scent, his voice, his face. It didn't matter that his insults still stung, it only made him seem more real. Aislinn grit her teeth and imagined Tobias was beside her, talking to her, stroking her hair. The iron slipped and moments later she was able to draw a gasping breath. Hope surged and she concentrated harder, imagining his strong arms around her and curling her nostrils as though his scent was real. The pain lessened.

More. She needed more.

They were children, romping in the meadow in wolf form.

Teenagers, stealing furniture for the den or treats for their midnight feast.

Whispering in the dark beneath their favourite quilt.

Lazing by the waterhole on hot summer days.

Slowly, slowly, the pain subsided, leaving her panting and spent on the bed. Exhausted but alive, Aislinn Redding closed her eyes and slept.

Six

Tobias stood ankle deep in the creek, his lupine body quivering with the aftershocks of whatever Aislinn had done to him. Desperation filled his spirit and he kept his nose low in the vain hope he'd stumble across her scent - her *actual* scent, not the fake trail she'd laid with such expert skill.

Zeke splashed over and together they scoured the open area on the other side of the creek, slowly making their way into the trees. After an hour or more with no scent or track to show which way Aislinn had gone, Tobias stopped in the shelter of a eucalypt and shifted back to human form. Zeke followed, golden-blonde fur receding to reveal the tall, lanky man instead.

"She got too good a start," Tobias sighed.

"I told you." Zeke ran a hand through his tight curls. "I've never seen anyone do what she did, man. She *disappeared*."

"Yeah." After he'd attacked her in a fit of uncontrolled rage which he couldn't remember, just like the scene in his house the day before.

As though sensing the train of his thoughts, Zeke laid a gentle hand on Tobias' shoulder. "Why didn't you say something?"

He shook his head. "I thought I had a handle on it."

"Dude, you weren't even you. How can you possibly have a handle on that?" Zeke dropped to his knees in the dirt, scooped up a handful of creek water and threw it over his face. "If Ash hadn't done… whatever it is she did, I reckon you'd have gone the lot of us."

"Probably."

His second scooped up another handful of water, staring at his reflection for a moment before raising it to his lips to take a sip. "I saw your eyes, man. Ain't no probably about it. We're just lucky Ash knew what was happening."

"She's a Den Mother," Tobias murmured, staring up at the cloudless blue sky. "A strong one, if she's got extra powers. I can't believe I didn't notice."

"Given that your current state of mind is questionable at best, I wouldn't worry about it. We all underestimated her - though I honestly don't know why." Zeke snorted. "Ash was always the brains of the operation and now… how the hell did she get mixed up with *bears*?"

Tobias clenched his teeth in preparation for the surge of rage but it didn't come. Instead, the cool, lingering essence of Aislinn's energy swept over him, soothing the feral beast inside him until it lay back down and slept. He was no fool - whatever Aislinn had done, she'd saved not only his own life but Zeke and Dominic's as well. They all knew the stories of what happened when a transitional Alpha lost control of his energy and he'd very nearly become one of those monsters.

Zeke had wasted no time recounting every horrifying detail, but Tobias couldn't remember a single living second after that lightning bolt moment when he'd realised the scent mingled with Aislinn's' had the same acidic undertones as the scents of the bears who had murdered Freddie and Macy.

Sweet lord of the light, Aislinn was mated to a *bear*.

Whatever scenario he'd imagined, this was definitely the worst. No wonder Andre had sent her back to Ireland shrouded in secrecy - if Aislinn was mixed up with bears, she was lucky the Kin High Council hadn't had her imprisoned or even 'taken care of'.

"We need to find her," he whispered. "Before someone else does."

"And if we do?"

Tobias looked up to find Zeke studying him impassively, and frowned. "Andre ordered us to protect her."

"That's not what I asked."

"You think I'd hurt her?" Tobias demanded, his temper flaring.

"Dude, you called her a slut." Zeke's gentle tone only served to enhance the impact of his words. "I've never heard anyone use that word aloud in my life, let alone someone I respect and admire. Someone I've sworn to follow into death, be it needed."

Tobias' temper bled away as quickly as it had come and he trembled with regret. "It wasn't me," he whispered. "I don't know what happened - ever since Ash arrived I've been coming apart from the inside."

"So you *don't* want to hurt her?"

"Of course not!"

"Good." Zeke nodded, his face etched with relief.

"You found a trace of her, didn't you?"

"Sure did, dude - but I wasn't sharing unless I knew she was safe. One of us has to keep their head on straight." Zeke pushed to his feet, clapping Tobias on the shoulder. "You ready to go after her?"

Tobias looked back the way they'd come, his sense of responsibility warring with the thumping drive to find Aislinn and apologise. "You think Dom's okay?"

"Yeah," Zeke nodded. "I told him to take the car and get a safe distance away before he called in Freddie's murder. There'll be a team up from Melbourne before you know it and they've got the address." He paused, squinting in the afternoon sun. "Besides, if the bears really are after Ash, that's where their attention will be. She's in way more danger than Dom right now."

Tobias frowned, worrying his lower lip. "Maybe she's going to meet up with them."

"If that's the case, why bother torturing Freddie? Who, by the way, obviously kept his mortal mouth shut," Zeke added. "We owe him."

"Yeah, we do. Okay, what did you find?"

"I caught a hint of her scent in some of the low scrub. I followed it a little way and found some fur. She's trying to be careful but she's also tired and sore." Zeke gestured off into the distance. "Ash is heading towards Kilpenny."

"*Kilpenny?*"

"It's the last place we'd have thought to look on our own." Zeke smiled, a show of teeth without mirth. Tobias merely nodded, his mind already racing ahead. Kilpenny. At this rate they'd have no chance of catching her before she arrived.

"What about the horsekin?" He said suddenly. "They have territory between here and Kilpenny and they own most of the town."

"What about them, dude? Joseph and the herd spend an awful lot of time in horse form - more time than we really have to lose waiting for them to return our call," Zeke said.

"I'm not going to call them, I'm going to go there," Tobias replied. "Andre helped them once before so they might be willing to help us now."

"You're nuts," Zeke protested. "There's only two of us and who knows how many of them."

"We're at peace, remember?"

"All right, bro, but I'm going on record as saying this is foolish." Despite his words, Zeke's eyes glittered with excitement.

Tobias nodded. "Noted. Let's go." He leapt forward, shifting as he went and trusting Zeke to follow. The landscape blurred as they accelerated, dodging amongst pale gums and shooting through low scrub. Though they moved at a right angle to the direction in which Kilpenny lay, Tobias was still certain he'd made the right choice. If he and Zeke pushed hard, they'd make Kilpenny some time in the middle of the night but they'd both be exhausted. And what if the bears were already there? He'd be no good to Aislinn after a whole night of running through the bush. But if the horsekin agreed to help, they'd reach Kilpenny much sooner - and in a car, meaning they'd be in ideal fighting shape if things got ugly.

Assuming, of course, that she was still there, or that she'd welcome their help. Tobias grimaced. He'd blundered badly – Ash was probably terrified of him, if she didn't hate him. He had so many things he'd wanted to say to her, wonderful things that he'd practised for over a decade; then she'd turned up covered in another male's scent and he'd gone to pieces.

But... a bear? It didn't make sense. Ash had always been independent, bordering on rebellious - but to mate with a *bear*? She was young, she was beautiful and though the idea galled Tobias completely, he was certain she could have her pick of almost any male in the world. If that was the case, why choose a species sworn to enmity with literally every human, Kin and creature on the planet? Unless... perhaps she met a nice bear? Tobias nodded to himself. Aislinn would never choose a mate who wasn't up to the challenge. More than likely Andre had sent her home because he disapproved - he'd always been the heavy handed sort - and Aislinn's mate had come looking for her. Something cold churned in Tobias' gut as he recalled Freddie's severed head. Maybe the bears, too, were unhappy about the union. Either way, Aislinn and her bear-mate were mixed up in something truly awful.

The horsekin grazing grounds loomed ahead and Tobias slowed. The herd had a reputation for wandering from one patch of grass to another and he and Zeke were between two possible locations. The bush itself gave him no hints, nothing but the oppressive heat of the late afternoon. He blinked. One of the flats nearby had a creek running through it. Surely in this hot weather, the shade of trees and the cool creek would make it an ideal place to graze? It was also slightly closer to Kilpenny – so if Tobias was right, *if* the herd were there, then he and Zeke already had a head start.

It was worth the risk. Tobias changed direction and within half an hour he could smell fresh water. He slowed to a gentle lope, flicking a glance over his shoulder to make sure Zeke did the same. The foliage became steadily greener as they approached and before long they stood in a thin line of trees overlooking a small flat. The grass was bisected at one end by the bubbling creek, and Tobias could see the faint outline of a roof and chimney beyond the treeline. He nodded to himself. They were Kin too - it made sense there would be a facility for those who preferred human form. He examined the chimney but couldn't see any smoke. Was it too early for a fire, or had he made a mistake? Were they alone here, after all?

Tobias was about to turn away when a large chestnut stallion stepped out of the trees beside the hut. He walked with swinging strides into the middle of the flat and stopped, one forefoot slightly raised.

He's scented us. Tobias nipped Zeke to tell him to wait, then loped out onto the flat. Stopping just out of range of the stallion's sharp hooves, he summoned his human form and held out both hands in a gesture of peace.

"My name is Tobias Greenwood and I'm looking for Joseph, leading stallion of the horsekin herd," He said, hoping he'd correctly accorded the other man's title.

The big chestnut stared down at him for a long moment and then shifted with a liquid grace that made Tobias feel awkward and primitive. Bright blue eyes sparkled from a frame of red hair that tumbled haphazardly about the older man's face. Whilst his expression was stern, laugh lines wrinkled the corners of his eyes.

"I'm Joseph," the man said. "You're brave to come here, wolf."

"I come bearing the spirit of peace that has reigned between my Alpha and yourself for so many years," Tobias answered.

"Ah, you're from the Redding pack. Tobias, you said? I think Andre may have mentioned you before. What brings you to the grazing grounds?" Joseph asked, his smile polite.

"Andre's daughter Aislinn has come home," Tobias said, unsure where to begin. "She was injured in Ireland and sent here to recover."

Joseph nodded. "Andre warned me she was coming."

"He did?"

"Yes, about a week ago." Joseph rolled one shoulder in a shrug. "He wanted to make certain she'd have somewhere to stay if the pack rejected her."

Tobias stared. Andre had expected the pack to reject Aislinn? It was a slap in the face that set his cheeks burning with shame. "The pack didn't reject her," he bit out. "She ran away."

"She ran *away*? Why would she do that?" Joseph demanded.

"I may have scared her off," Tobias answered, hanging his head. With his eyes firmly fixed on the ground, he explained about Freddie's death, the bearkin and his own reaction. "She was able to stop the energy surge but fled before I woke."

"I see."

"We believe she's heading for Kilpenny and were hoping you might help us find her," Tobias added, looking up into the other man's stern expression.

"So you can finish the job?"

"Of course not. I made a mistake but I'm not a maniac," Tobias growled, clenching his fists. "Transition or no, the safest place for Aislinn is with us. I swear I mean her no harm - I'd give my life for hers, if I had to."

Joseph studied his face for a moment, then nodded. "All right. You better call your second out of the trees, then."

Wondering how the horsekin had gotten the one up on him, Tobias whistled. Zeke loped across the flat, shifting into human form when he arrived at Tobias' side. Though Joseph was tall, Zeke was taller and the stallion was forced to step back in order to look him in the eye.

"Your Highness," Zeke inclined his head to Joseph.

"You must be Ezekiel Smythe. Andre speaks highly of you. Please, call me Joseph."

"No problems. And I'd prefer Zeke, if it's all the same to you," Zeke answered.

"Of course. Now, if we're going to find Aislinn, there's no time to lose - particularly if there are bearkin involved." Joseph's brow puckered in thought. "I own a Kin hotel in Kilpenny and chances are that's where she'll be. I'll make a call and we'll head there in the herd's car."

"What if the bears beat us there?" Tobias asked.

"They might, if they know where they're going," Joseph admitted. "Don't worry, though - I have a friend working at the hotel who can keep Aislinn safe until we arrive. Now if you'll excuse me, I'll make the call."

Tobias watched the stallion walk away, chewing the inside of his cheek. As soon as Joseph disappeared into the hut at the other end of the field he turned to Zeke and poked him in the shoulder. "What the hell did you call him your highness for?"

"Joseph is the leader of the Victorian horsekin. The head of all the herds is a king amongst horses," Zeke answered, looking surprised.

"Why didn't I know that?"

"Because you didn't listen when Grandma Redding was teaching us?"

"Dammit," Tobias growled. "At least you've got manners. He probably thinks I'm an idiot."

"Forget it, dude. He agreed to help us anyway, right? All that matters is getting Aislinn home and when we do, we'll find out exactly what sort of shit is going down."

****

Aislinn woke in a cold sweat, the bed sheets twisted around her legs and auburn-tinted hair plastered across her face. Stars peeped through the gap in the curtains and the bedside clock declared it was a little after midnight. She lay perfectly still, heart thundering as she tried to work out what had woken her. Something she'd heard, or half heard? There it was again – a knock?

Struggling upright, Aislinn flung the bed covers aside and dragged her hair out of the way. She could smell her own sweat, mingling with the stale odour of bear and horse. Yuck. Blinking the sleep out of her eyes, she struggled to the door and looked through the peephole but could see no more than a silhouette.

"Yes?" she managed, her throat thick with barely remembered nightmares.

"Miss, may I come in? It's very important."

Aislinn frowned. "I'm sorry, I think you've got the wrong room."

"Miss, please. I promise I mean you no harm." The silhouette stepped back a pace, arms wide to show he was unarmed and Aislinn recognised the lanky limbs and olive green eyes of the guard who'd let her in earlier.

"Do you know what time it is?" She asked, unlocking the door and opening it just enough to ascertain that he was, in fact, alone. "I've barely slept."

"Yes, Miss, and I'm sorry but… would you mind if I come in?" The youth wrung his hands for a minute, glancing up and down the corridor. "It'll be easier than talking in the hall."

Aislinn rubbed a weary hand over her face, then stepped aside to flip the interior lights on. "Okay, sure, why not? Come in."

"Thanks. I, uh... I'm Steve," the man said, following her inside and closing the door behind him.

"Hi Steve, I'm -" Aislinn stopped. What had she said her name was? "Lynne. What can I do for you?"

"I don't want to frighten you, but I know your name is really Aislinn Redding. I've been sent by Joseph, leader of the horsekin. The bears are coming," Steve added, twirling his cowboy hat in his hands.

"Shit," Aislinn whispered. The bears are coming. Just like that.

"Miss, you must trust me. I may not look like much but I'm here to help."

She took in his faded jeans and flannel shirt and snorted a laugh. "Have you ever fought a bear before, Steve?" There was no use doubting his story – her father had mentioned he'd be keeping Joseph apprised of the situation - but really? He looked like he was about sixteen years old.

"I'm older'n I look, Miss." Steve hesitated, then stepped a little closer, his expression earnest. "I've fought and killed more than my fair share of bears. I trained with Brax MacArthur up in Darwin."

"Brax?" Aislinn blinked, then narrowed her eyes. "He still collecting those damned bottle caps?"

"Only from Mexican beer."

"Huh." She gave him a second look. "All right, Steve. You still look like puberty's hitting hard, but you pass the test."

"I'm thirty-two," Steve snorted, then sobered. "Can you fight, Miss?"

"Aislinn. Call me Aislinn. And yes, I can fight," she added.

"I didn't ask if you knew how to fight, Aislinn. I asked if you could fight *now*." Steve tilted his head, scratching at his sandy blonde hair. "Joseph said you were injured."

Aislinn swallowed. The nervous boy had disappeared and the man looking out at her from behind those eyes had the cool calm of a warrior. What was he? "Yes. I can fight now."

"Good, because I have a feeling." Steve stood and walked towards the window, peeping carefully around the edge of the blinds. "Do you know any of the bears by sight?"

"Only a couple." Aislinn crossed to the table for a sip of water. She needed to clear the fog of sleep from her mind and she needed to do it *now*. "Broad shoulders, snub nose. Bald, tall… nothing really helpful."

"Hmmmm." Steve stepped away from the window and drew a phone from his pocket. "I'm going to send Joseph a quick text. Keep watch."

"Sure. Can you flick the lights off for me?" She asked. Steve complied without question, plunging the room into darkness. Aislinn sidled up to the window and, keeping a close eye on the street below, melted into the shadows. From here, it was possible to see the entire length of Kilpenny's single road and as long as she stayed away from the streetlight filtering through the gap in the curtain, she'd be invisible. The little town was quiet, making it impossible to miss the black SUV crawling down the street. The car slid out of sight around the corner of the next building but Aislinn had seen enough.

"Joseph says he's not far, maybe ten minutes. We just need to - Aislinn?"

She stepped back from the window and dropped her cloak of shadows. "I'm here."

"Woah." Steve blinked and then grinned. "Neat."

"Thanks." She strode to the door and slid the bolt across. "And we need a better plan than waiting for Joseph, because the bears are here."

"If they're here, I say we fight. You got a midform?"

"Wow, you sure know how to talk to a lady." Aislinn raised an eyebrow. "Yeah, I've got one."

"Good - me too." Steve's smile was cold. "What about we show these bears a good time?"

It was impossible to stop the answering smile spreading over her own face. "It's a date. Now all we need is some idea of exactly where they are."

"Oh, you'll know soon enough," Steve chuckled. "I prepped the steps specially for moments like this."

As though on cue, a loud creak sounded from the back of the building. Steve cocked his head, listening to the steady groan of floorboards, then held up three fingers. Aislinn took a deep breath. This was it. She reached inside herself for her wolf form and felt it rise towards the surface. All Kin could shift - it was part of their genetic construct. Some of the more powerful Alphas and Den Mothers were able to take the concept one step further, utilising a balance point between their two shapes to create a midform. Flynn believed it was because the stronger Kin were closer to their animal forms than their human ones and, therefore, had a better understanding of how things worked - all Aislinn knew was that her midform had saved her life on countless occasions, and that was more than good enough a reason to celebrate it.

Her skin itched and tingled as fur sprouted in waves, covering her entire body. Bones cracked and stretched as she grew taller. Fingernails lengthened into claws, teeth to fangs. In midform, Aislinn stood on two legs like a human, but was now over seven feet tall with all the natural weaponry and killer instinct of the wolf. This was the creature once labelled 'werewolf' – a strange cross between human and animal that was the best of both worlds and twice as deadly. Padding across to the door, Aislinn set her back to the wall, calling the shadows close so she could listen to the hushed whispers from the hall.

"- hear a thing," one voice muttered.

"Boss said she'd be asleep or unconscious," came the answer. "Just a snatch and grab."

"Well, get on with it then. Where's the pick?" The lock on the door clicked and the handle jiggled. There was a muffled curse and then the sound of wood creaking as something very large and very heavy leant against it.

"Just shift and bust it," the first voice hissed.

"It's the middle of the night. We're supposed to be quiet," growled a third - but his voice ended on a soft snarl and a second later, the door slammed open.

A large, dark bear lumbered into the room, heading straight for the empty bed. One of his companions kicked the door shut and the third, still in human form, headed for the bathroom and yanked the door open - only to leap back with a shout as a huge *thing* lumbered into the room. Lean legs and arms. Greenish brown, leathery hide. A thick, powerful tail and a long snout filled with razor sharp teeth.

Steve, Aislinn realised. Steve was a crocodilekin.

For a moment, their would-be attackers hung still and stared. Crocs were rare enough that many Australian Kin had never seen one, let alone one with a midform – for the foreign bears, Steve looked like a prehistoric monster from their nightmares. Aislinn slipped through that moment of shock, a ghost in the dark, and materialised behind the bear crouching over her bed. She tore out his throat with a single, well placed swipe of her claws and the spell of Steve's appearance was broken by the heavy thud of a body hitting the carpet.

"Shit!" The one in human form yelled - and crumpled as Steve bit his head off with one large chomp.

The third and final bearkin had shifted, his thick body already lumbering towards Aislinn - whether in a vain attempt to finish his mission or because he thought she was the less threatening of the two midforms, she had no idea. She braced herself, watching the bear's awkward stride in anticipation of an attack, but at the last moment the beast switched direction and made a run for the window.

Aislinn leapt, landing squarely in front of the bear and causing him to rear up, roaring in frustration. She struck at his gut, catching a handful of fur and feeling the scrape of skin separating as her enemy leapt backwards. He made a swipe for her head and she ducked, releasing her grip to avoid claws just as sharp as her own. Holding his wounded belly with one paw, the bear swung towards the door and drew to a skidding stop as he came face to face with Steve's snapping jaws, still dripping blood. No way out.

Speech was impossible, even in a midform, so Aislinn gestured for the bear to stand down. There was no need for any more bloodshed. The bear looked down at his blood-soaked paw and then back up at Aislinn.

She saw, as if in slow motion, the cogs turning in his mind and leapt forward, but too slowly.

With a roar of despair, the creature threw himself towards Steve, claws glittering in the light from the bathroom window. The crocodilekin ducked the clumsy swipe and slit the bear's throat with all the grace of a dancer, slithering out of the way as the third lifeless body crashed to the floor.

Aislinn stared at the carnage around her, then back up at Steve, whose expression was impossible to read. He took a squelching step towards her and suddenly swung to face the door, clawed hand held up in warning as the hotel's interior staircase creaked beneath the weight of several pairs of running feet.

The door burst open for a second time and three hefty figures barged in, one pausing to turn on the light. Aislinn's jaw dropped open as she recognised Tobias and Zeke, closely followed by Joseph, the Prime Stallion for the local horsekin.

"Ash?" Tobias' eyes widened as he took in her bloodied midform. His face was drawn with exhaustion - the aftermath of his Alpha explosion - but he looked otherwise healthy and safe.

Steve, seeing Joseph, shimmered back into his human form. "Hey, Joe. Talk about timing."

"Yeah. Glad you're safe, mate." Joseph dug a phone out of his pocket, tapped the screen twice and began barking orders for medics and a clean-up crew. "How severe?" He asked, eyes still on Steve's weedy form.

Naked, Steve was even more laughably non-threatening than he'd been before and if Aislinn hadn't seen him bite a man's head off with her own eyes, she'd not have believed it possible. The croc shrugged. "They're dead and we're not. Couple scratches, most like. Kim's only across the road, anyway - she'll be here before the bodies are cold."

In punctuation to his words, shouts echoed downstairs and moments later a trio of Kin medics rushed into the room. One immediately began checking Steve and the other two spread out to inspect the bodies.

"Ash?" Tobias said again, taking a step forward. Aislinn growled in warning, flexing her clawed hands. No. They had to go - *she* had to go. It would be safer. Tobias swallowed heavily, eyeing her combative stance. "Please, Ash. I'm sorry."

Sorry? Aislinn hesitated for a fraction of a moment, tilting her head to one side in question. She couldn't talk in this body but if she shifted back to human form she'd be naked – and that was *not* something she was prepared for right now. Or maybe ever.

"Aislinn, you're bleeding," Joseph announced, gesturing for a medic.

She looked down. Blood oozed from a slash she couldn't remember receiving but experience told her it wasn't serious. One of the medics made to approach and she growled a warning, stepping back.

"Aislinn, please. We're not here to hurt you." Joseph stepped in front of Tobias, his hands held up in a placating gesture. "Tobias is not going to hurt you."

Aislinn snorted a laugh at that and across the room, saw Steve grin. Tobias? In her midform, she could turn him inside out - literally - before he'd even blinked.

"Ash, babe, come on. I know Tobias went over the top but you can't just run." Zeke poked his head over Joseph's shoulder. "Come home. Please?"

She shook herself thoroughly, equally annoyed and amused. They thought she was afraid of *Tobias*? Angry and hurt, yes, but afraid? Aislinn blew out a gusty sigh and waved a dismissive hand, relaxing her stance. As the Kin medic rushed forward to dab at her open wound - already clotting, thanks to her body's increased healing ability - she looked over at Tobias and shook her head. No matter what she thought or felt, it was foolish to go back to the pack. Not if the bears were truly after her.

Joseph eased a little closer, as though sensing the direction of her thoughts. "Aislinn, we're here to help. If you cannot trust your packmates, place your trust in me. I swore an oath to Andre to see you safe."

He had. She knew he had. And she was suddenly very, very tired. Her scars ached beneath the safe disguise of her fur and her bones groaned a protest with every move she made. All that running and now the fight - it was too much and as the adrenaline wore off, Aislinn knew her body was going to give out. Which meant, whether she liked it or not, that she wasn't running anywhere. Still… was it safe to go with them, even for a little while? She flicked a worried glance at Tobias and he flinched as though struck.

"Wounds are clean," said the medic, patting Aislinn on the arm and stepping away. "Healing well. She just needs to rest."

"Aislinn?" Joseph held out a hand.

How many times was he going to say her name? She wasn't crazy, dammit, just exhausted. She understood her own name. Aislinn grunted, eyeing the men and shifting from foot to foot. Where would they take her? Home, probably. At least Grandma would be there and maybe, once she'd rested, she could convince them to let her go without a fuss. With all three of the bears dead, it would take their leader time to realise what had happened and initiate a new search. Surely that meant she could afford a day or so to recover? Her knees wobbled uncertainly and she knew there was no more time to think. With a sigh of defeat, Aislinn stepped into Joseph's arms and fainted.

****

Tobias watched Aislinn crumple and leapt forward to catch her even though he knew he'd be too slow.

"I've got her." Joseph swung her into his arms as though her enormous midform weighed no more than a newborn. "She's just fainted."

Rather than offend the stallion, Tobias bit his tongue, stepping close to Aislinn and stroking one soft red-brown ear. In that moment, he could've cared less about the dead bodies, the medics, even Zeke - all he could see was the way her claws had flared open when he'd entered the room, as though to defend herself. What had he done?

"You must be Tobias."

Tobias turned to face a lanky, rakish looking man with sandy hair and olive eyes. "And you must be Steve," he said, extending a hand. "I owe you a debt. Thanks for helping Ash."

"None needed," Steve replied, his handshake firm. "Besides, I'm pretty sure I was just back-up. She's got some mad skills."

Zeke sighed. "I wish I'd seen it."

Tobias shot his second a warning glare and then turned back to the newcomer. "So, uh... what are you?"

"Crocodile." Steve grinned.

"Holy shit, man!" Zeke waved a vague hand, sapphire eyes wide. "I thought you were some sort of dinosaur."

"I get that a lot when I use my midform," Steve answered. He jerked his chin towards the bears. "Sorry they're all dead. Aislinn tried to get one to stand down but he went kamikaze instead."

Tobias swept his gaze over the room. The medics had covered the bodies in blankets from the bed while they arranged for a clean-up crew. He'd expected to feel nauseous, as at the scene of Freddie's murder, but instead he simply felt satisfied. Because under the pervasive tang of blood, he'd already ascertained that at least one of these bears had been at Freddie and Macy's house earlier - meaning justice, as it was, had been served. At least for now.

"I'll put out a search order," Joseph said, following Tobias' gaze. "See if we can track down where they came from."

"There's a car downstairs - I'll look into it," Steve offered. "It'll only take me a minute."

"We'll wait," Joseph agreed, turning to place Aislinn carefully on the bed. He glanced up at Tobias. "I don't think we'll find anything, though."

"Neither do I," he agreed. "It was clearly a do or die mission."

"They had to come from *somewhere*," Zeke protested.

"Oh, yes - but for now, whoever's pulling the strings is determined to keep that location a secret. Whatever Aislinn knows, we need to find out." Joseph tapped a finger against his temple. "Now, if you'll excuse me, the medics are calling for my assistance."

"Not a problem," Tobias murmured. Andre might've warned Joseph that Aislinn was injured, but he'd clearly left it at that - not surprising, seeing as even Grandma Redding had used the word 'classified.' Everywhere he turned there were secrets and falsities and now, people were dying and there were bears in the Australian bush. The entire thing was enough to make him see red - literally.

Tobias grit his teeth and forced the creeping red fog away, his eyes wandering to Aislinn's midform. Auburn-brown fur clung to a body which was feminine and soft now that the fury of battle had gone, though no less deadly. A new and ravenous part of him found that particularly alluring. Everything, from the curve of Aislinn's hips to the swell of her breasts begged for Tobias' caress and he'd taken several steps towards her before Zeke jabbed him in the ribs with an elbow.

"Put a lid on it," his second hissed.

"Shit." Tobias took a deep breath and deliberately focussed on the golden torc still visible around Aislinn's neck. *Not yours, Tobias. Not yours.* "Okay. Call the Den Mother and have her arrange to meet us at the burnt shack with the boys. Nobody else needs to know about this - I won't take any chances with Ash's safety."

"You got it, brother." Zeke loped off.

Tobias dropped onto the bed by Aislinn's feet, deliberately facing away from the distraction of her body. A few hours' rest and she'd be up and well able to answer his questions. One of which was why she hadn't resumed her human form before passing out – such a thing was instinctive, which meant it had been a conscious choice to remain in her midform. Was she embarrassed at the thought of other Kin seeing her naked? Tobias frowned. Unlikely. Clothing was something that didn't shift, so nudity was an accepted part of Kin life.

"Could be the Mark, brother," Zeke said, dropping onto the bed beside him.

"What?" Tobias blinked.

"You're frowning, so I guessed you were thinking about the same thing I was. Why wouldn't she shift back?" Zeke's eyes glimmered as he looked over at Aislinn's fur covered form. "I'd guess she didn't want anyone seeing the Mark."

"Maybe. Did you make the call?"

"Yup. Just waiting on Steve and Joseph, now."

Floorboards creaked outside and moments later, the door swung open and Steve loped in. "Car's clean. It was a rental."

Across the room, Joseph nodded. "I'm not surprised. All right, let's clear out, shall we? The medics can wait for the clean-up team."

"Sure. Thanks again, Steve." Tobias pushed to his feet and strode to shake the crocodilekin's hand a second time.

"No problem." Steve smiled. "Aislinn seemed really nice. I hope she's okay. Would you pass on my number? Just in case she's ever in another spot without you guys around."

"Of course we will," Zeke said when Tobias remained silent.

Steve bummed a scrap of paper from one of the medics and scrawled a phone number on it, presenting the bloodied trophy to Tobias with a nod. "I appreciate it."

"I'll make sure she gets it," Tobias promised, struggling to speak through the shame engulfing him. If not for his behaviour, Aislinn would never have been alone in the first place - and now Steve, who'd known her all of fifteen gory minutes, was stepping in where he had failed.

"Prime Joseph? The truck is ready," a horsekin called from the doorway.

"We'll be right there," Joseph replied.

"I'll stay here and help clean up. See you guys around, yeah?" Steve shot them both a casual salute before limping away.

"Nice guy," Zeke commented.

"Yeah." Tobias bent and gathered Aislinn into his arms. A broad range of scents assaulted him, sweat and blood and wolf and horse and bear, each one tempting him with secrets that he didn't understand.

Fighting the urge to bury his face in Aislinn's fur and pretend the last twelve years simply hadn't happened, Tobias clenched his teeth and strode out the door.

Seven

Aislinn woke with a gasp, her hands immediately attempting to cover her naked body. She relaxed when she discovered she still wore her midform, and was alone in her bed at Grandma Redding's. She'd expected them to bring her here, of course, but the knowledge still tugged at her conscience. Every minute she spent on pack land was another minute that people she cared about were in danger. With that thought foremost in her mind, Aislinn released her midform and returned to her own skin, rubbing her eyes to clear the sleep from them. After taking a moment to readjust to the proportions of her human body and note that the clock read 4am, she swung out of bed and padded to the door.

She couldn't make out words but it was easy to pick individual voices downstairs. Grandma, Zeke, Tobias. Jaxon. Dominic, Rory. She sighed. Of course they'd all be here; the pack ran together for better or worse. If she called her shadows she'd probably be able to listen at the top of the stairs but what was the point? They were clearly arguing and after Freddie's murder, there would be more questions than ever before. Particularly since Tobias had worked out she stank of bear.

Should she run? No, she wasn't up to it; not yet at least. There was no sense in lingering, but neither was she foolish enough to think they wouldn't chase her - and catch her - all over again if she ran without more rest and a little preparation. That meant facing the music and doing the one thing she'd been avoiding thus far: telling the truth.

Grumbling under her breath, Aislinn went to her wardrobe and grabbed a fresh bra and pair of underwear. Her hand hovered over the summer dress that the weather dictated she should be wearing but she selected instead a pair of light yoga pants and a loose cotton windcheater. She ran a brush through her hair, grabbed an elastic and pulled it back off her face into the sort of messy bun that probably looked fashionable on Sienna Smythe, but made Aislinn look like she'd been in a tussle with a mugger in a back alley somewhere. The image made her think of Flynn and she smiled a moment, glancing out the window as though she could see all the way back to Ireland. If only he were here. She'd come to depend on his moral support and acerbic sense of humour and knew he felt the same. Still, wishing wouldn't make him magically appear any more than wishing for a pair of wings would enable her to fly away from all this mess.

Aislinn sighed, turning away from the window and crossing the room. Wolfkin hearing was excellent and the arguing downstairs stopped the moment she opened her bedroom door. She briefly considered going across to the bathroom under pretext of a shower and making them wait - but that would only prolong the inevitable and while she was many things, she'd never been a coward. Squaring her shoulders, Aislinn set her trembling hand on the banister and forced her feet to move. *Not a coward,* she reminded herself. *If you can face down slavering bears, you can look your birth pack in the eye.* Still, the walk down Grandma's carpeted stairs was one of the longest of her life.

"Aislinn, dear." Grandma leapt out of her chair and crossed the room to enfold her granddaughter in a fierce hug. "I'm so glad you're awake."

She squeezed her eyes shut at the wealth of emotion in Grandma's voice. "I'm sorry if I scared you."

"Don't you dare apologise!" Grandma Redding gave her a squeeze and stepped back, her voice pitched for Aislinn's ears alone. "I know you've had it hard, my sweet, but I think it's time."

"It is," Aislinn agreed, her voice trembling.

"You can do this, my girl." Grandma kissed her gently on the cheek and then moved away, dropping into a chair close by in a silent show of support which did wonders for Aislinn's courage.

Tobias stood and took half a step forward. "Welcome home. You look... better."

"Thanks." An awkward silence fell as Aislinn looked around at the rest of the pack.

Dominic looked away. Zeke smiled in welcome but Jaxon wore an openly unfriendly expression and Rory's face was as blank as a weather-smoothed stone. Tobias attempted to paste a friendly look on his face but Aislinn could see his nostrils twitching and knew her scent was permeating the room already.

"Let's just get this over with." She crossed her arms over her chest, affecting a bravado she didn't feel. "Who wants to go first?"

All five men stiffened as though they'd been struck. It was Jaxon, lip curled into a sneer, who leant forward to break the silence. "You stink," he announced. "Of bear."

"I know," Aislinn returned. "Imagine living with the stench all the time."

Another shocked silence.

"You don't *like* the smell?" Dominic said at last, sounding incredulous.

She snorted. "Would you?"

"If you don't like the smell, gorgeous, why did you accept the Mark?" Zeke's voice was soft, his brow furrowed in confusion.

Aislinn raised an eyebrow. "Did it ever occur to any of you that I may have been Marked against my will?"

Each male went still, their faces frozen with astonishment. No, they hadn't considered it. Not even Zeke, sweet Zeke whom she had trusted the most. Every one of them had believed, in their heart of hearts, that she'd turned traitor.

Tobias shook his head, unkempt brown hair flopping back and forth. "But..." his eyes drifted down and settled on the golden torc around Aislinn's throat. "Why mate with a bear and accept the Mark if you didn't want to?"

"Mate with a *bear*?" She repeated, taken aback. "You think I *mated* with a *bear*?" With trembling hands Aislinn grasped the hem of her windcheater and pulled it over her head, dropping it onto the floor to a chorus of gasps. The sounds only served to incense her and she tore her yoga pants off, flinging the shredded remains aside to stand before the pack in her bra and underpants. "Haven't you ever heard of *rape*?"

Aislinn wanted nothing more than to claw all ten of their eyes out but she stood still instead, allowing those eyes to rove her body and see, at last, the truth of it. Violent pink and purple scars crisscrossed her torso, starting from the base of her neck and flowing down over her chest. Mostly slash marks from claws and lower down around her ribcage, the unmistakable evidence of biting, tearing teeth. Puncture marks along her hips and thighs where they'd held her. More torn punctures around her calves and ankles where she'd fought the hold. Fought and fought whilst Olaf Gruybere, High General of the bearkin army, had raped and mutilated her.

"Here." Tears strangled her rage to a whisper. "Here I am. A *slut,* isn't that right, Tobias? Here's the evidence." She didn't need to look, her hands knew the way. Aislinn framed the Marking that covered her right hip, part of her thigh and part of her waist, thick and black and large as a dinner plate. It looked a lot like a tattoo, only it wasn't – it was evidence of possession and cruelty. "Marked and mated, as you so sweetly put it, to a bear."

The men all stared, faces white and jaws slack. Tears glimmered in Grandma Redding's eyes – she'd seen some of the scarring before but certainly not all of it. Tobias opened his mouth but Aislinn wasn't done, oh no. She growled low in her throat and was gratified to see his jaw snap shut.

"Listen and listen closely, because I'm only going to say this once," she warned. "I was working at home, studying a case file. I heard a noise but before I had a chance to turn someone stabbed me with a syringe. I fought the attacker off and turned to see five bears; three in human form, two in bear form. I called my midform but whatever they jabbed me with prevented the transformation. We fought and I killed two of the humans before the third – Olaf – managed to back me into the two bears."

"Olaf Gruybere?" Dominic's face went pale.

Aislinn awarded him a sharp nod. "Yes, Olaf Gruybere. He part shifted, just enough for claws and teeth. The other two held me down, chest and ankle. Olaf... enjoyed himself. The more I fought, the more he tore into me. I knew he meant to kill me and at first, when he Marked me, I didn't understand why - but death breaks the connection, see? Like an artist signs his painting before he sends it to the gallery, I'd be raped, mutilated, Marked and dead." She paused, her breath coming in great gasps, tears streaming down her face at the memory of that torturous nightmare. She wanted to stop talking, to stop *breathing* but the words tumbled out of their own accord. "I didn't care in the end, I just wanted it to be over. But Dad arrived with a bunch of other Kin and there was a fight." She shook her head, still unsure how he'd known to come, or why he'd bothered. "Olaf escaped in the chaos – it wouldn't have been hard. Kin were everywhere, there was blood and screaming and death. When it was over, I begged Dad to kill me himself but the cowardly bastard refused. Instead, the medics jabbed me with a sedative and I passed out."

"Aislinn," Tobias began, but she cut him off with a look.

"A month I tried to heal. A *month* and nothing worked. I couldn't shift, I couldn't sleep, I couldn't think for the stench. The shame. I begged again and again for Dad to put me out of my misery but in the end, after all I've done for our people, he couldn't even grant me that. After I caused enough trouble that his precious political reputation came under fire, the decision was made to send me home - where I swapped one lot of prejudiced assholes for another." She barked a laugh and felt a twinge of satisfaction when they all flinched. "I should've healed but somehow, Olaf's perverted the mating Mark to be used as an instrument of torture. Unless he either grants permission or dies, I'm carrying these half-healed scars for the rest of my pathetic little life."

There. It was out, it was said, it was done. And it didn't matter what they thought, because as soon as she was able Aislinn knew she'd have to leave. Again.

"Oh, Ash." It should have been Tobias but it was Zeke. He'd fallen to his knees on the floor, his face a mask of grief. "Gorgeous, I'm so sorry."

His gentle words and genuine emotion threatened the pillar of her rage and Aislinn blinked against a fresh wave of tears. "I wanted to tell you," she whispered, "but I couldn't. Every time I close my eyes I can see that room, hear the noises. I relive that day over and over and over and *over*. There's no escape from it. I'm sorry that I left everyone in the dark but I couldn't talk about it." She hesitated, then admitted; "I didn't think it would be a problem until Freddie ended up dead."

"So Olaf decided to track you down and finish the job," Rory mused, his clear brown eyes bright. She could almost see the cogs turning inside his mind and realised what she had mistaken for a lack of emotion was in fact a deep, dark pool with a still surface. He ran his gaze lightly up and down her body and said; "And he brought extra firepower because he knew it wouldn't be easy."

"I doubt he travels anywhere without an entourage of lackeys but if he knew who I was before the original attack, that's plausible." She sighed and shook her head. "I know for a fact that he didn't Mark me with the intent of letting me live."

"No. He didn't want you for a mate, he wanted you for a message." Rory narrowed his eyes thoughtfully. "In theory, he could Mark infinite amounts of women so long as he killed them afterwards. His message is delivered, and he's free to move on with his life."

"Exactly. There've been a steadily increasing amount of rape-Mark-murders over the last five years which, after my attack, we now know were carried out by Olaf." Aislinn rubbed at her forehead, suddenly tired. "The only bonus of my being alive is that he can't Mark anyone else."

"There are lots of bonuses to your being alive," Dominic protested, then flushed when Aislinn raised an eyebrow at him. "I'm sorry, Ash. I didn't even know it was possible to Mark someone against their will. Ma always said it was a sacred ceremony and the connection must go both ways."

Aislinn accepted the apology with a curt nod.   "Nobody knows how he managed to Mark me unwillingly, Dom. Trust me when I say I had a whole team of scientists following me around, analysing my every movement."

"Why didn't Andre bring you home himself?" Tobias asked.

"Because he couldn't stand the stink." Aislinn's top lip peeled back from her teeth. "He told me there were other matters to be attended, of course, but I overheard him arguing with Mum outside my hospital room. The word he chose was 'compromised'."

"Compromised?" Tobias repeated. He blinked, the golden starbursts in his eyes alight with sudden fury. "*Compromised*?"

Aislinn's smile was bitter. "I'm Marked and mated to a bear, Tobias, voluntarily or not. The Kin High Council suspended my contract of service 'pending a full physical and mental recovery.' Dad's stamp was on that order right next to everyone else's."

Dominic frowned. "But you're his daughter."

"No," said Aislinn quietly. "Not when he's busy being the Canis representative to the High Council."

"Enough." Grandma Redding leant forward in her chair. "Andre *is* concerned with Ash's safety but he's also concerned by the fact that she was injected with a substance that stole her ability to change forms." She gave her granddaughter a hard look. "Tell us about that instead."

"Fine." Aislinn closed her eyes, feeling all over again the jab of the syringe in her ribs and the horrible burn of the serum. "A few weeks before the attack, the High Council granted asylum to a female bear named Regina. She claimed to have stolen a formula which would prevent Kin from shifting and she promised to give it to us in exchange for protection from her own people."

"Let me guess - Regina was staying with you, in the house." Tobias' voice rumbled, a growl accentuating his words. "The attack was never meant for you, was it? It was meant for her."

"Yes. I'm assuming you've worked out by now that I wasn't a receptionist over in Ireland." Aislinn opened her eyes to find Tobias staring at her, his face filled with horror. "My team and I were Regina's bodyguards. She'd gone up to the lab with a couple of the others and I was studying case files, as I said earlier. The bears were pretty pissed when they realised their intel was wrong but Olaf recognised me as a Councillor's daughter. I guess he decided that if he couldn't get to Regina, I was the next best thing."

"So you didn't die and now they want to tie up loose ends by finishing the job," Jaxon spat, his lip curling. "It's a nice story, Ash. You still stink."

The other four men turned and stared, mouths open. Aislinn met Jaxon's feral glare and bared her teeth. "What's your recommendation, Jax? Kill me yourself?"

He flinched at her words then tried to cover the reaction by surging to his feet. "You know what they say; survival of the fittest. Why should we protect you when you put everyone else we love at risk?"

Grandma Redding rocked back as though slapped. "*What?*"

"Come on," Jaxon scoffed. "Think with your head for a minute. Aislinn's been here less than a week and the bears already tracked her to Freddie, then followed her to Kilpenny. How long before they realise she's here? Hours, days - a week maybe? How do we even know she's not leading them to us on purpose?"

"Watch your tone, pup." Grandma's voice was dangerously soft. "I don't like the implication that Aislinn is some sort of traitor."

"No, Grandma, it's okay." Aislinn threw up a hand, meeting Jaxon's green glare with one of her own. "You're right, I *am* putting everyone else at risk. That's why I ran away after Freddie's murder. The safest place for me to be right now is as far from here as possible."

Tobias blinked. "I didn't scare you?"

"*You*?" Aislinn laughed at that, shaking her head. "Mother Moon, Tobias! I'm an assassin, a Den Mother and a damper who's smothered Alpha energies stronger than yours. No, you didn't scare me, you idiot."

"You're an assassin?" Zeke jabbed a gaping Tobias in the ribs. "I *told* you we underestimated her."

"Assassin isn't the official word but it's the one Flynn uses, and it's accurate enough." Aislinn shrugged. "I work on a highly specialised team and in simple terms my job is to hide in the shadows and leap out on the bad guys while someone else is causing a ruckus. The bad guy dies and I disappear before anyone realises I was ever there."

Jaxon sneered. "If you're so shit hot, how did Olaf track you?"

"I'm not a superhero, Jax," Aislinn growled. "For your information, all my powers shrivelled up after the attack and have only just started returning the last day or so. And even if I was at full strength, there are a million ways Olaf could've found out I was coming back here. He's not a General for nothing."

Grandma cleared her throat. "Andre believes that the bears were keeping tabs on the hospital, waiting for security to lessen. Once they got wind of Aislinn's return to Melbourne, it wouldn't have taken long to follow and anyone asking for the Redding pack at the embassy would've been directed to Freddie." She paused for effect, then added; "This isn't Aislinn's fault."

"Solaeden save me, I do *not* need Dad getting involved in this," Aislinn groaned, rubbing at her face. "Please tell me he's not coming here. I'll end up killing him if he does."

"Not right now, no." Grandma's voice was gentle. "Don't be too hard on him, dear."

"Don't be too *hard* on him? He has to hold his breath when he's in the same room because he can't handle the - actually, you know what? I'm not going there right now. I can't." Aislinn waved her grandmother off with an impatient hand. "Look, we can back and forth about this for ages but the facts are: the bears are hunting me and Freddie's dead as a result. Unless one of you wants to kill me -" she paused and was rewarded with a collection of horrified expressions, "- then the safest thing for the pack is if I lead the bears away from here."

"Injured and alone?" Zeke shook his head in protest. "Andre will have our hides if we let you do that."

"Dad couldn't stop me running before and he sure as hell can't do it now," Aislinn growled. "If he thinks he knows what's best for me he can -"

"Don't go," said Tobias softly.

Aislinn blinked, corralling her chaotic thoughts. "What?"

"Don't go." He took a step closer, his eyes a deep, deep blue, the golden centres like miniature suns. "Stay with us."

"Are you *nuts*?" Jaxon exploded, at the same time Aislinn said, "No."

"The strength of the pack is the wolf and the strength of the wolf is the pack," Tobias said, edging closer. "Stay with us, Ash. Let us help you."

"It's too dangerous," she negated. "Jaxon's right."

"How far will you get?" Tobias countered. "Alone, no money, no allies and the scent of bear all over you. Come on, Ash - nobody is that good."

She begged to differ but kept the thought to herself. "So as long as I carry the Mark, Olaf will hunt me. You know that."

"We can protect you," he insisted.

Jaxon growled low in his throat. "Come on, Tobias, have you really done a complete one-eighty just because of a pretty story? Your family isn't here to be raped and slaughtered by a bunch of fucking bears but mine is! What if they do to my mother what they did to her?"

Aislinn winced. Sarah Heliope-Flint, mauled and murdered by bears? "Jax, I'd die before I'd ever let that happen," she murmured. "I swear it."

"And what good is your word?" Jaxon waved a dismissive hand. "You've been away for twelve years. We don't know you any more."

"How *dare* you," Tobias snarled, his hands clenching to fists. Fur rippled up his arms and the air around him crackled with static electricity.

"Stop!" Aislinn grabbed Tobias' wrist, slapping her dampening powers over his spirit with such force that he staggered. "Both of you, stop it right now. I'm not worth this, especially when Jax is right; you don't know me any more."

He blinked, Alpha fury fading to leave confusion in the golden starbursts of his eyes. "But -"

"Tobias, not two days ago you were standing in Jaxon's camp. Okay, now you're more educated and that's great. I've told the truth and none of you tried to tear out my throat and for that, I'm mostly grateful." She paused, drawing a deep, steadying breath. "I spent my entire time overseas wishing I was back here, with all of you, where I belonged. It's the time we all spent together in *this* pack that kept me going in the dark days. Believe it, don't believe it, I don't care - but it's true. When I arrived back here, however, I realised pretty quickly that those soft, sweet days were long gone and I no longer fit in. I thought for a little while we might mend the rift, but now Olaf's here I can see that for the pipe dream it was. However, you all still belong to each other and I'll be damned if I let a bunch of useless bears destroy that." Aislinn released her grip on Tobias' wrist and propped both hands on her hips. "I won't risk the lives of anyone here in the pack. I won't. End of discussion."

Silence. After a minute, Zeke cleared his throat. "So… what now?"

"I'll stay until I'm feeling better; two days, three at most." Aislinn tapped her chin in thought. "The bears who followed me to Kilpenny are all dead, so they can't report anything they saw or heard back to Olaf. He has to start fresh, with less information than he had last time."

"So, what, in the meantime we just hope they don't turn up?" Jaxon growled.

"Anyone asking for directions can get a map to pack land," Rory pointed out quietly. "If Olaf decides to come here, he could do it whether Aislinn was here or not."

"Exactly." She nodded. "Which means that when I go, I need to do it loudly and leave a trail that's easy to follow."

Jaxon stood and crossed the room, pushing into Aislinn's personal space until their chests were touching, regardless of the fact she wore only a bra and panties. "I'm sorry for what happened to you, Ash, I really am. But I have to protect not only the rest of the pack but also my parents and my siblings. So I hope you'll understand when I say that if you're not gone in three days, I'll run you off myself."

"Jaxon Heliope-Flint," Grandma roared, exploding out of her seat. "You will *not* threaten my granddaughter."

"I'm sorry, Den Mother," said Jaxon, without a hint of remorse. "If you don't like it, I'm happy to swear out."

"Don't be ridiculous," Dominic protested. "You can't leave the pack!"

Jaxon shrugged. "I can and I will, if it comes to that - but no matter what, after three days, she goes. How it happens will be up to the rest of you." And with that, the stocky wolfkin turned and stormed out.

The front door slammed so hard that the windows rattled in their frames. After a second's tense silence, everyone started talking and the room was a painful symphony of noise and agitated movement. Aislinn retreated to the edge of the room, waited until she was sure they were engrossed in their conversation, then cloaked herself in shadow and slipped up the stairs. She paused at the top but when nobody shouted in surprise, made for the sanctuary of her room and ghosted inside. Breathing a sigh of relief, Aislinn dropped the shadows and closed the door as quietly as possible, catching sight of herself in the mirror on the opposite wall as she did so. The scars were still as red and angry as the day she'd woken in the hospital, her life in shambles around her. Blinking back tears, she reached for a long, soft cotton dress and dragged it on. It boasted a crossover neckline and had no sleeves, leaving a great deal of scarring exposed but in the privacy of her own bedroom, she didn't really care what she looked like. After all, everyone in the house had seen the damage anyway - so long as she didn't look in the mirror, it didn't matter any more. None of it did. Sighing, she moved to the desk and began dragging out a notebook and pen when a soft knock had her freezing in place.

"Ash?" Tobias' voice was uncertain. "Are you in there?"

Of course she was, and he could likely smell it. "What do you want, Tobias?"

"Will you let me in? I just want to talk."

For a moment she debated telling him to go away but in the end her body betrayed her, walking to the door and tugging it open. Tobias hesitated in the doorway, his eyes so wide and soulful that Aislinn stomped back over to her desk just so she didn't have to look at him. She splayed both hands on the pale wood, waiting until he stepped inside and closed the door before she bothered to turn her head.

"Whatever you have to say, just say it." Her words were raw with emotion and Aislinn swallowed around the lump in her throat. "In the last couple of days you've hurt me more than Olaf could ever manage — if you have any decency left, be quick and be honest."

Tobias flinched as if he'd been struck. Several expressions flitted over his handsome face and he opened his mouth and shut it again without saying anything. "I'm sorry," he managed at last.

"You think you can call me a slut and take it away with 'sorry'?" Aislinn laughed bitterly. "What are you, five?"

"It wasn't me," he insisted, his expression full of desperation. "I don't even remember saying it, I swear."

Aislinn dug both hands into her hair and tugged, uncaring that the elastic slithered out and wine-brown locks tumbled around her face and over her shoulders in recalcitrant waves. "I know it wasn't you, Tobias, but here's the thing; those Alpha outbursts come from somewhere. They're all triggered by something. So you might not say that word on purpose but somewhere deep inside, that's what you were thinking."

Tobias sagged, tousled hair flopping down over his eyes. "I… I knew you were mated." From beneath the thick curtain of golden brown, Aislinn saw his eyes flicker up to her golden torc. "I just wanted to know who and I couldn't stop thinking about it. It was driving me crazy."

Slowly, so slowly, Aislinn raised trembling fingers to the necklace - still around her neck in spite of the fact that Tobias had twisted it irreparably in his feral rage. "*This* was triggering you?" He squeezed his eyes shut and nodded mournfully. She reached up behind her neck with trembling fingers, fumbling with the clasp until the torc slid free. "Twelve years without a word," she whispered softly, "and you're angry because I wore a *necklace*?"

"I didn't -"

"Mother Moon, Tobias." Aislinn laughed, and the sound was choked with tears. "If you had any idea what I went through - any idea at all -"

"You just told us," he interrupted, opening his eyes.

"No," Aislinn shook her head. "I wasn't talking about that. I was talking about *you*, and the fact that you couldn't be bothered to as much as pick up the phone while I was gone."

He blinked. "What? No, Ash -"

"Shut up," she snapped, shoving him towards the door. "Just shut up. I don't want to hear how you changed your mind. I don't want to hear how you had better things to do, how you were living your life and it no longer had space in it for me. I already know. But as for my necklace?

You have *no idea* what you're talking about, Tobias Greenwood. None at all."

"Aislinn please, wait," he protested, staggering backwards as she opened the door. "I know I messed up but I just want an opportunity to start fresh. Can't we talk about this?"

"I'm done talking." Aislinn planted her hand against Tobias' sternum and pushed him out into the hall. As he stared down at her out of those eyes - the same eyes she'd laughed with all those years ago - she dropped her twisted torc into his palm. "Goodbye, Tobias," she whispered, and shut the door in his face.

****

Tobias stared at the peeling paint barely an inch from his nose, the torc a living brand in his palm. What had just happened? He swallowed, turning his eyes down to the mangled necklace Aislinn had dropped so unceremoniously into his hand. She wasn't mated. Well, not really. Which meant her mate - or not - hadn't given her the torc. Which meant that he'd been very mixed up and angry and entirely inappropriate for a whole lot of nothing. All those revelations had hit him, very hard and very fast, while he'd stared at the horrific mess the bears had made of Aislinn's body. Pieces that hadn't made sense before had slotted into place while his new Alpha instincts had begun chanting mine, mine, mine.

He wanted to tear Olaf's head off. He wanted to bury his face in Aislinn's hair and mould her curves with his hands. He wanted to disembowel Jaxon for even daring to *think* about trying to run her off. He wanted to shout at Andre for being a miserable excuse for a father. He wanted to roar in fury at the idea of Aislinn leaving a second time but, more than anything else, he wanted to apologise for being an asshole and start fresh.

Except she'd thrown him out.

"Tobias?" Grandma's voice filtered up from the living room.

Pushing away from the door, Tobias shoved the torc into his pocket and stumped downstairs to find Zeke and Grandma Redding waiting for him. He looked around at the empty lounge room, then back to his second, still not quite sure what to do or how to be after Aislinn had dropped bomb after bomb on his head.

"I sent them off to sleep and patrol. No rest for the wicked and all that," Zeke said. His eyes flicked upstairs. "How was she?"

"I tried to talk to her. She's mad at me," he admitted, confusion and something a little too vulnerable making his voice creak.

Grandma squeezed his shoulder. "She'll come around."

"I don't know, Joanne." Tobias shook his head. "I said some unforgivable things. She came home to rebuild her life and look how I've treated her!"

"Keep your voice down, young man. She'll be trying to sleep," Grandma scolded.

Tobias turned away, running one hand through his hair. "Sorry."

"Listen to me, Tobias Greenwood, and listen well. This situation has been a learning curve for all of you and I don't want it ruined with your self-pity." Grandma Redding shook her finger for emphasis and neither Tobias nor Zeke were exempt from her glare. "Despite the fact that Aislinn's situation is something we've never seen before, you're all grown men – I expect you to start acting that way."

"Yes, Den Mother."

"Good." Grandma nodded. "Now, one thing is for certain; we absolutely must keep Aislinn here with us."

Tobias and Zeke exchanged an astonished glance. "What?"

"You telling me you want her to go?"

"No," Tobias replied slowly. "I was considering going with her, until she slammed the door in my face."

Grandma snorted. "Oh dear, she shut the door in your face? You poor, wounded creature. Do men these days honestly have no spine?"

He gaped and Zeke sniggered. "You deserved that one, dude."

"Get your shit together, Tobias!" Grandma snapped. "You're an Alpha."

Tobias passed a hand over his face and took a deep breath. "Right. Okay. You're right. If Aislinn leaves, I'm going with her."

"Me too." Zeke shrugged and grinned. "I'm sworn to you, dude. Where you go, I follow like that curry you shouldn't have eaten last week."

Tobias frowned. "I told you not to bring that up."

"Don't bring it up?" Zeke waved a finger under his nose. "I've been sniffing second-hand curry for days and I didn't even have any."

"Dammit, Zeke -"

"My point," Grandma said firmly, drawing their attention, "is that if you leave and take Zeke and Ash and probably at the very least Dominic with you, then who's going to stay and look after the rest of the pack? Even if Aislinn does run, there's no guarantee Olaf won't come here anyway."

Oh. Tobias screwed up his face. "Well, shit."

"While we're at it, holding an entire pack hostage would be a mighty good way to force her to come back," Zeke added, frowning. "And she would, too - you heard her earlier. She'd offer her throat in a second for the lot of us."

A cold shiver slithered down Tobias' spine. "I'll die before I let them have her."

"Chivalrous but illogical. I can request backup from the embassy, of course, but we'll need to go through official channels. If Andre gets a sniff that she's planning to run, he'll lock her up before you can blink." The older woman sucked on her teeth a moment. "Going above board means we can't state the real urgency of the matter, which means we'll be waiting a while for our case to be read, let alone answered. I'll hazard a guess that Aislinn can speed things up but in order for that to happen, we need her to agree to stay." Grandma Redding pinned Tobias with her steely gaze. "*That* will be up to you."

"Me?" He demanded. "What about Andre? Can't you get him to speak to her without clueing him in?"

Grandma's eyes shuttered. "I can tell you now, Aislinn will flat out do the opposite of whatever my son commands. No, we need to keep Andre out of this as long as possible - she *must* decide to stay of her own accord."

"Yes, Den Mother," Tobias murmured.

"Good. Now, seeing as it's after 4am, you should go home and get some rest. Aislinn is a warrior - she'll be up and planning early, which means you both need to be up and convincing early. The clock is ticking and I'm counting on each of you to do your part." Grandma glared a final time, then turned and walked into her kitchen without waiting for a response.

Tobias didn't bother following. He spun on his heel and hurried outside, turning his face up to the night and searching for the moon, hoping to catch a glimpse of Lunaida, the lunar goddess. There was nothing more than a pale sliver of light amongst a sprinkling of stars but even so, he drew comfort from it.

"I guess I'll be seeing you in a couple hours, brother," Zeke said softly, closing the door behind him.

"Yeah. Gather the pack in the den first thing – we need to think and plan."

"And Aislinn?" Zeke asked.

"I said gather the pack, didn't I?" Tobias growled. "She's part of us, no matter what she thinks."

"This isn't going to be easy, bro. She'll be wanting to plan her escape."

"I know." Tobias nodded, slipping one hand into his pocket where the golden torc rested. "I'm hoping that by helping, we might find an opportunity to make a case for solidarity. None of us are in her good books right now and trying to force a change of mind will only push her further away." He frowned down at the lawn. "The first thing - and the thing we should have been doing from the start - is to prove that she still belongs here. That we *want* her here. The rest will come later and… why are you looking at me like that?"

Zeke's ridiculous grin only widened. "Just glad to see you back, dude. I thought I lost you for a few days."

"You did. I'm such an idiot." Tobias glanced up at Aislinn's window and sighed. "Only thing I can do now is try and make amends."

"I think we're all in that boat, man. Sleep well." Zeke raised a hand and then loped away.

Tobias crossed the common lawn in silence, barely paying attention as he mounted the steps to his front door and slipped inside. There was nobody there, of course – discounting the intermittent visits from Zeke and Sienna, he'd been living alone since his parents had left for Ireland eight years earlier. For the first time the loneliness bothered him and he roamed the ranch-style house on restless feet. At last, for lack of anything better to do, he made a ham and cheese sandwich and sat down on his bed, looking out the window at the stars above.

Grandma Redding's two story house was easily visible against the skyline. Tobias knew without doubt where Aislinn's window was – he'd stared at the darkened glass almost every night for some twelve years now and tonight was no exception. There was only blackness to be seen but Tobias drew comfort from simply knowing that this time, she was actually there.

What a downright pig he'd been. Although, Ash's reaction to his attempted apology still didn't make any sense. Recalling the way her eyes had welled with tears right before she'd shoved him out the door, Tobias reached into his pocket and drew out the golden torc which had so infuriated him since her arrival.

It lay in his palm, glimmering gold in the moonlight and twisted out of shape by the fingers of his midform. Tobias fitted his human fingers into the indents he'd made and tried to imagine lifting Aislinn by the necklace alone, as Zeke told him he'd done, but his memory refused to co-operate and offered only the recollection of blinding, feral rage. Tobias clenched his fist and the bulk of the torc cut into his palm. Recalling at last that it was a locket, he opened his hand again and flipped the necklace over.

Sure enough, there was a catch at the back and a hinge where the body of the torc could be opened. He hesitated, wondering if it was an invasion of privacy - but Aislinn had given it to him, hadn't she? Haunted by the look on her face as she'd said 'good-bye, Tobias,' he swallowed his misgivings and flicked the locket open.

Nestled snugly inside the hollow cavity was a small piece of black fabric. Tobias prised it out and set the torc aside, gingerly unrolling the well-worn scrap to reveal an ancient piece of paper. Feeling less sure of himself as the moments wore on, he spent several minutes working out how to unfold the paper without tearing it, discovering at last a letter with a lock of thick, golden-brown hair inside.

Tobias raised a hand to his head, eyes wide. It couldn't be, surely. He lifted the letter to his nose and sniffed; paper, ink, Aislinn - real Aislinn, before the bear - and, faint but still recognisable, himself. It was a lock of his own hair. With a lump in his throat, he began to read.

Dear Tobias.

I don't want to go. I know I said we'd laugh all night and not think about it but I can't help it. Dad promises it's only six months but I just have this feeling, like something awful is going to happen and I'll never see you again.

I stole a lock of your hair while you were sleeping. Sorry. You'll never notice; you were too busy snoring and you never brush it anyway.

I just couldn't leave without something to keep with me always, to remind me that you're with me no matter what.

Whatever happens, wherever we end up, one day I'll find my way back. Who knows, maybe you'll come to visit me and we can go on an adventure together. Until then, I guess I'll wonder and wait and wish, with half of my soul here and the other half back home with you.

Always yours,

Aislinn.

Shit. Tobias set the letter and the lock of hair aside as though they were made of glass and swiped at the tears flowing freely over his cheeks. All this time he'd been worked up over Aislinn's imaginary mate, she'd been carrying *him* around inside that torc. No wonder she'd been so angry.

He glanced at the letter again, dated the day Aislinn had left and his world had shorn in two. All this time he'd thought she'd moved on, that she'd grown and changed and become someone else - and she had, but she'd taken him with her, the way she'd promised.

Tobias ate his sandwich in silence, reading the letter again and again and again. He set his empty plate atop a stack of similar plates on his bedside table and carefully gathered the lock of hair back into the letter, folding it up along the lines and tucking the whole thing inside the scrap of linen. He picked up the torc and hesitated. While still functional, the necklace was ruined, marred forever with the evidence of his petulant rage.

No, that simply would not do.

Tobias set Aislinn's precious things into the top drawer of his bedside table and grabbed his phone, tapping out a message. Now, more than ever, he'd die before he let her leave without him. It just wasn't going to happen. Still restless, he nevertheless undressed and got into bed, his gaze never leaving Aislinn's darkened window. Tonight might have been a write off but tomorrow, he'd start to show her that the boy she'd left behind was still here, and he was hers.

****

Aislinn woke to the carolling of magpies in the tree outside her window and, for the first time since she'd been home, wished they would go away. She groaned and rolled to one side, pulling the sheet over her head but it was no use. After a few minutes' grumpy silence, she pulled herself out of bed and went across the hall to shower. She examined herself in the mirror while she waited for the water to heat, trying to remember what she had looked like *before,* but it was no use. Eventually she sighed and completed her morning rituals, doing her best to ignore the way puckered, tender flesh pulled and ached with every movement.

After the previous evening's revelations, Aislinn was reluctant to pull on her long, body-covering clothes. Surely now that she'd told the truth, there was no need to hide her wounds and endure the suffocating heat of the day? Sienna's shopping assistance had been invaluable and had given her all sort of options which could be layered if need be or worn singly for when, in Sienna's words, Aislinn was 'back to normal.'

She glanced out the window, where the morning sun promised another mercilessly hot day and, trying not to think too much, dragged on her bikini, followed by a loose patchwork skirt in shades of blue and green and a soft pink peasant top. It was deliciously cool but Aislinn had to swallow her nerves as she turned to the mirror, where those awful red and purple scars poked out from neck and waistline.

"I can do this," she murmured. After a moment's deep breathing to calm her racing heart, Aislinn ran a brush through her hair in long, clean strokes and arranged the tumble of waves across her shoulders and down her back, covering up a few of the nastier scars.

She paused for a glance at her long sleeved tops and jeans, then set the brush aside and went downstairs for breakfast. Grandma Redding was nowhere to be found, only a note saying that Tobias had invited Aislinn to meet the pack in the den for breakfast at 8.30. She looked at the clock, stomach churning. It was a little after 7am, meaning she had plenty of time, but… *should* she? Tobias had probably opened the locket by now and whilst giving him the torc had seemed like an excellent idea from the safe cocoon of her rage, in the bright light of day it seemed like just one more way to make herself vulnerable.

Still, if she didn't go to breakfast, there'd no doubt be an avalanche of questions and probably even suspicion as a result. Aislinn sighed. Regardless of her intentions to leave and the smackdown she'd given Tobias earlier, it would be foolish to try and avoid her pack mates. She'd need their help with an appropriately obvious send-off when it was time to go, something that would be easier to achieve if there was less tension.

Breakfast it was, then.

The sun outside was already warm and by the time Aislinn arrived at the den she was soaked in sweat. It was empty and she assumed the men were either still sleeping or out on patrol, so she decided on impulse to sit by the waterhole and dip her feet in. The water was cool and clear, the rocky bottom covered in tumbled stones. Aislinn stared into the crystalline depths and wondered idly what day it was. Tuesday? Wednesday? Not that it really mattered - not out here, in the bush, where there were no missions to run and no Council to answer to.

Still, she missed Flynn, the pain so sharp it made her breath turn jagged. They hadn't been apart so long in years, and certainly not over such a great distance. Aislinn sighed, wishing her phone hadn't been confiscated when her term of service was suspended - it would've been nice to hear him gripe about the time gap, if nothing else. She pursed her lips. If she was going to flee, it'd be worthwhile picking up a new phone. In theory the bears could track her GPS signal but if she paid a visit to some ex-colleagues who owed her favours, they could fix that.

Sweat trickled down Aislinn's spine and she eyed the water longingly. She had time to swim but after the panic attack last time, did she dare? The day already shimmered with heat, promising to get hotter still – swimming was only natural. Gathering her courage, she stood, stripped off her skirt and top with trembling hands and dropped them onto the rock. Despite being alone, fear made her breathing quicken and Aislinn closed her eyes, resisting the urge to try and cover her Mark. It wouldn't work, of course, the damned thing was far too large. She cracked an eyelid and looked down. More than a month, and she still felt sick at the sight of it. Thick and black and jagged, the circular design was perhaps the angriest mandala she'd ever seen and more than one of her attendant physicians had flinched at the sight of it. Marks were supposed to be a blessing and a gift, something worn proudly to show shared love, not perverted to hurt and -

"Ash?"

Panic surged at the sound of that particular velvet rasp and Aislinn spun with a gasp, her hands splayed inadequately across her body in spite of her intentions otherwise. Tobias walked slowly out of the bush, dragging his singlet off over his head as he approached the water.

Aislinn sucked in a breath as she looked him over, her heart thundering and her legs twitching with the impulse to run. He wore his body broad and muscular, with an even tan that suggested he spent a lot of time shirtless. The faintest suggestion of dark hair dusted his chest and since his transitional episode at Freddie's, an aura of strength clung to Tobias like a second skin. His blue eyes with their golden starbursts were serious and deep, glimmering with concern as he caught her gaze and repeated her name.

"Hey," she managed, embarrassed by the fear clinging to her body.

"I just finished helping Brian load the truck for market and thought I'd cool off with a swim," he said, loping further into the clearing. "You look like you've seen a ghost. What's the matter?"

No mention of the night before. No mention of the torc, or the words which had passed between them. Aislinn searched his face, found genuine concern there, and forced herself to breathe normally. "Nothing. You just surprised me."

"Sorry." Tobias's eyes fell to where her hands covered part of the Mark and his face softened. "You don't need to hide that, Ash." He stepped closer, one hand out in supplication. "Can I see?"

"Um." She shook her head and backed up half a step. "I don't think that's a good idea."

"Ash," he murmured, his voice dropping several octaves and entering a register that sent shivers up her spine. Waves of power washed over her skin and Aislinn grit her teeth, well aware that Tobias had no idea of the energy he was exuding. With a proper mentor, he'd be a force to be reckoned with - without one, he'd be dangerous. She swallowed and looked up at his face, still earnest as he said; "Please?"

Oh, to hell with it. After all, he'd seen it already, right? And if she gave him a quick look, he might leave. "Go ahead," she choked out.

"Thank you." He immediately knelt beside her, peeling her hands away from the Marking with infinite care. When he stretched out one finger to brush lightly against her hip, she couldn't help but flinch. "Does it hurt?"

Aislinn shook her head. "No. Sorry, I... It's just, I guess I'm not used to being touched." When his brow furrowed, she stumbled on, embarrassed by her clumsy words. "I've not really been close to anyone since the incident." His frown deepened. Desperately, she added; "I mean, you haven't touched me at all since I've been back, and..." She bit her lip, aware it was trembling, and shook her head helplessly. Solaeden knew the absolute last person she wanted to be vulnerable in front of, after the last few weeks, was one Tobias Deklyn Greenwood. Sighing, Aislinn said; "Never mind. It's just ugly."

"I haven't touched you since you arrived home?"

"Not unless you count picking me up by the torc." She took a deep, steadying breath. "It's fine. I get it; the smell is awful."

Tobias blinked, a long, slow lowering of lashes - then stood and pulled her hard against him. Aislinn barely had time to glimpse the intensity in his expression before he lowered his head, grazing his cheek against hers as he buried his face in the mass of hair at her neck. One arm slid up to her shoulders, the other across her lower back, folding her into the curve of his larger, stronger body. "I'm sorry, Ash," he murmured, his chest rumbling against hers. "The smell shouldn't have mattered. The torc shouldn't have mattered. I'm an ass and you deserve better. I should have *been* better."

Mother Moon. It was the hug she needed, the words she needed - but fear slammed through Aislinn, stealing the breath from her body and making her tense. Suddenly all she could see was Olaf and his cronies holding her down. The hard surface of the desk pressed into her back, those now-cursed green walls with their photographs laughing down at her. Screams filled her, both the ones she'd voiced at the time and the thousands which had been trapped in her throat thereafter. Then... Tobias' voice echoed through the chaos, calling her name. Calling her home. All she had to do was fight. Fight and be free.

"Ash?" She was cradled against his bare chest, her feet trailing along the rocks beside the waterhole where he must have knelt to catch her when she collapsed. "Aislinn. Come back - I've got you."

She placed her hand against Tobias' warm chest but realised almost immediately that there was nothing forceful in his arms, no violence in the strength of his body. His familiar scent, burnt indelibly into the depths of her memory, offered comfort and his face was full of concern. Tears welled in Aislinn's eyes and instead of shoving him away as intended, she leant into Tobias and sobbed. He startled as her face pressed against his skin, but a moment later freed one hand to rub it awkwardly up and down her spine. How long they stayed like that she couldn't say, but when at last her tears had stopped and the awful memories faded, Aislinn pressed gently against the solid wall of his chest.

Tobias immediately straightened, set her on her feet and took a polite half step back. "Are you okay?"

"I will be." She cleared the huskiness out of her throat. "I'm sorry I didn't tell you straight away. I was ashamed of what had happened and what I'd become."

He sighed, reaching up to catch a tear on his thumb. "Ash, you have nothing to apologise for. I should've looked harder, thought more and been there to support you." He hesitated and Aislinn held her breath, worried he'd ruin the moment by bringing up the torc. Instead, Tobias simply said; "I might not have been there before but I'm here now."

"I don't mean to be a coward." She swallowed heavily. "When you touched me, I remembered -"

"I know," he interrupted, lips pressing into a thin line. "And that's not cowardice, Ash, that's natural. You experienced something traumatic - something nobody should ever have to experience. But I want you to remember that I'm not Olaf and I would never hurt you." Tobias' head tilted to the side and he pursed his lips. "Not intentionally, anyway."

"So, I'm supposed to just not count your Alpha outbursts?" She snorted and shook her head, unable to stop the wry smile tugging at her lips. "Good luck with that."

"There's the girl I remember." An answering smile spread over his face and, after a moment of intense scrutiny that she'd rather have done without, Tobias sighed. "I guess I'd better run and get changed."

"Yeah," she agreed, relieved at the opportunity to be alone and collect her thoughts. "Good idea."

"Well... I'll see you in the den for breakfast?"

"Sure."

"Great. Welcome home, Ash." Tobias turned and loped away, his muscles glistening in the sunlight as he went.

In the short time they'd been talking, the heat of the day had risen several degrees and Aislinn was once again sheened in sweat. Now that she was alone, she realised Tobias had never actually swum himself and in spite of her determination to be mad at him, another smile tugged at the corners of her lips. Now that the threat of being seen unclothed was gone and she'd had her good, old fashioned ugly cry, Aislinn found herself reluctant to abandon the idea of swimming. After a brief internal debate she turned and waded into the water, pausing to hiss every time the cool liquid slithered over her scars. With every step she expected the panic to rise again but it didn't and before long she was in up to her shoulders without any negative effects. Maybe sobbing all over Tobias' chest had helped?

Yeah, right. Tell the guy to piss off and then let him hug you. Real consistent. Setting her jaw, Aislinn took a deep breath and slipped under the water's surface, waiting for the terrible bands of iron which had assaulted her the last time. They never came. She broke the surface with a gasp and struck out across the waterhole, ignoring the pull of her injured flesh and simply revelling in the ability to move. She reached the other side and climbed out, dragging her hair over one shoulder to squeeze the water out. By the time she'd collected her things from the other side of the waterhole and wandered back in the direction of the den, her hair was merely damp and her bikini was completely dry. Aislinn dragged her clothes back on over the top of her bikini and tied her hair in a knot, then squared her shoulders and stepped into the den's shaded interior.

"Hey babe, good timing. Drink?" Zeke's voice greeted her from across the cave and though she was yet to spot him, Aislinn smiled in response.

"Sure. Iced water?"

"Iced water?" Zeke demanded, pushing himself up from one of the den's worn couches. His blonde hair was pulled back into a ponytail and he wore faded denim shorts and nothing else, revealing a lean, subtly muscled chest and stomach.

Aislinn laughed as she noted the amber hued liquid in his glass. "The sun's barely up," she chided, moving to the ice box.

"I've been patrolling since you went to bed, babe." Zeke raised his glass in a toast. "It's evening for me."

"Patrolling alone?"

"Nah, I had Dom with me. He went home to change and pick up the food." Zeke tilted his head to one side. "I'd watch that one, if I were you."

"Yeah, he was flirting with me the other day." She poured herself a glass of water and sipped slowly. "I'm not worried. It won't last."

"Really? Babe, we've had this discussion already," Zeke chuckled. "None of us are blind and you're about a fifteen out of ten."

"But last night -"

"Last night proved that we're all a bunch of assholes and that bad shit happened to you," Zeke cut her off, his sapphire gaze almost luminous in the half light of the cave. "Dominic's quick to bounce back from a shock and he was listening *very* intently to the part where you were Marked against your will."

"Solaeden save me." Aislinn passed a hand over her face. "I'm not... I can't do this."

"Why? Don't like boys?"

"*Zeke.*" She took a deep breath and dropped her hand. "A bit of harmless flirting is one thing, but Olaf issues notwithstanding, I'm leaving. Very soon."

The second quirked an eyebrow, taking a long swig of his liquor. "Maybe that's all the more reason to live it up a little."

"No." Aislinn prodded Zeke in the chest and he giggled, a high pitched, squeaking sound, and grabbed her wrist. "Ezekiel Smythe, are you drunk?"

"Little bit." Zeke tugged her close, releasing her wrist to slide his arm around her waist. "Should've eaten first. Dance with me?"

"Dance?" Aislinn's feet stumbled to catch up as Zeke swept her across the room. "What in the-"

"You know, I remember you being skinnier." He nudged his chest against hers, sapphire eyes sparkling with mischief.

"They're called boobs, you oaf," Aislinn growled, chuckling in spite of herself. "And they're annoying."

"I'm not annoyed by them in the slightest." Zeke's tone was so full of innocence that she rolled her eyes. "What do you remember about me, hmm? A thought for a thought."

"I remember a shy little boy with bright eyes and better manners," Aislinn replied and was rewarded with a laugh.

"Sorry to disappoint, baby girl."

"I'm not disappointed." Aislinn shook her head, digging her hand into Zeke's shoulder as he ducked and spun her with ease. "Since I got back, you're the only one who hasn't treated me like I was diseased."

He growled at that, the first truly aggressive sound Aislinn had heard him make. "Bunch of fuckwits, the lot of them." Tightening his grip on her waist, Zeke dumped his glass on a passing table and swirled them to a halt. His gaze was fastened on her chest but Aislinn knew he wasn't looking at her breasts. She wasn't surprised when, a moment later, he traced a gentle finger along the scarring at the base of her throat. "All night while I was running," he said conversationally, "all I could think about was what that must have been like for you. What you went through, alone. And I don't think I would've come out the other side, if it were me. Hell, just thinking about what Olaf did to you had me running straight for the liquor."

"Zeke," Aislinn whispered, her heart squeezing. His free hand clenched in her skirt and he dragged her impossibly closer, lowering his head until their foreheads bumped.

"I'm proud of you, little sister-wolf." His voice was hoarse and silver tears spangled his golden lashes. "And I'm going to tear Olaf apart, piece by piece, for what he's done."

She offered a trembling smile. "You sound like Flynn."

"I dunno who that is but I like him already."

"He's my other brother from another mother." Aislinn forced her smile to widen. "How long before everyone else gets here?"

Zeke took a deep, shuddering breath, rubbed his nose to hers, and straightened up. "Bout an hour, I reckon."

"An hour, huh?" Aislinn looked pointedly at the bottle of whiskey on the sideboard. "Wanna get roaring drunk before breakfast?"

Zeke's grin was slow, broad and filled with mischief. "Let me pour for you, babe."

Eight

A cold shower had done nothing to cool the raging furnace inside Tobias. He dressed simply; torn denim shorts and a black t-shirt, all the while consumed by the memory of Aislinn's skin beneath his hands. His intentions had been nothing but innocent when he'd pulled her into an embrace but he'd been ill-prepared for the warmth of her bared body, the intimacy of her skin brushing against his. The raised flesh of her scarring had stirred something strange inside of him, something dark and deep and protective.

"Shit." Tobias ran a hand through his hair, fingers snagging on tangles that had probably been there for months. He growled and tugged at the matted mess to no avail, thoughts completely derailed. Maybe he should brush it? Did he even *own* a brush? Wandering into the downstairs bathroom, he found the hairbrush Sienna kept for when she stayed over and set about trying to unravel the disaster zone which was his hair.

After ten frustrating and painful minutes, Tobias gave up in disgust and, rather than turf the brush across the room in a fit of rage, placed it carefully back on the vanity. He stared at his face in the mirror, noting with alarm that his eyes were almost glowing with energy. How long since Ash had damped him? Was that episode at Freddie's only the beginning? What if he flipped his lid and hurt someone without knowing?

"Shit," he said again, clenching his hands into fists.

"What's shit?" Sienna asked from the doorway.

"Mother Moon, Sens!" Tobias swung around, one hand over his suddenly thundering heart. "You scared the life out of me."

Sienna screwed up her pretty face. "But I knocked twice and even called out."

"Oh." Tobias pinched the bridge of his nose. "Sorry. It's been a long night."

"As evidenced by your weird-ass text message." Sienna held up her phone for emphasis. "Just wanted to pop by and make sure we're talking about the same thing."

Tobias took a deep breath and strode to her side, leaning on the door jamb so he could see the screen on her phone better. "Yeah, that's it," he said, rubbing his chin against the top of her head. "Can you sort it out for me?"

"Of course," Sienna chuckled. "Now get off me, your whiskers are getting stuck in my hair and it took me ages to get the curls right."

Tobias chuckled and stepped away, leading her back into the kitchen. He yanked open the fridge, pulled out a jug of water and, because it was his house and he could do as he liked, gulped straight out of the jug. "I'm heading down to the den for breakfast. You coming? Ash will be there."

"Oh, I wish! But I have to go to work. Ysera and I are planning a new collection." Sienna's eyes were alight with enthusiasm as she looked up at Tobias and after a few seconds, she frowned. "What happened to your hair?"

"I tried to brush it."

"Well, you've made a mess. Sit down and I'll fix it," Sienna commanded, pointing imperiously at the dining table.

"It's really not-"

"*Sit*."

Tobias grunted and sat. "Did Zeke give you the run down on Ash?"

"Of course, but I already knew about her injuries - just not how she got them," Sienna said breezily, combing her fingers through his hair.

"You did?"

"Yeah, well, she sort of had to show me when we went shopping, or I'd have never been able to help her with her clothes," Sienna answered, working through a particularly difficult tangle. "She asked me to keep quiet, so we traded a secret for a secret."

"What secret?" Tobias asked, tilting his head to try and see her face.

"Uh uh, Tobias, I don't think so." Sienna leant closer as she fiddled with his hair, her brow puckered in concentration. "Do me a favour, will you? Next time you get the wild urge to manscape, either call me first or don't bother."

"That bad?"

"Worse." She gave a long suffering sigh and flicked him on the nose. "You're a mess."

Tobias laughed at that because it was truer than Sienna knew, and rested his head against her ribs. "What would I do without you to nitpick at me all the time, Sens?"

"I don't know. You'd probably be dead by now," Sienna sniffed - but Tobias could hear laughter in her tone. Her thin arms draped around his shoulders and she leant forward to press an affectionate kiss to his cheek. "There, all done. Now I have to run, or I'm going to be late."

"Me too." Tobias patted her hand, glancing up at the clock. "Matter of fact, I'm already late."

Sienna bustled over to the kitchen bench and collected her purse. "Wine and popcorn tonight?"

"I dunno, Sens, I'm pretty bushed," Tobias admitted, raising a hand to run it through his hair - and freezing halfway as he caught Sienna's glare. "We were up almost all night."

She nodded. "Tomorrow night, then. Will you tell Ash or will I?"

"Er," he replied, blinking rapidly.

Sienna frowned. "She doesn't have a phone, does she? Okay, you tell her. See you tomorrow, spunk. I'll bring the wine." And with a coy wink, she danced out the door, pulling it closed behind her.

Tobias stared at the wood grain in his kitchen bench for a long moment, trying to work out exactly how he'd been talked into hosting wine and popcorn night when he still wasn't entirely sure what that was. Still, if the aim was to make Aislinn feel more like part of the pack, maybe it wasn't such a bad idea. Tobias worried at his lower lip as he shoved his phone in his pocket and moved to the door. Three days, she'd said - meaning that the night before she was due to leave, she'd be in his house again, same as the last time.

And last time, he'd let her go.

To be fair, he'd only been sixteen at the time and Aislinn fourteen - still subject to the whims of their elders. Tobias stepped out onto the common lawn with a snort, shaking his head at the shy, mournful boy he'd been. Now, however, he was an adult - both by Kin and human standards - and he'd be damned if he watched her walk away again.

He jogged towards the den, waving to Bill Deepwater as he passed and ducking behind the Heliope-Flint family's water tank to avoid an overly long conversation with Barbara Forthrite. When she was out of sight, cooing to the elderly cat wrapped around her neck, Tobias sprinted for the cover of the trees and didn't stop until he was safe inside the tea tree tunnel leading to the den. After a quick few moments to slow his racing heart and collect his thoughts, he shoved his hands in his pockets and strolled the last little way to the cave.

Laughter echoed from within but Tobias was not prepared for what he found: Zeke, wearing nothing but a chef's hat, holding a spatula in one hand and a glass of straight whiskey in the other. Aislinn, wiping tears of mirth from the corners of her eyes as she arranged fruit on a platter. Dominic, spreading a table cloth that had seen better days over a large, battered trestle table he'd gotten from Lunaida knew where. Rory and Jaxon, wrestling over silverware and debating exactly how to lay out a proper table setting.

What in the world?

"Tobias!" Zeke waved his spatula wildly and Tobias ducked as a half-cooked pancake sailed by his left ear. "You're late, cupcake."

Tobias eyed the little pan Zeke had propped over the den's fire. "Why are you naked?"

"I'm not! I'm wearing a hat," Zeke protested, flipping his pancakes with reckless abandon.

"Okay, why are you only wearing a hat?" Tobias rephrased.

"Because I set my shorts on fire," Zeke replied - causing Aislinn to burst into a fit of giggles.

"Better the shorts than the tackle," she managed. "It was the most spectacular undressing I've ever seen."

Tobias eyed the matching glass of whiskey in Aislinn's hand and then turned to Dominic. "Are they both *drunk*?"

"As skunks," Dominic confirmed, straightening up from the table and waving to Rory. "Okay, ready for cutlery. I'll grab the condiments."

"Remember - work from the outside in," Jaxon grumbled, brows beetled as he watched Rory calmly begin laying out a formal table setting. "I suppose, seeing as nobody else is doing it, that I'll go and get the chairs."

Tobias stared in astonishment as Jaxon stomped off, then sidled up to Aislinn. "What's going on?"

"Breakfast," she answered, turning to him with liquor-bright eyes and a wide smile. "Like you said. Want some fruit?"

"Er," Tobias looked down at the platter in front of her and blinked. "Is that…?"

"An incredibly accurate representation of Zeke's equipment? Sure is!" Aislinn winked and sashayed over to the table, setting the platter pride of place in the centre. "Perfect."

Zeke surveyed her handiwork, looked down, gave his hips a little swing, and nodded. "Not bad, little sister-wolf."

She grinned. "I'm particularly going to enjoy scooping your balls onto my pancakes." That set Zeke off into peals of uproarious laughter and Tobias leapt to catch his second before he fell into the fire. Aislinn watched in amusement. "Now you know how he lost his shorts."

Tobias stared from Aislinn to Zeke and back again. "Which one of you is responsible for this?"

"Aislinn," said Zeke, Dominic and Rory in perfect unison.

The woman in question swayed unsteadily over to Tobias and dropped a ridiculous curtsy in front of him. "At your service." She stood and blinked blearily up at him. "What happened to your hair?"

"I tried to brush it," Tobias muttered. "Sienna fixed it."

"Sienna?" Aislinn grabbed the front of Tobias' singlet and yanked him forward, nostrils dilating as she sniffed. "Before or after she licked your face?"

"She fixed my *hair*," Tobias repeated.

Aislinn sniggered and gave Zeke a conspirational elbow. "Riiiiight. Now we know why he was late. Sienna was 'fixing his hair'. Where is lover-girl, anyway?"

"She had to go to work," Tobias spluttered, completely and utterly out of his depth. "She said she'll see you tomorrow for wine and popcorn at my house."

"Oooooh!" Aislinn clapped her hands in delight. "I love wine and popcorn."

"And she's not my lover-girl," Tobias added, wondering where on earth Aislinn would get such a ridiculous idea. "It's Sens, for Solaeden's sake."

"Uh huh," Zeke guffawed. "Methinks our glorious leader protesteth too much."

"Hmmm." Aislinn pursed her lips and Tobias watched them glisten in the early morning sunlight. "I'm not sure protesteth is a real word."

"Prove it," Zeke growled, leering in her direction. "Now where's the plate? These are ready."

"Here!" Dominic rushed forward with a plate already laden with pancakes, deftly catching the new ones Zeke lobbed in his direction without bothering to look. "In case anyone was wondering, I've not had enough sleep for this."

Tobias tended to agree, stepping back as Jaxon arrived with chairs - and loud threats to thump anyone who got in his way. In minutes, Aislinn co-ordinated all five of them to set out plates, glasses, pancakes and condiments around the table. Before Tobias was entirely sure what had happened, he was sitting between an amused Rory and a still-naked Zeke with a glass of orange juice and a heaping serve of pancakes in front of him.

"Right, all of you, tuck in - who wants some of Zeke's turgid erection?" Aislinn stood poised over the fruit platter, her hair in glorious disarray and her soft pink top hanging off one shoulder. Jaxon leant towards her, reaching for some strawberries, and she thwacked the back of his hand with her spoon. "Manners, Jaxon Heliope-Flint. Just because I smell bad is no excuse for being rude."

To Tobias' absolute astonishment, Jaxon retreated. "Strawberries, please."

"Better." Aislinn dug the spoon into what appeared to be Zeke's fruit shaft and sniggered when the second groaned as if he were in pain. "Here."

"Thank you," Jaxon growled, snatching the maple syrup and dumping far too much of it on top of his pancakes. After a moment, mouth full of fruit, he looked over at Zeke and said; "Your dick is delicious."

Dominic snorted so hard orange juice came out of his nose and Aislinn, sitting beside him, gave him a matronly thump on the back. "It's okay, Dom. Nothing wrong with a little early morning cock."

"Especially if it's mine," Zeke added - and he and Aislinn dissolved into peals of drunken laughter all over again.

"Don't know how we're supposed to get anything done with them like *that*," Rory said quietly from Tobias' elbow. "But the show is totally worth it."

Tobias couldn't entirely disagree as he watched Aislinn, her face lit with mirth, digging into her pancakes - though he had to bite down on a growl when she dropped jam on Dominic's elbow and leant over to lick it off. The other male's expression wavered between shock and amusement but Tobias wasn't surprised at all when he deliberately dolloped jam on the other elbow less than a minute later and offered it up for the same treatment.

"That's on Jax's side, get him to do it," Aislinn replied breezily.

"Fuck off," Jaxon grunted - and blinked as everyone, even Tobias, laughed.

"What, you don't like jam?" Aislinn rolled her eyes, leaning bodily over Dominic to wipe the jam off with her finger and smear it down the side of Jaxon's face. "Chill out, princess."

Jaxon stared across the table at Tobias, his eyes wide. "She did not just do that."

"She did," Tobias answered.

Jaxon stood up. Beside Tobias, Rory said, very quietly; "Oh shit."

"Jax," Tobias warned - but Aislinn was already there, shoving Jaxon back into his seat and leaning over to whisper in his ear. What she said, Tobias didn't hear but the surly wolfkin eventually nodded and went back to eating his breakfast as though nothing had happened - and the jam stayed firmly on his cheek.

"What the actual fuck," Rory breathed. "*How* did she do that?"

Tobias just shook his head, reaching for his orange juice to take a deep swig, which he promptly choked on. "Does this have *vodka* in it?"

"Surprise," Aislinn grinned. "I thought it might loosen up those panties you've got twisted so tight."

Tobias growled deep in his chest. "You want my panties off, Aislinn Redding, you just ask."

To his utter astonishment - though by this time in the proceedings, he wasn't sure why he was surprised at all - Aislinn gave him a sultry look and said; "Tobias Greenwood, I'm willing to bet my left tit that if I got your panties off, you wouldn't have the faintest idea what to do next."

Really. Around him, the entire pack dissolved into peals of laughter but Tobias heard them from very far away, his heartbeat suddenly so loud it drowned out everything else. The edges of his vision turned red and he was vaguely aware of standing, his entire being focussed on Aislinn's laughing face.

****

"Tobias? Tobias!" Zeke yelped as Tobias wrenched his second bodily out of his chair and flung him across the cave.

Aislinn looked into Tobias' face and saw his pupils had all-but disappeared in a glorious blaze of blue and gold and when Dominic stood alongside her, she waved him down. "No, Dom. Don't."

"What the hell?" Jaxon demanded, watching as Tobias stalked towards Aislinn. "What's going on?"

"Transitional outburst," Aislinn answered, taking a slow step back from the table. "He can't hear you, or see you right now. He's not even really Tobias right now."

"I thought you already fixed him," Zeke said, pulling himself up and wiping blood from his split lip.

"It's not permanent," Aislinn answered, staring up at Tobias as he approached. "Hey there, big guy. Come to mama."

Tobias rumbled in his chest and Aislinn was surprised to hear there was no threat in it - at least, not the threat of violence. Oh, great. Here? Really? She summoned the cool, soothing shadows even as Tobias drew level with her, his fingers sliding the length of her jaw to cup her cheek. Aislinn sighed, nuzzling into his touch, inviting him closer with her eyes so that she could flatten her palms on his chest - and swiftly wrap him in shadows, using her energy to smother his like a fire blanket. Tobias staggered and she caught him under the shoulders, supporting his weight when he sagged almost to his knees.

"What - Ash?" He mumbled, slowly getting his feet beneath him. "Why am I over here?"

"Hormones," Aislinn said softly, waiting for Tobias' brain to catch up to his body. "Sorry about that. I know it's disorienting."

"I feel like someone threw a bucket of cold water over me," he admitted, looking down as if to check for evidence. Tobias looked at his packmates, still sitting at the table, and back at Aislinn. "Did I attack you again?"

"More or less," she answered, unable to stop the tugging at the corner of her lips.

142

Tobias frowned. "I don't remember being angry."

"You weren't," Aislinn shook her head. "What do you actually know about transition?" When Tobias looked confused, she turned her gaze outwards. "Anyone?"

"When an Alpha male's powers emerge, they need mentoring through the difficult stages," Zeke said, repeating verbatim what he'd clearly read in a text book somewhere. "The more powerful Kin can be prone to episodes that require closer management."

"Right," Aislinn nodded. "That's essentially correct but it's missing a whole lot of detail. So, when a stronger energy emerges and you get a transitional episode, the Alpha - in this case, Tobias - loses the ability to think cognitively and is slave to the drive of their instincts."

"Which is why I attacked you at Freddie's and you... restrained me," Tobias said slowly.

Aislinn nodded. "Yes, but like I just said to Zeke, it's not permanent and needs to be reapplied situationally. To top it off, I have to be touching you to do it."

"Which is why you didn't just -" Zeke waggled his fingers in the air, "- Abracadabra him?"

"Exactly." She hesitated, then added; "Powers like mine - the ability to absorb or smother those outbursts - are not common. Ones strong enough to deal with the big whompers even less so."

"Wait a minute... if your mojo isn't permanent, then what happens if there's nobody around to stop him?" Zeke blinked, staring at Tobias wide eyed.

"You have to fight him. People get hurt and sometimes they die."

"Shit," Tobias looked down at his hands. "So I'm dangerous?"

"You can be, but you weren't trying to kill me," Aislinn said gently. He frowned. "I wasn't?"

Aislinn stared at his adorable confusion and shook her head. "No. Violence and anger are the most common forms the energy uses but sometimes... other urges can take over."

"Oh," Dominic sat up straight. "So you were teasing Tobias about his panties and then -"

"Yeah."

"But then he - if you hadn't stopped him, then -" Dominic cut off, his face suddenly white.

Tobias' eyes widened as he realised the implications and the colour drained from his face. "Ash, I'm so sorry," he gushed. "I didn't mean to, I swear."

"Stop, stop." Aislinn held up her hands, unable to swallow the chuckle which slipped between her lips. "You look like you've seen a ghost. I said before and I'll say again, I'm not scared of you, Tobias. You'd have probably snuggled up to me like a big old puppy, nothing more." She winked. "Don't worry, I won't tell Sienna."

"Sienna," Tobias repeated, dropping white faced into his chair.

"She'll be perfectly safe. Just don't… Er… get too excited, or you might embarrass yourself on her leg."

Rory snorted a laugh. "Unlikely. Tobias is as calm and collected as they come." Everyone turned to stare at him and the wolfkin shrugged. "What? He is."

"So I'm not - you know - going to hurt someone?" Tobias repeated, his brows beetled.

"If you're referring to rape, no." Aislinn reached out to pat him on the arm. "You won't be co-ordinated enough to go all the way. Murder, though - I'm afraid that's still on the cards."

"Mother Moon, what do we do?" Dominic whispered.

Aislinn shrugged. "Don't piss him off - and if you do, come running for me."

"But you're *leaving*," Jaxon growled. "Remember?"

"Oh, yes." Aislinn pursed her lips. "Hmmm. I'll talk to Grandma later. She might know of someone in the area who can step in - but for now, don't worry. I'll be your fire blanket for the next few days."

Tobias swallowed heavily. "Are you sure you're up to it? Last night you said your powers had only just started returning."

"It's fine, I seem to be almost at full strength." She gave him a wide, reassuring smile. "Breathe. I've done this before, with Alphas stronger than you. Now, why don't we finish our breakfast?"

"My whiskey's worn off," Zeke complained, stumping back to the table and resuming his seat. "Bloody Kin metabolism."

"Tell me about it," Aislinn sighed, returning to her own chair. "Still, I'd rather that than a hangover. Have you seen what happens to a human when they drink too much? It's gross." She speared a mouthful of pancake and shoved it in her mouth and to her relief the men followed suit, but the jovial nature of the meal had definitely altered.

"So," said Jaxon, shoving his plate aside and leaning both elbows on the table. "What now?"

Aislinn leant back in her chair, cradling her vodka and orange juice. "Well, first step is I need a plan. And some supplies."

"We can take another trip into Gerup," Tobias offered, draining his glass in one gulp and setting it back on the table. "Pick up whatever you need."

"Yeah, that'd be good. I'll draw up a list." She stared off into the middle distance, mind churning. "I think the best route would be to trek north but I don't know whether to head straight for Canberra and try to leave the country, or cross the desert and head towards Broome."

"Broome?" Zeke frowned. "Why Broome?"

"I have a friend out there who's been off-grid awhile. Still on the Council payroll but she owes me a solid. I could lay low for a bit, make the bears mill about and potentially give up." Aislinn screwed up her face, discarding the idea as soon as it came out of her mouth. "No, they'll just start creating havoc. Better to lead them a dance, maybe even set a trap."

"Will they be expecting you to run?" Rory asked, his eyes narrowed. "I mean, given your injuries and all."

"Probably not, which is why we'll have to advertise it," Aislinn acknowledged. "Regardless of the intel he's gathered, Olaf will expect surrender at some point. Regina told me some pretty horrific stories about how they treat women in bearkin territory."

"A good bear…" Dominic shook his head. "It's hard to believe, isn't it?"

"Perhaps, but she intimated the bears aren't as solid a race as we've been led to believe," Aislinn replied. "Regina was part of a small but determined rebellion. According to her information, the bears are pretty classist and treat their own kind little better than the rest of us. When you think about it that way, three centuries is an awful long time to be downtrodden."

"If Regina was part of a group, why did the Council grant sanctuary to her alone?" Tobias asked.

"From what I've been able to cobble together, the short version is this: Regina and a group of other scientists were being forced to create a serum which suppresses the Kin ability to move between forms, trapping the victim in whichever body they are currently occupying.

They were road-testing several versions of the serum on a number of captured Kin of various species in order to perfect it when Regina managed to get it right." Aislinn took a sip of her juice, considering what she knew and how best to explain it. "The scientists were little better off than the subjects of their experiments and Regina, along with a couple others, had been trying to formulate an escape plan for some time. With the functional serum on hand, they realised they finally had the tool to enact it."

"They injected their masters," Zeke guessed, his sapphire eyes bright.

"Yes, and destroyed the other research while they were at it. Regina was the only one who knew the correct formula for the serum so it couldn't be replicated once she was gone. They took what remained of the finished product with them, determining to sneak out of bear territory and disguise themselves as humans."

"As long as they injected in human form, they could live as mortals in a human village and nobody would be any the wiser." Rory shook his head, admiration plain on his face. "That's ballsy."

"Desperate is the word Regina used, but the end result is pretty much the same," Aislinn agreed. "Anyway, the journey was a long one and they weren't particularly worldly. Somehow they ended up caught between the pursuing bearkin army and a group of rebels. The rebels saved them and after some pretty talking, convinced the little group they'd do more good helping the rebellion than sneaking away to hide."

"Clearly something went wrong somewhere," Dominic said, his soft brow puckering. "Or she'd still be there."

"Yeah," Aislinn toyed with the condensation on her glass and sighed. "Somehow - a spy, most likely - the bearkin army discovered their location and launched an ambush. Regina was able to escape but she had no idea if any of her fellow rebels survived. Considering Olaf now has the small stock of serum she'd managed to create for the rebels, we're assuming it was a slaughter."

"So Olaf has a store, but he can't make any more." Rory nodded. "That explains why he was after Regina."

"Yes." Aislinn shuddered. "Right now, the bears are more dangerous than ever but they have to be careful how they use the serum because it's finite. It also, according to Regina, has a shelf life - but I don't know how long that is."

"But what do they *want*?" Dominic asked.

"The bearkin? Same thing they wanted three hundred years ago, before the war. Open slather," Aislinn shrugged. "Surely you guys remember your history lessons."

"Survival of the fittest, eating 'lesser races' of Kin and humans, blah blah blah," Zeke waved a hand. "Yeah."

"Well, in the last thirty years, rumours of a new bear leader have begun circulating. Twenty years ago, the attacks started - mostly guerrilla warfare and terrorism tactics but they're steadily increasing in frequency and severity. Like Olaf and his string of rape-mark-murders," Aislinn gestured down at herself with a sardonic smile.

"But the bears are supposed to be exiled," Tobias frowned.

"They are but there's no wall, or bars, just inhospitable landscape." She shook her head at that particular fact. "Three hundred years ago the bearkin were basically decimated. When they claimed what was formerly known as Greenland for themselves and retreated there, shutting off from the world with nothing but the clothes on their backs, well - at the time, the human and Kin governments were happy to let them be. We set up border patrols and assumed the bears would be too busy focussing on their own survival to trouble anyone else."

Jaxon grunted, both arms crossed over his chest. "Stupid."

"Yes, but we paid a heavy price in that war, as did humanity. It was easier for everyone to believe they were locked away forever… and for humans, three hundred years is a long time and means several generations. Nowadays, some of them don't even think the war actually happened, that it's a Kin fabrication to keep humans in line. Others think the bears might be rehabilitated and should be offered a place back in society." Aislinn shook her head. "Kin have longer life spans so the memory of those days are fresher but we've been hampered by the humans' resistance. They've begun to pull their forces back from the bearkin borders and our own resources are spread too thinly to cover everything. It's frighteningly easy for the bearkin to slip through undetected."

"We should just feed the humans to the bears and be done with it," Jaxon grunted.

Aislinn laughed. "There have been times when I've thought the same, Jax - that's why I'm a warrior and not a politician." She paused, snatching a strawberry and chewing thoughtfully. "Because the bears have been smart, the humans aren't convinced that all the recent attacks are linked, or that they're the work of bears. The only thing either government agrees on is that, for now, they're trying to keep the activity quiet to avoid widespread panic. That's why teams like mine exist."

"So Freddie never really had a chance," Tobias murmured.

Aislinn stiffened but he didn't look angry, just sad. "Freddie knew the risks of his job," she said at last. "And unfortunately, he was in the wrong place at the wrong time. If the system was working properly, the bears should never have been able to get to Freddie in the first place."

"If they can get to Australia undetected then they've obviously got more than the clothes on their backs now," Rory said.

"Yes, and we've tried scanning but the snow and ice is so thick up there it's impossible to see anything," Aislinn replied. "They've learnt to use the environment to their advantage. We don't even know where the main settlements are."

Jaxon frowned. "Why bother telling us all this?"

"Because it might save your life one day," Aislinn returned. "Forewarned is forearmed. Things might be on the lowdown now but if the political situation escalates, the Council will begin conscripting anybody who can fight."

"What?" Jaxon's jaw dropped. "If they introduce conscription, who will protect the pack?"

"Not the Council's problem." Aislinn got to her feet, dusting her hands on her skirt. "Trust me, they're big picture types."

"Andre would never leave the pack undefended," Dominic said, puffing out his chest. "He's our senior Alpha, and he's on the Canis Council *and* the High Council; he'll look after us."

"Dad?" Aislinn snorted. "I learnt a long time ago not to put too much faith in him." She paused, swallowing her private feelings, and flashed them all a broad smile. "Now, who's going to help me clean the dishes?"

****

Returning the den to normal was a welcome distraction. The other men were mostly quiet and Tobias guessed he wasn't the only one mulling over the information Aislinn had shared and trying to apply it to their own view of the world. Ash, meanwhile, had taken up a seat in the corner with a pad and pen to try and work out what supplies she'd need. Rory had volunteered to help, his mousy brown head bent close to hers as they wrote and rewrote the list.

Jaxon jogged up to Tobias, dumping his tea towel in the den's makeshift sink. "I'm patrolling now - you good with that?"

Tobias nodded. "Be careful."

Jaxon, ever a man of few words, clapped him on the shoulder and left.

"He's not doing so bad," Zeke murmured, appearing at Tobias' elbow.

"Not so long as he thinks she's leaving," Tobias agreed, striding down the corridor to the training cavern. "If we ever convince Ash to stay, he'll go through the roof."

"We can handle him."

"I hope so." Tobias sighed, grabbing his favourite staff from the rack and twirling it back and forth. "I don't like the idea of a pack divided."

"Get used to it," Zeke grunted. "If Ash leaves, we'll go with her but some of the others might not. If Ash stays, Jax will be pissed at the very least - there's no way around a divide. All we can do is try and plan for how best to manage whichever scenario ends up being the outcome."

"Fuck." Tobias blew out through his teeth. "When did you get so wise?"

"Somewhere between the whiskey and the pancakes," Zeke elbowed him in the ribs and leant over to grab a staff of his own. "Come on, give me a couple bruises."

"Mind if I try instead?"

Tobias turned to find Aislinn standing in the tunnel entrance, arms crossed over her chest. "Try what?"

"Giving you a couple of bruises." She nodded at the staves. "I sparred a little with Dom yesterday and it felt good to loosen up."

"You're familiar with staves? Tobias is pretty good," Zeke warned, nevertheless tossing his staff in Ash's direction.

"I do okay," she shrugged, snatching the weapon out of the air. "Ask Dom."

Dominic appeared out of the shadows by Aislinn's shoulder, followed closely by Rory. He looked between the two weapons and grinned. "Oh, this should be good." And then, to Ash; "But shouldn't you be resting?"

"I don't want to rest." She crossed the room, flicking out a finger to prod Tobias in the stomach. "Besides, your Alpha's looking pudgy."

"What?" Tobias blinked, his hand instinctively moving to the place she'd touched. "*Pudgy?*"

"You heard me." Aislinn looked down at her nails for a moment, then flicked a glance up at him from under her lashes, blue-green eyes alight with mischief. "I saw how many pancakes you ate."

"Twelve years changes a man, you know. I grew some muscles." Tobias flexed his biceps at her, waggling both eyebrows. Aislinn laughed and the sound tingled all the way down his spine.

"Yeah, well, I grew some boobs. Pretty sure I can still kick your ass." She cupped her breasts a moment in emphasis before turning away and stalking into the centre of the cave without a backwards glance.

Oh, she wanted to play, did she? With a lopsided grin which was more a baring of teeth, Tobias followed her into the ring.

****

Aislinn thumped the butt of her staff on the floor, getting a feel for the balance of the wood. Tobias took up a position opposite, stance easy and staff held with confidence. "Sure you're happy with staves? We can choose something else if you prefer."

"No, this is fine. I don't get to use the staff much anymore - it's too big and obvious. Most of my stuff is done with the little, close range weapons." She curved her free hand into an imaginary claw. "This'll be fun."

Zeke snorted, taking up a place against the wall with his packmates. "Tell me that *after* you're finished sparring with Tobias."

"Oh?" Aislinn grinned, watching Tobias' shoulders ripple as he twirled the staff around his body in a few simple warm-up exercises. "Sounds like a challenge. You practise often, then?"

"Hard to impress the ladies if you keep hitting yourself in the head all the time," Tobias answered. Aislinn laughed, recalling a lanky youth with a shallow chest and unruly hair who'd spent more time walking into the furniture than around it. That boy was gone, though, as evidenced by the way adult Tobias moved.

"Ready?" Zeke called from the sidelines. "Go!"

Tobias reacted instantly, his staff whistling through the air. Aislinn twisted aside, feeling the wind of the weapon as it missed her by moments. Following her momentum through, Aislinn swept her staff around her body in a two handed slash at Tobias' feet. As he danced back out of the way, she reversed the direction of her slash and bought it up for a glancing blow across his shoulder.

Astonishment filled Tobias' face, only to be replaced moments later by determination. He drove towards her, swinging and spinning like a demon and it was all Aislinn could do to keep her feet. Sweat ran freely and her body ached and pulled with every movement but the rhythmic sound of wood against wood was a soothing balm for her soul. A month in hospital had done this to her, made her body weak. Olaf had done this to her. And the medics couldn't heal the damage - Olaf *wouldn't* heal the damage - but as Aislinn sunk deeper into the joy of the dance, she started to wonder whether she might heal herself, at least on the inside.

It would hurt, but two weeks ago she'd been barely able to breathe for the nightmares, the memories. A week ago she'd been unable to think past the pain. And a few days ago… A few days ago she would have still happily walked into the arms of death with the belief that she'd paid her dues. Aislinn parried a heavy strike, her feet sliding across the ground, and bared her teeth at Tobias. He wasn't going easy on her because she was injured. He wasn't going easy on her because he believed he was better. He wasn't treating her like she stank, or was compromised, or made of glass that might shatter at any moment.

He was treating her like an equal and attempting to beat the stuffing out of her.

Aislinn laughed out loud, sliding her staff along Tobias' and revelling in the way her arms trembled - and held. A second wave of strength surged and she danced on the spot, changing her stance to promote attack rather than defence. Tobias' jaw dropped as she drove forwards and this time it was he who retreated beneath the force of her blows, ducking and weaving and twisting. The steady thwack of the staves increased to a frenzy as Aislinn swung and struck and swung again. Several times Tobias was forced to twist his body and accept blows, sacrificing the less vulnerable parts of himself to protect the areas she'd originally been aiming at.

This, she thought. This was what she was made for - not to sit on the sidelines and wait for death to come at the hands of the bears, or the order of the Council as they deemed her unfit for duty and suspended her service. Aislinn grinned as Tobias misjudged her feint and instead of ducking to retreat, she tucked the staff horizontally against her chest and dove forwards. Tobias' staff whistled over her head as she rolled, coming up inside his guard and trusting to her momentum to thrust herself – and her staff – into his broad chest. Tobias staggered and fell. Tucking her feet beneath her, Aislinn followed him down and landed crouched on his chest, one foot thrust out to pin his staff, her own white oak pressed hard beneath his chin.

He stared up at her in astonishment, chest heaving with effort. For a moment his muscles tensed as though he'd throw her off but Aislinn slithered against him, skirt hiking up her thighs as she straddled his ribs, blocking the attempt with a well-placed knee in his shoulder. She leant forward until those blue and gold eyes filled her vision, her hair falling around them like a curtain. "Gotcha."

Tobias' staff rattled to the floor in a silent admission of defeat. His eyes were impossibly wide, his entire body trembling as he exhaled; "Always."

Applause echoed through the cavern and Aislinn sat up abruptly, flushing as she realised she'd forgotten her audience. Kicking her staff aside, she offered them a broad grin before rolling off Tobias' chest and flopping down beside him on the floor.

"Now that was something else," Zeke laughed, strolling over and propping both hands on his hips. "You two always did know how to put on a show."

A laugh rumbled from somewhere in Tobias' direction. "Glad to amuse."

Aislinn raised a hand to wipe her sweaty face and blinked. Blood ran freely down both arms and, after further exploration, across most of her body. "What in the world?"

"You didn't know?" Tobias levered into a sitting position, brows drawn as he looked her over. "I assumed you did."

"No, I didn't notice." She screwed up her face. "This was the first time I've really moved since the attack, so I guess it's normal." Tobias' nostrils flared and he opened his mouth but Aislinn held up a hand in warning. "If that's an apology on those lips, I'm going to punch them."

He shut his mouth.

Zeke crouched down beside her, fingers gentle as he pried at the shoulder of her top. "The scar tissue's split but it's already healing. I'd say ten, fifteen minutes and you'll be back to normal. Well, you know - as normal as can be, given you look like you wrestled a lawn mower."

Aislinn looked up in surprise to meet those sapphire eyes and a heartbeat later, burst out laughing. "You flea-bitten excuse for a floor rug," she growled, and tackled Zeke to the floor. "Just for that, I'm going to bleed all over you."

"Mother Moon, she's got me," Zeke yelped, not even bothering to defend himself as Aislinn rolled him through the sand, wiping blood and sweat all over his chest. "I'm infected! I'm melting! Someone tell my mother I love her!"

"You deserve all you get, you rogue," Aislinn laughed.

"Oh yeah?" With a swift move she didn't quite see coming, Zeke flipped upright and tossed Aislinn into the air. She spun as she went, tensing for the landing - only to have the steady, strong arms of one Tobias Greenwood catch her and cradle her against his chest.

"Huh," she managed, heart racing as she stared up into eyes that blazed gold. "You really did grow some muscles. Who'd have thought?"

His face split into a wide, boyish grin and Tobias rumbled another laugh. "Told you," he murmured, sliding her down to the floor.

Dominic jogged up with two glasses of iced water and Aislinn accepted hers with a nod of thanks, tipping her head back to down the lot. It was only when she finished that she realised her whole body still shook and she was gripping Tobias' arm for support, her fingers digging in hard enough to bruise. "Sorry," she said, locking her knees and releasing him. "That took more out of me than I thought."

"Apologise again," he teased, "and you'll have to pay for it - isn't that what I just heard?"

"Oh please," Aislinn snorted, looking to Dominic for support. "Like he could take me." Dominic merely winked broadly, accepting her empty glass and wandering off. She looked down at her body and grimaced. "I think I'm going to head home and shower."

"Me too," Zeke growled. "I'm covered in crap and I didn't even get to fight."

"You brought that on yourself," Aislinn laughed, jabbing a finger in his direction. "That's what happens to smart asses."

Zeke flipped her off with a wicked grin and stalked out to the main cave, his voice echoing back down the tunnel. "I'm going to see if there are any pancakes left first. All that watching made me hungry."

"You sure you're okay?" Tobias asked.

Aislinn nodded. "For the first time in a long time - yeah, I am." She paused, chewing the inside of her cheek. "I think I'll spend the afternoon laying out some itinerary ideas and finalising the supply list. You good for a trip to Gerup tomorrow?"

"Me?" Tobias looked surprised.

"No, the other Alpha in the room." Aislinn rolled her eyes. "Are you rescinding your earlier offer?"

"No, but you and Rory -"

"You can read a list just as well as Rory, can't you?" She raised a brow. "Your transitional energy is running wild, Tobias. You could have another episode at any moment. I'll chat to Grandma this afternoon about what we can do in the future but for now, we need to stick relatively close together."

"Oh." He looked vaguely disappointed. "Sure. I don't want to hurt anyone."

"Am I ruining your plans with Sens?"

"What? No - I mean, unless you're pulling out of wine and popcorn night," he replied. "Which, by the way, I'm not entirely sure I understand."

Aislinn rolled her shoulders in a shrug. "It's wine and popcorn. What is there to understand?"

Brow furrowed in adorable confusion, he simply nodded. "I guess I'll have to take your word for it. What time do you want to head out?"

"Well, it's about an hour's drive, right? If we head off early we can do the shopping, grab lunch and be back with plenty of time to get ready for wine and popcorn," Aislinn suggested.

"Nine am, then?"

"Sure," she nodded and turned for the tunnel.

"Wait." Tobias grabbed her wrist, swinging her around in a move that was both alien and familiar, for it'd been twelve years since he'd last done it. "What about at night? What if the transition attacks while I'm sleeping?"

Aislinn cocked her head. With Flynn, she'd just - well, better not to mention that to Tobias. "You live alone?"

"Yeah."

She pursed her lips. "You'll be fine - just make sure you lock all the doors and windows before you go to bed."

"What?" Tobias blinked. "Why?"

"Because that way, if the energy takes you over while you're asleep, you'll have to break down the doors or smash a window to get out. The noise will wake me and the delay will slow you down enough that I'll be able to get to you before any real damage occurs. Got it?" Aislinn stared up into his horrified expression and pulled her wrist from Tobias' nerveless fingers, reaching up to pat his cheek in reassurance. He nodded, very slowly, and she smiled. "Good. See you in the morning."

Nine

Aislinn snuck upstairs to shower and change as soon as she arrived back at Grandma Redding's. Feeling suitably refreshed afterwards, she entered the kitchen to find Barbara Forthrite sitting at the table, complaining over a steaming cup of entirely too-strong tea and some lemon slice.

"Aislinn, surely you remember Barbara," Grandma said by way of introduction.

Aislinn pasted a smile on her face. "How could I ever forget?"

"Oh my dear, you've certainly grown. How long has it been?" Barbara looked over the top of a pair of tortoiseshell glasses that took up most of her pinched face, her brown eyes sharp for all her hair was white and her body hunched.

"A couple of years," Aislinn answered, pouring herself some berry-infused water from the glass urn Grandma kept on her kitchen bench. "I hope you and the cats are keeping well."

"It's been twelve years, eight months, twenty days and six hours," Barbara corrected. She adjusted the tabby cat that hung around her neck like a scarf and humphed. "And I'll bet you can't even remember the names of my kitties."

"Jupiter, Neptune, Nebula, Osiris, Norcross Babbington the Third and Mr. Stripington." Aislinn smiled sweetly, reaching out to tickle the aforementioned Mr. Stripington under the chin. "Does he still like oat cakes?"

Barbara simply sniffed and returned to her cup of tea.

"Barbara was just asking me about Tobias," Grandma said, hiding her smile behind her mug. "Apparently he's been exhibiting some unusual behaviour lately."

"Oh?" Aislinn blinked. "Like what?"

"Well, yesterday I saw him jogging across the common lawn and I'll be darned if he didn't have a shirt on. Then this morning, thank my sweet Lord, he *was* dressed but I saw him snuggling up against Sarah and Brian's rain tank." Barbara pressed her lips together in disapproval. "It simply will not do."

"Of course not," Aislinn replied, managing to keep a straight face only from years of practice. "Surely you've seen a man without a shirt before, though, Barbara? It's the middle of summer and the men often go shirtless; I'm sure Tobias is no exception. And he *is* your Alpha, for now - likely he was doing a little maintenance for Sarah and the pups while Brian's out at market. The round trip to Melbourne and back takes a couple of weeks, as I'm sure you're well aware."

"I had no need to see a shirtless man before Gavin died and I've less need for one now," Barbara snapped. "Who knows what might happen if Tobias is wandering around with only half his clothes on all the time? As you say, he's the Alpha now, and others will follow his example. Before you know it all the men will be stark naked and the women won't get a thing done. It's not proper, I tell you, and it's your fault."

"My fault?" Aislinn repeated. "I didn't strip anyone."

"Don't take that tone with me, young lady," Barbara growled, the sound echoed by Mr. Stripington. "It was always you causing the trouble as a youth. When you went swanning off around the world, things became lovely and peaceful. Now you're back without so much as a 'Hello, Mrs. Forthrite' and suddenly everything's going to pot again. I'm no fool; I know trouble when I see it."

"Really?" Aislinn glanced at Grandma, who merely shrugged. "Well then, I'm ever so glad you stopped by - I'm always on the lookout for trouble. It's my specialty."

"I knew it," Barbara exclaimed, triumph writ across her elderly face.

"I thought you might. It's the duty of a Den Mother to ensure everyone in the pack is comfortable and whilst I've been away some time, this is still the pack into which I was born." Aislinn smiled widely enough for Mrs. Forthright to see her slightly elongated canines - both top and bottom. "I take my duties very seriously."

Barbara leant back slightly in her chair, eyeing Aislinn's teeth as though she might actually bite. "A... a Den Mother? *You?*"

"Amazing, right? And I can do all sorts of helpful things. Watch." Aislinn snapped her fingers and, as if by magic, Mr. Stripington stood, meowed, and jumped into Aislinn's open arms. "Look at that, he's up and about. Not bad for an old cat, although I do believe he's a little overweight. For shame, Barbara - Mr. Stripingon's hips will give out if he's too heavy."

"Hips," Barbara repeated, eyes wide as she watched her cat purring and rubbing against Aislinn's chin.

"Yes. I think, if I were you, I'd exercise him a little more." Aislinn placed her mouth against the cat's ear and emitted a sound - somewhere between a growl and a purr - that Flynn had once taught her. Mr. Stripington yowled in delight, rubbed against Aislinn a final time, then leapt from her arms and raced out the door. "There we go."

"Oh!" Mrs. Forthrite stood suddenly, one hand to her mouth. "Where -"

"Don't worry, he's just gone for a quick jog; Mr. Stripington will be waiting for you at home," Aislinn reassured, draping a friendly arm around the older woman's shoulders and steering her out of the room. "In the meantime, I promise I'll look into Tobias' troubles. We can't have our Alpha acting out of character, now, can we?"

"No," Barbara agreed uncertainly.

"If you see anything else out of the ordinary, do be sure to let me know; while I'm here, I'd love to help ease Grandma's Den Mother burden." Aislinn opened the door and propelled Mrs. Forthrite outside with a gentle push. "Until next time, Barbara. Give my regards to the other kitties, won't you?" And she shut the door in the old woman's face.

After a solid ten seconds to be sure Barbara Forthrite had really gone, Aislinn returned to the kitchen to find her grandmother collapsed in a chair, covering her face with both hands to mask her laughter. "Oh, Aislinn, that was too good."

Aislinn snorted. "I've been talking myself out of trouble for years, Grandma; that was nothing. Silly old busy body."

"Ah, she's never been the same since her husband and daughter died." Grandma sighed, her laughter fading. "The cats give her a modicum of peace. Nice trick, by the way."

"I've learnt to get on well with felines." Aislinn smiled, dropping into the chair beside her grandmother and reaching for a fresh piece of lemon slice. "I do, however, need to talk to you about Tobias."

"Don't tell me that *you* don't know what to do with a handsome man who hasn't got a shirt on."

"Tobias? Handsome?" Aislinn frowned. "Well yeah, he is, but what about Sienna?"

"I have no problems if you prefer Sienna, dear," Grandma replied, patting her hand in a matronly fashion. "It's a free country."

"What? No, Grandma, I mean - never mind. I wanted to talk to you about Tobias' transition," Aislinn clarified. "He had another episode in the den this morning."

"Ah." Grandma frowned, leaning back in her chair and cradling her mug. "It's begun in earnest, then; so much for thinking he'd skip by under the radar. How strong is he?"

"One of the strongest energies I've ever encountered - and growing. Not the biggest whammy, but he'll be incredible when he's done." Aislinn pursed her lips. "It's probably going to be a rollercoaster, considering he's such a late bloomer."

"He always has been. Tobias was almost twenty before he grew into his shoulders, let alone the rest of him."

"Hmmm." Aislinn chewed her thumbnail for a moment. "He needs a full time damper, Grandma. In my experience, the episodes are going to get stronger and more frequent - it's not safe for him to wander around unsupervised."

"Lucky for Tobias that we have the Council's best damper right here, then, isn't it?" Grandma reached out to pat Aislinn on the shoulder. "Did you tell him the dangers?"

"Sort of - I didn't want to scare him." Aislinn sighed and shifted uncomfortably on her chair. "I can mentor him a couple of days, I guess, but then I'm leaving. Who's local?"

"That's strong enough? Nobody," Grandma shook her head. "Joseph's got a damper coming through but she's going to be mildly talented at best - and far too young."

"The embassy will have someone, surely."

"Not strong enough, Aislinn." Grandma Redding shook her head. "If he's as strong as you say, and I have no doubt he is, then there's likely nobody in the world strong enough, let alone the country. It has to be you, and you know it."

"But I'm *leaving*," she growled.

"Then you're sentencing Tobias to death," Grandma's tone was clipped. "Even if there *was* someone else strong enough, it'd take weeks - months - for the Council to approve their release and send them out here."

"Mother Moon." Aislinn dropped her head into her hands, squeezing her eyes shut. "What am I going to do? He'll likely take out at least Zeke if he loses it totally. Oh, who am I kidding? I'd be killing them all."

"What you're going to do," Grandma said quietly, "is help him."

"But what about Olaf?" Aislinn threw her hands up in the air, feeling suddenly as though she were choking. "And let's not forget we haven't spoken in over a decade - Tobias' choice, not mine."

"Ah, yes, I heard the two of you arguing the other night. Tell me, Aislinn, did you actually sit down and talk to him?" Grandma Redding tilted her head to one side. "You're a grown woman now and you're capable of making your own decisions. Would you really see Tobias dead for your own petty revenge?"

"Of course not." Aislinn slammed both her hands on the table, teeth bared. "I don't hate him, Grandma."

"Then why aren't you with him right now? You said yourself he needs supervision." Grandma waved a vague hand in the direction of the common lawn.

"I told him to lock the doors and stay inside." Aislinn slumped in her chair, tipping her head back to study the ceiling. "I don't know if this is a good idea, Grandma."

"You and I both know locking the doors is like trying to catch the ocean in a stocking," Grandma snapped. "Has he truly done something so unforgivable that you'd leave him like this? Really?"

"No," Aislinn growled. "You know I'm not going to let him die - or anyone else, for that matter. But I'll be dooming the pack to a different kind of horror if I stay."

"Something we can work out in time. For the moment, however, Olaf is an extraneous threat and Tobias is a very real one." Grandma's voice softened. "Go to him, Aislinn. He needs you more than you know."

"Fine," she sighed. "But will you at least touch base with Dad on this? I'm not about to drag the pack down with me if he thinks I'm acting outside the scope of my suspension."

"I'll mention it," Grandma nodded. "I'm due to speak to him later today - unless you'd prefer to."

Aislinn made a face. "No thanks. He'll only ask questions I'm not in the mood to fight about."

Grandma pressed her lips together and Aislinn tensed for a new fight but after a long moment the older woman sighed and nodded. "I know this is hard for you, my sweet. One thing at a time - focus on Tobias first."

"Yes, Den Mother." Aislinn rose, dropped a kiss on her grandmother's cheek and went upstairs to pack a bag.

****

Tobias flipped the latch on his front door with one hand, fumbled with the chain and finally, after hunting for the deadbolt key, yanked the damn thing open. Aislinn stood on the front step, a floral tote slung over one shoulder and an apprehensive expression on her face.

"Ash." He blinked up at the sun and then back down at her. "I wasn't expecting you until tomorrow."

She chewed her lip a moment. "I know. Sorry."

"Do you... want to come in?" Tobias stepped back from the doorway, stifling a yawn and adjusting the shorts he'd dragged on during his run down the stairs. Aislinn didn't move, staring into the dim interior of the house as though it contained her doom. "Ash?"

"I should never have told you to go home alone and lock the doors," she said finally. "That wasn't fair."

"It's fine, I was only sleeping anyway." Or trying to. Tobias frowned, tracing the tension in the lines of her shoulders with his eyes, the words finally sinking in. "So I'm not dangerous after all?"

"Oh, you're dangerous." Aislinn looked at him at last, her smile sardonic. "It's just that if I was doing my job properly instead of being selfish, I'd have explained that you need supervising at all times, not just when it's convenient for me." She sighed, shifting her bag on her shoulder. "Letting you go home on your own puts not only you but the entire pack in danger."

"So what's the solution?"

"I'm strong enough to damp you." Aislinn straightened suddenly, looking him in the eye. "But it means I'm going to have to stay with you all the time."

"Here?"

"Everywhere."

"What, like, on the toilet?"

"Mother Moon, Tobias." Aislinn ran a hand over her face and snorted a laugh. "No, not on the toilet. I have no need to see you taking a dump."

"Hey, I was just kidding." Tobias stepped onto the porch and, ever so gently, took her bag from her shoulder. "I'm really grateful that you're here. I don't want to hurt anyone."

Guilt flashed over her face. "I know."

"And for the record, I don't think you're being selfish," Tobias added, waving her in through the open door. "I know you've been through a lot and the last thing you probably want to worry about right now is an Alpha with out of control hormones."

Aware that she'd stopped walking, Tobias dropped Aislinn's bag on the kitchen bench and turned back to see her standing in the lounge with tears shining in her eyes. "It's exactly the same," she whispered.

"Of course." He propped a hip against the counter and smiled. "Not much changes around here." Tobias tilted his head as she slowly sank to her knees on the faded rug. "Ash, what's really wrong? This morning in the den you were fine."

"If I stay, Olaf will come here. He'll come for me and he'll come for the pack." She closed her eyes, one hand clenching in the fabric of the soft cotton dress that hid Olaf's Mark. "But if I go, you die. They die. No matter what I do, I'm bringing ruin. Death and ruin."

Words tumbled through Tobias' brain, a million logical arguments that he'd normally apply to such a situation but instead, he crossed the room and dropped to his knees beside Aislinn, reaching out to tip her chin up with one finger. "Don't say that."

"It's true," she whispered, squeezing her eyes shut. "You know it's true. I'm trapped, with no way out, and I'm going to kill you all as a result."

This wasn't the Aislinn he knew, nor the one he remembered. Tobias watched her body begin to shake, terrible tremors that worked from the inside out. The stench of bear rose around him, growing stronger by the moment. Aislinn began to wheeze, her body curling in upon itself as she struggled for air.

"Ash?" Tobias gathered her body into his lap, horrified to find her skin as cold as ice and her bones like concrete. Zeke had described something similar, a thing which Aislinn had called a panic attack but felt very different to what he would've imagined. Her scent - no, Olaf's scent - rose thick and heady around them and Tobias growled, trying desperately to focus on Aislinn as his vision began to turn red. Why was he angry? He buried his face in her hair, searching for something solid to grip onto. He wasn't angry, Tobias realised. He was… defensive. He wanted to *protect* Ash. He wanted to kill in her name and bask in the heady, gory afterglow.

But there was nobody here.

The moment that thought crossed his mind, the red fog thickened and fur rippled across his arms. No, no, no - he couldn't afford to lose his mind now, not when Aislinn was locked in her own silent struggle against… Olaf. How he knew, Tobias couldn't say, but with the bearkin's name ringing in his skull and his acidic scent thick in the room, there was no doubt in Tobias' mind that Olaf was behind the assault in some unusual way.

"Aislinn, listen to me." His voice was mostly a growl, his instincts thumping at him to do something, even though their enemy was invisible. "You have to fight. Come back to me. I'm right here, Ash. I want to help you but I can't do it alone." Tobias wrestled with the rising tide of sensation sweeping his body, his vision narrowing until all he could see was the dark crescents of her lowered lashes. Energy surged and sparked and he tightened his arms as though he would somehow mould them into one being. "Dammit, Ash, *fight him.*"

The scent of Olaf was now so dense it was almost unbearable. Someone was howling, or growling, or something in between. Driven by instinct alone, Tobias' hand slid up Aislinn's leg, under her skirt where his fingers splayed across the Mark Olaf had branded her with. It burned with cold fire, searing his skin, and he snarled a challenge back, blind but for the feel and the sound of Aislinn's faltering heartbeat, stuttering and slowing as though being slowly and inexorably crushed. Cold. She was cold - but that wasn't right. She should be warm. Deep in the grip of his own crushing energy, Tobias focussed on that one, simple fact; she needed heat. She needed to be warm and alive and smiling and his.

"Ash," he begged, no longer sure if he spoke aloud or inside his own head. Beneath his hand, Olaf's Mark flared in time with the sluggish beat of her heart. Tobias' roaring, tempestuous instincts seemed to hone in on that cold flame, spitting and shoving. The icy grip flickered, faltered - and he felt something underneath, a glimmer of light trapped beneath a sheet of black ice. Aislinn. He didn't know what he was doing but his vast, furious Alpha energy did; it gathered around him in a seething cloud of fire and fury and struck out. The two energies collided and Tobias flinched beneath a backlash that felt like a punch in the gut, but the barrier between Aislinn and himself wavered. Tobias' energy gathered itself again and this time he urged it on, throwing every ounce of his conscious determination into the wild storm. Roaring in feral delight, the energy struck home - not much, just a crack, but enough for Aislinn's glimmering essence on the other side to leak out. Her shadow-cool energy burrowed into Tobias', drawing on his wild strength. Where he'd fumbled blindly she moved with confidence, twisting their two powers together and smashing at Olaf's death trap again and again until, with a final, heart-wrenching lurch, it let go.

Aislinn drew a deep, shuddering breath, her lashes flying open and her blue-green eyes wide. "Tobias," she breathed - and it was perhaps the purest thing he'd ever heard. He tried to answer but couldn't, well and truly lost in the waves of chaotic energy which, now that Olaf was gone, had nothing to focus on.

She cupped his face in trembling hands, their breath mingling, their hearts racing. Aislinn's fingers were cool but it was no longer the awful, frigid chill of death - it was a soothing, gentle balm that danced across his spirit, wrapping him up in a soft blanket of shadows that felt like coming home.

Tobias was vaguely aware of her fingers tightening and Aislinn began panting with effort, her powers washing over him in a shadowy wave. The red fog immediately began to lift, succumbing to that siren song and bringing the room back into startling focus. Ash's eyes rolled back in her head and she sagged, but Tobias' nose told him it was only exhaustion, that she'd spent whatever was left over from fighting Olaf on soothing his raging spirit. Her body rolled backwards and he tried to arrest the fall but managed only to lay her out on the carpet, his arms like lead. Whatever had happened during that silent battle had drained him drier than any physical fight would've done and his body was already shutting down in response. No wonder Aislinn was always so tired after her attacks - somehow, Olaf was stealing her very life force.

Or trying, anyway. Together, they'd turned the tide and beat the asshole bearkin back.

A feral grin split his lips and Tobias was startled to feel the scrape of fangs along his flesh. He briefly considered investigating but his arms were still full of Aislinn and even if he'd wanted to let her go, he was pretty sure he'd never lift his hands to his face in his current condition. Rather than try, Tobias slithered down onto the floor, buried his face in waves of luscious, red-tinted brown hair, and surrendered to the restorative powers of sleep.

****

Aislinn woke with a start, sitting bolt upright in bed. Pale sheets wrapped her still-dressed body and the butterscotch and cream scent of one Tobias Greenwood hung heavily in the air. Chest heaving and heart thumping, she stared around wide-eyed and realised she was alone in Tobias' bed, in the same room he'd occupied as a child.

"Tobias?" When there was no immediate answer, she flopped back on the pillow, waiting for her racing heart to slow. The crinkle of paper caught her attention and Aislinn turned her head, snatching at the folded note poking out from the edge of the pillowcase.

Ash,

I know you're going to be pissed but I was due on patrol and didn't want to wake you. I can still feel your energy inside me, so I figured I'm probably safe for now. I've taken Zeke as backup and he promises that if anything goes wrong, he'll bolt straight for you rather than trying to intervene. You can take the rest out of my sorry hide later.

Feel free to make yourself at home; what's mine is yours. I'll be back about 11pm.

Tobias.

Aislinn stared down at his elegant, flowing handwriting, forcing sluggish thoughts into motion. She remembered arriving at Tobias' house and feeling unusually out of sorts, then a panic attack had stolen all sense of reason. Except... Aislinn frowned, one hand straying to her hip. She had a vague recollection of Tobias' voice, his hands on her body, his energy reaching for hers when she'd been lost. She shook her head. That made no sense; when she'd opened her eyes it was clear Tobias was caught in the grip of a transitional surge and she'd used the last of her powers to smother it. Perhaps the rest had been a dream?

Not entirely convinced by her own thoughts, she shoved them aside and read the note again. Damned right she was pissed at Tobias for running off - but at the same time, Aislinn couldn't help smiling at his promise to accept punishment without protest. She could look for him, of course, but the Redding Pack's land was huge and she'd be more likely to exhaust herself pointlessly than she would be to find Tobias before he finished his rounds and came home again.

Rolling out of bed, she looked at the bedside clock. 8.15pm. Aislinn took a deep breath, her eyes sliding around the bedroom she'd spent almost half her nights in as a young girl. Why hadn't Tobias moved to the master bedroom once his parents had left? Curious, she wandered the house, noting that whilst there was evidence of Tobias in the ensuite, the master bedroom itself contained only the scent of clean sheets. One of the two guest rooms smelt of both Sienna and Zeke but the other echoed with emptiness. Rupert's study, though free of dust, was strewn with papers dating from eight years ago and judging by the size of the cobwebs in the upper corners of the roof, it was likely Tobias rarely came inside.

Aislinn's feet took her downstairs to the sprawling living areas that, at last, contained evidence of use. Whilst Tobias hadn't bothered to change the furniture or any of the decor, she found his laptop and other papers on a little desk against one wall in the rumpus room - whose furniture had been removed in favour of a rubber martial arts practice mat. The lounge smelt mainly of Tobias but Aislinn caught snatches of a variety of other pack members, some more recent and others older. The scarred dining table was clean but for some ancient cork coasters and a wire basket with salt and pepper inside. The kitchen was dominated by an enormous, custom made wooden bench, a shining silver stove that looked too clean to be lit regularly, and a deep sink piled high with sandwich plates. The main bathroom held a variety of ablution tools that smelt mostly of Sienna but apart from that, it seemed Tobias truly lived alone.

Padding back to the kitchen on silent feet, Aislinn tugged open the refrigerator to find half a loaf of bread, a carton of milk, butter, ham and cheese. Having not eaten since breakfast, she dug out the food and a frypan and made herself some toasted ham and cheese sandwiches, leaning on the bench while she ate and contemplated her accommodation options. It seemed rude to use the room that Sienna and Zeke favoured, and the other guest room was incredibly cramped and small so, once her sandwiches were gone, she reluctantly lugged her tote bag into the master and dropped it beside the bed.

A knock at the front door had her racing back downstairs with her heart in her mouth. Fearing it would be Zeke with news of a transitional surge, Aislinn flipped the locks and yanked the door open as fast her fingers would allow.

"Hey, Ash." Dominic offered a broad smile, stepping through the door before she'd finished opening it. "Zeke said you'd be here."

Right. Tobias had obviously told everyone where she was staying, which made total sense except that Aislinn was still trying to come to terms with it herself. She straightened her spine and cleared her throat. "Is everything okay?"

"Oh, yeah, fine." Dominic smiled again, moving to the kettle and flipping it on. "Tea?"

"Does Tobias even *have* tea?" Aislinn asked, following the other male into the kitchen. "The fridge was terrifyingly empty."

"He's the resident Alpha. He might not have real food, but he has tea and coffee and even hot chocolate on hand for any pack members who decide to pop by."

"Hot chocolate?" Aislinn's ears pricked up and Dominic chuckled, reaching up to one of the overhead cupboards to pull out two mugs. He was dressed simply, in light jeans and a burgundy t-shirt that smelt of a fresh shower. "So, what brings you by at nine o'clock on a school night?"

He flashed a lopsided grin, scooping way too much chocolate powder into the mugs and winking when Aislinn grunted in appreciation. "Zeke said you'd been unwell. I volunteered to swing past and check on you - I was going to offer you some dinner, but I see Tobias' fridge already beat me to it."

Hence the shower. She smiled. "Sorry to disappoint."

"I can handle it." He stirred the mugs and tilted his head in thought. "If dinner's out of the question, how about dessert?"

"Dessert?"

"Sure." Dominic placed Aislinn's mug on the bench, turning the handle towards her. "Nothing too fancy, but Tobias always has ice cream."

"There's never a bad time for ice cream," Aislinn declared, and was rewarded with Dominic's hearty laugh.

"That," he said as he stuck his head in a cupboard under the bench, "is exactly what Tobias says."

"Then he has good taste." Aislinn sipped her hot chocolate, humming in appreciation. "This is delicious."

"Thanks. My sister takes hers the same way," Dominic chuckled, withdrawing two bowls and depositing them on the bench. "Deanna thinks that making a decadent hot chocolate is an important life skill."

"She's right," Aislinn agreed, watching him retrieve the chocolate ice cream from the freezer and portion it out. "Tell me there's topping."

"Maybe." Dominic frowned, rummaging in the mostly bare pantry. He emerged a moment later with a bottle of chocolate topping and a triumphant grin. "Voila!"

Aislinn chuckled as he made a great show of adding topping to her bowl, presenting her the spoon with a flourish. "Thank you."

"Welcome." Dominic led the way out onto Tobias' back patio, throwing himself onto one of the wicker lounge chairs that graced the deck. "So... do you miss Ireland?"

"That's a tough question," she admitted, perching on the chair beside his and staring out at the darkened bush. "There are aspects I miss. People, mostly - but I've spent a lot of time missing being here, too."

Dominic stirred his ice cream, pale blue eyes almost glowing in the light from the porch. "Nobody special, then?"

"Oh, Dom," Aislinn shook her head. "Subtlety doesn't suit you. Out with it."

"I just thought - I hoped, perhaps, you might like to go on a date with me." Dominic flushed as he spoke, meeting her eyes from behind the curtain of his sleek black hair.

Aislinn hid behind the armour of her dessert, spooning quietly in the warmth of the evening. "I don't know," she said finally. "I'm a bit of a mess right now. I can't even look at myself naked, much less contemplate the idea of someone else doing it."

"I said a date," Dominic protested, back stiff with indignation. "Nothing else."

"For which I'm grateful - but my point stands. It wouldn't be fair to either of us." She stood, setting her now empty bowl on the outdoor table, and crossed to press a kiss to his forehead. "You're sweet, Dom, but you're also my friend. For now, more than anything else, that's what I need."

He sighed, shoulders slumping. "I thought you'd say something like that."

"I'm sorry." Aislinn swept silken hair back from his brow in a comforting gesture. "Surely I'm not the only single woman in the pack?"

"Of course not, and there are others in town and the surrounding areas, too," Dominic agreed. "But they're not… I mean, I haven't…" He sighed and shook his head. "I don't know what I need, Ash, but none of them are it."

"And you think I am?"

"I don't know," he frowned, fingers tightening around the edge of his bowl. "But when I saw you that first day… you have all these hidden depths and more fire in your soul than all the girls in the local pub put together."

Aislinn blushed. "I think that's one of the nicest things anyone's ever said to me."

"It's the truth." The corner of Dominic's lip twitched. "I just - I guess when we were kids I just knew you as you, if that makes sense. Not as a woman whose actions match her swagger, and who wields a staff and turns invisible and uses the word 'turgid' in an actual sentence."

"It's an awful word, isn't it?" Aislinn ignored the flattery in favour of screwing up her face on a manufactured giggle. "But it seemed to fit the situation."

"It did." Dominic thumped his bowl down on the deck and leant back in the chair, staring up at the stars. After a long, drawn-out moment, he said; "Do you ever feel like you don't belong? Like something's missing?"

"Oh, only for the entire last twelve years of my life," Aislinn snorted. "Why do *you* feel like that, though? You've always had a place here."

"Do you know I've never been out of Victoria?" Dominic rolled abruptly to his feet, moving to the porch railing and leaning against it. "Much less the country. It's so quiet here, you know? I mean, there's nothing wrong with it but I guess I just always thought there'd be… more."

"There is more." Aislinn crossed to lean on the balcony beside him. "A whole lot more - but it might not be what you think. Life out there isn't tourism and selfies, Dom. The bearkin are dangerous and the Kin High Council are actively trying to recruit anybody worth their salt." She sighed. "At least it's peaceful here."

"Maybe peaceful isn't all it's cracked up to be." Dominic frowned and shook his head. "This is entirely too deep a conversation for ice cream and hot chocolate."

Aislinn laughed. "That it is - see what happens when you ask out a girl who's wrestled a lawn mower?"

"You really think that badly of yourself, don't you?" Dominic shoved off the railing, backing up a few steps and using his hands to make a picture frame. "Do you realise you're about a fifteen out of ten? I'm being serious, here."

"You boys and that damned numerical scale." Aislinn blinked, then laughed and patted self-consciously at her body. "Don't tell me you're chauvinistic enough to actually use that in your daily life, or I might have to hurt you."

"Of course not, but it serves to get my point across," Dominic returned. "Really, Ash - you see scars, I see courage. You see wounded, I see a fighting spirit. You're not looking at this right; it's what's inside that makes the outside glow and you've always been a bonfire."

"Sweet again." She smiled gently. "You're going to make someone very happy one day, Dom."

"I hope so." He turned and wandered back inside, collecting the dishes on the way and stacking them on the bench. After a moment staring at the plates piled up in the sink, Dominic shook his head, pulled them out and started running the hot water. "Bloody man never does his fucking dishes. Deanna would kill me."

"I'm assuming from that comment that you still live with your sister?"

"Yeah," he nodded. "She never really recovered from Keelin's death. Mum and Dad tried to help but she couldn't stand the pity on their faces. She begged me to move in with her and I wasn't sure, but… she was so broken, Ash. Couldn't get out of bed, was frightened of the phone, forgot to eat, was barely sensible. A ghost."

"So you went to her." Aislinn laid a comforting hand on his shoulder. "That's beautiful, Dominic. If Deanna's still breathing today, it's because of you."

He accepted the praise with a slight flush and a nod. "She says that, too. I only ever planned to stay until Deanna got back on her feet… but she hasn't yet, not entirely, and I'm still there." Dominic pursed his lips. "She did meet a nice guy from the local foxkin pack, though. I'm hoping."

"As long as they don't blame us all for Macy's death," Aislinn murmured, grabbing a tea towel.

"I shouldn't think so - not if the bears' names are all over it." Dominic scrubbed at the plates, muscles bulging beneath his t-shirt. "Deanna needs someone peaceful."

Unspoken was the declaration that he, Dominic, did not.

"Don't give up, Dom. We're only young," Aislinn said, accepting the plate and scrubbing it dry. "You're a good man and I'm sure you're a great warrior - staves notwithstanding, of course."

"I'm better hand to hand," he admitted. "Since we've been doing all these extra patrols, it's hard to find anyone to practice with."

"I'm frightfully out of shape but I'll spar with you if you like," Aislinn offered. He raised an eyebrow and she grinned. "As friends."

"I'd like that." He flicked his head in a well-practised gesture that shifted his hair out of his face. "But first, let's finish these dishes. Tobias only has eight plates."

Aislinn accepted the next plate and saluted him with it. "To friends?"

"To friends."

Ten

Taking the pack's ute to Gerup for supplies had seemed like a good idea at the time, but as he drove, Tobias wished he'd picked a car with working air conditioning. Not because he couldn't handle an open window or two, but because Aislinn had yanked her harem pants up above her knees and opened her loose crossover top to reveal the form-fitting singlet underneath, the neckline of which was low enough to show off the leading lace edge of her bra - a sight which, every time he glimpsed it, had him struggling for air.

She was trying to kill him again.

Maybe she really didn't know, Tobias mused, flicking another glance at her out of the corner of his eye. Gods knew she'd been oblivious to his clumsy attentions as a teenager, and Zeke had mentioned Ash's surprise when he'd commented on her figure a couple of days ago. But surely, *surely* she couldn't still be so clueless? He tried to imagine what her life might have been like in Ireland, realised he knew absolutely nothing, and gave up. Yeah, safer to assume she had no idea, as she'd always had no idea. Not that it mattered; there still wasn't enough air in the godsdamned ute for his liking. Tobias took a deep breath - the third one in almost as many minutes - and once again swallowed his words.

"What?"

He jumped, hands tightening convulsively on the wheel. "What, what?"

"You're clearly not saying something." Aislinn slid her sunglasses down the bridge of her nose and pinned him with her blue-green eyes. "Did I pick the wrong room to sleep in or something?"

Yes, but he dared not say that out loud. "You can sleep wherever you want, Ash," Tobias replied, hoping it was truthful enough that his scent wouldn't give him away. "I'm just worried about you after that episode yesterday."

"And I'm still pissed you skipped out on me for a patrol," she growled.

"I took Zeke with me!"

Aislinn snorted, reaching across the gear stick to poke Tobias in the thigh. "If Zeke was free for backup, then Zeke was also free to take your shift so that you could hang around."

True, but he hadn't trusted himself to keep his mouth shut when she woke up, so risking Aislinn's wrath and going for a very, *very* long run had seemed the safer alternative. "Okay, fine, but I don't like to shirk my duties." True enough. "Besides, didn't Dominic pop by?"

Aislinn sighed, turning her head to watch the countryside slip by out the window. "Yeah, to ask me out."

"Out?" Tobias blinked, grinding his teeth as the edges of his vision turned pink. "Like, on a date?"

"Yeah. Crazy, I know." She drummed her fingers on the window sill. "Don't worry, I let him down gently."

"You don't like him?" Now why did he say *that*? Even trying to picture Ash and Dom together was like a red flag to a homicidal maniac.

"Of course I do." Aislinn tossed her head in annoyance. "Just… not like that."

"Oh. Fair enough." Tobias' hands tensed on the wheel as another possibility popped into his head. "You're seeing someone else?"

"Nah, not for ages." She waved a negligent hand. "Besides, I'm pretty much damaged goods, now." Aislinn recrossed her feet on the dash, rolling her head to look over the top of her glasses again. "Thanks for your help yesterday, by the way. The panic attacks are further apart now but they're more intense."

"About that," Tobias said, frowning down at the speedometer but not really seeing it. "I don't think they're panic attacks."

"What do you mean?"

"When you collapsed, you were really cold. Literally freezing. The Mark was so icy it burnt my hand and Olaf's scent got stronger the longer it went on." Tobias shivered at the memory. "Your heart was slowing and you weren't breathing. I think… I think Olaf was attacking you through the Mark."

Aislinn's jaw dropped open. "Are you sure?"

"Very sure." Tobias nodded, even more certain now the words were out of his mouth. "I've been thinking about it all night. I know it sounds strange, but there are stories of Kin who can sense or share their mate's energy through an almost psychic bond."

"Yes, but…" she trailed off and frowned. "You're talking about a heartmate connection, Tobias. Those are so rare as to be almost mythical; and that shared energy, I mean, surely he'd have to be an Alpha - an Ursar, rather - at the very least? Besides, this particular mating Mark only goes one way."

"Doesn't anyone else know how it all works? Isn't there some sort of file on him somewhere?"

"Not really." Aislinn's brow puckered, her gaze far off in a way that suggested she was searching her memory. "Very little is known about Olaf beyond his military rank and merciless bloodlust. Until my attack, the Council didn't even know he was the one preying on Kin women. He's a master at keeping secrets."

Tobias ran his hands across the surface of the steering wheel, pairing what she'd said with his thoughts on yesterday's incident. "He has to be an Ursar, and a strong one. We already know Olaf's been able to pervert the Mark in other ways; why shouldn't he be the sort of Ursar who could use it to steal energy instead of sharing it? It'd also explain his ability to Mark women against their will."

"Son of a bitch," Aislinn murmured, laying her hand over her heart. "You're right. You have to be. Olaf's trying to kill me through the Mark and making it look like a panic attack."

"I think so. Considering you're the first woman to have survived the initial Marking process, it's likely he didn't know he could attack you from afar." Tobias clicked his tongue against his teeth. "All the attacks seem to have happened when you've been upset - maybe moments of vulnerability or stress make it easier for him to get in."

"Which means the attacks aren't getting worse because I'm getting sicker, they're getting worse because as Olaf gets the hang of it, he can sap my energy more effectively," Aislinn whispered. She snatched her sunglasses off her face and crushed them in her fist, face twisted into a snarl. "I'm going to rip his useless throat out with my teeth."

Tobias rumbled in agreement. "At this point in time it seems like the best solution."

"Wait. I was completely defenceless yesterday. If Olaf *was* trying to kill me… why didn't it work?" Aislinn opened her hand, grimaced at the crumpled plastic and dumped the remains of her sunglasses into the empty cup holder. "Remind me to buy a new pair in town."

"Okay." He hesitated, then; "You don't remember what happened yesterday?"

"The attack? No. I remember freaking out on the lounge room floor, then waking up in your bed." She set about picking tiny shards of plastic out of equally tiny cuts in her palm - which, in sharp contrast to the injuries Olaf had given, were already healing. "Why?"

"We-eellll," Tobias drawled, chewing on his lip, "I'm not an expert in these things but… I helped you." He told the tale of the encounter as best he could, watching as Aislinn's mobile face went from curious to concerned to outright astonished.

"I didn't think something like that was possible," Aislinn murmured, massaging her healing palm with one thumb. "I'm grateful, though," she added, shooting him a brief but scintillating grin. "Looks like you're officially my hero."

"I didn't do it," Tobias denied, flipping his hair out of his face. "It was the transitional fever or whatever you call it."

Aislinn was silent for a long time, studying the road and the few houses that began popping up as they entered the outskirts of Gerup. Finally she said; "There are a lot of holes in your education."

"What do you mean?"

"I don't really know yet but I intend to find out." She rolled towards him, tucking her legs up beneath her. "Up for a quick lesson? I don't want to come across as a snooty know-it-all."

"I'm yet to think that about you," Tobias reassured. "In this instance you're pretty much the expert. Educate away."

"You need to stop thinking about the transitional energy as something 'other'. It's not - it's you. You're not a man and a wolf trapped in the same body, you're Kin, meaning that you are both man *and* wolf, blended into one." She reached out to run a finger down his forearm. "Those of us who are Alpha or Den Mother get a stronger dose of whatever mojo makes Kin tick. We see better, hear better, perform better. The strongest sometimes develop skills which would, in more archaic times, be likened to magic."

"Like what I theorised with Olaf's attacks, and your ability to blend into the shadows and disappear?"

"Yes. Exactly like that. I can also use those same powers to blend another person or even an object into the shadows instead of myself."

"Okay. Some of that I kind of knew." Tobias swallowed as her hand dropped into her lap, leaving behind a wave of tingling flesh. "So regarding the transition, you're saying… what, exactly?"

"Transitional energy is the by-product of those extra abilities developing. As Alphas, we're closer to our animal sides, wilder, freer - but the trade-off is that we have to learn to find our balance and maintain it. We're more animalistic than normal Kin and the stronger ones even exhibit some animal features." Aislinn bared her teeth and Tobias was startled to see her top and bottom canines were extended and sharp. "Don't worry, you're not blind. I've learnt to smile so they only show up if I want them to."

"I thought… yesterday, I thought my teeth were funny," he said, "but after I woke up they were normal."

"You're strong," Aislinn nodded. "They'll likely come back and are even more likely to stay permanently. Teeth are a common identifier, but I've seen others. Hair, eyes, ears, skin… the list goes on. The upper echelon of Alphaism is relatively rare, with most of our knowledge coming from history books."

Tobias ran his tongue along the inside of his teeth and stopped when he heard Aislinn's chuckle. "So I thought the energy was something extra but it was actually me all along? How did it - I - know what to do?"

"That part I can't answer, seeing as I don't actually know what you did. However, I can tell you that the transitional phase won't end until you accept the extra energy and find a balance point that allows you to harness it." Aislinn sighed, stretching languorously. "We're almost there, right? My butt is numb."

Tobias burst out laughing, shaking his head as he pulled into a public car park. "You know for a fact we're here. You weren't always this restless - what changed?"

"I transitioned. Now I don't like sitting still." She shrugged, popping the door and jumping out. "You get used to it."

Tobias sat for a moment, staring out the window as Aislinn re-wrapped her crossover top and fixed her pants, covering the majority of her scars. He ran his tongue over his teeth again. All four of her canines were pointed - *pointed* - and he'd not noticed at all since she arrived. Come to think of it, nobody had. What else was there to discover that he'd simply not noticed so far?

"Are you coming or what? It's only getting hotter, you know." Aislinn poked her head back in the window, finishing with the ties on her top. "I might be more restless but you're still as slow as ever, Tobias Greenwood. I'll have grey hair and wrinkles and you'll still be sitting in that seat, staring at the speedometer - which, by the way, is broken."

"Keen eyes." Tobias chuckled and, on impulse, reached over and flicked the tip of her nose. "As always."

Aislinn winked. "I've got to look at something other than your muscles or the car would fill up with drool. Now come on, get that sexy ass out of the ute - we've got a hardware store to raid."

****

Gerup's idea of a hardware store was, in fact, a general store with a home improvement aisle. Aislinn paced up and down in front of the few supplies, chewing on her lip and going over the list of things she had in her head. Some of it was here but a lot of it most definitely was not. She sighed, twisting one hand into her ponytail and tugging indecisively. Grandma had all-but ordered her to stay with the Redding Pack, but fear for the people she cared about made her reluctant to completely relinquish the idea of running. The phone conversation with her father had been postponed from the Ireland end, so on the off chance that Grandma was able to secure a strong enough damper when she spoke to Andre this morning, Aislinn had decided to take the trip to Gerup anyway.

The more she spoke to Tobias, though, the harder it was to think about leaving him behind. He was clearly clueless about what was going on, and Aislinn wasn't being immodest at claiming the title of the Council's best damper. Whether because her Den Mother powers were so strong, or by sheer luck, her damper abilities were off the scale and there truly was nobody else - that she knew of - who could handle an energy as powerful as Tobias' was shaping up to be. She sighed, her thoughts turning to Flynn. Was he getting by, without her around to damp him? His episodes had become few and far between, but if he were to lose control - Aislinn cut off that train of thought immediately, snatching a roll of duct tape from a clip strip and examining the strength of the weave. No. She wouldn't borrow more trouble for Flynn or herself and really, much as she craved him by her side, if things went south the Council would send for her. Wouldn't they?

"Hey." Tobias' head popped around the edge of the aisle, thick brown hair flopping over his eyes. "Find anything?"

"I forget how country we are," she grumbled, clenching her hands around the roll. "I'm going to have to rethink my list."

"Well… why don't we go grab a coffee and talk it over?"

"Coffee's for chumps."

"Aislinn," Tobias slid out from behind the shelf and propped both hands on his hips. "You've been here for almost thirty minutes, just staring at hooks full of nails. Come on."

"These are very interesting nails," Aislinn returned, thwacking him in the chest with the tape. "Look, those ones have a screw thread on the end."

He raised an eyebrow, stepping in close and tugging the duct tape out of her hand. "I know a place up the road that sells ice cream."

"Ice cream?" Aislinn straightened suddenly. "Wait, wait - real ice cream or just re-tubbed ice cream?"

Gold and blue eyes twinkled with mischief and Tobias held out a hand. "Real ice cream. They even have tables and chairs where we can discuss that precious list of yours at length."

She took his hand. "Let's go."

Barely had they taken two steps when the general store's enormous front window shattered, spraying shards of glass throughout the shop. Aislinn ducked, vaguely aware of Tobias dragging her into the shelter of his body as a brick hurtled overhead and thumped into the back wall, smashing a refrigerator full of canned drinks.

Hard on the heels of the projectile were two men, both in drill shorts and button-down shirts and wearing thick, wrap-around sunglasses. One palmed a large knife and, as he strode past the sales bench, flicked out with his weapon to slit the throat of the store attendant. She crumpled to the floor, clutching uselessly at her ruined neck as blood gushed down the front of her uniform.

Aislinn twisted in Tobias' arms, leaning into the strength of his body as she bought both feet up to kick at a stand of mobile phone accessories. The display toppled onto the second stranger's head, knocking him to the floor - only to be thrust aside by the shaggy black bear which rose up on hind legs in his place.

"Shit," Tobias hissed, trying to drag Aislinn backwards. "Bears. We better go."

"No," she shook him off. "More people will die if we run. You take the asshole with the knife, I'll get this one."

Aislinn reached into the shelf beside her and palmed a screwdriver, ducking under the bear's razor sharp claws and burying it deep in the beast's side. The bearkin roared in fury as she danced away, grabbing a bottle of boutique cordial from an oak barrel by the counter. She smashed the base of the bottle against the side of the counter and spun in the wreckage, kicking glass up at the bear's face. He flinched and roared again before dropping to all fours and charging. Aislinn watched the bear approach, clumsy at first but gaining speed. When he was almost on top of her she dropped to the floor, ignoring the pain of the glass slicing into her flesh, and cloaked herself in shadows. As the other Kin's body passed by overhead, Aislinn relinquished the shadows and raised her arms, pressing her shoulders into the floor - and the damned glass - for leverage as the sharp edge of the broken bottle cut into the bear's vulnerable underbelly. The bearkin's rage quickly became agony as his gut tore open and he staggered into the wall, sliding to the floor in a dazed mess of blood and his own insides.

A second roar, this one canine in nature, was all the warning Aislinn had and she dematerialised moments before a knife thumped into the floor where her head had been. Without flesh to dig into, shards of bloodied glass tinkled to the floor, leaving her swift and silent in her shadows. Taking advantage of the dim interior of the store, Aislinn swept around behind the sales counter and drew herself up, looking for Tobias.

He was glorious. No longer human or wolf, thick brown fur covered his entire body, which had expanded to encompass the muscular structure of his midform. Blue eyes with golden centres glittered in a furred, lupine face whose lips were drawn back from two rows of razor sharp teeth. Hands had become claws, feet transformed to a wolf's hind legs, and a bushy tail swished back and forth at the base of his spine.

Over seven feet tall, Tobias loomed above his opponent, who was still in human form after throwing his knife at Aislinn. As she watched, Tobias swung his scimitar claws, clumsy as he adjusted to a larger, heavier body. Ungainly or otherwise, he was still fast, and the bearkin swore as a line of bloody scratches appeared down one cheek.

Fur began to ripple down their enemy's arms and Aislinn materialised on top of the counter, snatching up an umbrella-shaped stand of chewing gum. She swung it like a club and the heavy end connected with the back of the bearkin's head. He stumbled forward, expression horrified as Tobias leant down and tore out the Kin's throat with his teeth. As the corpse slumped to the ground, Tobias looked up at Aislinn with glassy eyes devoid of any pupil, his lips curled into a murderous snarl.

"Shit," Aislinn muttered. If she damped Tobias now, he'd lose his midform and may not be able to regain it - and judging from the screams out in the street, she was going to need his help. "All right, big boy. Follow me."

Sliding off the counter, Aislinn dove between Tobias' legs and rolled to her feet, sprinting into the street. The screaming came from the restaurant across the road, where she'd eaten only a couple of days before. Trusting that the growling and snarling behind her belonged to Tobias, Aislinn flung herself across the road and in through the restaurant's open double doors.

The dining room was a mess, with smashed furniture and discarded food all over the floor. A couple of diners lay inert on the ground, while still more had taken shelter in the kitchen, which was being guarded by a pair of women in waitress uniforms. One wielded a knife she'd clearly swiped from the chef, greying hair escaping from her tight bun in wisps. The second, younger woman had wide brown eyes filled with terror and her hands clenched tight around a meat fork.

Three bearkin, all in shades of brown and gray, rolled and growled in the centre of the restaurant while flashes of russet fur dashed around and over them.

"Stay back," Aislinn yelled to the women, calling her own midform as she dove into the fray. The first bear didn't see her coming and dropped like a stone as she landed square on his spine, snapping it in two with a well-placed heel and all her considerable Kin strength. The other two bears leapt aside, one clawing at a bleeding fox clinging with grim determination to his face while three more yipped and leapt at his sides and belly.

A howl echoed from behind Aislinn and she ducked as Tobias swiped at her from behind. One of the bearkin sensed an opportunity and lunged forward but Aislinn had already swept Tobias' feet out from under him, shoving her shoulder into his gut and launching him bodily into the approaching bear. Tobias yowled as he went, his claws raking a long trail up the outside of Aislinn's arm, but he hit his new opponent square in the chest and they both went down in a roaring mass of claws and fur.

Aislinn straightened in time to see one of the foxkin flung free, and snatched his small body out of the air as razor sharp claws sliced through the space where he'd been. The fox yipped in thanks as she set him down, disappearing into the mess of smashed furniture with his three companions on his heels.

A low, deadly growl issued from the bear who was now Aislinn's problem and he took slow, heavy steps towards her. One eye was bleeding from the fox's work and yet more blood streaked the fur at his shoulder but it was impossible to tell whose. Aislinn seized a broken chair leg and threw it but the bear dodged easily, using the momentum of his turn to catch a tabletop in his front claws and hurl it back at her.

Aislinn lowered her shoulder and deflected the flat surface, grunting against the weight. To her surprise, the bear continued his slow advance, watching and growling, proving himself much smarter than his companions. He took a step to the side and Aislinn went with him, mirroring the movements, refusing to give ground. Again he moved, again she followed. The bearkin shifted his weight, his growl growing louder - and then disappeared from Aislinn's sight as a heavy weight cannoned into her from the side.

Son of a bitch, Aislinn thought, tumbling end over end through the wrecked dining room. The bear had used his voice to mask the sound of the other Kin growling in the room, the one whose body was now twined around hers, his snapping teeth inches from her neck. Tobias.

Devoid of options, she twisted in her packmate's arms until she was on his back, arms wrapped over his chest. Tobias snarled, his claws digging into her shoulder as he reached back over his head to try and tear her off. Aislinn yelped in pain, drawing desperately on her shadows and smothering Tobias with everything she had. His midform dissolved in an instant and she caught his naked body as he slumped, the slamming weight of her power rendering him instantly unconscious. Cradling Tobias in her arms like a child, Aislinn turned to look for the bearkin.

"He's gone." A middle aged man with auburn hair and a neatly trimmed beard limped out from behind a pillar. "I bit him on the balls as he went, though."

Aislinn laid Tobias gently on the floor and resumed her human form, snatching a tablecloth from the ground as she went in an attempt to cover the worst of her scars. "You're the foxkin."

"One of them - the others have gone after our fleeing bearkin friend." He gave Tobias a scornful look. "That fucker almost killed you."

"He's transitional." Aislinn sighed, sweeping tumbling hair off her face with a blood-streaked hand. "I'm his damper."

"Hmmmph." The foxkin shrugged Tobias off with a roll of his shoulder and Aislinn was suddenly glad he was face down, his identity hidden. "You okay?"

"Fine." She looked towards the kitchen, where the older of the two women had a phone in her hand and was talking rapidly. "Looks like emergency services will be on the way soon. Will you watch these people in the meantime?"

"Wait - you're leaving? Looking like *that*?" The man raised his eyebrows. "You have an odd definition of fine, lady. Your arm was almost torn off. By your friend."

"It's not as bad as it looks," Aislinn lied, "and I heal fast. If that bear gets away he might come back with friends, which would be much worse."

"My boys are on it. Some bears murdered a friend of mine, and her partner, and we're calling in a blood debt." The fox pursed his lips. "Hey, you're a wolf, right? Did you know Freddie?"

"Yeah. We all knew Freddie. He was a good guy."

The foxkin nodded, his brown eyes turning sad. "He was. Mace was my friend and even though it was weird for her to date a human, they loved each other. Never did anybody any harm."

"I'm sorry," said Aislinn, and meant it.

"They will be." The fox nodded, his face grim. "Name's Hart, by the way."

"Ash," she returned. "Are you officially investigating the murder, then?"

"Nah," Hart waved a hand. "Higher ups are taking too long - always fussing over one thing or other. Right now they're caught up chasing some Kin agent who's gone rogue and seeing as Mace and Freddie are already dead, they've been shoved to the back burner. We decided to call in a blood debt, like I said earlier, and look into the murder ourselves."

"Blood debt makes sense."

He gave a crisp nod. "Sanctions any bloodshed, at least, and bypasses the red tape. Still, not a great time for one of our own agents to go rogue."

"A rogue agent." Aislinn frowned, wondering why Grandma hadn't mentioned it earlier. "That doesn't happen often."

Hart tilted his head to one side, eyes narrowing. "It ain't you, is it?"

"No." Aislinn forced a laugh and pointed at Tobias. "I'm a damper, remember? He's only just started transition, so I've not been on Pack land very long - but I grew up around here."

"Yeah, you don't look like an out-of-towner." Hart nodded and then offered a grin which lit up his handsome face. "Welcome home, eh?"

"Something like that," Aislinn murmured, her heart sinking as she looked out at the wrecked restaurant. All this had happened because the bears were chasing her, she was sure of it. "I should probably go."

At that moment three orange-furred shapes blew in through the front door, yipping and tumbling over each other before shifting into three jostling people.

"Hart! We lost him," a woman declared.

"Ah, shit." Hart frowned. "He was our best lead for Mace."

"I'll go after him," Aislinn said. "I've got a midform, I might pick up something you missed."

"Steffie's got the best nose around here," one of the other foxkin said, jutting his chin out. "Who're you, anyway?"

"The wolfkin who saved your sorry ass from being sliced in half, Greg," Hart snapped. "Now back off." He turned to Aislinn, eyeing her shoulder. "You sure you're up for this?"

"I'll do." Aislinn adjusted her tablecloth self-consciously as the other three foxes began staring at the leading edge of her scars. "When the emergency services get here, tell them what you saw. There are two more dead bears in the general store across the street - but they got the saleswoman before I had a chance to stop them. Make sure you request extra muscle in town in case they come back."

"Sure." Hart elbowed his closest companion. "I'll hold the fort here. You idiots go up the street and make sure everyone else is okay - bring any wounded into the restaurant, it'll make life easier on the medics." The three other foxes nodded in unison and ducked out. "Sorry about that. They're a nosy lot."

"It's fine." Aislinn offered a watery smile. "I know they look bad."

"Eh, warrior's life," Hart shrugged. "I dig a chick who fights. You coming back after your hunt?"

"No." Aislinn shook her head. "If I find anything, I'll send word to your Vixen. In the meantime, I need to take my friend home, where he'll be safe. He's going to have a hell of a headache when he wakes up."

"Shame," Hart grinned impishly. "I would've liked to buy you a drink. Maybe another time?"

"Maybe," Aislinn answered, taken aback.

"Cool." Hart nodded, turning towards the kitchen. "Good luck, then."

"Thanks," Aislinn replied, calling her midform again. Fur rippled over her body, cloaking the scars, and she dropped the tablecloth to pick up Tobias. Blood dripped from her fur and onto his bronzed skin but she had no time to think about that, nor the fact that it meant she was losing more than she ought. She had to catch that bear.

Outside, the street was in chaos. People were swarming the general store and yet more were pointing west and shouting. Guessing that was the direction the bearkin had gone, Aislinn loped the same way, ignoring the gasps and stares from other Kin as she went by in her midform. In a country town where everybody knew everybody and midforms were even rarer than usual, she'd be a talking point for months. Holding Tobias close to her chest, Aislinn tried to follow the bear's scent but it disappeared quickly into the hubbub, people pressing in on all sides. She rumbled a growl - too many rubberneckers - and blinked as the crowd was abruptly parted by a woman with skin so pale it seemed unnatural, long, straight black hair obscuring her face from view. The woman didn't look up, simply waved a deathly white hand and motioned the crowd in another direction. Whether thrown by her unusual pallor or some other symbol of authority, the gawping passers-by turned away. Growling her thanks, Aislinn picked up her pace and loped on, hoping for a miracle. After a few laps of the nearby shops and houses with no scent or sign, however, it was clear the bear had slipped away.

Sirens blared in the distance and Aislinn sighed. If she was still here when the authorities arrived, she'd need to answer questions that she really didn't feel like answering. Hart could handle it, she decided, cutting behind a row of houses towards where Tobias had parked the ute. She'd made it most of the way there when she realised she couldn't drive in her midform, and had no spare clothes - meaning an hour's drive home in the nude. Provided, of course, that she didn't pass out from blood loss first.

Great.

At least she had somewhere to put Tobias, she reflected, flicking back the soft canopy on the ute and depositing him inside the tub. In the relative shelter of the car park, she checked him over for injuries and was relieved to find only surface scratches that were already healing. He'd likely bruise from where she'd had him in an almost-headlock but if that was the worst of it, Aislinn was glad.

"Ash? Is… is that you?"

She swung towards the voice and blinked to see Sienna Smythe jogging towards her through the trees. Reluctant to relinquish her midform in public, Aislinn growled in what she hoped was a non-threatening manner and nodded.

"I was in the boutique when the attack happened. Some jumpy foxkin named Greg came by to check in and said a woman with scars and a crazy ass attitude was in the restaurant, saving everyone's lives - didn't take much to figure out it was you. Is Tobias with you?" Sienna added. "This is where he always parks."

Aislinn motioned to the ute, wincing as the smaller woman squeaked in alarm, her hands quick and sure as she checked Tobias over herself. Sienna breathed out a sigh of relief and turned, eyes rounding as she finally noted all the blood. "Solaeden save us, Ash… are you okay?"

Figuring it was safe to admit the truth, Aislinn shook her head, bending slightly to display her wounded shoulder and arm.

Undaunted by the blood, Sienna reached forward and prodded carefully at the rent flesh. "That's a mess. Okay, get in the back with Tobias and keep him steady. I'll come back for my car later."

Rumbling her thanks, Aislinn vaulted into the back of the ute and laid down on the floor beside Tobias' unconscious form. For a moment she was worried about the key being in his clothes - wherever they'd gone - but a few seconds later the ute rumbled to life and pulled out into the street.

It was a long, agonising drive back to pack land and several times Aislinn had to grit her teeth against the black maw of unconsciousness but she refused to put anyone at further risk by slipping into sleep. Instead, she drew the vinyl canopy of the ute's tub over herself and Tobias like a blanket, tucking his smaller human body against her longer, stronger midform.

Blood - mostly hers - covered Tobias' chest and shoulders but there was nothing she could do for now. Unable to stop the whine of pain as Sienna hit a particularly large pothole, Aislinn poked her snout into the crook of Tobias' neck and closed her eyes, breathing in his familiar, comforting scent. Here, like this, it was easy to forget the argument they'd had in her room and the twelve years of gut-twisting distance he'd chosen to put between them.

Coward, Aislinn scolded herself, and blew out softly through her nose. She really should confront Tobias about the past, but couldn't quite bring herself to have the conversation which would invariably shatter what precious little remained of their childhood bond. He'd been her everything, once - sun, moon, water, air. Part of her very self. And somewhere, somehow, he always would be; but the man Tobias had become had, at some point along the way, decided he didn't want her in his life.

The knowledge hurt more now, with him curled sleeping in her arms, than it had done all those years ago in Ireland when Aislinn had thrown herself out into the rain with nothing but her pyjamas and her grief for company.

"Ash?" Tobias stirred and she tensed as those blue and gold eyes swept slowly, almost lazily open. He frowned, taking in the blood covering them both. "Bears."

She nodded. Tobias groaned, both hands creeping up to cover his face. After a solid minute of the ute bumping down the road, he peeped out between two fingers, his eyes searching her face. "Why are you still in your midform? Did we miss some?"

She nodded again, wishing for about the millionth time she could talk with her lupine mouth - but no. Tobias dropped his hands, reaching out with a frown to touch her fur, still sticky with blood. "This is your blood," he realised, his nostrils curling. "You're hurt."

He tried to sit up and Aislinn growled a warning. They were driving down the highway! Was he insane?

Tobias fixed her with a steady glare. "Let me look."

Ugh. Fine. Aislinn flattened herself against the base of the tub, rotating her shoulder so that he could see it. Tobias' fingers were gentle in her fur, his chest rumbling where it pressed against her arm. "Who did that?" A moment later his hand splayed and she heard his gasp. "Ash... did *I* do that?"

She rolled sideways to meet his eyes, wondering how much he could remember. Judging from the furrow between his brows, not a lot - perhaps just an instinctive recollection of teeth and fur and unbridled rage. Since he'd smell a lie, Aislinn huffed out softly through her nose and attempted a casual shrug with her uninjured shoulder.

"Shit." Tobias rolled onto his back. "I'm sorry, Ash. I don't even - *how* did I do that?"

Aislinn grunted deep in her chest. This conversation that was not a conversation was a pain in the ass, but there was no way she was shifting back at this late stage in the game. She was saved from replying as the ute slid smoothly through a set of enormous, open doors, jerked to a halt and shut off.

"Aislinn? We're here." Sienna leapt out of the driver's seat and came racing around the back. "Is he - oh! You're awake!"

"Sens?" Tobias blinked up at her in surprise. "What are you doing here?"

"I was at work, you big idiot," Sienna snapped. "I tracked Ash down after the bears attacked and offered to drive you both home. Should I call Zeke?"

"No, I'm fine." Tobias pulled himself up to his knees and rolled out of the tub. Morning sunlight streamed in through one of the massive garage's grimy windows, glistening off the blood and sweat caking his naked body. "I can carry Ash."

Carry? *Carry?* Aislinn bared her teeth and vaulted out of the ute, covering her stagger by leaning on the side of the tub and growling low in her throat. She needed a lot of things, but carrying was not one of them.

"I don't think she wants you to do that," Sienna said, handing Tobias a pair of shorts from the spare clothing kept in the garage for that exact purpose.

"She's lost a lot of blood," Tobias returned, dragging on his shorts. "It'll be better for her this way."

His voice faded into the background as Aislinn slipped into the shadows and disappeared, floating out of the main door and around the side of the garage. The shadows halted soon afterwards but it was enough to put some distance between herself and the other two Kin so Aislinn let them go, re-materialising in the blistering sunlight. Carry her, would he? Not to mention talking about her like she wasn't even there, or capable of making her own decisions? Oh, no. Not in this lifetime. Drawing strength from her temper, Aislinn returned to Tobias' house at a steady, ground eating lope. It wasn't a swift journey but she managed, sticking to the trees where possible and calling her shadows when anyone came near.

The interior of the house was cool and Aislinn dropped her midform as soon as the front door closed behind her, racing up the stairs in a vain effort to minimise the blood dripping onto the floorboards. She'd just made it into the ensuite and shut the door behind her when she heard Tobias' voice downstairs, filled with righteous indignation as he called her name.

Served him right.

Aislinn allowed herself a vindictive grin as she locked the door and turned on the shower. The water cascaded over her wounds, drawing a hiss from between her lips, but she squeezed her eyes shut and bore the sensation until it eased. By the time she'd scrubbed herself clean and stepped out, the jagged mess her shoulder had been was little more than faded lines hidden beneath her older scars. Thank Lunaida for that, she thought. Now that her skin was sealed, her body could begin to regenerate blood and the worst of the danger was over.

Tobias was waiting in the bedroom, arms crossed over his chest and a scowl on his face. "Did you have to run like that?"

"Mother Moon, Tobias, what if I was naked?" Aislinn demanded, clutching more tightly at the towel wrapped around her body.

He blinked. "So? I've seen you naked before."

"When we were kids!" Aislinn exclaimed, striding across the room to smack him in the arm. He was still covered in her blood, hair mussed and borrowed shorts rumpled. "Voluntarily naked and a surprise after-shower visit are two different things, you asshat."

Tobias ignored that, reaching out to run his fingers over the raised scars on her shoulder. "What did I do to you? Are any of these mine?"

"Dammit, Tobias, did you hear anything I just said?" Aislinn growled, jerking away from him.

"Of course I did," he growled back. "And I'm not looking at your body, okay? Not at all. I'm worried about you being hurt."

Aislinn took a half step back, breath catching at the sting of his words; though exactly why, she couldn't say, seeing as she'd been the one to scold him in the first place. After a long moment of shared glaring, she sighed and dropped onto the bed. "Fine. We were ambushed in the general store and you shifted into your midform."

"I still can't believe that I, of all people, ended up with a midform."

"I don't see why - you're more than strong enough. It was just a matter of time, really." Aislinn looked out from under her lashes as Tobias sank to his knees on the floor. "You went completely feral. Killed one bearkin, then turned on me. I could have damped you but I knew there were more, so I lured you into the restaurant. We got two more bears but the third tricked me and then ran for it after you tumbled us both into a big mess of smashed furniture. I had no choice but to damp you then, hard and fast. You passed out." She sighed. "I went looking for the bastard but he was better than his peers. He got away."

"I could have killed you," Tobias murmured.

"Unlikely." Seeing the devastation on his face, Aislinn leant over to grip his chin. "Stop that right now, Tobias Greenwood. I know that expression - this is *not* an excuse to sulk. Look at me."

Gold and blue eyes flicked up to hers. "I don't remember. I could have killed you and I wouldn't even have known."

"You could've killed me but so could the bears, or a bus, or a bad case of food poisoning, or one of Zeke's farts. And let's not forget I chose to leave you in your midform, okay? I needed a weapon and you were it." She released his chin to pat him gently on the cheek. "You did good."

"You have a weird definition of 'good.'" He frowned. "How many people died?"

"I'm only really sure of the one, but there were other bodies on the floor at the restaurant." Aislinn shrugged. "Grandma will get a report. We'll find out eventually."

"How can you be so… okay with that?" Tobias asked, catching her hand in his and rubbing his cheek on her palm.

"Two reasons," Aislinn returned, smiling sadly. "One, it would've been a whole lot worse if we hadn't stepped in. Believe it or not, you saved lives today. And two, this is not my first rodeo - far from it. I've seen much worse."

Tobias took a deep breath and then blew it out between his teeth. "Do we go looking for Grandma?"

"I'm pretty sure she'll come to us," Aislinn chuckled. "If I were you, I'd shower now, while you have the chance. Where did Sienna go?"

"Home." Tobias waved a hand vaguely in the direction of the Smythe household. "She wanted to change and grab some stuff for wine and popcorn night."

"Wine and popcorn night?" Aislinn raised an eyebrow. "We're still doing that?"

"Sienna insisted. And, really, we may as well - neither of us are in any shape to patrol. Injuries or not, we'll be too tired." Tobias sighed, then shot her a firm look. "And don't try and tell me otherwise."

"No, you're right," Aislinn agreed. "Now get out."

He blinked. "What?"

"I told you, Grandma will be hunting us soon and I'd like to be dressed when she arrives. Also, if we're really having Sienna over, I'm going to need some time to clear my head - which is not going to happen with an overbearing half-Alpha glaring at me from the bedroom floor."

"Half-Alpha?" Tobias protested, but he nevertheless got to his feet. "I'll have you know I'm *all* Alpha, young lady."

She followed him to the door and offered her sweetest smile. "You sure about that? I saw you naked in the back of the ute, remember."

And while Tobias boggled at her in astonishment, Aislinn laughed and closed the bedroom door in his face.

Eleven

As Aislinn predicted, Grandma Redding turned up with Zeke in tow a bare thirty minutes later. Tobias had managed a quick shower and fixed some sandwiches without really seeing what he was doing; his mind was firmly back in the bedroom where Aislinn, clad only in a towel, had been teasing him.

Flirting, even?

No, surely not. Tobias shook his head for the fourth time, trying to pay attention to whatever Grandma Redding was saying - something about the nutritional value of a ham and cheese sandwich and how, really, he ought to eat better.

"It's fine, Grandma." Aislinn accepted her own plate of sandwiches and plunked down at the kitchen table, beckoning everyone else to follow. "Meat, dairy, grains - it's a balanced meal."

Tobias hovered by the kitchen bench, his gaze travelling the length of Aislinn's body. She'd dragged her hair into a haphazard almost-bun at the back of her head but thick, luscious waves were already escaping to tumble over her shoulders. In sharp contrast to her previous wardrobe choices, she'd selected a tight, floral tank top with spaghetti straps and a plunging neckline which showed off her curves, the full weight of her breasts and the spectacular crisscrossing of her vivid scarring. Bare feet were tucked beneath her backside, which was covered by an ancient denim mini that rode low on her hips, revealing yet more of those scars and the occasional glimpse of Olaf's Mark - something Tobias didn't dare point out for fear she'd go and change.

Zeke shot him a warning look from the table and Tobias bit his tongue to cut off the soft, rumbling growl echoing in his chest. He really, really needed to get a grip. Pasting a smile on his face, he forced his legs to carry him to the table, where Grandma was flipping open a manila folder.

"I finally spoke to Andre," she said by way of opening. "He's excited to hear that Tobias is finally transitioning, particularly because Ash is on hand to help out."

"Woah, wait - I thought you were going to ask about a replacement damper?" Aislinn's brow furrowed, her sandwich hanging from limp fingers. "Tell me you did, Grandma."

"I asked," Grandma Redding nodded. "But as we suspected, there's nobody else. Even if you weren't already here, you're the strongest damper the Council has. Andre's had you officially signed on as Tobias' mentor. The medics thought it would be an excellent way for you to continue working whilst you heal and have agreed to reinstate you conditionally, at half pay."

"Dammit," Aislinn snarled, thumping her fist on the table. "Bunch of meddling busybodies, the lot of them."

Tobias raised an eyebrow. "Sorry to be such an inconvenience."

Aislinn froze at the hostility in his tone, then sagged back into her chair. "No, Tobias, it's not you. It's just - you saw what happened in Gerup. I'm a walking target. I don't know how to handle this situation as it is but tying us together officially just makes it all the more difficult."

"Before you get too far into that," Grandma said, holding up a hand to forestall Tobias' reply, "I should also tell you there have been several spot raids on small towns in the local area in the last two days. There aren't confirmed sightings of bears at every attack but the men responsible seem to match the descriptions of the ones at Gerup."

"Meaning they likely *are* bears," Aislinn muttered. "Great."

"Meaning," Grandma's voice firmed further, "that it doesn't matter if you stay or go, Aislinn. The bears are here and they're going to cause a ruckus regardless of your location."

"You don't know that," Aislinn returned, crossing her arms over her chest. "I still think I can lead them away."

"For how long?" Grandma quirked an eyebrow. "You'd be safer here - we'd all be safer here. If you leave, you divide the warriors in the pack and then everyone is in far greater danger."

"Divide the pack?" Aislinn tilted her head. "What are you talking about?"

"She means," Tobias broke in quietly, "that if you leave, I'm going with you."

"And where he goes, I go, gorgeous." Zeke looked thoughtful. "I'm willing to bet Dominic would follow too, at the very least."

"What? Why?" Aislinn stared at the two men, her expression somewhere between rage and horror. "Who will defend the pack if you're gone?"

"Jax and Rory - unless they come too," Zeke answered, his voice carefully casual.

Aislinn hissed in a breath, her eyes flickering with fury. "If Dad put you up to this…"

"No," Tobias cut her off, his own temper bristling. "I'm capable of making my own decisions, Ash - and even if you discount the fact that I could kill every single person here and not even realise it the next time I can't get the lid off a jar of jam, I'll be damned if I'm letting you waltz off into the sunset a second time." He leant over the table, fingers digging into the wood. "You go, you get me too. The only thing you get to choose is whether we stay here, together, or whether we run together - but you can bet your scarred hide that whatever the decision is, it'll be *together.*"

There was a long, pointed silence during which Aislinn, her eyes never leaving Tobias' face, slid her hand across the table and twined her fingers in his. A moment later cool, soothing energy swept up his arm and Tobias looked down just in time to see his clawed hand return to a human one again.

"How long ago," she said quietly, "did you all take it upon yourselves to decide this?"

"The night you told us the truth," Tobias returned. Her fingers were warm and soft against his, turning his breathing ragged - but he figured that was just fine, seeing as everyone would assume it was his near-transitional apocalypse that had caused the reaction rather than the touch of the woman who was driving him mad. "You might not want me, Aislinn Redding, but you're getting me nonetheless."

She flinched at that and Tobias felt a perverse sense of satisfaction as she withdrew her fingers. Aislinn closed her eyes, reaching up to massage her temples with trembling fingers. "Okay," she said at last. "Okay."

"Okay what?" Grandma asked, her voice softer than Tobias had heard it in years.

"I surrender. We'll stay." Aislinn dashed at a lone silver tear, shaking it off her hand as though it were acid. "I'm going on record as saying this is a bad idea, but we'll stay. There's a better chance of survival if we're all together." She pressed her lips into a thin line. "Reinstated me conditionally, you said?"

Grandma nodded, her voice pitched to soothe. "That's right, dear."

"Good. Give me your phone."

Blinking at the command in her granddaughter's tone, Grandma nevertheless pulled her phone out of her pocket and handed it over. Tobias held his breath as Aislinn punched in a number, holding the handset to her ear.

"Janina? It's Ash." She paused as a female voice chattered double-time, the words so fast and tinny it was impossible for him to catch what was said. "Yeah, I know, I know. Everywhere - had a bust up with them myself earlier. I know, Janina, I know. Doing my best. Look, can you do me a solid?" She paused again, one eye narrowed as Janina all but shrieked down the phone. "Hmmm. Really? Okay, listen up. You do this and I'll owe you double, yeah? I've got a four fifty and a sixteen thirty. Can you send teams to…" Ash flipped the manila folder towards her and rattled off a string of co-ordinates. "And I want you to beef security at the embassy, too. Yeah, requisition extra hands from wherever you need. I know we don't keep that many agents on hand." Aislinn's eyes narrowed as Janina gibbered on again. "No, I don't think they'll be that stupid but it pays to be prepared, yeah? Bill it to the usual account. Mmmm hmmm, that's the one. Okay babe, perfect - I'll bring a tub of double choc chip next I see you." Aislinn hung up the phone and handed it back to Grandma with a nod. "Thanks."

"I don't know what just happened but I feel like I'm in a spy movie," Zeke whispered loudly.

Tobias couldn't help but agree. "What's a four fifty?"

"Pain in my ass, out of control, transitional Alpha," Aislinn replied dryly. "Codenamed Tobias Deklyn Greenwood."

Zeke guffawed loudly and Tobias glared at him across the table. "And the sixteen thirty?"

"Bear invasion," Aislinn shrugged. "Janina will get things moving and send help to Gerup and Omeo. Hart said the Council have been dithering around and I'll be damned if I let more innocent Kin and humans die while they work out which is the most politically correct breakfast cereal to eat."

A growl rumbled in Tobias' chest. "Who's Hart?"

"The foxkin in Gerup who wanted to date me," Aislinn returned, shaking her head with a bemused chuckle. "I don't think I've ever had so much attention as now, when I'd rather not have it. The irony is not lost on me."

Zeke kicked Tobias under the table and he swallowed the rest of his growl, along with the ridiculous urge to find Hart and rip his balls off. "I think I'm losing my mind," he announced, rubbing a hand across his forehead. "How long is this energy going to drag me around by my hair?"

"Until you learn to control it, or you turn thirty," Aislinn answered with another shrug. "And like I said before, it's not 'this energy' - it's yours. The sooner you come to terms with that, the sooner you can start to get a handle on it. Don't worry, I've got you if you lose your shit."

Tobias forced himself to take a deep breath and nodded. "Okay, I guess that's the best we can hope for right now. What's next?"

Aislinn turned to Grandma. "Hart mentioned a rogue Kin agent. What do you know?"

"A rogue?" Grandma blinked in astonishment, sitting ramrod straight in her chair. "Nothing."

"The foxkin knew all about it; Hart said it's the reason Freddie's investigation is going so slow. Dad didn't mention anything?"

"No," Grandma frowned. "I'll have to call him back later and ask."

"I'm pretty sure that considering I just signed all Janina's orders over to him, Dad will be in touch with you real soon," Aislinn returned - and grinned suddenly. "For once I'm glad I don't have my phone anymore."

"What happened to it?" Zeke asked.

Aislinn rolled her eyes. "Council confiscated it when they suspended my term of service. Apparently it was theirs - funny, since I bought it myself. Personally I think it was because they decided I was a security risk after the attack." She sighed, bravado abruptly disappearing. "Traitor and all that, you know?"

"Surely Andre would never stand for that," Tobias protested.

"You really don't know him anymore, do you?" Aislinn shook her head. "He took the phone off me himself. Nobody else was game."

Feeling like he'd suddenly found himself naked in a thunderstorm, Tobias looked to Grandma Redding for clarification, only to find the older woman had her mouth firmly shut. "For someone who's supposed to know what's going on, I'm feeling decidedly lost," he said.

"Welcome to real life," Aislinn muttered, grabbing the remains of her sandwich and offering it up. "Here, this'll help."

"It will?"

"Yeah, watch." Aislinn tore the sandwich in half and tossed her portion up in the air. As it tumbled end over end, she snatched a butter knife from the table and threw. The silver shot through the air like an arrow, skewering the sandwich to the back wall of the house. "See? I feel better already."

Tobias gaped at the casual display of skill while Zeke roared with laughter. "Oh, little sister wolf, I've missed you."

Aislinn blew him a kiss, her eyes never leaving Tobias. "Go on, Alpha-pants. Show me what you've got."

"You want me to impale a sandwich?"

"Sure, why not? Get it next to mine and I'll cook dinner tonight," Aislinn offered. "Miss and you're cooking me pizza."

Knowing better than to mess with Aislinn when she was in a mood, Tobias went to the kitchen and retrieved a second butter knife. He weighed the sandwich in his hand, lobbed it into the air and threw; the knife thunked into the wall by Aislinn's but the sandwich landed on the floor some feet away with a pathetic splatting sound. "Dammit."

"Hah! Pizza it is." Aislinn grinned, craning her head towards Zeke. "I hope someone taught him how to cook."

"There's a reason he always eats ham and cheese sandwiches," Zeke replied.

"Hey!" Tobias protested, one hand on his hip. "I'm right here, you bunch of twerps."

"Bunch of *twerps*? Really?" Aislinn dissolved into a round of giggles. "What are you, five?"

"As enlightening as this has been," Grandma interrupted, pushing to her feet, "I'm going home; I've got things to do. You," she added, levelling a finger at Aislinn, "are to rest. Just because we now have a direction doesn't mean you get to ignore the fact you lost a lot of blood today. And you," she turned her finger on Tobias, "need to practice throwing your knives." With a wink in Zeke's direction, Grandma Redding saw herself out.

Tobias wandered over to the wall, yanking the butter knives out and rescuing the scattered remains of the sandwich. A chaos of thoughts and feelings were racing through his mind, none of which he dared voice, so he busied himself with cleaning the dishes while Aislinn and Zeke chortled together at the kitchen table. He was glad Ash had agreed to stay but it galled him that he was now her duty, a shitty job handed over to someone who clearly didn't want it. He growled and flinched as the plate he was scrubbing snapped clean in half.

"Tobias?" Aislinn was by his side in an instant, her fingers cool on his arms and her shadows cool in his veins as she fished his hands out of the water.

"I'm fine," he grumbled, tugging free of her grip precisely because it wasn't what he wanted to do. "Sorry to be a pain in your ass."

"Oh." Aislinn sighed, then, and tugged on her hair. "Look, Tobias, you've got it all wrong. You know I'd never leave you to transition alone."

"Do I?" He returned, leaning on the bench. "It's been a long time, Ash."

"Let's not throw stones in glass houses, shall we?" She blew out between her teeth and Tobias watched as Aislinn sorted and discarded replies behind the safety of those blue-green eyes. "I approached Grandma about a replacement because I was trying to keep you safe. Nothing more, nothing less. I'd expected her to have someone lined up already but you're such a late bloomer, she assumed you were going to sail on through transition without so much as a ripple and end up in a fairly low power range."

Not sure whether to be comforted or offended, Tobias considered her words and frowned. "Meaning I wouldn't need a damper at all?"

"Exactly. There's only a handful of dampers around, but there are also very few transitional Alphas who need constant intervention." Aislinn shook her head. "I'd say you were poised and ready to go and just needed the right trigger to set you off."

Tobias blinked. "You mean... you?"

"Maybe. More likely the scent of bear I brought with me," Aislinn grimaced and waved a hand down at herself. "It wouldn't take much to tip you over the edge and it would only have been a matter of time. It's lucky I was here."

"What would happen if you weren't here? Or if there was nobody strong enough?" Zeke asked, sauntering over to lean against the bench.

"Depends on the individual. Someone as strong as Tobias, though? He'd have to be locked up until he learns to sort himself out. It's a tough way to transition but it's too dangerous to leave that sort of energy wandering around unchecked." Something must have shown on Tobias' face, because Aislinn reached out and flicked him on the arm. "Hey, don't. It's fine. No matter what history lies between us, I'd never leave you to that." She stretched and yawned. "We good? I really need a nap. Lost more blood than I thought."

"Yeah, we're good," Tobias rumbled. "I'll wake you for dinner or Sienna - whichever gets sorted out first."

Aislinn waved over her shoulder and sashayed up the stairs. As soon as her bedroom door snicked shut, Zeke chuckled under his breath and tugged out his phone. "Dude, you are in such deep shit."

"What are you talking about?" Tobias whispered. He had no idea how good Aislinn's hearing was and wasn't about to risk being overheard.

"You know what I'm talking about," Zeke returned, his voice just as quiet. "You're lucky she's blissfully ignorant, because if you wag your tail any harder it might fall off."

"You're being ridiculous," Tobias hissed. "I'm fine."

Zeke snorted, tapping his screen as he wrote out a message. "I don't need to be an Alpha to smell that lie, man. You gotta talk to her."

"And say *what*?" Tobias growled. "Think about what she's been through. She wasn't even interested in Dominic, for Solaeden's sake - and girls are always interested in Dominic."

Zeke shook his head. "Dominic's already in her friend zone. He doesn't count."

"Right, and I was her closest friend, remember? If that hasn't changed by now, I don't see that it ever will," Tobias returned, wondering when they'd moved on from his denial to a strange acceptance of unspoken facts.

"You have to make her see, man. Lift the veil on her memories so that she understands you're not that shy little kid anymore. Besides, you don't know what she feels. I'd wager even Ash doesn't know what she feels." Zeke's phone beeped and he looked up at Tobias with a grin. "Just heard back from Sienna. She's going to bring pizza ingredients with her in a couple hours."

Tobias shook his head, marvelling anew at the way his second was always one step ahead. "Thanks."

"No probs. It's my job," Zeke shrugged. "I'm due on patrol in half an hour. I'm going to have the rest of Ash's stuff sent over, now that we're officially keeping her, and then I'll head out. You right here?"

"Yeah, I'll be fine." Tobias looked down at his broken plate and grimaced. No matter how hard he tried, he couldn't shake the feeling that it was a lie.

****

Aislinn set her wineglass down on the coffee table and patted her stomach in satisfaction. "Now that," she announced, "was the best pizza I ever won in a sandwich stabbing competition."

On the couch opposite, Tobias grunted - but the twinkle in his golden starburst eyes said he didn't mean it. Sienna, perched so closely beside him it was a wonder either of them could eat or drink without bumping arms, giggled prettily. "You're just lucky I had all the stuff on hand."

"I'm very grateful," Tobias told her, lip quirking as she bathed him in a radiant smile.

"Grateful enough to make the first batch of popcorn?" Sienna asked, her face pulling into an attractive pout. She fluttered her eyelashes. "Pleeeease?"

"Fine." Tobias rolled his eyes, the muscles under his shirt rippling as he pushed upright, collecting the plates. "I trust you two can look after yourselves while I'm gone."

Aislinn chuckled. "Because the kitchen is so far away."

"Boys," Sienna snorted. She jumped up from the couch and grabbed her wineglass, sashaying over to sit down next to Aislinn as Tobias left the room. Zeke's younger sister had arrived several hours ago wearing another retro throwback sundress in vivid red that set off her sapphire eyes, her blond hair arranged in artful curls that sat just above her shoulders. As the evening cooled she'd drawn on a soft cream cardigan and announced that seeing as they were all drinking wine and chatting until the early hours of the morning, she may as well stay the night in her usual room.

"So," Aislinn leant in conspirationally close to Sienna. "How's it going?"

The other woman tucked her legs up beneath her, leaning into Aislinn's shoulder. "About as good as you'd think," she whispered. "After he scented me the other day I thought maybe… but nothing, you know?"

"Maybe you just need to relax and let things happen naturally," Aislinn suggested quietly. "Tobias has always been reserved when it comes to discussing his feelings but I promise he does have them. Besides, surely he's dated other girls before?"

"No," Sienna shook her head, brow puckered. "He's been with women, I'm sure of it, but no actual relationships."

"Damn, so you can't even borrow past experience to know what'll get his attention." Aislinn frowned. "Sorry, but I can't help. I mean, he used to like marshmallows dipped in chocolate in front of the fire but that was twelve years ago. Plus, we never dated, so that's probably useless information anyway."

"Really? The way I remember it, you two were attached at the hip," Sienna giggled, giving Aislinn a prod. "I always just figured."

"Which is why you waited for me to leave?" Aislinn teased - and chuckled when Sienna blushed. "Don't worry, he was never interested in me."

"What are you two scheming about?" Tobias placed an enormous bowl of buttered popcorn in the middle of the table, eyes narrowed.

"Old boyfriends." Sienna sighed, reaching forward to snatch a handful of delicious, buttery goodness. "Which, by the way, are none of your business."

"Old boyfriends?" Tobias screwed up his face in recollection. "Like that guy with too many elbows you dated a couple years back?"

Sienna squealed in mock rage and pelted him with popcorn. "Sean was sweet, you take that back!"

"No way," Tobias chuckled, looking to Aislinn. "Poor guy was yet to grow into his height - had lumps and bumps and bones poking out in all the wrong places."

"And one bone in the right place, presumably," Aislinn raised an eyebrow in Sienna's direction.

"Oh yes," she sighed, flattening one hand over her breastbone. "He did have that, at the very least."

Tobias choked and Aislinn grinned. "You brought that one on yourself. Poor, lanky old Sean clearly knew how to show a lady a good time."

"What about you?" Sienna asked, prodding Aislinn in the side. "Surely you've had a string of boyfriends."

"Me? No," Aislinn shook her head. "My job is dangerous and pretty much all-consuming when it comes to time. Relationships are almost impossible but, that said, I've not really had any admirers."

"What? Whyever not?" Sienna demanded.

"Because… well, honestly, I don't know." Aislinn shrugged. "I hung around with a lot of dangerous people and I like a man who can keep up. I probably scared them all off."

"Oooooh, you're into bad boys?" Sienna clapped her hands. "Leather and bikes and all that?"

"Hah! Not exactly," Aislinn replied, wondering why she was confessing even as she spoke. "I just want someone who's not afraid of me, or who doesn't mind my constant mischief. Someone who wants to spar, and laugh, and go on adventures. Not to mention accept my unusual profession. I guess I've just never met anyone who… fit."

"But you've had a boyfriend before," Sienna pointed out. "I can tell from the way you're talking."

"Yeah, one. We're still great friends," Aislinn added, smiling. "In fact, we realised that was what it should've been all along. Made us a stronger unit." She reached for the popcorn, shoving a handful into her mouth and chewing. "That was a few years ago now."

"Here I am thinking it's hard for *me* to meet people," Sienna mused. "I never thought about all that sort of stuff." She turned to Tobias, who was standing very, very still by the unlit fireplace. "What about you?"

He blinked, as though surfacing from deep underwater. "Me?"

"Don't think you're getting off that easily," Sienna chuckled, lobbing another piece of popcorn at him. "Drink up and fess up."

Tobias snatched his glass of wine and tipped it back, swallowing noisily. Aislinn watched the corded muscles in his throat working, her eyes drifting lower to the strong planes of his chest, clearly visible beneath those t-shirts which all seemed ridiculously small - as though he was still wearing the same clothes he'd owned before he grew into the body of a man. "Nothing to tell," he said finally, setting the glass firmly back on the coffee table.

"Lies," Aislinn said immediately, grabbing the bottle of wine and refilling his glass. "I don't even need to smell it, your face is a dead giveaway."

"There's been no relationships," he said, shaking his head, "so it's not a lie. Nothing to tell."

Sienna and Aislinn shared a long look and then, as one, turned back to him. "Uh huh."

Tobias took his refilled glass and swigged again. "What is this, an interrogation?"

"Depends on if you're telling the truth," Sienna teased.

Aislinn merely raised an eyebrow in silent challenge. "Don't tell me you're still a virgin, Tobias Greenwood."

Tobias choked on his wine. "I beg your pardon? I'm twenty-eight!"

"Stranger things have happened." Aislinn waved a dismissive hand and Sienna giggled. "Well? Do you know how to stick your pointy end into the other person or what?"

"I know," he admitted, his cheeks flushing a rather becoming shade of red. "I just don't like doing it for no reason."

Sienna giggled again. "I'm pretty sure it's a reason in and of itself."

"Don't forget he can shift to a wolf and suck his own dick," Aislinn reminded her. "That'll take care of the odd itch here and there."

"I can *what*?" Tobias stiffened in indignation, his jaw dropping open.

"You heard me," Aislinn grinned. "Nobody ever talks about it but I'm one hundred percent certain everybody's tried it at least once."

Tobias coughed and spluttered, his confusion and embarrassment perhaps one of the sweetest things Aislinn had ever seen. Chuckling low in her throat, she stood and swayed over to him. "Spar with me."

He gathered himself visibly. "I'm too busy sucking my own dick."

"Your loss. Sienna?" Aislinn tossed a glance over her shoulder. "You game? I'm a little drunk and I want to play. If Tobias isn't sharing his glorious shaft, then fighting's the next best thing."

"Oh." Sienna clutched at the bowl of popcorn as though it were a lifeline, her enormous eyes growing larger still. "I don't know how."

"You don't? Not even basic self-defence?"

"I… well, no. I mean, I'm a wolfkin, right? I've got teeth." Sienna bared her perfect, human teeth as if it were proof of her ability to defend herself.

Aislinn snorted. "Gods above, no. All right, Tobias, come on. It's lesson time."

"No. You just want to beat me up."

"Tobias, get your ass onto that training mat right now, or so help me I will tear your clothes off with my teeth and throw you outside in the nude," Aislinn growled.

Tobias hesitated, as though considering which option was worse, but eventually he shuffled into the open rumpus room and cracked his knuckles, jumping up and down on the mat in his bare feet. "Okay."

"Right. Sienna? Watch. Tobias is going to attack me and I'm going to defend." She looked at Tobias. "Bear hug."

After a moment's hesitation, he loped in and wrapped both arms around Aislinn from behind. His body was deliciously warm and hard against hers, and she blinked rapidly past the wine-induced shiver of delight. Ignoring how good he felt, Aislinn shoved her hips back against Tobias, set one heel on the top of his foot, spun, wrenched and… a second later he hit the mat with a loud thump.

"Oh!" Sienna exclaimed, both hands flying to her mouth.

"Again," Aislinn instructed, reaching down to help Tobias to his feet. "Slower this time."

"Are you sure?" He growled in her ear as they resumed their places, his arms strong and warm across her chest. "I don't know if I can handle this. I think I'm losing my mind."

"Oh, please." Aislinn grinned over her shoulder at him, his face so close their breath mingled; wine and popcorn and static electricity. "Don't worry, I can damp you any time. Now, Sienna - watch again." They repeated the movements slowly, so slowly, until the last moment where Aislinn flipped Tobias over her head and dumped him on the mat.

"Amazing," Sienna squeaked, her eyes wide.

"Now you try." Aislinn waved Sienna off the couch, making her stand on the mat and waiting while Tobias gingerly wrapped his arms around her tiny body.

"I don't want to hurt her," he said, looking desperately up at Aislinn.

"Sweet," Aislinn replied, "but it's not going to help her learn. You didn't go easy on me."

"No, well - you're you," he replied, frowning. "Of course not."

Not sure whether the remark was a compliment or not, Aislinn nevertheless guided Sienna through the steps, choking on her laughter when the wolfkin utterly failed to remove Tobias from about her person.

"Sorry," Sienna said at the end, stepping back with a blush.

"You need some serious lessons, Sens." Aislinn shook her head. "If you can't even throw Tobias on the mat, we're in trouble."

"Hey!" Tobias protested.

Aislinn grabbed her wine and downed it in one gulp. "You heard me, pretty boy. Want to prove me wrong?"

"You have no idea," Tobias growled, and launched himself right at her.

Sienna squealed, scrambling furiously backwards as Tobias tackled Aislinn square in the chest, rolling them end over end until he had her pinned on her back on the mat. His hips crushed hers, his hands captured her wrists and his body loomed above her, lips twisted with laughter. He was warm and muscular and smelt incredible - surely Tobias had never smelt like *that* before - but the instant his weight landed on top of hers, Aislinn's heart seized in her chest. The walls bent inward, turned the same shade of green as her study in Ireland. And someone was growling, ripping and tearing at her clothes in preparation for -

"Aislinn," Tobias' voice. "Ash, I'm here. Come on, come back to me." The weight disappeared and Aislinn blinked up through a fog. Gradually the green faded back to the old wood of the homestead, the soft mat beneath her. Though Tobias' weight no longer bore down on top of her, he lingered nearby, his face a mask of concern and his warm fingers twined with her own. "I'm sorry, Ash, I wasn't thinking. Are you okay?"

"Fine," she croaked, sitting upright and tugging her hand free so she could check herself over. Scars and all, completely intact. "Holy shit, I'm a mess."

"No, I shouldn't have done that." Tobias held up his hands in apology. "I didn't think-"

"Dammit, Tobias, I'm not made of glass," Aislinn snarled, levering herself upright. "Or I shouldn't be. I wasn't. I'm *not.*" She strode over to him, bumping her chest against his. "Why does that happen? You're not Olaf."

"No, I'm not," he said softly.

Cursing, she swung away, suddenly and completely sober. "I need five minutes."

"We'll make more popcorn," Sienna volunteered.

Aislinn nodded in acknowledgement, dashing up the stairs and into the relative safety of her room. Leaning against the closed door, she squeezed her eyes shut and took deep, calming breaths. Tobias wasn't Olaf - was, in fact, the furthest thing from him. Why, then, did the memories keep happening? Why did that day haunt her so, when she wanted nothing more than to be rid of it? Aislinn's hands strayed to the Mark at her hip, wondering if it was another attack, but no - the Mark was as warm as the rest of her. Meaning it was only her own mind playing tricks on her. Great.

What if she couldn't stand to be close to a male ever again? That was all-but impossible in her line of work - and what would she say to Flynn? To call him tactile was an understatement. No, she had to work this out, had to get a grip. Aislinn placed her ear against the door, listening to the deep rumble of Tobias' laughter and Sienna's answering tinkle. She could do this. She could. Filling her chest one last time, Aislinn tugged the door open and made her slow way back downstairs. Their voices were coming from the kitchen, bright and cheerful, so Aislinn swung around the corner to join them and immediately wished she'd stayed in her room.

Sienna had the popcorn bowl held high above her head, face flushed, laughing and incredibly pretty in the soft lighting of the kitchen. Tobias, his shirt slung halfway across the room on the back of a chair, had her backed up against the bench, pinning her in place with his hips while he growled in good-natured warning, making a half-hearted attempt to swipe the bowl out of Sienna's hands. She'd steadied herself against him by wrapping a leg around his thighs, the skirt of her dress rucked up almost around her waist to accommodate the movement. As Aislinn watched, very much aware she'd stumbled in on an intimate moment but completely unable to tear herself away, one of Sienna's hands dropped to Tobias' muscular shoulders, clinging on for dear life as she tried to move the empty bowl out of his reach - a movement he thwarted by sliding his hands up her ribs, his sun-bronzed skin a dark contrast against the vivid red of Sienna's dress and her pale complexion.

And then Sienna looked up, her eyes meeting Aislinn's across the room, and she froze. "Oh."

Tobias half spun in place, Sienna's leg preventing him from completing the movement entirely. He blinked at Aislinn, then looked down at himself, then back up again. "Ash-"

"No, no, it's fine." Aislinn held up her hands, shocked to see them trembling, her breath coming in gasps. "I'm sorry. I didn't mean to intrude. I - I'll leave you two in peace."

"Wait," Sienna called, her voice shaking. Oh, yes, the transition. Wouldn't be safe to just waltz off and leave her to the mercy of a homicidal maniac, would it? Aislinn felt a sudden and horrid wrenching feeling in the approximate location of her heart.

"Don't worry," she said, her voice hollow even to her own ears. "Tobias won't hurt you - transitional energy has its benefits, too, you know." She cleared her throat, tried to smile through suddenly blurry vision. "I'm happy for you both. Enjoy."

Unable to stand even another moment, Aislinn slipped into her wolf form and bounded swiftly out the nearby doggy door and into the night.

****

"Oh," Sienna managed again, her voice very small.

Tobias could only stare at the swinging flap set into the wall by the back decking, his heart stuttering as though it might stop. He looked down at Sienna, who was staring up at him from very wide, sapphire eyes brimming with tears. "Shit."

"It's not me, is it?" She whispered, a tear slipping free.

"What?" Tobias blinked, then looked down at their bodies, caught in what could be easily mistaken for something a little more than a friendly fight over an empty bowl. He took in Sienna's flushed face, her trembling lips and did some very quick maths that led him to an astonishing and completely unexpected answer. "Sens, I-"

"Don't," she whispered, shaking her dainty head. "I knew. I always knew. I guess after the restaurant I just thought… maybe I stood a chance after all."

The restaurant - when he'd scented her, and she'd blushed, and he'd been so caught up in his own problems he'd not bothered to consider what she might have thought or felt. "Shit," he breathed again. "I'm sorry."

Sienna cupped his face and pressed a soft, sad kiss to his lips. When she leant back again, she dropped her leg from his hips and laid dainty hands on his chest. "Don't apologise, Tobias. I was ever in her shadow and I knew it." Taking a deep, shuddering breath, Sienna jerked her chin in the direction Aislinn had gone. "Chase her."

Tobias took a step back, then another, his heart in his throat. "Sienna -"

"Chase her, Tobias Greenwood, and don't you dare come back alone," Sienna growled, baring her teeth as more tears silvered her cheeks. "Get out of my sight before I kick you out. Go!"

Tobias drew on his wolf form and went.

Trees and scrub sped by in a blur, the hard-packed ground still warm beneath Tobias' brown-furred paws. Aislinn was ahead - he could smell her unique blended scent in the still summer air. He thought he might catch her at first, then she entered the wilder areas of pack land and became harder to follow. After a few minutes' back and forthing, he realised he knew where she was headed and flung his body through tunnels of scrub and between gnarled trunks with an agility that surprised him.

A small fissure in the earth appeared as if from nowhere and Tobias leapt it without a second glance. The ground became uneven and the sandy earth changed to rock and grit. He hopped nimbly over several large cracks, dodging tree trunks that rose swiftly out of the dark until he came to an almost sheer cliff face.

Standing at the foot of the rocks, Tobias paused. What if Aislinn didn't want him to follow her? What if - no. Whatever was between them, for better or worse, it had to be sorted out. This half-life was no life at all, just a torture he could no longer endure. Tobias shoved through a particularly thick bush, crawled under a half rotted log and emerged in a small clearing at the foot of the cliffs. A barely-there goat track, marked by tufts of grass and tiny summer flowers led the way and Tobias followed it with his eyes, bunching his haunches and leaping straight upward. The tiny ledge was all-but invisible from underneath but he knew where to look, and after a moment's inelegant scrabbling, Tobias was up and climbing. Here, at last, he caught a snatch of Aislinn's scent and knew she was ahead, her slimmer wolf body having an easier time of the narrow track.

After a harrowing few minutes hanging over empty space, Tobias reached a narrow slit in the rocks which was hidden from below. The walls on either side dug painfully into his flanks as he squeezed through the entrance, dropping onto the narrow tunnel floor with a measure of relief. The passage was wider here and he trotted along, heading for the patch of moonlight at the other end. Tobias paused at the doorway, measured his distance and jumped neatly down to the grassy area below.

The hiding place was in fact a small valley of sorts, although now that he was older Tobias wondered if it was even big enough to warrant being called that. A roughly crescent-shaped hollow in the rocks, sheltered for the most part by the overhanging cliffs above and carpeted by soft grass and a few straggly bushes. Why it had appealed to them both as children Tobias never knew, only that they'd returned again and again in times of distress, cocooned in the knowledge that nobody was likely to find them. Aislinn was already there, wrapped in a thick blanket in spite of the heat, her back turned and her auburn hair tousled.

"What are you doing here?" She whispered.

Tobias drew on his human form and took a few tentative steps forward. "We need to talk."

"I don't want to talk." Her voice was weary, heavy in a way he'd never heard it. "Go back to Sienna."

"For fuck's sake, I don't want to go back to Sienna," he snarled, temper flaring. "I don't *want* Sienna, Aislinn."

Ever so slowly, she turned towards him, her face silvered by the moonlight. "What? But in the kitchen -"

"That was the secret she told you, wasn't it?" Tobias guessed, one hand on his hip. "A secret for a secret, you said. You showed her your scars and she told you how she felt. But did it ever occur to you I might not feel the same?"

Aislinn's brow crinkled. "Of course, but when you scented her at the restaurant I assumed it was more likely you just didn't know how to tell her what you felt."

"I scented her to get away from *you*," Tobias growled and was glad, for a wild moment, when she flinched. "Twelve years I waited for you, Aislinn Redding. Twelve years of staring at the stars every night and wondering where you were or who you were talking to. I imagined your curves, the way you would grow in all the right places in all the right ways. I pined for you every waking moment and your face haunted my dreams. When I was older I searched for you in the local towns and their pubs but I never found another girl who had your fire or your smile. Every day we were apart I felt as though something was missing and I treasured your memory more than my own life - so don't you dare sit there and stare at me like I've done something wrong. I wasn't the one who walked away, Aislinn. *That was you.*"

She stared up at him, eyes wide and tearful in a pale face. With her hair mussed and her feminine curves hidden by the wool, Aislinn looked more like her old self than at any other moment since she'd returned to the pack. She swallowed heavily and shook her head, the blanket falling off one shoulder to reveal the scarred flesh underneath. "I… Tobias, that makes no sense. Why didn't you call? Or write?"

"I did!" He shouted, throwing both arms up in the air. "I tried to tell you that the other day, but you threw me out. Every time I called, the housekeeper told me you weren't home. Every letter I wrote went unanswered. I tried, so help me Aislinn, I did. And then one day Dad told me to let it go - you'd moved on, grown up, didn't need me anymore. 'Time to be your own person, Tobias', he said. 'She's not coming back for you.' But it was too late by then, the damage was done." Tobias dug both hands into his hair, his breathing ragged. "I was already a wreck; I'm still a wreck. Then you show up and start telling me I didn't try hard enough? Mother Moon, Ash, what more did you want?"

Aislinn's face was aghast, her body trembling. Tobias couldn't look at her, he couldn't - too much pain and anger and now, he didn't even have his dignity, because he'd all-but told her everything. He swung away, heading towards the tunnel before he said something even more stupid.

"Tobias." Rocks clattered and a moment later, Aislinn grabbed him by the arm, swinging him back to face her with a well-practised flick of her wrist. "Wait. Please, wait."

He should wrench his arm free and go, but Tobias already knew he wouldn't. He'd wanted this talk, they both needed it - but he was already mourning the inevitable outcome. So he was completely unprepared when Aislinn said; "We never had a housekeeper."

"What?"

"Never," she shook her head. "And I never got a single letter. I...." Aislinn trailed off, chewing her lip. "It's a long story, Tobias. Will you listen?"

"All right," he said quietly, and allowed her to lead him to the most sheltered area of the hollow, where a time-worn rock had served many times as their couch in the past. Aislinn settled herself under her blanket and, after a long moment, tugged at Tobias' hand until he dropped down beside her.

"I cried every night," Aislinn said by way of opening. "I had a lock of your hair and that stupid letter in a little bag I'd made out of an old pillowcase. I turned it into a necklace with a bit of string and I wore it under my clothes." She pressed a hand to the blanket, over her chest. "Dad promised it was only for six months, you know? Just the introductory term. Once the formalities were over, he was going to quit and we could come home again. He wanted me to go to school while I waited, but they told me to wear a prissy little uniform and smile and nod and I hated it. I went for two days and then started skipping."

"That sounds like you," Tobias snorted. She'd ever been the handful.

Aislinn simply nodded. "It was easy enough to hide; I went to the park, to the market, to the river, to the sea. I befriended a couple of street urchins and played with them fairly often, giving them my school lunches so they had something to eat. Dad was so busy with his duties and Mum with hers they never even thought to question, so long as I was home at the right time of day. Then the bears blew up the peace summit."

Tobias shivered; he remembered the day himself. The pack had been so quiet, because well over half their members had flown, at Andre's request, to a summit commemorating three centuries since the end of the Kin wars. There was to be a feast, a presentation, a great festival - but the bearkin had set explosives and blown the entire thing to smithereens, killing everyone. The Redding Pack had been among the worst hit, with almost every active warrior slaughtered.

"Dad was supposed to be there," Aislinn recalled, "but I'd caught millpox during my wandering of the streets and he'd come down sick the day before he was meant to leave. So he survived, when he shouldn't have. And Rupert was back here with the skeleton crew that had stayed to watch over the pack, like he was supposed to be, but…" Aislinn blew out through her teeth. "Everyone, including me, expected Dad to resign his position and come back home the way he'd promised, but that attack changed him. He became consumed with the need to repent for what he saw as his failure to the pack, and he pledged to stay on as the wolf representative after his six month probation was up. I wanted to come home on my own, but the Council put a freeze on all international travel that lasted nearly a full twelve months."

She paused, pulling at a fraying thread on the blanket, then looked up at Tobias from under her lashes. "I wrote you a lot of letters, in a diary. Once a week, from the day I landed in Ireland, I chose my favourite and wrote it out and posted it. You never answered a single one."

"I… never got one," Tobias murmured.

"Somehow I thought you'd say that." Her voice hardened for a moment and then Aislinn cleared her throat and went back to the story. "I was miserable, knowing I couldn't get back to you. Dad and Mum were so busy with the cleanup effort that they didn't notice I wasn't even bothering to put my school uniform on anymore. I went to my little urchin friends and told them I wanted their help making money in exchange for food."

"What? Why?"

"Because I had determined to get home under my own steam. If I could garner enough money for an airline ticket, when the ban was lifted I'd be able to fly back here and leave the absolute misery of my life behind." Aislinn chuckled without mirth. "The urchins took me to meet their friends - they were a scraggly bunch of orphans, street rats with nobody to look to who'd grouped together under the care of a couple of older kids. One of them, a boy about your age, was named Flynn."

"Let me guess, he was charming and sweet?"

"No," Aislinn snorted. "He was a fucking asshole and I hated him. Suspicious, rude, completely out of line. We fought, verbally and physically, on a daily basis. Apart from friendly romps in the sun with you and the boys, it was the first time I'd ever been in a scrap and Flynn fought dirty. He'd rail on me over and over about how I didn't belong and should just go back to where I came from. The day I kicked his ass was one of the most satisfying days of my life."

"And then he left you alone?"

"Not a chance." Aislinn smiled and Tobias was surprised by the warmth in her expression. "He just came back harder and nastier and after a few months I realised he was training me. We began working together, stealing food for the young who couldn't look after themselves and doing odd jobs around the city for cash. Not a lot, but it was enough to make a start. I kept the money in a jar inside my mattress - inventive, I know. But it was working and I thought I'd be home in a matter of months."

Intrigued, Tobias leant forward, propping both elbows on his knees. "Something must have gone wrong."

"Not really, other than it took a lot longer than I thought to save. Mum and Dad started getting suspicious about my daytime activities and placed a couple of calls to the school, but they didn't know who I was and Flynn and I had already forged a document saying I was doing brilliantly, which sounds completely ludicrous but it worked." Aislinn shook her head. "Then one day Dad said that Rupert was coming to Ireland. I was so excited; here I'd thought I was going to have to fight my way to you but instead, you were coming to me. And suddenly I didn't care that you'd never answered my letters, I just knew you were going to be there, in Ireland, and there was nothing we couldn't tackle together."

"I don't understand," Tobias shook his head. "Dad said we were under orders to stay behind and protect the pack."

"Nobody bothered to tell me that," Aislinn growled. "Four years of hell and when Rupert and Stephanie finally arrived, they did it without you."

"What happened?"

"I lost my shit," Aislinn recalled. "I demanded to know where you were. Dad got down on his knees and told me you didn't want to come. You were happy with your life in Australia, with the pack, and you didn't want to see me." She paused and Tobias watched that old grief contort her features. "I told him I didn't believe him. I threw myself at Dad but Rupert pulled me off - so I turned on him and you better believe I used every dirty trick Flynn had taught me. It was probably mostly surprise, but I got the upper hand and managed to get away. I raced upstairs, grabbed my money and leapt out the window with only my pyjamas and that makeshift locket around my neck."

"You went to Flynn," Tobias guessed.

"I went to Flynn," she confirmed. "I was angry, and lost, and sad. I hated you in that moment, hated my life, hated everything. I ranted and shouted and Flynn just stared and stared and stared and then…"

"What?"

"I'm not sure you want to know."

"Aislinn," Tobias said gently, reaching out to tug at a lock of her hair.

She blew out a long breath. "He kissed me."

Tobias blinked. Whatever he'd expected, it hadn't been that.

"We fell into bed almost at once - four years is a lot of time to build up tension and we'd been kids when we met but I was eighteen by then." Aislinn stared down at her hands. "He was the exact opposite of you, which was everything I needed. And in complete contrast to the Flynn I'd known, as a lover he was sweet and generous and patient." Her hand fluttered to her neck. "I'd torn off my locket in a rage and thrown it into a corner. We spent three days in bed and then Flynn went and picked it up, brought it over and said, 'We're going back to Australia and we're going to give this fucker a black eye.' He put the necklace back around my neck and that was that; we set about planning to come home. Both of us."

Tobias swallowed his instinctive, irrational rage and managed a credible imitation of calm. "You were coming back just to punch me?"

"Essentially." Aislinn chuckled at that, leaning into him with a friendly shoulder bump. "My life revolved around you, Tobias. I was pretty pissed off."

"And Flynn?"

Aislinn barked a short laugh. "Flynn is permanently pissed off. Are you sure you want to hear this through? You don't look impressed."

"I'm not, but I want to hear it," Tobias replied, "and I think you need to tell it to me."

"Right. Well, I had some money and Flynn had some money but he mostly used it to feed the other orphans, so it was nowhere near enough. We started stealing, money and goods, some of it to feed our growing collection of mouths and the rest to save for airfares." Aislinn's hand clenched into a fist. "During one of those expeditions, we got caught. Dad had been searching for me, obviously - and even though it'd been a month, he was patient, waiting for us to get cocky. He and the Council raided the hideout, scattered the urchins and confiscated all the money we'd saved up. We should've gone straight to prison but Rupert pleaded clemency and after a brief but explosive interview with the High Council, Flynn and I were made an offer: sign an eight year contract to work for the Council or get locked up indefinitely. If we finished the contract without a hiccup, our ledgers would be wiped clean; but if one of us slipped up, both of us would suffer."

"You took the deal."

"We did. Flynn would never have survived being caged; he's a wild creature and always will be. The only caveat we made to the deal - and I can't believe they accepted it - was that we remain together. Rupert was set up as our trainer and you can bet your bottom dollar he was surprised to learn as much from us as we did from him. A couple years went by and Flynn began to transition. At that point, through sheer luck, we discovered I was a damper - which was excellent, because Flynn is the strongest transitional Kin in recorded history." Aislinn blew out between her teeth. "If he'd been half feral before… trust me when I say your episodes thus far have meant nothing, Tobias. There were other dampers around but none of them could get close to him, and you need physical contact for the damping power to work. Flynn would only let me in, so I became assigned as his official damper and the Council, though it must have killed them, eventually built a team around us."

"That's why you're so confident damping me," Tobias nodded. "Because Flynn is stronger and more dangerous."

"Right." She sighed and wrapped both arms around herself. "A few months later, I transitioned in a short but horrific episode which Flynn nursed me through. We enjoyed a solid, fulfilling relationship for a few years but in the end realised we were better off as friends and separated, excepting a few hiccups now and then. That torc you hated so much? Flynn spent his first legitimate pay check to buy that for me because I insisted on still wearing my old necklace, even though you'd moved on.

In his words, he was tired of staring at that ridiculous scrap of linen day in and day out." Aislinn laughed, her fingers raising to the spot where the torc had once rested. "I hoped, when I came home, that it was somehow all a lie but you were so nasty and I just - dammit, what happened to us, Tobias?"

What, indeed. Tobias chewed at the inside of his cheek, weighing her words in his heart. He was an Alpha, and he could scent if she was lying… and as incredible as the story had been, it was all true. His own anger had deserted him at some point while she spoke, leaving a strange calm. They'd both ripped the scab off an old wound and now that the junk had been expelled, beneath it was a deep pool of emotion Tobias knew he would no longer be able to conceal. But she was damaged and, whether intentionally or not, he'd contributed to part of that. So he very carefully wrapped an arm around her shoulders and said; "The only thing I can think of is that both of our fathers intentionally conspired to keep us apart. But why would they do that?"

"I don't know, but I was thinking the same thing," Aislinn whispered. She hesitated, then; "Maybe Grandma would know. She is the pack's resident Den Mother, after all."

"Surely she would've told you."

"Maybe not, if the reason was good enough. Also, I was pretty wild," Aislinn admitted.

Tobias chuckled at that. "When have you not been?"

She turned to look up at him and for the first time since her return, Aislinn's eyes glowed with the same vibrant life Tobias had remembered in his dreams. The darkness curled around them, soft and warm and intimate and before he knew it, he'd cupped her face in gentle hands and pressed his lips against hers.

For a single, crystalline moment time stood still and with it, Tobias' heart. What was he doing? She was injured and lost and alone but he'd wanted to kiss her for so very long, it was a temptation he couldn't ignore. Aislinn's body stiffened with shock, her eyes very wide as he drew away and Tobias knew without doubt that he'd ruined whatever had once laid between them - but for once, just once in his life, he'd wanted her to *see* him, not as a childhood friend and playmate but as a man who'd waited half his life to kiss her.

He made to drop his hands, waiting for her wrath, but Aislinn grabbed his shoulders tight enough to bruise. Her voice was breathy, a tone he'd heard only in his imagination as she said; "Again."

Tobias froze, that simple, single word echoing inside of his skull. Fire lit in his veins, crawled across his flesh but he forced himself to move slowly, to lean in just as gently, brushing his mouth against first one corner of hers, then the other. Aislinn growled low in her throat and wrapped her arms around Tobias' neck, her body twisting sideways until she was almost in his lap. Her lips were hot against his own, demanding far more than the questioning caress he'd first offered.

He was lost. He knew it even before he gathered her, blanket and all, into his arms, being careful not to hold Aislinn too tightly lest he accidentally cause a recollection of her horrific attack. She melted against him, the coarse weave of the blanket tickling Tobias' chest as her lips opened and her tongue swept into his mouth with a passion that threatened to overwhelm him. Anyone else and he'd have given in but this was Aislinn, *his* Aislinn and Tobias was not about to mess up the miracle that was blossoming in front of him. So he squashed his wild instincts and kissed her gently, tenderly, answering her fire with just enough of his own to fan the embers between them.

"I didn't know," Aislinn said, drawing back just enough to lean her forehead against his. "I didn't know you tried. I didn't know you waited. I'm sorry, Tobias."

"You're sorry?" He gave a shaky laugh, reaching up to wipe gently at the tears streaming down her cheeks. "*I'm* sorry. I should have tried harder, Ash. When I heard you'd moved on, I - I should never have doubted you."

She shook her head and Tobias knew that just like that, their twelve years of shared pain was forgotten. "But when did you… how long have you…"

"Solaeden's balls, I don't know." He reached up to brush her hair back from her face and pressed a kiss to the corner of each eye. "As long as I can remember. Longer."

Aislinn stared up at him, stunned, so Tobias kissed her again, soft and sweet and lazy. No need to frighten her by confessing everything, all at once, he decided. But… "When did *you*?"

She made a choking sound. "I don't know. I was even encouraging Sienna to try and loosen you up. It wasn't until I saw the two of you in the kitchen that I realised I very much did not want your hands on her, or hers on you. But I - Tobias, I don't know if I can... after the attack, I..."

"Stop," he murmured, nipping her lower lip in emphasis. "I don't want anything you're not prepared to give me, Ash. Even if this is it, I'll take it."

"Surely you can't mean that," she squeaked, leaning back from him. "And the smell! I stink, Tobias. I know I do."

He fisted his hand in her hair and leant forward, burying his face in the crook of her neck and inhaling to full capacity. "I smell bear," he admitted at last. "I also smell sweat, and rage, and desire, and the apples in your shampoo. Mostly, I just smell you. Olaf is there, Aislinn, but you're underneath - and I'm clinging to that. I know that scent and it's in my veins. Not even Olaf can truly pollute it."

She shivered at that, uncertainty writ plain across her face, but he knew she'd be able to smell the truth in his declaration. After a long moment, Aislinn nodded and curled into his chest, tucking her head under his chin. "How long can we hide here?"

"As long as you want," Tobias replied, "but it's bound to get a little cooler when we hit the early hours of the morning."

"I don't want to leave you. Not now, not again," she whispered.

"Then don't. Come back to bed with me," he said, stroking her hair gently. "No pressure, no questions - just us, like we used to."

Aislinn sat up straight, searching his face with her unfairly large eyes. "You mean that."

"I told you I did."

Her nervous facade fractured and underneath, a glimmer of light peeked through. "All right, Tobias. You're on. Let's go home."

Twelve

Aislinn woke, not to the sound of magpies as she'd become accustomed, but to the steady rhythm of Tobias' breathing. His fur was warm against hers, their snouts touching and wolf bodies twisted into a shape reminiscent of the yin and yang. Her head was pillowed on his lupine shoulder and his on hers, all eight paws tucked in and tails lazily draped over one another's backs.

Twelve years since she'd spent the night like this and it still felt as familiar as her own beating heart. Aislinn opened her eyes, content to lay still a few moments longer, the folds of their favourite quilt a comforting warmth beneath her. She'd not paid attention the last time she woke here, but Tobias' room was almost exactly as it had been in their youth; neat and minimalistic bar a few old photographs of the pack, some drawings from various members of the Heliope-Flint horde and the bedside clock.

Mother Moon, those photos. Aislinn stifled a laugh as she saw a picture of herself and Tobias in the waterhole, she covered in freckles with her hair unbrushed and he so skinny it looked as if he'd not eaten in a month. Tobias was barely acknowledging the camera - he'd always been shy - and instead had his face angled towards Aislinn, whose arm curled lazily around his waist and was laughing at whoever was taking the picture.

His warmth shifted slightly and she turned to see familiar blue and gold starburst eyes watching her. Tobias blinked and shook his head as though she were a dream and when she didn't immediately evaporate in the morning sunlight, he wagged his tail and nuzzled into her fur.

Aislinn rumbled the lupine equivalent of a laugh, nipping affectionately at his ear. Last night, she'd felt as though someone had torn a blanket off Tobias and she'd seen him for the first time. Tall, with broad shoulders and bronze skin silvered by the moon that had hung above them. A powerful frame sculpted with muscle and thick brown hair she had a sudden itch to plunge her hands into. Full, high cheekbones, a strong jaw and a dimpled smile that did embarrassing things to the butterflies in her stomach - and of course those eyes. The same eyes now peering up from beneath a curtain of Aislinn's own fur, watching her with an intensity that was, if she was honest, a little bit terrifying.

Tobias raised his head and yawned, displaying an impressive array of teeth, then stood and shook himself thoroughly, sending tufts of brown fur up into the air. Even his wolf form looked different now; deep chested, long legged and cloaked not only in the undefinable charisma that all Alphas carried but a strong masculinity Aislinn hadn't noticed previously. She watched him stretch and thought back to the kiss they'd shared the night before.

It had been entirely too much and not enough at the same time, the merest brushing of lips sending a fire through Aislinn's soul unlike anything she'd felt before. And seeing as she'd spent an awful lot of time kissing Flynn in the past, she was fairly confident it wasn't the standard sort of pre-passion enthusiasm. She'd demanded more and he'd obliged, in the soft, sweet way that Tobias had somehow turned from gentle boyhood into complete masculinity - and it'd been all Aislinn could do not to fling the blanket aside and beg him to give her everything he had. There'd been no bad memories, no nightmares, not even the merest hint or thought of Olaf; only the absolute, borderline overwhelming energy of Tobias seeping into her bloodstream and filling up nooks and crannies that had been cold and dark for over a decade.

Tobias hopped down onto the floor and a moment later straightened up in his human form, his back to Aislinn as he looked out the window. "Looks like another hot day."

She frowned. Was that... a tremble in his voice?

"Tobias Greenwood, are you nervous?" Aislinn asked, shimmering back into her human body and pulling the quilt over her scars.

"Is it that obvious?" He flicked a look back over his shoulder, golden sunbursts blazing. "I half expected to wake up and discover you were just a dream. Or worse, that you were real but you'd changed your mind and snuck out in the middle of the night."

"Looks like you were wrong on both counts," Aislinn chuckled, waving a hand down at herself. "Here I am."

Tobias' eyes drifted over her scarred shoulders and then back out the window. "Do you want to know why I never changed rooms?"

"I had wondered."

He pointed to Grandma Redding's house. "Because I can see your window from here. Sometimes, when I was lonely, I'd pretend you were in there, asleep - and that I'd see you soon." Tobias shook his head, brown hair whispering across the nape of his neck. "Silly, I know."

"Tobias," Aislinn murmured, and when he didn't turn; "Come here right now."

Slowly, he stepped back from the window and came to perch on the edge of the bed. Aislinn could hear his heart racing and felt hers automatically ratchet up in response. This was a new beginning for them both, something fragile and familiar and alien all at the same time - and in truth, it was a great comfort to know Tobias was just as out of his depth. She leant back on the pillows of the bed, allowing the seductive scent of butterscotch and cream to curl around her, and waited.

"I'm worried that you won't… that I can't…" Tobias's eyes flickered down, picking out some invisible speck on the carpet. "I don't really know what I'm doing."

"You think I'll compare you to Flynn," Aislinn guessed. Tobias tensed and she nodded. "I suppose that's fair enough. We were together a long time, are still together in a lot of ways. He's my friend and he's going to continue to be in my life in the future. And you've never had a relationship, not really. Right?"

He rumbled an agreement, eyes never leaving her face. "One night stands, enough to take the edge off."

"And after a little soul-baring and a single kiss," Aislinn continued, interlacing her fingers behind her head, "you're suddenly worried I might… what? Think you're not up to the job?"

"I just -" he cut off with a growl, tensing both fists. "I don't want to screw this up. I'm still not sure it's even really happening. And after everything you've been through, I don't want to hurt you. Not like that, not ever, not at all."

Aislinn fell silent, staring up at the cracks in the roof, mulling over his words in her mind. "Come up here," she said at last, patting the bed beside her. Tobias moved silently, crawling onto the mattress until he dropped down next to her, unabashed by his nudity as all Kin were. It was Aislinn who was the oddity, covering the scars that crisscrossed her skin, but if he thought it unusual, Tobias didn't comment. Instead he propped his head on one elbow and simply waited, quiet and patient as he'd always been.

Words were no use here so Aislinn didn't even bother; instead she unlaced her fingers and reached up to trace his jaw with one hand, listening to his sharp intake of breath and the way Tobias' heart swept into a far more rapid rhythm. Keeping her eyes firmly entrenched within his, Aislinn slid her fingers into Tobias' hair and tugged him downward.

Fire.

It swept her veins, all encompassing, the moment Aislinn touched her lips to his, the moment her fingers tightened in his hair. Tobias was trying to be gentle but it was clear he felt the same connection because his hands clenched in the sheets and his chest rumbled with a purely Alpha growl. Raw, tingling energy caressed Aislinn's skin and she hummed in response, pulling Tobias closer when he would have withdrawn, nipping at his lips until he opened his mouth and allowed her entrance. As her tongue swept over his teeth, she reached for his hand, guiding it around her back until Tobias could no longer deny the temptation to pull their bodies close, rolling back on the bed and tugging her atop his chest.

"Ash," he panted, breaking the kiss to bury his face in her hair. "I'm losing it."

"No," she soothed, smoothing her hands across his chest and with them, the cool, damping energy that was opposite to Tobias' wildfire. "You're not." Aislinn leant forward again and this time, it was a gentle brush of lips before she said; "I don't know the answers either, but I can tell you now that I don't want to ruin this any more than you do. I worry that you'll need something I can't give you; I'm not whole anymore and I'm not the girl you remember. She exists, but I've grown and changed. So have you. It's impossible to imagine we could go so long apart and not feel the keen edge of that time. But," she added, putting a finger over his lips when he would have interrupted, "I also believe we're still the same. So I think the best option is to just be ourselves, both old and new, and see if perhaps things just might work out in their own way. I don't know the answers but I *do* know that the ache I've carried since the day I left has finally gone because I'm here with you - not anyone else. I might have been blind a long time but my eyes are open now, Tobias, and you're all I can see."

He stared up at her for a long, long moment, one hand bunched in the blanket which, as though in testament to his chivalry, was still wrapped around her body. "You mean that."

Aislinn laughed, thumping him none too gently in the shoulder. "Of course I do. Now all you have to worry about is the stink of bear irritating you all day long."

"Bear?" Tobias blinked and frowned. "What bear?"

"Me. The stench. Remember?"

A low thrumming in his chest was all the warning Aislinn had; a moment later they were halfway across the room, Tobias' body pinning her upright against the wall. His hands caged her ribs, sliding over the blanket to brush the underside of her breasts while he buried his face in her hair, burrowing ever deeper until his teeth nipped at the curve of her throat. Power swept across her in a wave, strong and warm and scented with butterscotch. When Tobias spoke, his voice crackled with energy and a dangerous edge that sent glorious shivers up her spine. "I don't smell anything but you."

Trapped, trapped, trapped, her instincts shrieked. But it was impossible to believe, because whilst Aislinn could feel all that power centred very much on her, Tobias' hands were soft, his skin like silk, his body pressing without pressuring. Leashed. At her disposal, should she choose, rather than striving to possess her. The walls wavered and for a moment she feared they'd turn green but Tobias was there, irrevocably so, the feral fury of his Alpha energy crackling through her veins and calling the shadows forward to dance.

Aislinn tipped her head to the side and Tobias bit down on the join of her shoulder, just enough pressure to draw a groan from her lips and set a very different kind of fire burning in her gut. Not a declaration of dominance as was so often assumed but an allegiance, an offering - because to get that close to one throat meant also baring your own. Aislinn's knees went weak and she wrapped a leg around his hips for balance, feeling his satisfied chuckle all the way to her core. Tobias lifted his head, then, his tongue sweeping over the place he'd bitten. He whispered something against Aislinn's skin which she didn't quite catch and then kissed his way up her neck, taking her lips with the desperation she'd sensed him intentionally banking the night before. Their tongues twisted briefly before Aislinn nipped his chin and Tobias bared his throat, groaning as she scraped her fangs across vulnerable flesh. His fingers bunched in the quilt, muscles quivering with tension as Aislinn's tongue followed her teeth, tracing a line along the hollow beneath his jaw.

"If you don't stop me," he growled, "I may not be able to stop myself."

"Yes you would," Aislinn whispered, but answered his plea nonetheless, washing the cool shadows over his energy until it subsided to manageable levels.

"You have more faith in me than I do," Tobias rumbled, dropping his forehead against hers.

"I think that's a mutual feeling." Aislinn's laugh was shaky but he returned it and they stood for a long moment in shared, comfortable silence.

"Do you really need this?" He asked, tugging at the quilt. "Because it's not a turn-off, if that's your intention."

"It's not for that," Aislinn answered, feeling a blush creep up her skin. Kin were so often naked in each other's company that clothing was commonly used to promote intimacy, to entice a potential lover. "It's just…" she cleared her throat. "I don't like seeing the scars. So I cover them up, even when I'm alone."

Tobias' eyes narrowed and before she knew it, he whipped the quilt away with a lightning fast flick of his wrist. Aislinn squeaked a protest but he tugged her tight against his body, angling his hips so that the weight of his erection didn't press against her belly. "Sorry," he added, almost as an afterthought. "I'm trying, but you're incredibly sexy."

Dizzy from the sensation of all her flesh pressed against all of his, Aislinn could only gasp and shiver. He waited, watching with gentle concern, until at last she said; "I'm not frightened of your boner, you idiot."

Tobias laughed, a hearty, full sound that reverberated through her bones. "I guess I'll take that as a compliment," he murmured, his voice dropping into a register reserved for velvety midnights and too much scotch. "Can I look? Please?"

He'd already seen most of it at the watering hole but this was an infinitely more intimate, difficult thing to give permission for. Tobias was requesting a trust she'd not yet given to anyone since the attack, not even the doctors - they'd had to tranq her to get close while she was truly naked. Aislinn swallowed, furious with her own cowardice. "Okay, but I might freak out and try to chop your head off."

Ever so slowly, Tobias peeled his body back from hers. He made sure to keep his hands on her biceps, a light, gentle support as his attention moved downward. The golden centres blazed with a mixture of fury and desire and Aislinn shivered as he assessed her ruined flesh. She couldn't bear to watch so she shut her eyes and was therefore completely unprepared when he pressed a kiss to her ribs, on the left, just below her breast.

"Tobias!"

He was grinning up at her, having gone to his knees on the carpet, his hands sliding down to her wrists. "What? Can't I admire you, just a little?" Tobias tugged her palms to his lips and laid a kiss in the centre of each. "It's me, Ash. Just me. I won't hurt you."

Just Tobias. Not Olaf, not the doctors, or her father or the scientists or all the other people who stared as though she were a circus sideshow. Just Tobias, his smile soft and his hands gentle and his eyes very much appreciating what he saw, scars or no. And he'd always looked at her that way, Aislinn realised with a shock. Always - she'd just never understood the intensity lurking in the back of his expression.

A tiny sob escaped her lips and she threw herself into his lap, curling into his comforting embrace. Humming in satisfaction, Tobias pushed to his feet as though Aislinn weighed no more than a feather, carrying her through to the ensuite and turning on the shower. He slid her down his body, followed her into the hot water and with careful hands and a gentle smile, washed her thoroughly from head to toe, pausing now and again to press a kiss against one scar or another.

Aislinn trembled as he worked, heart in her throat. For fire and fury and laughter and tears she had answers, but for tenderness? It was a concept that took on new meaning as she allowed Tobias' hands to roam her skin with gentle reverence. For one Kin to wash another was a sacred, rare gesture of trust that not even all mates and lovers granted. It was an enormous thing to allow someone else so close to your most soft, vulnerable parts, to be so dreadfully exposed in so many ways. Yet here in the shower with Tobias, it felt like coming home. A little voice whispered that she was in well over her head but when Tobias straightened, reaching to wash himself, Aislinn held him still with a single finger to his wrist.

"Are you sure?" He asked, nevertheless handing her the soap and wash cloth. There was no hesitation in his eyes, no questioning her intentions or her honour; something her assassin's dark soul appreciated like nothing else. She could kill him six different ways in as many seconds, but Tobias' face was open, not a single trace of nerves in his scent.

Not quite trusting her voice, Aislinn merely nodded and began. His body was smooth and warm and, for all he'd grown, familiar. She felt clumsy and free all at once, working slowly down his chest and arms, blushing as she discovered all sorts of dips and hollows and muscular curves that certainly hadn't been present twelve years before. Tobias stood still as a statue, though his frame hummed with tension and Aislinn couldn't help but smile as she smoothed her hands along his thighs. He was as uncertain as she, feeling his way through a ritual as old as the story of Lunaida, goddess of the moon, and her consort Solaeden, god of the sun.

When she straightened again, Aislinn set the soap and wash cloth down and melted into Tobias' arms, closing her eyes as the water cascaded over the both of them, content to simply *be*. He set his chin atop her head, rumbling deep in his chest, hands kneading the tension in her shoulders and down the length of her spine. In the soft shadows behind her eyelids, Aislinn could almost feel the threads of their souls reaching for one another, mending the gap that time had put between them for so long.

Tobias held her silently until the water began to go cold, then he flicked the taps off and swept Aislinn's wet hair back from her face. His lips pressed softly to her forehead and he whispered; "Thank you."

Aislinn opened her eyes and tipped her head back until she met his gaze. "For what?"

"Trusting me," he replied, giving her a final squeeze and stepping out of the shower. "I wasn't sure I'd get a second chance."

Aislinn smiled, accepting the fluffy towel he offered. "I wasn't sure you would, either. Guess I'm a sucker for a pretty face."

Tobias looked so astonished that she laughed, flicking him playfully in the ribs. He stared down at the place she'd touched and then blinked once, very slowly, before raising burning eyes to her face. "Do that again."

She obliged and he snatched at her hand but Aislinn danced away, laughing. "Too slow, Tobias."

"Oh, really?" He bared his teeth in a feral grin and tackled her bodily to the floor, both of them laughing as they rolled out into the bedroom in a tumbled mess of arms and legs - and fur, as Aislinn shifted in order to wriggle out of Tobias' grip. "That's cheating!"

"You're just jealous because you didn't think of it," she teased, melting back to her human form and dragging one of her bags onto the bed. "On the topic of thoughts - we should go and talk to Grandma this morning."

"You really think she knows why Andre and Dad kept us apart?"

Aislinn shrugged, frowning as she rummaged in her bag for something suitable to wear. "She's the Den Mother. She either knew, or helped - and I can tell you now, out of the three of them, she's most likely to answer our questions."

"Okay," Tobias nodded. "I'll make breakfast and we'll head over. After yesterday we both need a good - what on earth are you doing?"

"I don't know," Aislinn growled, kicking at the growing pile of clothing on the floor. "I don't know what I feel like wearing. Sienna was a great help with my wardrobe but heat and scar coverage don't go hand in hand, you know."

"Sienna." Tobias' face fell. "I should probably go and see her."

"Actually, it should be me," Aislinn contradicted. "You were upfront with her."

"Debatable," he replied, propping one hand on his hip. "Neither of us intended her to get hurt. We just…"

"I know. Still, I think it should be me. Sens has been a good friend since I've come home, and I'd hate to lose her. I'll go after we see Grandma and try to get to the bottom of this shit show." She ran a hand through her hair, picking up and discarding a maxi dress. "Bah! This is stupid. Bears want to kill us, our parents are keeping secrets, the world is upside down and I can't decide what to *wear*?"

Tobias crossed the room and extricated a bunched up tank top from her white-knuckled grip. "Relax." He dug into the chaos of her suitcase and tugged out the denim mini she'd been forced to wear the previous day because the main bulk of her clothes had still been at Grandma's. "I like this one."

"So do I but it doesn't cover everything and I don't really think it's leggings weather."

"Why do you need to cover anything?" Tobias raised an eyebrow. "You wore this yesterday and I thought you looked good."

"I didn't have any other choices yesterday, and I knew we weren't leaving the house." She pressed her lips together in a thin line and waved a vague hand at her scars. "Like I said before, I don't like looking at them."

"Why?"

"Why? I'd rather not see the evidence of my own failures, that's why."

"Failures?" He blinked rapidly. "*Failures*?"

Aislinn shook her head, yanking out a black and gold bikini and tugging it on, wrestling her breasts into position. They were too bloody large for a warrior by far but Tobias watched her progress with fascination. "Look," she said when she was done. "See?"

"I am both looking and seeing," he agreed equably. "And in a minute, if you don't stop waving those in my face, I'm going to be motorboating."

She growled low in her throat and gave him a shove. "Dammit, you're missing the point, you hormone-ridden fleabag."

Tobias rolled his eyes. "I fail to see how surviving horrific wounds inflicted by someone else make you a failure, Ash. Were you supposed to fight off all those bears by yourself?"

Aislinn wrapped her arms around her ribs and shivered. "I should've heard them coming. I should've been paying better attention. I should've had my weapons closer. I should've reacted faster. I -"

"Stop." Tobias grabbed her shoulders and swung her to face him. "There was nothing you could have done. Nothing. You're only one person and Solaeden knows what all those officious medics and scientists and lab rats said to you but dammit, Ash, you're incredible. You *lived*. How many other women before you can't claim the same thing?"

"Thirty seven that we know of," Aislinn muttered.

"Thirty seven families that buried their loved ones. Thirty seven mates who lost the other half of their hearts. Thirty seven lives stolen -"

"I get it!" She shouted, snatching the skirt from his hands and throwing it back in the case. "I wish I could've helped them. I do. I wish I could help *anyone* who's been through something like this. It's lonely, Tobias. Cold and lonely and awful."

"Then step into the sun," he said softly, anger bleeding from his body as though it had never been. "Fight, Ash. For yourself and for those women. You survived, and every single one of these scars is proof of that. Every second you draw breath is a second you're one up on Olaf." Tobias stepped closer, tipping her chin up with one finger. "As for cold and lonely, that officially ended last night - and I will tear out the throat of anyone who says otherwise."

Aislinn's heart stuttered and for the second time that morning she found herself incapable of words. Tobias bent and brushed his lips against hers, a brief, tantalising show of affection and support.

"I'm going to get dressed and make us some breakfast," he said softly. "You choose whatever *you* want to wear and I'll see you downstairs."

* * * * * * *

Tobias looked up from the stove as he heard Aislinn's feet on the stairs. His hand tightened on the spatula to the point of pain, his lungs wheezing almost to a halt. She'd put on the denim mini he'd selected, with a loose, sleeveless crochet top in khaki that hung off one shoulder and revealed the black and gold bikini underneath. Her hair hung loose, tumbling over her shoulders in thick glossy waves of red-tinted brown that fell well past her waist.

"What do you think?" Aislinn asked, hesitating at the bottom of the stairs.

"I think you're trying to kill me," Tobias managed and was gratified when she laughed and ducked her head. "Also, I made French toast sandwiches."

Her eyes widened. "Really?"

"With cream cheese and jam in the middle."

She was suddenly at the bench. "Like you used to?"

"As much as I can remember," Tobias admitted, shoving a sandwich onto a plate and pushing it in her direction. "You'll have to be the judge."

Aislinn's smile was bright and she demolished her sandwich amidst squeals of delight, promptly demanding a second. Tobias leant on the bench with his own sandwich, juggling molten cream cheese and jam and a glass of iced water. He dusted his hands on faded black shorts and reached over to steal Aislinn's top crusts - she'd never eaten them, even as a child - and then looked up to find her laughing. "Are you planning to wear a shirt today?"

Tobias looked down at his bare chest and then back up again. "Should I?"

"Barbara Forthrite complained the other day that you're half naked all the time. Apparently it's my fault," Aislinn added, her grin widening as she leant over to poke one of his biceps with a finger dusted in icing sugar. "Although *why* you were hiding behind a water tank, of all things, has got me stumped."

"I was in a hurry and she talks for hours," Tobias replied, raising an eyebrow. "And also, I rarely wear a shirt all day. Shifting in and out of wolf form all the time makes clothing a pain and anyway, Barbara's Kin, like the rest of us. I could be naked in a room full of naked people and that wouldn't be weird in the slightest. Why is she worried if I'm only half dressed?"

"She was looking for something to complain about. And I've just covered you in sugar," Aislinn added, leaning closer to rub at the mark on his arm and, rather than cleaning it off, smearing jam over the top instead. "Oh, for Lunaida's sake."

Tobias raised his arm to his mouth and, watching Aislinn's face over the top of his own flesh, licked the jam and sugar off with a long, single stroke. "Fixed."

"Tobias Greenwood, are you flirting with me?" Aislinn demanded, eyes sparkling.

"Only took you twenty years to notice."

Rather than blush, she burst out laughing. "Doesn't say much about your skills, now, does it?"

"Hey!" Tobias vaulted over the kitchen bench, but Aislinn was suddenly gone. Laughter had him turning towards the front door, which was now open, with Ash leaning casually against the frame. "Okay, you gotta explain how that works."

"Magic," she shrugged, and laughed when he growled. "All right, all right. If there are shadows, I can… melt into them, I guess. My body becomes part of the darkness. It's good for assassinating nasties and escaping lecherous men."

"Lecherous?" Tobias lunged again and she danced out of the way. "No disappearing that time? Is it a limited use talent?"

"I need shadows." Aislinn paused for a moment and pointed to where she'd been standing in the full sunlight. "In the dark I'm pretty much sorted but in full light, natural or otherwise, I'm limited. When I said I melt into the shadows, I mean it, but I need actual shadows or true darkness for it to work."

"So all I have to do to catch you," Tobias mused, stalking her across the room, "is back you into a spotlight?"

"Something like that - but I've had a lot of practice," she returned, lips twitching. "Catch me if you can, big boy."

Tobias rumbled deep in his chest, herding her backwards into the full light of a window. "Keep talking like that and I'll have to go full Alpha on you, young lady."

"Really?" Aislinn's head tilted to the side and he heard her heart kick up a notch. "I didn't think you had it in you."

"You'd be surprised what I've learnt while you were away," he returned, his voice dropping into a register that, until a few days ago, Tobias hadn't known he was capable of - but he'd noticed the way it made Aislinn shiver in delight, as she was doing right that second, the fire in her eyes taking on a decidedly bedroom gleam. Harnessing that velvet rumble, he added; "Want to play, Ash? Careful you don't bite off more than you can chew."

He had her against the window now and Aislinn stopped as the hard edge of the sill collided with her buttocks. "You have no idea what I'm capable of."

"Then show me," he growled, pushing into her personal space.

Aislinn grinned and slipped her arms around his neck, twisting her fingers into his hair in a way that sent tingles of electricity shivering down Tobias' spine. "All right, I'll set you a challenge. Consider it part of your training to master those naughty transitional tendencies." She paused, chewing at her lower lip with one pointed canine, then said;

"Catch me and I'm yours for five whole minutes to do with as you will."

"Fifteen," he countered, resting his forehead against hers.

"Eight."

Tobias clenched his hands around the window sill on either side of her hips, struggling to keep his breathing even. "Twelve."

"Ten," she whispered, her breath tickling his chin. "That's my final offer."

"And the rules?"

"None. Anytime, anyplace - catch and restrain me somewhere I can't get away." Aislinn's blue-green eyes were wide and very, very close. Her tongue flicked out, sweeping across his lower lip. "Starting now."

Tobias' hands slid over the wood to twist in her skirt, despite his demanding them otherwise. Since when did his body not do what it was told? Since forever, where Aislinn Redding was concerned - and she was only making it worse by teasing him into a frenzy. He tugged her hard against his body with a low growl. "You've got yourself a deal."

"Good." And just like that, she was gone. Tobias staggered forward, his head thumping against the window pane, breath whooshing out of his body in a rush. Barely had he blinked when Aislinn was tapping against the window from the outside, smile broad and fingers crooked in a little wave. "Come on," she said, her voice muffed by the glass. "Let's get to Grandma's before she decides to head somewhere else."

Straightening up with a rude gesture that she laughed off, Tobias glanced at the clock. Almost 10am - Grandma would, indeed, be done with her chores and having a quick morning tea before carrying on with the rest of her day. Running a hand through his hair in a useless attempt to settle it, Tobias followed Aislinn out into the bright sunshine and tugged the door closed behind him. "I had you in the sun," he said as he joined her at the bottom of the porch steps.

"You made a shadow with your own body," she returned, skipping ahead of him onto the common lawn. "I don't need much, not for a little trip."

"This is going to be harder than I anticipated, isn't it?"

"Mother Moon, I hope so," she chuckled, waving at a naked Rory as he loped up the steps to his grandfather's house. "Morning, Rors."

"Hey, Ash," the other man called. "Tobias."

"How was patrol?"

"Fine." Rory gave himself a shake, water flinging from his blond-streaked hair. "I've switched with Jax, had a swim, now going for a nap. Bush is quiet."

"Normal quiet or oh-shit quiet?" Aislinn asked as they drew level.

Rory paused, expression thoughtful as he toyed with the chain on Bill's porch swing. "Nothing I'd say was unusual," he said at last. "Just quieter than normal."

Tobias noted the way Ash's lips pursed and frowned. "What are you thinking?"

"I'm thinking that being prepared is better than being surprised." She looked up at Rory. "Can you organise a pack lunch in the den?"

"As long as you don't mind a temporary lapse in the rounds, sure." The other man nodded. "Jax doesn't finish patrol until almost one o'clock, though."

"Late lunch, then," Aislinn shrugged. "No skin off my nose."

"It'll be done."

"Thanks, spunk monkey." Aislinn blew the wolfkin a kiss and then skipped away, leaving Rory blinking after her in surprise.

"Spunk monkey?" He repeated, then shook his head and glanced up at Tobias. "You look different today."

"I do?"

"Yeah. More…" Rory's brow puckered and Tobias waited, long accustomed to the other's thoughtful silences. "More you." And with the hint of a smile on his face, he slipped into his grandfather's house and closed the door.

Tobias snorted softly and jogged after Aislinn, catching up to her by the steps outside Grandma's front door. "I'm more me, apparently," he said in response to her raised eyebrow.

"Well, we wouldn't want you being less you than you should be, would we?" Aislinn returned, mounting the steps and swinging the door wide. "Otherwise it'd just be an imposter. Nobody has time for fake Tobias."

"Helpful," he drawled, bumping her playfully with his shoulder as she flitted into the house.

Grandma was sitting in her kitchen, a steaming cup of tea in front of her and a plate of melting moments to one side. She looked up from her daily organiser as Aislinn and Tobias wandered into the kitchen, the former leaning over to press a kiss to her grandmother's cheek and the latter pulling down two extra cups and a plate from the overhead cupboards.

Joanne Redding, ever the astute type, dragged her eyes over first Aislinn, then Tobias and said; "Well. It's about time."

Aislinn dropped into a chair and Tobias deposited a cup of tea and some biscuits beside her. "You've been expecting us?"

"In one form or another."

Tobias carried his own tea to the table and slid into the chair next to Aislinn, leaning over to snatch a melting moment from the plate he'd set out for them to share. "Sounds ominous."

Grandma watched them both very closely for another long moment, a tiny smile tugging at the corners of her lips. "That depends on what you want to know."

"Hmm." Aislinn glanced up at Tobias, then faced her grandmother and visibly gathered herself. "Have our fathers been trying to keep us apart on purpose?"

"Yes," Grandma answered, curling both hands around her cup and staring into the depths. "They have."

"Why? I mean I know Dad's a lunatic, but why Rupert?" Aislinn demanded, her tone thick with hurt. "And you, Grandma. Why didn't you say something? Why didn't you *do* something? You knew I was hurting - you have to have known Tobias was, too."

Tobias slid his fingers down Aislinn's forearm and twined them into hers, squeezing gently. "Let's hear her speak before you lose it, Ash."

Grandma's gaze slid to their joined hands and she sighed. "It's a bit of a tale but if you promise to sit through it, I'll answer all those questions."

"I'm going to need more biscuits," Aislinn groused, snatching a melting moment from the plate for emphasis. Grandma Redding picked up her own plate and tumbled the rest of the melting moments onto Aislinn's. "All right. I'm listening."

"Do you know how a new representative is chosen for the High Council seat?" Grandma asked, leaning back in her chair.

"Of course." Aislinn nodded. "The names of all the Alphas and Den Mothers of that breed of Kin go into a ballot and the rest of their species make an anonymous vote. Alpha or Den Mother with the most votes goes into the council for their denomination; in Dad's case, the Canis Council. From there, those lesser Councils vote to elect a representative who speaks with the High Council on their behalf. The new councillor gets a six month probationary period and then, provided they do a reasonable job, have the option to either take the seat permanently or step down, triggering the ballot process again."

"Correct. When Kit Theyron retired from the Canis Council, nobody was more surprised than your father to be elected as replacement. Even more so that he was offered Kit's High Council seat as well." Grandma sipped her tea thoughtfully. "Truth be told, it's always puzzled me, too. We were a reasonably sized pack but certainly not the largest and out here in the bush, we're very remote. Andre had only been senior Alpha a decade or so and was still relatively untested; he knew he was under-qualified for the job and told me before he went to Ireland that after the six months was up, he'd be coming back."

"That's why he left my dad behind," Tobias guessed.

Grandma nodded. "Yes. No need to take your second if it's only a short jaunt - and Rupert was a good, stabilising energy on the rest of the pack in Andre's absence. It made sense. The High Council, however, would've seen his turning up alone as an affront, so Andre took his wife and daughter as a show of goodwill instead."

"Too bad he didn't ask us first," Aislinn muttered.

"Your parents thought six months seeing the wider world would be good for you," Grandma shrugged. "You must remember your mother's from Sydney and was used to city living. She worried that without some external stimuli, you'd be barefoot and pregnant before your teenage years were over."

Aislinn rolled her eyes. "Because I'm so like that."

"It was intended to only be a short trip," Grandma reiterated. "Put you into a normal school, give you a little break from the isolation of pack land. Your protests over going only served to harden both of your parents' resolve."

"I was fourteen," Aislinn protested. "I wasn't having sex with anyone."

"No, but you were wild and independent and your mother knew that when the time came, whatever decisions you made would be done wholeheartedly. She went to university as a youngster, as you know, and worked as a lawyer for several years before she met your father. There's something to be said for the independent freedom of such a lifestyle and though Marguerite never regretted scaling down when she came here, she worried a personality as big as yours would end up stifled and any intellect you possessed would be wasted. So you went, whether you wanted to or not." Grandma rubbed at her brow for a moment, then shrugged. "I know you didn't want to go but at the time, it didn't seem like it would do any harm."

"I hated it," Aislinn hissed.

"I know," Grandma soothed. "But you may not have. Anyway, shortly before Andre's six month term was up, there was the peace summit. The Council have a mandatory number of attendees for each representative's pack, then another again for other relevant guests. Suffice it to say that in order to fulfil the numbers in question, your father had to gather almost every active warrior we had plus a couple of 'honorary guests' - well over half the entire Redding Pack. Rupert stayed behind to maintain the skeleton crew left to guard the rest of us; working with myself, of course."

Aislinn sighed, slumping back into her chair. "The peace summit was a disaster."

"Yes, and whilst you'd been a handful yourself, I have never been more grateful for your shenanigans than when you gave your father those millpox," Grandma rumbled. "If not, he'd have been at that summit too and he'd be dead right now. I know you're probably familiar with the figures but it's worth mentioning, for the sake of the tale, that every single one of our pack members who attended that summit died there. Mothers, brothers, fathers, children, aunties and uncles all gone in one terrible explosion. And we weren't alone, of course, many others suffered heavy losses. I know of several groups who lost leaders and even had to merge into new packs or herds because there simply weren't enough of them left to go on."

"It was awful here," Tobias shuddered at the memory. "So many people just never came back. Both Rory's parents and his older brother, Leif. Gavin, Brooklyn and Stella Forthrite. Draco Heliope-Flint. David Smythe, Lucy Brexton. Keelin, Bess and Jett Arthknott - the list is almost endless. We didn't have enough people to work the farms, let alone fulfil the higher security protocol Dad wanted to put in place. It was the day after the summit that he rounded up the five of us boys and put us straight to work - on the land during the day, in the training ring at night. There were memorials, people grieving and breaking down all over the place. Jemima Smythe trying to counsel everyone when she herself had lost her father and her father in-law."

"Complete shit-show," Grandma nodded in agreement. "And Andre blamed himself entirely."

"I know he did, but I never understood why." Aislinn frowned. "It wasn't his fault."

"We all deal with grief differently, dear. He lost a great deal of friends and family that day and was consumed with the idea that he should have been there, as though it would have made a difference." Grandma sighed. "Your mother tried to convince him to come home but the threat to Kin worldwide was so great that the Council slapped a ban on international travel. Then the bears started sending threats to all the High Council members - pictures of their families, locks of hair, personal items, that sort of thing. The moment your father saw a picture of you in the marketplace handing out apples to orphans, he blew his lid and swore to stay on as the wolfkin representative that very day."

"He knew?" Aislinn startled, then looked thoughtful. "That's why he contacted the school."

"Yes, but you were already one step ahead, even then," Grandma chuckled. "Anyway, it was about that time he told me he wasn't coming home. Because you'd never wanted to go in the first place and had been making trouble from the start, your mother and father had ordered a stop on your mail and Tobias'. Calls had been redirected, correspondence intercepted. At first, it was meant to make a short time apart easier; your mother believed that if you had constant contact with the life you'd left behind, you were less likely to embrace the new possibilities in the world around you."

"I… she… *what?*" Aislinn's voice was choked with rage and Tobias felt his own temper flare in response.

"Stop, or I won't tell the rest," Grandma warned. "Eat another biscuit."

Aislinn grabbed a melting moment and crushed it in her fist. "You eat a biscuit."

"Ash." Tobias leant closer, nuzzling at her hair, and felt his heart leap when she instinctively relaxed into him. "Let her talk."

Grandma's lip twitched but when Aislinn remained silent, she sobered and continued. "I know it's aggravating, dear, and I'm afraid it gets worse. Andre was in an awkward position; with the exception of

Tobias and the other four boys, he had no youth of trainable age, and the few warriors he'd left with Rupert were already requisitioned by the High Council. Kin in general were at a disadvantage and the bears had made a clear and aggressive statement, forcing the hierarchy to demand all hands on deck. Andre wanted to repair what he saw as damage he'd been responsible for, so he bargained hard and managed to get a four year extension on the pack's conscription, citing grief and under population. He then instructed Rupert to train the five boys in secret, so that when the time came, there would be someone to defend the pack when the other warriors left."

"Why not just train some of the working adults who'd remained behind?" Tobias asked.

"The Council would have conscripted them immediately and Andre believed they'd already paid too high a price. So Tobias and the other boys became Andre and Rupert's dirty little secret and everyone else was pointedly left out of the equation. But you two," and Grandma inclined her head at both Aislinn and Tobias, "had the potential to ruin everything. If Aislinn went home, she'd have had a Council escort and the boys would've been spotted. Likewise, if Tobias came to Ireland as he once requested, he'd have been conscripted by the Council. That would've had a series of knock-on effects, including the exposure of the other boys and the revelation of Andre's treachery."

"Ultimately leaving the pack undefended," Aislinn whispered, "and Dad up on charges."

"Correct. So Andre decided, with Rupert's reluctant support, that the best way forward was to keep you both apart. The stage had already been set with Marguerite's well-meant meddling so they simply stepped it up another notch, continuing to intercept all communique and fobbing the two of you off anytime somebody asked a difficult question." Grandma paused, her lips pressed into a thin line. "For what it's worth, I disagreed and I told Andre so. He was - and is - consumed with determination to seek justice for the dead members of the pack and I believed, I *still* believe, that it's unhealthy. But he was getting results and had the full support of the Council, which only made him more zealous. He told me I could swear to keep my mouth shut about the arrangement, or he'd see to it that I never spoke to Aislinn ever again."

Aislinn hissed low in her throat. "I'm going to kill him."

"I felt the same," Grandma agreed. "I wanted to make a fuss, reveal the truth - but I knew that more than anything, you'd need someone to support you as time went by. So I swore I wouldn't initiate a discussion with you about it. Which, I might add, I haven't."

"Because we came to you." Tobias barked a sharp laugh, rubbing his chin on Aislinn's head. "Smart, Joanne."

"I have my moments," she smiled bitterly. "Suffice it to say that when the four years were up and Rupert returned to Ireland with his handful of warriors, you were rightfully incensed but your father believed he was prepared. He thought if he and Rupert explained that neither of you had any interest in ever seeing the other again, that given it had been four years, you'd all shrug and accept it and life would just go on. But he underestimated you, Aislinn - and I have never been more proud of you than the moment your mother called me in a panic because you'd disappeared without a trace. I'd warned them you were stronger and smarter than they gave you credit for, but nobody listened and it served them right."

"And when they caught me... the contract Rupert bargained for Flynn and I?"

"Was pushed to the maximum length of time to stop you coming home sooner," Grandma nodded in agreement. "Yes, that's correct. Your father doesn't approve of Flynn on a number of levels but I think he was hoping the two of you would end up mated and save him an awful lot of trouble."

"That's why he let us keep working together, even after we proved difficult," Aislinn breathed. "Son of a bitch."

"I happen to be the bitch in question, darling, so I'd be grateful if you'd choose a more imaginative insult next time," said Grandma drily.

"But why go to all this trouble just to send Aislinn home after Olaf's attack?" Tobias asked, frowning. "That makes no sense."

"Well, the answer to that is as simple as it is cold," Grandma responded. "The medics told Andre that there's no cure for Aislinn's condition save Olaf's death - and even then, they couldn't promise it would heal her scarring, only perhaps the Marking. Aislinn may never recover to her peak physical condition and with her altered scent was declared a liability on the battlefield. After she and Flynn tore up the hospital where she was staying, Andre wanted her out of Ireland as fast as possible to protect his reputation. Losing traction with the Council meant his plans for revenge would be stymied at best and ruined at worst."

Aislinn smiled without humour. "That'd explain why he made such a public show of cutting me off."

"Yes. With the way you were broken, the Council no longer had interest in sending an escort and Andre talked them into viewing your return to Australia as some sort of isolated, comfortable prison sentence. He, meanwhile, privately believed that he could send you back here, where the five boys were living in secret, and not only would you be out of his hair but you'd also have bodyguards - or prison guards, I suppose, depending on the view." She tapped her nails on the side of her cup and sighed. "He's a damned fool but I agreed because I wanted you back. You've suffered enough."

"But?"

"Well, I was bound by my oath, so I couldn't say anything unless one of you asked - and I've been waiting, believe me." Grandma chuckled, though the sound was without humour. "I knew there'd be some animosity between you two to start with, but I didn't anticipate Tobias' strong reaction to Olaf's scent nor that your return, my dear, would trigger his transition. And *nobody* thought the bears would try to follow you here, much less succeed."

Aislinn remained silent, her body trembling with violent emotion - the strongest of which, according to Tobias' nose, was unbridled fury; something he felt on the brink of himself. And so, uncaring of what Grandma Redding thought on the matter, he gathered Aislinn into his lap and wrapped both arms around her, offering support as best he could.

Contrary to his expectations, Grandma's face went immediately soft. "Damn fools, the lot of them," she whispered, "not to have seen from the start what's as plain as the nose on my face. Absolute idiots."

Tobias opened his mouth to query that cryptic comment but cut off when Aislinn, her head still buried in his chest, loosed a long, vicious growl. "I'm really going to kill him. That fucking bastard!"

One of Grandma's auburn brows rose. "No torturing first?"

"How dare he?" Aislinn demanded, her head snapping up, eyes alight with feral fire. "How *dare* he decide for me? How dare he thrust me into that world and now, when I'm no longer useful, brush me aside like a broken toy? So consumed with his pathetic quest for revenge that even his own daughter is collateral!" She swung towards Tobias. "You were right. Fuck the lot of them - this is *my* life. Our lives. I'm done being the pawn, the victim, the servant."

"Agreed." Tobias reached up to tuck a loose strand of hair behind her ear. He'd always loved her wildness, the way she took the bit between her teeth and ran. It had drawn him then as it did now, like a moth to the light. "I assume you've got a plan."

"Yeah. Olaf dies," Aislinn snarled, "and then I'm going to mail his head to my father with the word 'compromised' tattooed on his face. Time to show him where he can stick his fucking *liability*."

"We're undermanned," Tobias pointed out.

Ash grinned and it was more a baring of teeth, one that showed off all four of her pointed canines and hit Tobias straight in the gut. Fire roared through his veins and it was all he could do to tamp it down as she said; "I'll bet there are a lot of people here who'd like justice for their lost loved ones. We won't be undermanned for long."

He couldn't help it anymore, he had to kiss her. His instincts were screaming, his blood was boiling and there, on his lap, Aislinn had never looked more ferociously alive. Uncaring of the fact that Joanne Redding sat less than a meter away, Tobias crushed Ash against his chest and covered her lips with his. Her hands came up either side of his face, fingers digging into his jaw as she returned the kiss with equal passion, moulding to his chest as though she'd climb inside. Stars danced behind Tobias' eyelids as he swept his tongue into her mouth, testing the edge of those pointed teeth and finding something feral inside of him that sat up and begged for more. Energy roared through his body and he gasped into Aislinn's mouth but she was there, soothing him with her shadows even as her lips and tongue lit a very different kind of flame. Then pleasure and pain mingled and Tobias drew back with a start.

"Well, now." Aislinn, chest heaving from exertion and lips inexplicably bloody, grinned up at him. "Open wide, handsome. Show me what you've got."

Taking a long, sluggish moment to perceive her meaning, Tobias opened his mouth, running his tongue across his own four pointed canines. "What -"

"Shhhhh," Aislinn leant in and brushed her lips over his, giving him back his own blood. "It won't hurt for long. Told you they'd be back."

Tobias looked over at Grandma, wondering if he should be embarrassed now that his simmering power was cooling - and was shocked to see tears in her eyes. "Joanne?"

Aislinn turned, looking equally startled. "What's wrong?"

"Reminds me of your grandfather and I when we were younger." Grandma's smile was broad, even as a tear slipped down her cheek. "So, is this the part where I give you my stamp of approval as Den Mother to rally the pack?"

Aislinn clicked her tongue against her teeth. "I'm going to rally them anyway, but I guess it'd help."

"Consider it done." Grandma inclined her head, her face curiously intent as she looked them over and smiled again. "It's about time."

Thirteen

The sun was blisteringly hot as Aislinn stepped onto the common lawn with Tobias beside her. It was almost noon, the sky a perfect shade of cerulean, yet she couldn't shake the whispering shadows that lingered just out of hearing range. A soft breeze lifted her hair from her neck and Aislinn turned her face into the air current.

"I think it's going to storm," she murmured, searching the horizon with a furrowed brow.

"Really?" Tobias straightened to his full height, squinting into the light. "It's crystal clear out there."

Aislinn shivered. "I don't know; I just have a feeling."

"Do you have a weather sense?"

"No," Aislinn chuckled. "Not even a bung knee that aches before it rains." She shrugged and turned to smile up at him. "It's probably all that heavy talk at Grandma's table."

"Yeah. About that: are you okay?" Tobias asked, jamming his thumbs in the waistband of his shorts as they set out across the lawn. "It was a lot to take in."

"I'm angry," Aislinn replied, her hands clenching so tightly to fists that her nails cut into her palms. "But Dad and I have been on rocky ground for a lot of years now so the temper's nothing new. It's just... to manipulate our lives for over a decade? That's insane."

"He did it for the good of the pack," Tobias offered, but it was clear from the tone of his voice he didn't agree.

"Trying to see both sides is admirable but in this case, pointless. You and I both know the pack is no stronger than its weakest member - and by setting things up this way, he's disadvantaged everyone." Aislinn drew to a halt, her eyes on the immaculately painted weatherboards of the Smythe cottage. "How do I know Sens is in there?"

"Just a guess. After yesterday's attack, I don't think Gerup will be opening for business," Tobias replied, "and Sienna rarely leaves the house before midday on her days off. She's a professional sleeper."

Aislinn snorted. "That was us too, once upon a time."

"At least we had the sense to sneak away and hide where nobody could disturb us." Tobias brushed a knuckle over her cheek. "Are you sure you're up to this?"

"Yeah. I'll meet you at the den afterwards."

"Okay." He looked as though he'd say more, then flashed her a brilliant smile and walked away. Aislinn watched until Tobias was out of sight, then drew a deep breath and sauntered the rest of the way to the house.

Several knocks on the door went unanswered, so she moved around the back of the cottage, skipping over delicate flower beds until she reached a window with the curtains still drawn. Inching closer to the wall, Aislinn set her ear against the glass and closed her eyes, blocking out her other senses. The moment she focussed on the interior of the house and identified the sounds inside, she called her shadows and dissolved, streaming through the narrow gap between window and sill.

Sienna was curled on her bed, still wearing the same red dress from the night before, albeit rumpled. A tissue box balanced on her knees and a veritable sea of used tissues littered the quilt and floor. Her makeup was streaked and smudged, her hair a mess and a half eaten block of chocolate lay on the bedside table.

Aislinn dropped her shadows at the end of the bed. "Sens?"

Sienna squeaked in surprise, jamming a fist into her mouth and flipping the box of tissues across the room as she scrambled suddenly backwards. "Ash? Mother Moon, how long have you been standing there?"

"I'm sorry," Aislinn waded through the tissues and retrieved the abandoned box. "I didn't mean to frighten you. I just wanted to talk, and I heard you crying."

"Oh," Sienna blinked and swallowed. "Hayfever, you know how it is."

"Sienna Ellyse Smythe, don't you dare lie to me." Aislinn sank to her knees beside the bed, offering the tissue box like a tribute. "I'm so, so sorry. I never meant… I didn't know."

Sapphire eyes closed and Sienna drew a deep, shuddering breath. "I'm not angry. You had no idea how he felt, but I did. It's just that -" she choked off and shook her head.

"The restaurant," Aislinn murmured. "I thought the same thing."

"I was so worried you'd be angry at me," Sienna whispered.

Aislinn's jaw dropped open. "Me? Angry at *you*?"

"Sure. I mean, Tobias never said anything but it's pretty common knowledge - at least among those of us that know him well - that he was carrying a torch for you before you went to Ireland. Hells below, he's been carrying a torch for you since he was old enough to carry anything at all."

"That part is still a revelation for me," Aislinn admitted. "Actually, the entire thing is a revelation. I always thought we were just friends, you know? Two only children who formed a strong bond because we didn't have siblings."

"Siblings don't do the stuff you guys did, Ash." In spite of her tears, Sienna giggled. "Sweet lord of the sun, poor Tobias. He was trying so hard and you just never noticed!"

Aislinn blushed at that, scrubbing at the back of her head. "I swear I didn't realise there was more to it until I saw the two of you in the kitchen. I'm sorry if I hurt you, Sens."

"I'm hurting," Sienna allowed, "but it's not because of you. I was the one stupid enough to fall in love with a man who was never mine to begin with. It's just… Tobias is so sweet and generous and strong and handsome and… well, if I'm honest, he's the only one who never treated me like I was Zeke's annoying little sister." She offered a trembling smile. "I never had a chance, but I couldn't help it."

"I still feel guilty." Aislinn shook her head. "I don't know if I'm ready for this, either. What if I don't live up to his expectations? What if I've changed too much? What if I can't - you know - go through with it?"

Sienna cleared her throat and stretched out her legs, kicking a mountain of tissues aside to reveal a small cooler unit at the end of her bed. "Flip the lid; choose a flavour. We'll share."

Aislinn leant over and did as she was told, gasping in delight as she discovered the little freezer was stocked with tubs of boutique ice cream. "You keep ice cream in your bedroom?"

"No judging," Sienna ordered. "Just choosing."

"As if there's a choice," Aislinn dug out a tub of triple chocolate fudge and handed it over. "Chocolate or bust, baby."

"My favourite, too." Sienna smiled, reaching into her top drawer and pulling out two spoons. She flipped the lid on the tub with a one-handed motion Aislinn could only envy, then set it on the bed between them and scooped out a big spoonful. As she chewed, her eyes ran critically over Aislinn's body, taking in scars, outfit, the lot. "I guess if you really didn't know how Tobias felt, it would be pretty scary. What happened after he chased you?"

Feeling uncertain of her footing and not wanting to hurt Sienna any further, Aislinn nevertheless accepted her spoon, then recounted the events of the night and morning right up until the moment she and Tobias had separated out front of the house.

"I can't believe Andre and Rupert did that," Sienna whispered, eyes wide with astonishment. "And you're really going to get the whole pack together and tell them? Like, everyone?"

"Yes and no." Aislinn frowned, savouring the way the ice cream melted in her mouth, leaving fudge sauce behind. "I need to talk it over with Tobias but I'm not here to badmouth the choices their Alpha has made - I'm more interested in addressing the current emergency."

"The bears." Sienna swallowed heavily. "You really think they're coming here?"

"They were in Gerup, Sens. And at Macy's place, and in Kilpenny. They've been spotted in other places, too - they're already here. Just because they haven't attacked pack land doesn't make it less of a threat." Aislinn sighed. "It's only a matter of time."

Sienna fell quiet and for a few moments, there was only the sound of their spoons digging into the tub of ice cream. "Bears aside, I can already say you made the right choice with Tobias."

"What? Why?"

"You're a different woman than the one who first arrived here," Sienna said, shrugging. "Different, even, than the one curled up on the couch last night. It's like a weight has been lifted off your shoulders."

"And you think… it was Tobias?"

"I think it was you," Sienna contradicted, "taking a step down the road to recovery. Which, I might add, appears to be paved by Tobias Greenwood."

Aislinn laughed at that. "Letting him wash me was one of the most terrifying things I've ever done."

"I don't know if I could trust someone like that." Sienna shivered, hugging both arms around her pencil thin waist. "It's like… I don't know. I'm not even a warrior, so I guess it must be worse for you, but… I'd feel so vulnerable."

"I guess that's the point of the ritual," Aislinn agreed. "And you're right - after Tobias and I spoke, after we reconnected, I do feel lighter. I was worried about you, though. I feel like I betrayed your trust, encouraging you to go after Tobias and then getting upset when you made a move."

"No, Ash, no." Sienna dropped her spoon to clutch at Aislinn's hands. "Don't say that. You just didn't realise what was in front of you until it was at risk. Or appeared to be, anyway, because Tobias literally had no idea what was going on."

Aislinn raised an eyebrow. "At all?"

"Nope," she shook her head, mouth curving in a silly grin. "Not until you got upset, at any rate."

"He had no shirt on!"

"He turned the tap on too hard and covered himself in water while trying to rinse his glass," Sienna chuckled. "And I stole the popcorn bowl while he was undressing because I was tipsy and it seemed funny at the time. It really was completely innocent; from Tobias' point of view, anyway."

"I'm sorry," Aislinn muttered, digging at the bottom of the tub.

"Stop saying that!" Sienna snapped, slapping lightly at Aislinn's shoulder. "I told you, it's not your fault. Or mine, or Tobias'. It's just one of those things that was never meant to be - not for me, anyway."

"You'll meet someone someday," Aislinn said, hating the words even as they tumbled out of her mouth. "Shit, that sounded so trite. Please slap me again."

Sienna giggled, sapphire eyes sparkling through her smudged make-up. "No, I get it. Maybe you can introduce me to that sexy Flynn of yours?"

"*Flynn?*"

"You said he was cute, right?"

"Sienna, he's sex on legs, but he would eat you alive," Aislinn said, waving her spoon in alarm. "He's not a bad boy - he's a Very Bad Boy.

Capital letters, teeth and claws bad boy. Unless you can kick his ass from here until next week, I wouldn't even consider it."

"Will you teach me?"

"Teach you what?"

"To fight," Sienna clarified. "To really fight. Not to attract a man," she added, seeing the look on Aislinn's face. "But because I feel like… after what you said about the bears, maybe I should know. Maybe we should all know."

"It's not an easy thing," Aislinn warned, biting her lip. "It's nasty and dirty and it hurts."

Sienna merely nodded. "I figured as much after watching you throw Tobias on the floor yesterday."

"That," Aislinn said, "was not even a taste. But yeah, if you want to learn, I can teach you."

"I don't want to be a warrior or anything, I just want to know that if something happens, maybe I could help. If not myself, then someone else." Sienna reached out and brushed a scar on Aislinn's exposed shoulder. "Nobody deserves to be treated the way you were."

"I agree. And there are at least thirty-seven other women who didn't survive," Aislinn murmured. "When this is all over I think I'd like to set up some sort of outreach program for abuse victims and their families."

"I can help with that," Sienna nodded enthusiastically. "I have a degree in fashion design - which is irrelevant - but also a minor in business and I already handle all Ysera's books. I'd love to set that up with you, if you'll have me."

"Sens, that'd be fantastic." Aislinn grinned, feeling her heart lighten just that little more. "Friends, then?"

"Of course!" Sienna cried, throwing herself into Aislinn's arms and squeezing tightly. "Oh shit, sorry, did I -"

"It's fine," Aislinn reassured her, surprised to find that it actually was. "Wow. I might get a handle on this after all."

****

When Tobias arrived at the waterhole, Zeke was already there. His second swam swiftly across the deep pool and hoisted himself onto dry land, shaking the water off as though he wore his wolf form.

"How was last night?" Zeke asked, brushing curly golden hair out of his face. "You don't look like you've had too much wine and popcorn."

Tobias blinked. His world had been irrevocably altered the night before but, naturally, nobody else knew. He filled Zeke in as best he could, keeping his voice low in case anyone else happened to wander past. The more he spoke, the further his second's jaw dropped open. "Ash just went to see Sienna and then she'll meet us in the den," he finished, then shook his head. "I still can't believe that all happened in the space of one night."

"But… *Sienna*?" Zeke screwed up his face. "How did none of us notice?"

"I don't know," Tobias shrugged. "I guess I always thought it was, you know, sibling love."

"Dude, all you see is Ash so I wouldn't expect you to notice if a parade of women wearing 'we want to fuck Tobias' signs marched past you - but the rest of us should've seen it." Zeke frowned. "I wonder if I should check on her."

"Ash is handling it," Tobias managed, wondering if he should be miffed or pleased by Zeke's comment about parading women. "She seems to have a knack."

Zeke waved a dismissive hand. "She's a Den Mother - a strong one. Ash could charm a petrified turd."

"You're in a mood today."

"Yeah. Come see." Zeke jogged off towards the den and Tobias, still shaking his head, followed after.

Dominic was already inside the cave, setting up the trestle table they'd used for breakfast. Several ice boxes sat on the floor beside him and he waved cheerfully at Tobias before beginning to unpack cold roast meat, bread rolls and other sandwich fillings. As Tobias followed Zeke across the den to the far wall, he couldn't help but grind his teeth. Only two days ago, Dominic had asked Aislinn on a date and been turned down. How was he going to react now that she was covered in Tobias' scent? Even if neither of them said a word, a couple of sniffs and some quick maths and everyone would know that *something* was going on.

"Hey," Zeke waved an impatient hand in front of Tobias' face. "Earth to Alpha. Did you hear a thing I just said?"

"Sorry," Tobias rubbed at his face. "I was thinking."

Zeke narrowed his eyes for a moment and then turned to the wall, where someone had nailed a map of Victoria. "I *said,* all those pins are reported bear attacks over the last couple of days. Look at it and tell me what you see."

Tobias obliged, staring at the map and at last raising his finger to run a line down the rough semicircle the pins created. "They're trawling."

"That's what I thought. Probably lots of small groups, like you saw in Gerup, spread out in a net and slowly working their way across." Zeke pointed again. "Red pins are where they met no opposition. Black pins are where at least one bear was either injured or killed."

"You think they're most likely to hone in on those areas," Tobias murmured, then nodded. "Of course. If Olaf's looking for Ash, he's going to assume she's well guarded. Meaning the areas where Kin resist are more likely to have a connection."

"Yup. Three separate places including Gerup, but... Ash said one of the bears got away. Reckon he knew who she was?"

"I don't remember anything about the attack," Tobias muttered, clenching his hands into fists. "I was well and truly swamped by transitional rage."

Zeke sighed. "Maybe Ash can tell us."

"Tell you what? That you're dripping water all over the floor?" Aislinn's voice preceded her into the cave, her face twisted into a lopsided grin. "Haven't you people ever heard of towels?"

"You like a wet man, don't lie," Zeke leered, shaking his head and spraying water in her direction. "It's one of the few things I know about women. Slick up and they get all woogly."

"Really?" Aislinn stalked closer, giving Zeke a critical once over. "Do I look woogly to you?"

"Pfft, wrong guy. Here, try this," Zeke said - and snatched a jug of water from the nearby sideboard, upending it over Tobias' head.

Water cascaded over Tobias' body and red fog clouded his vision. He was vaguely aware of Zeke laughing uproariously but it came from a distance, as though he stood at the other end of a long, echoing tunnel. He growled, long and low, and *that* felt right, felt good. Heat flooded his veins and he flexed a suddenly itchy body, half expecting his skin to split open and reveal something else, someone new.

Cool shadows washed over him and Tobias blinked rapidly down into Aislinn's face, one of her hands splayed across the centre of his chest and the other cupping his cheek. "Easy, tiger," she murmured, her blue-green eyes steady. "Breathe."

"Can't," he managed, still fighting that strange, itching feeling.

"You can. Come on, don't make me knock you out. Breathe and let it go, Tobias."

Let what go? He shook himself, almost dislodging her hand, disoriented by the curious mix of hot and cold blending over his flesh. As he wriggled, Tobias caught sight of his arms and froze. Fur covered his skin and his hands were claws. Part of his chest and a section of his ribs, too - in fact, anywhere he itched. Zeke and Dominic were on the other side of the room, very pointedly standing still, eyes wide. Tobias frowned and made a concerted effort to concentrate on Aislinn's shadows, embracing the cool energy and closing his eyes as it washed the itch away. When he felt better he opened his eyes again and looked down at Aislinn. "Midform?"

She nodded. "Partly."

"Gone?"

"Of course." She looked over her shoulder at the other two males. "We're all good."

"Dammit, man," Zeke shook his head. "New skills at every turn."

"I'm still the same me." Tobias reached up and ran a hand through his sodden hair. "Just wish I had a better handle on my shit."

"And a towel," Zeke sniggered. "Still no woogly, Ash?"

"You and your woogly - that's not even a real word." Aislinn rolled her eyes. "You want to see weak knees? Watch this." She stepped closer to Tobias and bent over, licking a long trail up the side of his torso and over one pectoral. She paused by his nipple and blew out softly, a cool breath of air that, had he not already been covered in a wave of goosebumps, would have certainly caused more. "You're right, Zeke," she purred - and her voice did indeed cause Tobias' knees to wobble. "I do like my man wet."

Tobias' hands shot out but she was gone, nothing but smoke and shadows. He leant against the wall of the den for support, trying to still his racing heart as Aislinn appeared next to Zeke and elbowed him in the ribs.

"Solaeden save us, babe." Zeke's eyes were wide, his face caught somewhere between astonishment and amusement. "I don't know what you just did but I surrender - you win."

"*You*," Tobias growled, finding his voice at last. He levelled a shaking finger at Aislinn's laughing face. "Are trying to kill me. You realise you're only going to make things worse for yourself when I catch you?"

"Words, words." Aislinn waved a dismissive hand and winked at Zeke. "Now, what were we asking me about?"

Zeke pointed over Tobias' shoulder. "The map."

Aislinn narrowed her eyes, leaning one hip against the trestle table. "It looks like a net."

"Zeke was wondering if the bear who saw you in Gerup could've recognised you." Tobias pushed upright and dusted himself off, moving to join them. "If so, it'd give them a pretty big clue."

"Hmmm." Aislinn frowned at that, tapping one bare foot on the floor as she thought it over. "I don't think so - I was in my midform by then and Olaf never saw that. They're more likely to have a description or picture of my human form, if anything."

"But you were definitely wolfkin," Dominic pointed out, his eyes skating between Aislinn and Tobias. "Wouldn't that narrow the search?"

"Forget that - they have my name. The entrance to Redding Pack land may be concealed but our approximate location is known well enough and the connection is obvious. So… Why isn't Olaf centreing all his efforts here? Why not just sweep in and finish us off?" Aislinn frowned. "Unless he's trying to flush me out."

Dominic screwed up his face in confusion. "You mean he *wants* you to run?"

"Maybe. I mean, if there's an attack on the pack, it's a giant shit-show. War, righteous anger, yada yada yada. If I disappear without a trace, however, the fear surrounding the bears only grows, giving them power without having to risk their numbers more than necessary." Aislinn stalked over to the map, opening her hands above the pins and pushing in a north-easterly motion. "This isn't a net - it's a set of spot fires designed to drive me in a particular direction."

"I thought he just wanted you dead," said Dominic, crossing his arms over his chest. "That's not the movements of someone who wants someone dead."

"Oh, he wants me dead," Aislinn murmured, "but it looks like there's more to it than that. I just don't know what."

Bracken snapped by the door, preceding both Jaxon and Rory into the den. The former curled his lip and snarled; "I thought you were leaving."

"I was." Aislinn turned to face him and pursed her lips. "But things have changed and as a result, I've decided to stay."

"Things have changed," Jaxon mocked, stalking closer. "What makes you think I won't run you off, like I promised?"

"You can try," Aislinn replied, tilting her head at him. "Before you do, though, I want you all to listen very closely - *then* decide if you want to shed blood or not."

"I'm not interested." Jaxon stomped closer and drew up suddenly short as Rory appeared in front of him, one arm across Jaxon's beefy chest.

"I want to listen," Rory said simply. He glanced back at Aislinn and nodded. "Talk."

Someone was growling; Tobias realised with a start it was him. Aislinn took a deep breath and smoothed her hand down his arm, her shadows washing over him and cooling the Alpha energy which seemed intent on surfacing. "In case you haven't noticed, Tobias is transitioning. The Kin High Council have assigned me to officially be his damper. It was one of the jobs I did for them in Ireland and even though I requested a replacement, there's nobody else strong enough to manage it."

"Oh come on, we can manage him," Jaxon growled. "He freaks out, we hit him on the head. Simple."

"Tobias is not only possessed of a midform which he cannot control, but Lunaida knows what other powers as well," Aislinn returned equably. "You would all, to the last one of you, be dead in minutes. Transitional energy is wild at best and disastrous at worst and continues to increase in intensity until either the Kin in question gets a handle on it, they turn thirty, or they die. A damper - in this case, me - can help Tobias maintain control until he learns to find his own balance and accept the energy. If we don't, he won't live to thirty; he'll kill everyone here and then be shot like a rabid dog by the High Council."

"So if you leave, you'd be sentencing Tobias to a very grisly end," Dominic murmured.

"Not to mention the rest of the pack, at the very least."

"Do it remotely, then," Jaxon jerked his chin off in the distance. "From wherever the fuck you end up."

"I can't." Aislinn shook her head. "I told you before, I need to be in physical contact with Tobias - or whoever it is I'm damping - for the power to work."

"I don't believe you," Jaxon hissed.

Tobias growled low in his throat. "It's true, Jax."

"Was that your opinion before or after she sucked your cock?" Jaxon snapped. "I can smell you all over each other."

Tobias clenched his fists, striving for calm - and was astonished when a slap rang out in the den, followed by the sound of something heavy hitting the floor. Jaxon groaned as he rolled across the den's tattered rug, body curled into a foetal position and eyes squeezed shut. Aislinn seemed to have disappeared, then the shadows over Jaxon thickened and she materialised beside him, crouching down to dig her fingers into close-cropped black hair and wrench his head back to look at her.

"You're all wolves - you can shift and suck your own cocks," she growled, her voice hitting a register that carried the merciless chill of death. "Tobias certainly doesn't need me to do *that* for him. Here's the deal, Jax: I stay, and we get our shit together and try to formulate a defence against the bears. Because they're coming and they're going to do it whether I'm here or not. The best chance we all have of surviving is by working together, not shouting at each other. Option two; I go and Tobias goes with me. And Zeke, and whoever else decides to follow. Then who's left to protect your family, Jaxon Heliope-Flint? Who keeps your siblings alive and prevents your mother being raped and mutilated like the thirty-seven other women who went before me? You? *Alone*? Don't make me laugh." Aislinn dropped Jaxon's head and it thumped heavily against the rug. "Your choice, asshole, but whatever it is, remember that for better or worse, this is your pack. Fussing and fighting is fine but if you ever speak to Tobias - or anyone else - like that again, I will rip off your balls and turn them into ear muffs."

Aislinn stood to walk away but Jaxon gathered himself and leapt, tackling her onto the floor. Fists flew and people swore but Aislinn was already gone, Jaxon's punch slamming into the stone floor of the den. He howled with agony, the sound cutting short as she materialised behind him, picking the stocky wolfkin up by the back of the neck and flinging him against the far wall. Her blue-green eyes glittered with predatory intent and Tobias leapt between them, restraining Jaxon with one arm while holding up the other until Aislinn paused. "Enough," he snarled, turning back towards Jaxon, "or I'll finish you myself."

"Fuck you," the other male grunted. "You're not my Alpha."

"I am while Andre's away," Tobias growled, baring his teeth to show newly pointed canines. "And you'll do what you're told."

Jaxon shoved at the arm pinning his chest and blinked as nothing happened. Green eyes narrowed and he snarled, "I hereby renounce my oath to the Redding Pack and take up the mantle of lone wolf. My pack is no longer my home, my heart wanders where it wills. I am freed of the burden of my people and they are freed from me, from this moment forward, for the rest of my days."

Silence reigned in the den, save for Jaxon's ragged breathing. The ritual words fell like hammers on Tobias' ears and after a long moment, he dropped his arm and took a step back. "Get out."

"Jax," Dominic's voice was filled with shock. "You can't-"

"I can and I have," Jaxon growled. "Fuck the lot of you, each and every one." He narrowed his eyes on Aislinn. "Fuck you most of all, you useless bitch."

Her answering grin was filled with righteous fury. "You can't do me any worse than Olaf already did, you pathetic excuse for a swamp dog."

"I can't," Jaxon agreed, then pointed to Tobias. "But he can. I hope you all get what you deserve."

The last thing Tobias remembered before the red fog of rage overcame him was the black fur of Jaxon's wolf coat as he shifted and bolted out the door.

****

Mother Moon but Tobias was *fast*. Aislinn followed the scent of butterscotch and cream through the bush, lungs straining and paws reaching, trying to catch the Alpha ahead. Her only consolation was that the three males behind her, also in wolf form, were having just as hard a time of it.

Damn Jaxon. She'd warned them not to piss Tobias off and the fool had done it deliberately. Aislinn ducked her head and shot beneath a low hanging tea tree, barely gathering herself to leap a fallen log on the other side. A small, dark part of her contemplated letting Tobias rend his former packmate limb from limb but she dismissed the notion as soon as it surfaced. Neither Tobias nor Sarah Heliope-Flint deserved to live with the outcome of that scenario, regardless of how far out of line Jaxon had stepped.

Aislinn dodged a tumble of boulders, growling in frustration at the delay. If only she knew where Tobias was going - or more particularly, where Jaxon was leading him - wait. She leapt up a slight incline, nose raised to scent the wind. He was heading for the burnt shack.

With a yowl at Zeke to keep going, Aislinn flowed into her midform and leapt straight upwards, powerful legs carrying her high into the branches of the nearest gum tree. Making a point not to look down, she leapt into the cradling arms of the next tree, and then the next, flying through the canopy at breakneck speed. On the ground she was limited by the lay of the land and the thick, overgrown bush but up here, provided she didn't misjudge and plummet, she could move in a straight line.

Branches groaned beneath her weight and the thinner trunks swayed unsteadily, causing her heart to leap into her throat - but up ahead, Aislinn could see the faintest outline of fire-blackened corrugated iron. She pushed harder, scrabbling uncertainly for purchase when several branches proved to be almost beyond reach. She was rapidly running out of trees but also caught a glimpse of brown fur flashing through the undergrowth below, hard on the tail of a heavier-set black wolf. No time to think. No time to plan. If Tobias caught Jaxon, he would surely kill him.

Aislinn threw herself out into the air, streamlining her body like an arrow as she plummeted towards the ground. She was ahead now, but there was nowhere to land, only the jagged ground and partially cleared bush at the edge of the shack. Holding her breath lest she let out an undignified scream, Aislinn called the shadows and prayed to Lunaida for luck. Foliage slapped her fur and then, with the ground only inches from her nose, the darkness claimed her and she dissolved, streaming across a carpet of fallen leaves and dry bracken.

Jaxon shot past, his paws a thundering drum and moments later, Tobias. Aislinn materialised beneath him, wrapping the arms of her midform around his chest and tucking her larger body around his wolf form as they bounced and rolled and crashed into the undergrowth. He fought, teeth tearing and claws slicing but Aislinn concentrated solely on stamping out the transitional episode. They slammed into the base of a fallen tree and she howled in pain, barely managing to keep her grip on the golden-brown wolf clutched tightly against her chest.

A howl answered hers, then another and a third; the others were coming. She pushed harder with her shadows, grappling the enraged transitional energy until Tobias began to turn sluggish in her arms. His wild attacks slowly lessened until he abruptly sneezed, shook his lupine head and stared quizzically up at her from those blue and gold eyes. Aislinn relaxed her hold, dropping the wolf into her lap and leaning back against the tree trunk, her breath bubbling in her chest. She didn't need to look to know a wayward piece of trunk had jammed into her side, pushing up beneath her ribs to puncture a lung. It would heal, provided she could get the offending stake out before she bled to death.

Zeke erupted out of the bush, his golden-furred body skidding to a halt in front of them, teeth bared for a fight - until he saw Tobias lying dazed in Aislinn's lap. Dominic appeared beside him and the two of them went to their Alpha, nudging him with their noses and receiving muffled grunts in response.

"Ash? Can you hear me?" It was Rory, his wolf form melting away as he knelt by her side. "We need to get this out."

Aislinn blew out through her nose; she *knew* that. But knowing you had to remove the thing impaling you and having the courage to actually do it were two different things, and Rory had ruined her decision to wait a little longer by emerging from the bush at such an angle that he'd seen her wound before anyone else.

"Get what out?" Tobias' voice, wobbly but otherwise fine. "Oh, shit. Dammit, Ash!"

What? It wasn't her bloody fault; Jaxon was the one who'd lost his mind and precipitated the whole incident. She bared her teeth at Tobias and growled.

"Holy fuck, that thing is huge. No, Ash, don't move yet," Zeke warned, steadying her with one hand on her shoulder. "Let Rory get a better grip on it."

Tobias straddled her legs, taking her furry face in his hands. "Look at me, Ash. Just look at me, okay?"

She obliged, rolling her eyes in the process. He might not know it, but she'd had plenty of things stuck in her before that had needed pulling out. Tobias' face was creased in concern, his brown and gold hair messier than usual and Aislinn snorted a laugh to see bits of twig and leaves poking out of the chaos; remnants of their breakneck tumble through the undergrowth.

"Ready, Ash?" Rory's voice was quiet by her ear and she nodded. A moment later agony tore through her side and she howled again, digging her claws into the dirt - dirt which rapidly became slick with her blood. Tobias held her steady, leaning forward until his forehead pressed against her own, murmuring softly against her snout. Rory grunted and threw a bloodied shard of wood on the ground. "Done."

Aislinn shimmered back into her human form, sagging sideways into Zeke's steadying arm. "Thanks, Rory."

"You're welcome." Brown eyes travelled over the rest of her wounds, now revealed by the lack of fur. "Damn Tobias, you did a real number on her."

"It's fine," Aislinn sighed as Tobias gathered her into his arms, her body heavy with fatigue. "Not on purpose."

"I'm sorry, Ash," He rumbled, getting to his feet. "Whatever it was I did, I -"

"It's fine," she insisted, smoothing a hand across his chest. "It'll heal."

"She doesn't sound good," Zeke murmured, his voice somewhere behind her head. "Maybe we should take her back to Grandma's."

"No," Tobias and Aislinn, simultaneously. Tobias cleared his throat. "She stays with me. Rory, fetch Grandma and Jemima and have them meet us at my place. Dom, Zeke, with us."

"What about Jaxon?"

"Let him go." Tobias sighed, his chest moving against Aislinn's cheek. "He swore out. There's nothing we can do unless he changes his mind."

"All right," Zeke's voice was reluctant. "But he's a sitting duck if he goes too far."

"He almost got himself and Ash killed," Tobias growled, his temper evident in his voice. Aislinn burrowed closer, vaguely aware they were moving through the bush once again. Tobias' lips pressed briefly against her temple. "I'll worry about Jax once she's stable."

"Sleepy," Aislinn declared, her voice sounding muzzy even to her own ears. "Going to rest."

"That's okay," Tobias answered, his arms tightening. "I've got you."

Aislinn mustered the last of her strength and forced her eyes open, searching for his. "No doctors. No hospital."

"We're too far from a hospital anyway - but Jemima's okay, right? You know Jemima," Tobias soothed.

Her heart thumped in her throat and Aislinn fought back a wave of dizziness, clutching desperately at his arm as wave after wave of cold, clinical memories swamped her. "Don't leave me."

Tobias lowered his head again, his response so soft that Aislinn, sliding helplessly into unconsciousness, wasn't sure if she actually heard it. "Never."

Fourteen

Tobias hovered in the doorway of his room, watching as Jemima Smythe carefully checked, cleaned and dressed Aislinn's wounds. He'd promised not to leave her and he wouldn't - but he also knew, logically, that standing over the bed would only hinder Jemima's ability to do her job as pack medic.

"What do we do now?" Zeke muttered, pressing a cold glass of home-made lemonade into Tobias' hand.

"Wait," Tobias rumbled softly, "and plan."

Zeke sighed. "What I saw back in the den… she risked her life for you."

"No." Tobias took a long sip of his lemonade and then looked up at his second. "She risked her life for Jaxon."

Zeke fell silent at that and they watched while Jemima finished with her bandages. Zeke's mother was a petite woman, with Sienna's willowy frame and a head of curly black hair that had been tamed into a tight bun atop her head. Though both of her children had inherited their father's light colouring, Tobias could see Zeke in the sharp bones of her face and the quiet, purposeful way she moved.

"A few hours and she'll be awake - less if I know Aislinn," Jemima said at last. "She lost a lot of blood so she should be resting for a few days but the current climate may make that an impossibility."

"Any suggestions, then?" Tobias unhitched himself from the wall and strode further into the room, staring down at Aislinn's too-pale face. "We need her."

"I have a tonic," Jemima said reluctantly, pulling a bottle out of her apron pocket. "It will speed up her immune system and provide all the nutrients her body needs to recover the blood quickly."

"But?"

Jemima dipped her chin, rolling the bottle in her hands. "It's not kind. Side effects range from dizziness through mania."

"Mania?" Zeke frowned. "Real speak, Ma."

"Mother," Jemima corrected absently. "And mania as in hyperactivity, my son, only far worse."

Tobias looked from the bottle down at Aislinn. "I think we can handle it."

"There isn't much choice, but… don't say I didn't warn you." Jemima unscrewed the cap and decanted the thick, dark liquid into a dosage cup. When the cup was full, she set the bottle aside, jerked Aislinn's mouth open and tipped the contents inside. Aislinn immediately choked and then a moment later, her body swallowed on reflex and she settled back into sleep. "If she gets symptoms - and with a dose like that, she will - they'll last about twenty four hours until her metabolism catches up and absorbs the tonic."

"What do I tell her when she wakes?" Tobias asked.

Jemima filled her cheeks with air for a long moment, then said; "Tell her it's battle blood. She'll know what that means."

"Thanks, Jem." Tobias bent to press a kiss to the cheek of the woman who, for better or worse, had stepped into the role of his foster mother for the last eight years without complaint.

Jemima Smythe patted his cheek softly and then turned her dark sapphire eyes on Zeke. "Anything else before I go?"

"How quickly will that magic juice work?" Zeke asked, jerking his chin at the bed. "We need to gather the pack."

"It's hard to estimate, but someone like Aislinn?" Jemima pursed her lips. "If she's not up in an hour, I'd be surprised."

Tobias looked out the window, then at the bedside clock, then at Zeke. "Five o'clock. On the common lawn. Everyone."

"Everyone?" Jemima startled, eyes going wide. "I have appointments -"

"Change them," said Tobias quietly, softening his interruption by taking Jemima's hand and squeezing gently. "It's not a request."

The older woman ducked her head. "Yes, Alpha. I'll pass the word along to those I see."

"Thank you." Tobias watched her leave and then looked up as Grandma Redding strode in. "I hate having to do that."

"Unfortunately it's part of the job," Grandma grunted, her eyes on her grand-daughter. "Do I want to know what happened here?"

They waited until the front door slammed downstairs, evidence of both Jemima's temper and her absence, then Zeke straightened. "Jaxon swore out."

"Solaeden save us." Grandma passed a hand over her face. "Where did he go?"

"We don't know," Tobias growled, crossing to the bed and dropping down beside Aislinn. "He provoked a transitional episode and then ran in the confusion. Ash was injured in the process of calming me down and I decided to bring her here first."

"You did the right thing." Grandma chewed on the inside of her cheek for a moment. "Damned fool of a man."

"He's frightened for his family," Zeke replied. "I don't think he'll go far."

"Agreed." Grandma nodded. "For now, I say we wait. Jaxon's likely to turn up tonight after cooling down but if not, we'll search for him tomorrow."

"What about the bears?" Tobias jerked his chin out the window, where the bush basked in the afternoon sunlight. "If they catch him…"

Grandma Redding followed his gaze and sighed. "We don't know where they are and Jaxon is one wolf alone. As long as he keeps his head down, he's unlikely to run into trouble. A night stewing in his own juices might be just what he needs to come to his senses."

"I've told Zeke to assemble the pack for five o'clock," Tobias said, his aching heart reluctant to discuss Jaxon further. "Ash should be awake by then."

"Good idea." Grandma pursed her lips in thought. "All right, I'm going to finish the last couple of things on my to do list, and I'll meet you later. I'll arrange some food to be sent for Aislinn, too. She'll be hungry when she wakes."

"Thanks, Joanne. I'll call if anything happens," Tobias promised. Grandma Redding nodded once and saw herself out, her sturdy work boots thumping all the way down the stairs and out the front door.

"Man, I need a drink. Today's been balls to the wall." Zeke tipped his head back, staring at the cracks in the ceiling. "You should have seen you, dude."

"So you keep saying," Tobias muttered. "I don't remember a damned thing."

Zeke rolled his head to the side, eyes focussed over Tobias' shoulder where Aislinn slept. "She was incredible. Leapt through the tree tops like some crazy-ass wolf-monkey and then poof - out into mid-air. I thought I was going to die just watching."

"We need her," Tobias whispered, unable to stop his hand inching across the quilt to brush against Aislinn's leg. "For better or worse."

"I agreed with you before, but after today? Ash would blow all five of us out of the water - damned right we need her." Zeke let out a low whistle. "On a side note, you better buckle up, cupcake, because you're in for one hell of a ride."

Tobias snorted. "Your counsel is, as always, incredibly insightful. Don't you have something better to be doing?"

"Yeah, I'll start putting together the whole pack pow-wow." Zeke grunted. "Five o'clock on the common lawn, like you said."

"Thanks. I promised to stay with Ash but I can call anyone who's not already hanging around," Tobias offered.

"That'd be good." Zeke nodded, then quirked his lip in a grin. "At least one of us gets to hang out with a sleeping princess."

"What about that Kin who gave you the chocolate cake?" Tobias asked. "I'm sure she'd be willing to let down your hair."

Zeke's grin widened and became predatory, the sort of expression he made sure his mother never saw. "It had her number on the bottom of the container."

"Call it."

"I dunno," His second chuckled. "Pretty sure she was a kangaroo… I might accidentally eat her."

"That wound up?" Tobias quirked an eyebrow. "She might enjoy it, fur-brother."

Zeke's chuckle grew into a laugh which he hastily stifled behind one hand. "I think we've got enough on our plate for now; maybe once this is over. All right, I'm out - peace."

Tobias returned the lazy salute with one of his own, staring at the door long after his second pulled it shut. Not that bad things ever happened at a good time, he reflected, but Jaxon's sudden departure couldn't have been worse than now, when unity was going to be critical. According to Kin law, once sworn out Jax was no longer the pack's responsibility - but a few fierce words couldn't turn off a lifetime's friendship and Tobias knew beyond doubt he wouldn't be the only one eager to search come the morning.

As long as Ash recovered first, of course; because promise or no, with his transitional energies so chaotic, the safest place for him to be was by her side. Tobias sighed, digging his phone out of his pocket and scrolling through the contacts. Some pack members were easy to find - those who worked out in the fields, with the livestock or down in the sheds. Others, those who worked abroad or had no set schedule, would be more difficult to track down. Tobias began at the top of his list and called as many Kin as he could, then shot Zeke a text with the list of those he'd missed.

"Planning a party?" Ash's voice was sleepy, her eyes half-lidded.

"Packwide meet," Tobias answered, crawling up beside her and dropping his phone on the bedside table. His body curled around hers and he slid one arm under her pillow, wriggling in close. "How are you feeling?"

"Like I got stabbed," she answered, bumping her head against his. "Why do I taste ginger?"

"Jemima gave you some battle blood," Tobias said, feeling ridiculous using such a dramatic term. "She said you'd know what that meant."

"Shit." Aislinn sagged against him, staring sightlessly upwards. "I hate that stuff."

"I'll be honest, I've never heard of it."

"You wouldn't have." Aislinn rubbed sleep out of her eyes and turned to face him. "Battle blood is the slang term. It's a herbal concoction that's part medicinal, part hang-on-to-your-hat. The official name is…" she screwed up her face in thought. "Arraine's Remedial something-or-other."

"Helpful," Tobias chuckled, his heart lifting when she grinned in response.

"I know, sorry. Everyone just calls it battle blood - it got that nickname back in the Kin Wars. It's a potent mix of bits and pieces that work a bit like an adrenaline shot for a human; gets you off the ground when you're on your last legs, starts the repair process, gives you just enough fire to keep going and then knocks you out like too much bad curry when it's over." Aislinn grimaced, levering herself into a sitting position. "I've had to take it enough times to know I hate it."

"Sorry," Tobias murmured, watching the way her hair shimmered in the light as she shook it out. "But we need you back on deck."

"It's fine. I would've done the same." Aislinn patted herself down, tugging at bandages and checking poultices. "These will need to go."

"They stay for now," Tobias said firmly, catching at her wrist. "Jem said so."

"Fine." She tossed a smouldering look over one shoulder. "Don't think this whole episode qualifies as catching me, by the way."

Tobias blinked - it had been farthest from his mind. "The way Zeke tells it, you were the one who caught me."

"I had to. You would've killed Jaxon otherwise. Still," she shoved him in the shoulder and waved at the bandages. "I could have done with gentler treatment, you barbarian."

"Mother Moon, I'm sorry." Tobias made to reach for her on instinct, then hesitated and threw himself back on the pillow instead. "This is ridiculous."

Aislinn was silent a long moment and then her body, naked bar for the bandages, was sliding across his chest. She propped her cheek on one hand and stared down at him. "No sulking."

"I'm not sulking."

"You are and it won't help. This is going to keep happening until you get a handle on things. If not for our unfortunate landing, I'd have walked away from these injuries without a problem."

Tobias' eyes rolled downwards without his permission, where the swell of her breasts was sandwiched rather magnificently against his faded blue t-shirt. He blinked. "Where are your bandages?"

She grinned. "They were cramping my style."

"Your 'almost died saving an idiot's life' style?"

The grin became a giggle. "That's the one. Hey, don't pout - you told me they stayed for now and they did. That was then and this is the new, bandage-free now."

"How did you even get them off without me noticing?"

"Magic, obviously." Aislinn dragged herself further up his chest, eyes widening as she ran curious fingers along his hairline. "Did you know you have a tangle in your hair that looks like a map of Switzerland?"

Tobias pressed his lips together in a thin line as she yanked his head forwards to get a better view, all but thrusting his face into her cleavage. "Ash-"

"Shhhhh," she dropped his head back on the pillow. "No talking."

He opened his mouth to say he thought the battle blood had most certainly kicked in and they should think about going downstairs to help Zeke, but Aislinn twisted one hand into his hair and pressed her lips against his. Tobias' mind said no, bad idea - but as Aislinn palmed his cock through his shorts, Tobias' body said yes, yes, *yes.*

She hummed low in her throat, attacking him with lips, teeth, tongue, hands. Helpless to resist, Tobias kneaded her shoulders, her waist, her buttocks, pulling her harder against his rapidly growing erection. Aislinn growled in response, leaning back far enough to transform one hand into a claw and slice his t-shirt clean apart, her mouth kissing a trail of fire across his chest. She made it almost to the waistband of his pants when Tobias clutched her biceps in both hands and hauled her upwards, pinning her chest against his.

"Ash, stop," he panted. "We can't."

"Sure we can," she returned, lowering her head to nip at his jawbone.

Tobias groaned as her teeth scraped his skin, his hips twitching against her body of their own accord. "No, Ash. No. This isn't you - it's the tonic."

"It's me," she replied, wriggling sensuously in his arms. "Just… uninhibited."

"I'm not doing this," Tobias returned, though his straining erection demanded otherwise. "Not like this."

Aislinn paused, raising her head to stare down at him. "This might be the only chance we get, Tobias. The tonic has got fireworks going off in my brain - without it, I might think too much. I might freak out. I might not be able to go through with it."

"I'm willing to take that chance. I won't risk this - *us* - on a potion induced frenzy."

She wilted, eyes silvering with sudden tears. "You don't… you don't want me?"

Tobias barked a laugh. "Ash, I want to be inside you so badly right now I think I might die, but that's my point. I want *you*, all of you, for better or worse. Not some trumped up medicine that's making you crazy and giving you ideas you might regret later." He softened his tone, catching a silver tear on the back of one knuckle. "If I have to wait a hundred years, it'll be worth it to know you chose this on purpose, with a sound mind."

Aislinn drew a deep, shuddering breath and flicked a glance downwards, where Tobias' erection shoved uncomfortably against the prison of his shorts. "A hundred years? He won't like that."

"He does what he's told," said Tobias firmly, "whether he likes it or not. I'm not a feral beast, Ash. Don't ask me to be."

She sagged against his chest with a sob and Tobias released a gusty sigh of relief, stroking Aislinn's hair as she curled against him - not for release but for comfort. "I'm sorry. I just want to be back to normal."

"You will be," he murmured, pressing a kiss to her temple. "You just have to be patient."

"Do *not* say that to me right now," Aislinn growled, lifting her head and baring her teeth. "In fact, if we're not doing this, you better give me something else to do before I set the house on fire."

Tobias released her and Aislinn rolled upright, shaking herself thoroughly. "That bad?"

"Imagine a million ants crawling through your veins with hammers and nails. They're fixing everything but it's about as comfy as it sounds. Everything else is too bright, too loud and above all, too slow. I feel like I need to shout to be heard over the noise of my own thoughts, which can't work out what order they want to go in." She turned to face him and laughed suddenly. "I hope you didn't actually like that shirt."

Tobias yanked the offending garment off and threw it at her. "Bit late now, isn't it?" He glanced at the clock. "We've got about forty-five minutes before people will start gathering for the meet. Grandma promised to send food."

"I need a shower first. I stink like bush and bear and sweat and whatever Jemima rubbed in my cuts before they closed up." Aislinn shuddered, then paused. "Thanks for not leaving me, even though I was asleep."

"I promised," Tobias shrugged, eyeing the curves of her body as she disappeared into the bathroom, still chattering uselessly about nothing. He knew he'd done the right thing by not going along with her craziness, but both gods - and his poor erection - knew it was one of the hardest things he'd ever managed.

Blowing out a breath, Tobias adjusted his shorts and rolled off the bed. He'd barely made it downstairs and lifted the lid on a casserole dish full of slow cooked beef when Aislinn appeared by his side, damp hair twisted into a thick braid and wearing soft, paisley harem pants in shades of navy and white and a clinging black singlet top with spaghetti straps. "Oooooh, that smells good."

"Did you even shower?" Tobias asked, grabbing a ladle and scooping out two serves of casserole.

"Of course. What use is preternatural speed if I don't use it when I'm wired?" Aislinn returned. "Besides, you're prettier to look at than the bathroom tiles."

Tobias glanced down at his bare chest and then back up at her sparkling gaze. "I'd bloody well hope so."

She laughed at that, already well into her bowl of stew. By the time Tobias had taken a few spoonfuls of his own, Aislinn's bowl was empty and she stood to refill it. "Bastard tonic makes you hungry, too."

"Because the body's working overtime?"

"Something like that. Want me to speak at this meet?" She asked, settling back into her chair and tucking into the stew. "I'm not planning to throw our fathers under the bus, if you're worried, but I do know the bears better than anyone else here."

"Yeah, I think it would make more sense coming from you," Tobias said. "Unless you feel uncomfortable?"

"Of course I'm uncomfortable - but people's lives are at risk. I'll just let the tonic talk." Aislinn shrugged it off as no big deal but Tobias noted the faint shiver which worked up her spine.

He reached across the table and took her free hand in his. "I've got you," he murmured.

"I know." Aislinn's face broke into a blinding smile that stole the breath clean from Tobias' lungs. "Well, are you finished? Let's go address the pack."

****

Zeke had arranged for the pack to gather in front of Grandma Redding's house and by the time they arrived, there was already quite a crowd. Hyper-aware of Tobias close behind her, Aislinn lowered her head and threaded between milling bodies until Zeke, standing by

Grandma atop the porch steps, barked a command that had people stepping back to let her through.

Aislinn flashed the second a bright smile as she stepped up beside him, reaching out to tug an errant corkscrew curl that had escaped his half-ponytail. *Maybe we should have jumped Zeke instead,* said a voice in her mind. *Don't be ridiculous,* another answered, *he's nowhere near as lickable as Tobias. You'd get bored after five seconds.* There was a short silence. *But Tobias,* the first voice reminded, *is decidedly No Fun.* The first voice snorted. *Just as well, or who knows what would have happened?* The second voice loosed a throaty laugh. *We all know what would have happened. But credit where credit is due, the man's got morals.*

"Exactly," Aislinn muttered, stepping forward to embrace her grandmother in a quick hug.

"What, my dear?" Grandma asked.

"Nothing. Just talking to myself. Selves? Selfses."

Grandma pulled back and gave her a once over. "Are you sure you're up for this?"

"Of course." Aislinn smiled and swung back to the pack, reaching for Tobias. He was there instantly, without so much as a squeak of protest when she twined her fingers through his and held on tightly enough to make his bones creak. She looked over the small crowd and raised her voice. "Is everyone here?"

"Near enough," someone called, "and it's past five."

"In that case, let's begin. I'd like to thank you all for coming on such short notice," Tobias said, his voice carrying easily over the assembled wolfkin. "You will all, no doubt, remember Aislinn Redding, Andre's daughter?" A murmur of assent greeted his question and Tobias nodded. "Some of you have already welcomed her home in person, others have yet to be reacquainted. Unfortunately circumstances have arisen which have made Ash's reintegration into pack life a little complicated and it's for that reason I called you here today."

"Six weeks ago, I was attacked in my home in Ireland by a guerrilla team of bearkin." Aislinn took a half step forward, gripping Tobias' hand as tightly as she dared while thrusting her chest out, knowing her scars would be livid in the light of the setting sun. "This is the result. I was sent back here to heal but the bears are not content to let us live in peace any longer - they intend to finish what they started at the peace summit eight years ago."

A deathly hush fell over the crowd and Aislinn saw more than a few Kin flinch in mournful memory. "I know how much you all lost back then; believe me, in Ireland I saw much of it firsthand. I've fought and fought for our freedom, to avenge the memories of our loved ones, but I alone am not enough. Now, I need your help." She swallowed heavily. "You've all heard the reports or know someone who's seen or been involved in an attack. The bears are here and they're not going away. I know you're all hurting, but if we don't band together and work as a unit, when the bears come here - and if they're not stopped, they *will* come here - then we'll die, like our loved ones before us."

Bill Deepwater stepped forward, straightening his red flannel shirt. "What would you have of us, lass?"

"I want to know who's willing to fight," Aislinn returned evenly. "I want to know who's willing to protect themselves and their pack. I want to know who has experience, who doesn't and who's able to help the rest of you learn." She looked back out over the rest of the crowd. "The pack is only as strong as its weakest member. I don't want the bears to show up here and tear what's left of your community to shreds - rather, I think it's high time they paid for the sins they committed at the peace summit."

"But Andre's not here," a wavering voice from the back called.

"I'm here," Tobias said firmly. "Den Mother Redding is here, as she has always been. And Aislinn herself is a Den Mother too, in addition to being an accomplished warrior. We will protect you with our lives but three alone are not enough."

"I'm in," Zeke said loudly, projecting his voice for the benefit of the assembly.

"And us," Dominic shouldered forward, followed closely by Rory and his murmured assent.

Bill Deepwater looked his grandson up and down, then hoisted himself onto the bottom step. "I never saw the Kin Wars but my Ma did, and she remembered 'em even though she were young. She lost family and friends, everyone did. Then at the peace summit, we lost again. Bearkin are not to be trifled with," he said loudly. "They'll kill and eat you soon as look at you and they hate wolves most of all." Bill turned to Aislinn, his eyes bright. "I might be older now, but I were fully trained and served active duty as a youngster. I'd like another chance to draw blood for those we lost - I'll fight, and I can train those who don't know how."

An undercurrent of uncertain murmuring threaded through the pack; Bill was well respected and his word carried a lot of weight but Aislinn could scent fear on the evening air. She opened her mouth and paused as the crowd parted and Sienna Smythe, immaculately dressed in a floral blouse and a pleated white skirt, stepped out.

"I want to fight," she announced, high-pitched voice firm and delicate chin held high. "I want justice for our lost and I want justice for Aislinn."

Several gasps went up through the crowd but Sienna's decision dragged others forward and before Aislinn knew it the entire pack had pledged to fight. She was pleased to find several ex-warriors amongst the older members, Bill and Grandma Redding included. Though the crowd had dissolved into a hubbub of conversation, when Aislinn raised a hand for silence she got it immediately.

"Thank you, everyone," she said and meant it. "If nobody has any objections, I'm going to put Bill and Rory Deepwater in charge of training sessions. Grandma, would you be willing to draft a roster of who visits the ring and when?"

"Of course," Grandma gave a sharp nod. "But there's a lot of us. Where will we work?"

"Once 'pon a time, that's what the common lawn were for," Bill said.

Grandma looked down at Bill and smiled softly. "So it was. How could I forget? Very well, the common lawn it is. Bill, will you and Rory pay me a visit first thing in the morning so we can set things in motion?"

Bill clicked his heels together and snapped a smart salute. "Gladly."

"All right, go home and get some rest," Tobias called, his eyes roving restlessly over the assembled wolfkin. "You'll be notified of your training times when the roster's done. In the meantime, make sure you eat well, sleep well and bring everything you have to your sessions. All our lives depend on it."

Aislinn watched as the crowd dispersed, returning the nods of several Kin she'd yet to greet in person and giving Sienna a grateful smile. The petite woman blew her a kiss and then linked her arm through Dominic's, allowing him to escort her away.

"Did you notice who wasn't here?" Zeke said quietly, his head appearing in the blank space between Aislinn and Tobias.

"The Heliope-Flint horde," Tobias answered.

"Correctomundo." Zeke sucked on his teeth a long moment. "I'm willing to bet we know why, too."

"You think Jax is back already?" Tobias frowned. "It's only been a few hours but I guess it's possible."

"Why don't we go and see?" Aislinn offered. "Let's call it a triple date."

"You're on, little sister-wolf." Zeke grinned and bumped his head against hers. "I love being the third wheel."

"Don't be silly, you're Tobias' second." Aislinn prodded him in the ribs. "Someone has to be around to hold his hand when things get scary."

"Hey," Tobias protested, raising the hand he still had interlinked with Aislinn's. "Who's doing the hand holding?"

She grinned without remorse. "Fingers numb yet?"

"About ten minutes ago," he acknowledged. "I'm proud of you for speaking up. You handled everything really well."

"Not my first speech." Aislinn shrugged, releasing Tobias' hand and skipping lightly down the stairs. "Just the first time it's been personal like that." She glanced back over her shoulder and winked. "Thanks for the support. Now come on - and try to keep up."

Fifteen

The common lawn's grass seemed to blur into a smooth carpet as Aislinn jogged towards Sarah and Brian's sprawling ranch-style home, her hyper-sensitive ears picking up the sounds of Zeke and Tobias following along behind. The first thing she noticed was that the house was dark, curtains drawn and lights off. Aislinn knocked as a point of courtesy but didn't bother to wait and see if anyone answered, instead trying the door.

"Locked," she announced, following the verandah around the side of the house. Aislinn tried every window she passed, finally coming to the back door and pausing. "Even the dog flap is sealed."

Zeke frowned. "That doesn't bode well."

"Wait here," Aislinn told them, and shrugged on her cloak of shadows. The world shimmered and flattened and a moment later she'd streamed under the gap between the door and the floorboards, rematerialised and flipped open the locks.

"That shit is really something else," Zeke snorted as the door swung open. "I guess it doesn't matter if you lose your keys, huh?"

Aislinn stepped aside so the boys could join her in the laundry. "Something like that."

"Sarah?" Tobias called, tugging the door closed in his wake. "Kids?"

"They're not here," Aislinn said, already moving deeper into the house. "It smells empty. A couple hours at least."

"I'll check upstairs," Zeke volunteered and disappeared into the shadows.

Tobias followed Aislinn into the kitchen, flicking on the lights when she didn't bother. "What is it?"

"Why would they leave? If Jaxon was here, what would he…" Aislinn trailed off, stopping in front of the fridge. "Son of a bitch. Absolute, pig-headed, flea-ridden, pathetic excuse for a cattle dog!"

Tobias appeared at her side in an instant, reaching up to yank a note off the fridge. "This is just Brian's market timetable."

"Look at the dates," Aislinn said, leaning into the warmth of his body and pointing. "He's at market right now, isn't he?"

"Yeah, for another couple weeks," Tobias answered. "So?"

Zeke's footsteps preceded him down the stairs. "Kids' rooms are all packed up neat, clothes are on the light side. Looks like they've gone somewhere for at least a week - and I found this taped to the ensuite mirror."

Aislinn took the envelope out of his hand, reading 'Den Mother' on the front in an elegant script. "I'll bet this is for Grandma, but to hell with it - I'm a Den Mother." She tore the flap open and slid out a small notecard with a few lines written on it, barely glancing before handing it to Tobias. "I was right."

"Barbara - Jaxon organised a surprise trip into Melbourne for the whole family to meet up with Brian! Didn't have time to drop by, didn't want you to worry. Will call when we arrive. Sarah." Tobias blinked and looked up in horror. "Solaeden save us, he's got all the kids with him."

"And I'm willing to bet everything I own that the bears are watching the roads," Aislinn growled. "What's the quickest route to Melbourne from here?"

Tobias dug his phone out of his pocket and swiped at the screen, revealing a black and white picture of himself and Ash as teenagers; she pressing a kiss to his cheek and he blushing furiously. Aislinn elbowed him in the ribs and he grunted in response. "Now you know why I didn't want to lend you my phone in the car last week."

"He's hopeless," Zeke said, leaning in to look at the map Tobias pulled up. "Has been for years."

"So I'm discovering," Aislinn said drily. "Is that the main road through Gerup?"

"Yeah. I'd say it's probably the quickest under normal circumstances but surely Jax wouldn't go that way? Not after the attack, anyway." Tobias frowned. "Look here - this road is single lane and curls around the back of Old Tom's Hollow. It's almost as fast as the route through Gerup."

"That's the way he'll go," Aislinn nodded. "Don't suppose either of you want to try his phone?"

"I did upstairs," Zeke replied. "Called Sarah, too. No answer. I'll bet Jax left his phone in the den and didn't bother going back."

"Fucking idiot," Aislinn growled, heading for the door.

"Where are you going?"

"After him, of course - I'm not waiting until morning with Sarah and the kids out there." She yanked the front door open and looked back at the two men. "Come on! Every minute you spend gawping is another minute they're in danger."

"Wait!" Zeke cried. "Come out the back."

"Why?" Aislinn nevertheless closed the front door and jogged through the kitchen, where Zeke was already letting himself out.

"Because we have a spare car up behind the den for emergencies," Tobias answered, winking. "One of my better ideas."

"Only because Ash once said it was too bloody far to run to the garage if the shit hit the fan," Zeke panted as they raced through the twilight.

Aislinn's blood sang in her veins as they cleared the back of the houses and crossed the fringe of the orchard to a small, well maintained shed set at the base of the sheep paddock. Tobias whizzed the combination lock holding the door shut and pulled it aside, dragging the door open to reveal a sleek black car inside.

Aislinn frowned as Zeke reached under the front right wheel arch and drew out a key. "I don't remember this."

"You wouldn't," Tobias said softly. "It belonged to Leif Deepwater and went to Rory when he died at the summit."

"Oh." Aislinn was silent as Zeke unlocked the door and slid into the driver's seat. "I liked Leif."

"Everyone liked Leif," Tobias answered, opening the back door and ushering her inside. "Rory couldn't face the car for years so we stashed it here. In the end it became our oh-shit vehicle."

Zeke turned the key and the car started with a roar. "Seatbelts on, assholes puckered - here we go!"

In spite of the situation, Aislinn whooped as the car shot out into the twilight, speeding down the narrow dirt path so fast the scenery was soon a blur. *It'd be faster if we ran,* one voice said. *Don't be ridiculous, we'd have nothing left once we get there,* scoffed the other. *Get where?* Asked the first voice. *Wherever we're going,* answered the second. *There better be blood,* the first one groused. *Oh, yes,* the second purred. *On that, we are in agreement.*

"Shut up," Aislinn hissed, shaking her head to clear it. She caught Tobias giving her an odd look and grunted. "Battle blood is making me batshit crazy. I blame you."

"I'll take it," Tobias nodded, expression resigned. "I thought we could handle the side effects but to be honest, now I'm not so sure."

Aislinn gave him her best lecherous grin. "You could have handled all of it, tall-dark-and-handsome, but you turned me down."

In the front seat, Zeke made a choking sound and his eyes went wide in the rear-view mirror. "Please tell me you guys did *not* spend the last four hours humping the pictures off the walls."

"No," Tobias growled, his cheeks darkening with a blush. "We didn't."

Aislinn pouted. "I tried, Zeke, I really did."

Tobias passed a hand over his face, his butterscotch and cream scent sharp with embarrassment. "I told you, Ash, I don't want you when you're drugged out - there's no way I can be sure it's really you saying yes. Especially after what you've been through."

"That's what *I* was worried about," Zeke nodded, yanking the steering wheel hard to the right and fish-tailing the car out onto a road. "Tobias is right, gorgeous. Although when Mother said the tonic might make you manic, I'll admit I didn't think she meant it like *that.*"

"She's just a prude." Aislinn waved a dismissive hand, watching the intriguing way her own fingers flashed in the last rays of the setting sun. "Battle blood puts your entire body into overdrive and floods your fight or flight system with go-juice. I've seen Kin I thought were dead literally leap up off the floor and tear heads off with their bare hands and once, some poor guy's balls. Not a nice way to go, in case you were wondering."

"Holy fuck," Zeke muttered. "No wonder Ma was reluctant to give it to you."

"Unfortunately there's not a lot of other options in a pinch," Aislinn shrugged. "So I'm just going to babble and burn and whatever else happens for a while longer and then when the tonic fades from my system, there'll probably be some sort of epic fainting episode and I'll have a nice nap."

Tobias went pale. "Please don't do that until we get back home."

"Nah, takes about twenty four hours." Aislinn reached out to bop him playfully on the nose. "Want to ride on the roof of the car for a while? It'll be fun."

"No." Tobias shook his head and then, when Aislinn reached for her seatbelt, clutched her wrist in an iron grip. "*No.*"

"Party pooper." Aislinn poked out her tongue then leant almost her entire body weight over Tobias' lap as she squinted out the windscreen. "Where are we?"

"Almost at the turn off," Zeke answered. "Are you sure this is the way you want to go?"

"Yeah." Tobias' chest rumbled against Aislinn's shoulder, his voice sending zaps of electric energy through her supercharged veins. "There's no way Jax will go through Gerup. We're more likely to spot him if we follow the same road, even if he's a couple of hours ahead."

"Won't be quite that long," Aislinn negated, fascinated by the way the car's headlights dipped and flashed over the trees bordering the road. "He'd have had to hide out for a while to make sure we weren't following, then sneak the long way around the farms to get back to the house, then convince Sarah to go without contacting Grandma first, then pack everyone up and actually leave, and hang on, Zeke, didn't you speak to Sarah when you were organising the meeting?"

"No," Zeke shook his head, wrestling the car around a corner that he should have been going far slower to navigate properly. "She didn't answer the door so I just sent her a text - no answer."

"Jax probably has her phone," Tobias muttered.

"Did you see that?" Aislinn sat up suddenly, straining at her seat belt and the restraining arm Tobias flung around her waist. "Look! There's a mattress on the side of the road. Why is that there? Who drives around with a mattress?"

"Old Tom's Hollow isn't too far from here. The homestead, I mean," Zeke answered. "Probably some young dumbshits braving the haunted house."

"Haunted," Aislinn scoffed, twisting to stare out the back window as they whizzed past the abandoned mattress. "Old Tom's Hollow has been closed since before I went to Ireland. That mattress is new - the sort of thing you might roll up and strap to the roof of a car for a horde of young pups if you were heading on a trip."

"Pups don't sleep on the roof, Ash," Tobias drawled, laughter threading his voice.

"No, but if they took the station wagon, they could pull over and lay it down inside the back for the pups to sleep on," Aislinn answered. "Which means you need to consider - stop!"

Zeke slammed on the brakes and the car slid to a halt, tyres squealing and smoke pouring from the wheel arches. "I see it."

Aislinn was already moving, throwing her door open and leaping out of the car. An ancient, two-tone station wagon was barely visible from the ditch it had driven into, but she'd spied the flash of silver on a bumper as Zeke's headlights had swung around the bend in the twisty road.

One of the roof racks was torn clean off, the roof itself dented as though something heavy had landed on top. The car's nose was buried in stagnant mud and gnarled undergrowth but enough of the bonnet was visible for Aislinn to see it wouldn't be going anywhere anytime soon. The windscreen and several windows were smashed, bags and debris scattered throughout the cabin. Aislinn stuck her head through one of the windows and inhaled, trying to sort through the mixture of scents.

"I smell Jax," Tobias said from the window opposite.

"And the pups," Aislinn agreed. She spotted blood on the sharp edge of a shattered window and leant closer, nostrils curling. "Bearkin."

"Fuck." Zeke ran a hand through his hair, face pale. "We're too late."

"My left tit we are," Aislinn growled, straightening up and scanning the nearby bush. "If there's no bodies, it's not too late."

She called her wolf form and leapt the ditch, scrambling up the embankment on the other side. The Heliope-Flints had gone into the bush, and Aislinn followed the scent as quickly as she dared. A few moments later Tobias' nose touched her hindquarters in silent support and then, a few moments beyond that, Zeke repeated the same motion on her other side. The scent of blood and fear led her onwards through the darkness and in less than five minutes the bush opened out onto the tumbledown estate of Old Tom's Hollow.

Old Tom had been an eccentric wombatkin with a passion for model trains, and he'd turned his homestead into a tourist attraction of sorts. It had been popular enough to provide an income but Tom had no living relatives and after he died, the homestead and his collection had fallen into disrepair. Rumours said it was haunted by the old wombat's ghost, who had loved his trains so much that even death wouldn't keep him away - and whilst Aislinn hadn't seen any ghosts herself, the one time she and Tobias had crept through the hollow as youngsters, every hair on the back of her neck had stood straight on end.

Now, she thought only of the Heliope-Flint pups as she raced across the open ground, keeping her body as low to the grass as she could. The homestead itself was dark and silent and though smashed windows gaped like open mouths, instinct and a keen nose told Aislinn that Jaxon had led his family away from the tumbledown homestead. She turned her ears forward, straining to hear over the rustling of wind in the trees, certain she could hear whimpering up ahead. The house passed by on her right and Aislinn paused in the concealing shadows of the back verandah to consider her options.

The scents here were a chaos of bear and wolf and blood, the churned ground behind the house testament to some sort of struggle. The gut-wrenching scent of death was absent but that was cold comfort to Aislinn, whose scars ached beneath her fur as though to remind her that there were other things than death to worry about.

Aislinn shimmered into human form, pressing hard up against the peeling weatherboards of the homestead while she waited for Tobias and Zeke to follow suit. "It's a trap," she whispered, her words no more than a breathy exhalation. "I can't see the bears from here but I'm willing to bet they're lurking in and around that large barn."

Tobias squinted into the night. "How many?"

"Impossible to say. Probably more than there are of us," Aislinn answered. "Just means we have to be careful."

"We have two midforms," Zeke reminded quietly.

"I can't summon mine on purpose," Tobias returned, and Aislinn heard him grinding his teeth in frustration. "It's only ever surfaced when I've lost my mind - which might not be ideal right now."

"Not yet," Aislinn agreed, "but when the shit hits the fan, if you feel that itch you grab hold of it, understand?"

Tobias was silent a long moment. "I don't like that gleam in your eye."

"It's a trap." Aislinn shrugged. "I'm going to spring it. When I do, the bears will come running from wherever they're hiding to provide backup. Wait in the shadows and take out as many as you can before they get inside."

"And leave you in there alone?" Tobias hissed. "Are you crazy?"

"Right now, yes," Aislinn nodded, her blood already howling for battle. "But it makes the most sense. Olaf wants me - I'm the best one to spring the trap." She gave him a pointed look. "And you're the best ones to clean up the mess."

"This is the most fucked up thing I've ever heard," Zeke whispered. "What do I do when he loses it?"

"Tobias will attack the largest, loudest target. Lure him towards the bears, keep your mouth shut, and you'll both be fine." Aislinn paused to let that sink in, her eyes on the barn. "No more talking now - every second is another that those kids could be suffering."

She drew on her cloak of shadows and dematerialised, leaving the two males cursing softly behind her. Aislinn whispered across the darkened ground, thankful the moon was covered by clouds. The barn seemed as dark as any other but as she curled her way through a gap created by a broken paling, she discovered the bearkin had several battery-powered lamps illuminating the interior. Blankets and old farm equipment had been used to cover any areas the light might have leaked out, with all the window shutters and doors firmly closed.

Jaxon, naked and in human form, knelt in a clear space before the back wall with his family. Sarah was in human form as was young Achilles, with the remaining six children in wolf form hunkered mournfully between them. Sarah had a nasty bruise to one side of her face and Achilles one in the ribs but it was Jaxon who bore the brunt of the injuries, his skin pale and sweaty beneath a variety of cuts, bruises and lesions. His green eyes - one almost swollen entirely shut - were focussed grimly on two bearkin, one human and one in bear form, who stood guard a few paces in front of them. The bear sat with his legs splayed in a position that would have been comical if he wasn't licking blood off his long claws and huffing in delight. The male in human form lounged in a rickety wooden chair with a book in one hand, sipping casually from a steaming thermos. An empty syringe lay discarded on the ground by his feet and Aislinn guessed that Jaxon, at the very least, had been injected with the same serum that had stolen her own ability to shift during the ambush in Ireland.

There was no sign of any other bearkin or syringes but Aislinn was no fool - the needle had to have been left there on purpose, either to goad her to anger or frighten her into making a mistake.

Twisting incorporeal lips into a nasty grin, Aislinn flowed up the back of a support beam and into the rafters of the barn, where the light from the lamps either did not reach or cast shadows between herself and the roof. The intense illumination meant she couldn't enter the area and remain part of the shadows, but there was more than one way to spring a trap to her advantage. Careful to remain in the protective darkness of the beam, she positioned herself directly above her two foes and eyed the clear space in front of Jaxon with a calculating air. *It'll work,* one voice whispered. *It's perfect,* agreed the second.

Hoping those tonic-induced voices were right, Aislinn slipped off the beam and began to drift downwards. As soon as she hit the light, her cloak of shadows was stripped away and she fell, tucking in her legs to land neatly in a crouch between Jaxon and the bearkin. "Surprise," she announced, straightening up for a fraction of a second - just long enough for the bearkin to recognise her - then fur swept up her body as she assumed her midform, lashing out with razor sharp claws.

"Shi-" the human bearkin was too slow. Aislinn's claws raked him from groin to chin, slicing his throat in the process and toppling the body backwards out of the chair. The other bear was faster but it was still too late; Aislinn's other hand swept through his fur and tore open the vulnerable belly that had been left exposed while the bear licked blood off his claws.

"Ash!" Jax cried, part in relief and part in horror. "It's a trap!"

No shit, Aislinn thought. She looked over her shoulder to where Jaxon crouched with his family and growled in a way she hoped meant 'Stay.' Then there was no more time to think, because a nearby crate exploded and two more bearkin in bear form erupted, roaring loudly - the cue, no doubt, for their backup outside.

"Solaeden save us," Sarah sobbed.

"Sit, Mum." Jaxon's voice, though thick with fear, was firm. "Whatever they jabbed us with, we're useless like this. If we run we'll only get in Ash's way."

Well, well. He did have a brain after all. Aislinn bent and scooped up the heavy syringe, weighing it in her hand. The needle was thick and wickedly long, the barrel which had contained the serum heavier than expected. As the bears lumbered towards her on all fours, she changed her grip on the syringe and, with a flick of one powerful wrist, threw it like a dart. It flew straight into the eye of one of the bears and he dropped to the floor, slapping at his face with clumsy paws.

"Kill them, Ash!" Achilles shouted and Aislinn huffed a lupine laugh as she lowered her shoulder, braced her legs and caught the second bear head on. Due to their immense natural size and strength, bearkin held an advantage that was unmatched bar for Kin with large midforms. As a result, they were exceptional fighters, needing no more than their claws, teeth and vicious nature to win every battle they waded into.

Whilst the bear who slammed chest first into Aislinn was no exception to this rule, he was faced with the sudden and distasteful realisation that her midform was as tall as he was, and equally strong, rendering his natural advantages moot. He tried to shy away but Aislinn slipped her slimmer frame inside the bear's embrace and used his own momentum to swing him around and toss him away. He smashed through one of the barn's windows, disappearing into the night with a roar - a roar which very quickly became a gurgle. A howl went up from outside and Aislinn peeled her lip back from her teeth as she recognised Tobias, though the tone of his voice suggested he was struggling to control the Alpha energy that was no doubt coursing through his veins.

"Duck!" Jaxon shouted and Aislinn dropped to the floor, lashing out with her legs as the other bear, one eye now a bleeding ruin, swiped his claw through the space where she'd been standing. Aislinn's legs tangled with the bearkin's fur and he staggered, throwing himself on top of her with a growl. She thrust up one knee, driving it into the bear's groin even as she caught the rest of his weight on her forearms, twisting sideways. They rolled and Aislinn was suddenly kneeling on the other's chest but the bear was quick; he curled his claws around her arms and pinned them against her ribs. Blood ran freely, turning her fur slick and Aislinn squirmed in his grip, snapping at the bear's snout with her teeth. He twitched his head up and away - revealing his throat, which she tore out with a guttural growl.

She wrenched out of the bear's grasp and leapt upright, listening to the howls and roars echoing from outside the building. It was the noise of battle rather than the noise of impending doom, and she allowed herself a moment's sharp relief; her two boys were still very much alive. Which was good, really, because there were three new bears waiting at the edge of the lanterns' light, growling and prowling the fine border between bright and shadow. Aislinn glanced over her shoulder at the Heliope-Flints, still cowering on the floor, and then back at the bears. Three of them, one of her, with a distinct advantage to the bearkin in that she had innocents to protect and they did not. Why, then, were they waiting?

"Hello, Aislinn."

That voice. She froze, instantly transported back to her study in Ireland, where those green walls and that awful, deep voice had haunted her nightmares ever since.

Olaf Gruybere, elegantly clothed in a tailored suit which did nothing to conceal his powerful frame, stepped into the lamp light. His bald head gleamed in the harsh illumination, brown eyes so dark as to be almost black. He adjusted the cuff links at one wrist, stepping neatly around a bloodied corpse. "My, my; you've made quite the mess. Is that three - no, four of my men? For shame, young lady. What would your father say?"

Aislinn growled deep in her chest, flicking her claws into an attack position and moving to place herself squarely in front of the Heliope-Flint clan. There was no way, *no way*, that she was going to let Olaf anywhere near Sarah or the pups, no matter the cost.

"Still defiant? How interesting," Olaf mused, his thick accent laced with laughter. "I rather fancied I'd beaten that clean out of you." The words were intended to wound and Aislinn knew it - but she still couldn't help her flinch, or the way her lips drew back into a snarl. Olaf laughed. "Come now, why don't you slip back into that human body? I've heard the scars are incredible."

The bearkin slid one hand behind his back as he spoke and Aislinn's growl rose in response. He had a syringe, she was certain, and needed her in human form to render her as helpless as Jaxon and Sarah. As helpless as she'd been back then, on that day when he'd burned her life to the ground.

"No? I can't say as I'm surprised. You know, when you first got away from me alive - I'll admit I was furious." Olaf shook his head as though speaking to a naughty child caught raiding the cookies. "After all, I had such a glorious time tearing you to pieces and I was quite looking forward to snuffing out your life and leaving your broken husk behind."

Aislinn roared in rage, her body trembling, only the battle blood's fireworks preventing her mind from being swamped by the memories Olaf sought to elicit. *No.* She would not be a victim. Never, ever again, no matter what it took.

"Well now. Such strength," Olaf clicked his tongue between his teeth. "I'm impressed. You know I really ought to thank you, Aislinn. Your escape, whilst entirely unsatisfying, revealed a rather intriguing number of new skills I never knew I had." He flexed one hand and then pointed at her hip, where they both knew the Mark lay, concealed under her midform's thick coat of fur. "Imagine my delight when I realised I could steal your energy through our one-way connection. I thought I might be able to kill you - but alas, you managed to elude me. The echoes of your energy, however, came with snatches of sight and sound that gave me clues to your location. It didn't take long to deduce you'd been sent back here, to this hovel of a community."

He'd been tracking her through the Mark? Aislinn paused at that. It can't have been a perfect pinpoint, because why else would he have gone to the trouble of luring her out? Her thoughts cut off when Olaf removed his free hand from behind his back, palming, as expected, a second syringe of serum. "Despite my haste to be free of our noisome connection, I've recently discovered there's a little something I need from you. So, if you don't mind, I'd like you in human form so that we can be on our merry way."

Aislinn widened her stance and sank into her knees, growling low in her throat. There was no way she was going anywhere with Olaf - not without a fight, not without her death. Never.

"I was hoping you'd refuse." Olaf nodded, lips pursed thoughtfully. "I've been looking forward to seeing how well this works in person." He clenched his free hand into a fist and Aislinn gasped as bands of iron secured around her chest. Cold. Freezing cold, the cold of ice and snow and death, swept over her body and stole the breath from her lungs. She choked, spots dancing in front of her vision, and her midform faded almost instantly. Aislinn wobbled in place for a moment and then dropped helplessly to the floor.

"Ash!" Achilles cried. "No! Get up!"

"Don't worry, little pup," Olaf chuckled, his footsteps clicking across the barn's stone floor as he approached. "I won't kill her yet. Although, I must admit, seeing my handiwork does make me a little… eager for an entree. Should we show your packmates what's in store for them, my dear?"

Aislinn's blood froze in her veins, heart stuttering as she realised Olaf meant to repeat his performance in Ireland. And once she was out of the way, what was to stop him moving on to Sarah as well? She struggled uselessly against the ice imprisoning her heart, longing for Tobias' warmth. *Tobias,* whispered a voice. *Yes, yes, think of Tobias,* added the second. *Fight!*

Tobias. His blue and gold eyes, his thick golden-brown hair, that ready smile that was slightly crooked and boasted an unfairly adorable dimple when unleashed at full strength. His voice, soft and gentle, reaching into her soul and loosening those heavy bands of frigid iron a fraction. Aislinn wheezed and lifted her head, pinning the bearkin General with her most feral glare.

"Do you have something to say?" Olaf loosened his hold and air rushed back into her lungs. "Do share."

"Fuck you," Aislinn gasped. "I won't let you touch these people, you filthy prick. You can do what you want to me but I will never, *never*, let you hurt them."

Olaf blinked and then laughed, a smooth, musical sound which sent chills down Aislinn's already frozen spine. "Oh, my. So keen to have me all over again?"

"I'm already ruined," Aislinn replied, her throat raw from the ice of his psychic touch. "You can't hurt me any more, you flea-ridden excuse for a floor rug."

Olaf's expression didn't alter but his eyes glittered with malice and a moment later his psychic grip intensified, the pain so strong she dropped face-down on the floor. Outside, the sounds of chaos and howling drew ever closer and out of the corner of her eye, she saw one of the bears cut a nervous glance towards the barn door.

"My dear," Olaf said, moving close enough that Aislinn could see her own face reflected in the patent leather of his shoes. "That sounds like a challenge." He grabbed her by the hair and dragged her head up, half-lifting her limp, useless body off the ground and twirling the syringe in his fingers.

Fight! The voices screamed, their desperation mingling into a symphony of horror. *Break it, smash it!*

Aislinn filled her mind with images of Tobias, drew on the memory of his heat as though it were a favourite blanket. Olaf's psychic grip loosened and she sucked in a breath, drawing enough energy to spit at his face. Her aim was off and the spittle went wide, but the bearkin's expression hardened into one of pure, unadulterated fury and his hold on her fractured that little bit further. "Why, you -"

A roar split the air, a new, different and yet incredibly familiar roar. It shook the barn so fiercely that dust trickled down from overhead and the windows rattled in their panes. In the aftermath, everything was silent.

Olaf frowned and glanced over one shoulder. "What was that? I thought I said I wasn't to be disturbed."

The bears never got a chance to answer because the barn door imploded in a shower of wood and Tobias stood framed in the doorway, wearing his midform. Aislinn didn't need to see his eyes to know he'd long lost his grip on reality but it didn't matter. She drank him in, every glorious inch of muscle and fur and teeth and fury, her lips stretching into a rictus grin as that alien roar rang out again.

Now.

The window to her left exploded and an orange-white blur flew through the wreckage, tumbling into one of the bears standing guard and slamming them both into the shadows at the back of the barn. Still staring at Tobias, Aislinn dragged up every ounce of her considerably complicated feelings and *shoved* at the icy bands which held her still.

They shattered.

She surged upright, catching hold of the syringe in Olaf's hand and twisting up the length of his arm until her shoulders pressed into his chest. Wrenching his wrist back on itself, she slid the syringe free and slammed it into the bearkin's body. Aislinn jammed down on the plunger even as she kicked her feet up off the floor, sliding out of Olaf's grip and flipping backwards over his head. She drew on her midform as she went, howling in triumph - with his own foul serum running through his veins, the bearkin could no longer change forms or attack her psychically through the Mark.

"Bitch!" Olaf roared, yanking the syringe out and smashing it on the floor. He turned towards the cowering Heliope-Flints, drawing a wicked looking knife from his belt. "Now they die."

Or not. Aislinn called her shadows and dissolved, reappearing in front of Olaf with a growl. He dodged her swiping claws, slashed with the knife, and then disappeared as Tobias landed a vicious blow to the side of the bearkin's head which sent him flying out the window.

Aislinn turned to follow but Tobias was in front of her, roaring and gnashing his teeth. The barn was empty of bears now - bar the dead ones - and Zeke limped into the lantern light with his tongue hanging out between his teeth. His sapphire eyes were wary as they locked on Tobias and a low growl slipped his lips as he circled behind his Alpha, muscles tensed for a fight. Despite her towering desire for revenge on Olaf, Aislinn settled herself solidly between Tobias and the Heliope-Flints. She wouldn't abandon them now, even if it meant losing her enemy - and then that roar sounded again, from outside the barn, and she curled her lips back in a lupine grin. Maybe there *was* a way to have her cake and eat it too.

Tobias twitched toward the sound and Zeke shimmered into his human form, planting both hands on his blood-slicked hips in a deliberate distraction. His eyes were hard but his voice flippant as he said; "Who the fuck *is* that?"

There was a hesitation as Tobias glanced between the window and the vulnerable man in front of him, trying to weigh up what he wanted to destroy first. Aislinn seized the moment, throwing herself onto his back and wrapping her legs around his waist. He twisted and howled but to no avail - she flattened her hands over his chest and smothered his fire with her cooling shadows, keeping hold until his eyes rolled back in his head and Tobias sank to the floor, midform dissolving into humanity before her eyes.

Aislinn stepped away, chest heaving, and returned to her own human form. "That roar belongs to a friend who, with any luck, is going to catch Olaf for us. And Tobias is fine," she added. "He'll come around in a minute."

"Ash!" Achilles leapt out of his mother's grip and raced over, throwing his small body into her arms. "You saved us! That was amazing!" He leant back to stare up at her with wide, green eyes. "Are you okay?"

Aislinn brushed sweaty black hair back from Achilles' face and offered a soft smile. "I'm okay. How about you? Did he get you with the needle?"

"Yeah and it hurt." Achilles' face crumpled. "He got Jax and Mum and then I bit him and then he kicked me and I lost my wolf and then he jabbed me." The small boy held out his arm, where a puncture mark was clearly visible.

"You were very brave," Aislinn murmured, pressing a kiss to his brow. "I know it hurts but it will wear off, I promise. You'll be wearing your fur coat again in no time." She looked over to Sarah. "Are you okay?"

"Yes, but…" Sarah's hands strayed to her belly. "What will that awful stuff do to the baby?"

"Hopefully nothing," Aislinn soothed, "but we'll get Jemima to check you thoroughly as soon as we get home."

"Oh," Sarah dropped her face into her hands, shoulders shaking. "Whatever will I tell Brian?"

Aislinn turned a hard stare on Jaxon, whose green eyes were wide and shell shocked as he watched his mother. "Yes, Jaxon, what *will* you tell Brian?"

The wolfkin swallowed and turned to Aislinn, tears glistening in his eyes. "I wanted to keep them safe," he whispered. "I just wanted them to be safe and… all of that, because of me."

"Yup," Aislinn nodded, her face hard. "I tried to warn you, Jax, I really did."

"Jaxon? What is she talking about?" Sarah's voice wobbled with tears.

"I lied," Jaxon whispered. "I never arranged with Dad for a holiday. I thought Ash was bringing the bears to us and I didn't want you to end up like her. So I tried to make her leave but she wouldn't go." He swallowed, tears rolling down his cheeks as he stared up at Aislinn. "I said some terrible things and I swore out of the pack. I thought I could keep you safer by myself so I convinced you to leave but then the bears, they -" he squeezed his eyes shut. "If Ash hadn't come, we'd all be dead."

"Oh, Jaxon." Sarah's shoulders sagged and she shook her head. "You great, sweet fool. Now what do we do? I can't take you home if you've sworn out."

"I don't care, Mum, as long as you're safe."

Peeking out between her fingers, Sarah's gentle eyes flickered with sudden steel. "And I *am* safe, we all are, but it was a close call. How many times have I told you to think before you act?"

When Jaxon flinched as though struck, Aislinn held up a hand for peace. "Nothing here is beyond fixing, Sarah. Jax might've sworn out of the Redding Pack but he can swear to Tobias, who's here, or we can ask Grandma to consider taking him back in. All he needs is a Den Mother or an Alpha and the courage to set things straight."

Sarah relaxed with a sigh, closing her eyes and rubbing at them. "You're right, of course."

"Jax?" Achilles twisted in Aislinn's arms, pinning his older brother with a wide-eyed gaze. "What will you do?"

Jaxon swallowed and got to his feet, stumbling towards Aislinn. He paused half a pace away from her, face pale. "I'm sorry, Ash. I was a massive jerk and you still came for us. You saved my family when I couldn't. Can you ever forgive me?"

"You big idiot," Aislinn murmured, reaching out to ruffle his short hair. "Of course I forgive you. We all knew you were only frightened for your family and there's no harm in that - but I meant what I said. The pack is stronger together. *We* are stronger together. No matter what you'd said, we'd have still come for you."

"But Olaf - he would've - those things he did to you, he would have done them again," Jaxon choked. "Because of me."

"I'll die before I let him near me again," Aislinn said quietly, "or anyone else."

Jaxon was silent for a long moment, then dropped to his knees at her feet. "I, Jaxon Heliope-Flint, hereby pledge my life to you, Den Mother Aislinn Jaide Redding, by the light of the Mother Moon. I vow to walk in your shadow, defend your honour, and give my life, should it be necessary, for the keeping of yours. I offer my strength, my will, my soul, into your keeping from now until the end of my days." He lifted his chin, baring his throat. "For the pack."

Aislinn stared, her heart in her throat, until Achilles poked her in the shoulder. "He's joining your pack. You're supposed to say yes," the boy hissed.

Indeed. Well, she was a Den Mother, wasn't she? Very slowly, Aislinn shifted Achilles in her grip and bent to place her teeth over Jaxon's jugular. She scraped the flesh ever so gently, then straightened and said; "Welcome to the pack, Jaxon Heliope-Flint. May time make me worthy of your choice."

Jaxon got to his feet and nodded. "It already has, Ash. It already has."

Sixteen

Tobias woke with a gasp and sat bolt upright on the cold stone floor, adrenaline surging through his veins. He had a vague memory of tearing teeth and ripping claws, of stars and bears and someone calling his name.

"Steady." Zeke's hand, slicked with blood and dirt, gripped his shoulder. "We're good."

"Where are we?" Tobias blinked owlishly around him, relieved to see all the Heliope-Flint horde safe, some in human form and some in wolf form but all of them milling around Aislinn, who had Achilles in her arms and Jaxon close by her side. "What'd I miss?"

"We're inside the barn. I'm not sure of the specifics but Olaf was here throwing his jerk-ass weight around. He jabbed Sarah, Jax and Achilles with a needle and now they can't shift. Ash saved them, Jaxon swore to her and there is some crazy-ass fucker running around in the dark somewhere." Zeke considered his words and then shrugged. "Other than you, that is."

Tobias rubbed at his face. "Wait… Jaxon swore to Ash?"

"She *is* a Den Mother," Zeke reminded him. "It's not that weird."

"No, that isn't what I meant," Tobias waved a dismissive hand, clambering stiffly to his feet. "I was referring to the part where he hates her."

"Turns out he doesn't," Zeke shrugged. "In fact, after she saved his worthless ass and kept his family out of Olaf's jaws, I'm pretty sure he's now her personal shiny-eyed zealot."

Tobias brushed grit from his hands and flinched as an earth-shattering roar quite literally shook the building around him. "What the-"

Something large and angry stalked out of the shadows and Tobias could only stare, mouth agape. It was humanoid, covered in orange and white fur accented by black stripes. An elegant tail whipped back and forth above powerful, feline legs whose claws clicked across the stone. Incredibly tall, the male - definitely a male - with a tiger's head and very much a tiger's mouth full of tiger's teeth stopped just inside the circle of lantern light, his body half hunched like a wild beast and blood dripping from his claws.

"Holy shit," Zeke said into the silence.

Aislinn, looking for all the world like she were out for a picnic, calmly transferred Achilles to his mother's arms, nudged Jaxon aside and crossed the room towards the male with a midform unlike anything Tobias had ever seen. Power poured off the tigerkin's fur with such strength that Tobias' eyes watered, and to call him muscular was the understatement of the century. Still looking completely unconcerned, Aislinn held out her hands, palms up. The male leant forward, his great amber eyes flicking between her hands and face as he sniffed. Long, feline whiskers tickled Ash's skin and lips peeled back from teeth that made Tobias feel decidedly inadequate.

The creature made a sound somewhere between a yowl and a purr and straightened, giant clawed hands dragging Aislinn against his body. She spread both hands across his chest, humming tunelessly, while the tigerkin mrowled and rubbed against her like a lost kitten. Slowly, slowly, the movement slowed and stopped. Then the creature lifted his head, shook it and abruptly dissolved, returning to his human form.

At least, as human as he could be. Tobias couldn't help but notice the faint stripes that covered the man's body, nestled just beneath the surface of his skin. Tiger stripes. And those amber tiger's eyes? Also still there, not at all human and fixed intently on Aislinn. In human form, the male lost most of his impressive musculature and height, retaining instead an athletic figure more suited to a runner than a warrior. Pale skin and a long, elfin face that was unfairly handsome was capped by a shock of glossy black hair that looked more like liquid satin than actual hair. A collar - an honest to the gods, real life, studded leather collar - hung loose around his neck and, before Tobias had so much as drawn a breath, the male gripped Aislinn's jaw in long fingers and kissed her soundly on the mouth.

"Easy, tiger," she drew back with a laugh, reaching up to flick him affectionately on the nose. "You're late." He rumbled something under his breath which made Aislinn laugh and shove at his chest - but Tobias was too busy trying to swallow the red fog of his rage to pay much attention.

The man's eyes flicked over the rest of the room and he hissed, drawing lips back from teeth whose elongated canines still put Tobias' to shame, even though they were now in a human mouth. Aislinn looked over her shoulder and immediately freed herself from the tigerkin's grasp, shaking her head as she crossed the barn to slip into the circle of his arms. "Stop it, Tobias," she murmured, smoothing her hands - and her shadows - along his shoulders and up the sides of his neck. "He doesn't know."

"Who," he growled, "is that?"

Aislinn sighed and took a step back, gesturing at the tigerkin who had shadowed her part way across the room. "Flynn, this is Tobias. Over there is Zeke, Jaxon, Sarah and her children. Everyone, this is my friend Flynn."

Tobias blinked. *This* was Flynn? The Flynn she'd run away with, had slept with and laughed with. The Flynn who'd bought her that golden torc, fought by her side and kept her safe for almost twelve years. The tigerkin in question appeared to be giving Tobias the same skeptical once-over he was receiving and after a long moment, he stepped past Aislinn with liquid grace, snatched Tobias' arm and pressed his nose against the soft flesh inside his wrist.

A growl rumbled in Tobias' chest but Aislinn shook her head and, against his better judgement, he remained still while Flynn scented his skin. A moment later the tigerkin straightened, blinked slowly and offered his own arm in return. Swallowing down the million questions he wanted to ask, Tobias gently accepted the other male's forearm and lowered his head, scenting the proffered wrist. Cloves, a hint of coffee - rich and dark and exotic.

Flynn retrieved his arm and blinked again. "So, you're him." His voice was a velvety rasp, like finest sandpaper, with a thick Irish accent. "I thought you'd be taller."

"Don't be a jerk," Aislinn growled, elbowing Flynn and earning a faint grunt in response. "Now, what happened to Olaf?"

Flynn's amber eyes narrowed. "He had a car waiting. I tore off the roof but lost them at the bend." He rolled one shoulder, revealing a blistering burn. "Asshole had an over-juiced taser."

Aislinn sighed, giving the wound a swift check. "Well over-juiced. You're lucky your circuits didn't fry."

"They did - that's why I came back feral," Flynn snorted, then cut a glance at Tobias. "Too bad I can't say the same for tantrum-pants over there."

Aislinn spread a hand over Tobias' chest even as he pushed into it. "I'm not in the mood to break up a brawl, Flynn. You're both riding the trailing edge of transitional surges and this place isn't safe. Behave."

Flynn huffed a laugh, eyes glittering in a way that said he would make no such promise. "He did all right for a brainless beast - got at least four. You," and the tiger turned his attention to Zeke, "did a good job leading him around by his balls and making him kill stuff. I like you."

"Thanks," Zeke returned, looking mildly off-balance. "I don't want to sound rude or anything, but where the fuck did you come from?"

Flynn tilted his head. "Ireland."

"*Flynn*," Aislinn growled.

The tigerkin rolled his eyes. "You really want the story here, while the pups are looking at dead bears?"

"All right," Aislinn relented. "Let's get them home first."

"We won't all fit in the car," Zeke pointed out.

"You take Sarah, Jax and the kids," Aislinn returned. Jaxon made a sound of protest and she whirled, levelling her finger. "Jaxon Heliope-Flint, you will get in that car and present yourself and your family to Jemima Smythe immediately for a check. If I hear from Zeke that you stepped so much as a hair out of line, I will nail your hide to my wall. Understand?"

Jaxon grunted. "How will you get back?"

"I'm still hyped on battle blood so we'll run - provided you two are up for it?" Aislinn shot a glance at Tobias and Flynn.

"All I care about is getting the pups out," Flynn growled. He caught Achilles staring at him with wide eyes and grinned, showing those impossibly long fangs which, Tobias thought, should have distended his lips and made him ridiculous to look at but somehow didn't. "You good, little warrior?"

"Your teeth are real long," Achilles announced.

"Wanna feel?" To Tobias' astonishment, Flynn's aggressive air disappeared completely as he sidled up to a pale-faced Sarah, opening his mouth to display his fangs.

"Cool," Achilles breathed, running his finger down one long, jagged edge. "Can I pat you?" Flynn obligingly lowered his head and Achilles squealed in delight, running his fingers through the tigerkin's silken hair. "It's so soft!"

Flynn purred, a deep, soft rumbling in his chest - and before Tobias had quite registered what had happened, he'd carefully extricated the wriggling Achilles from his mother's arms. "Go gently, mama wolf," Flynn rumbled, leaning close to sniff Sarah's hair. "You have a puppy in there?"

Sarah nodded mutely, looking to Aislinn, who smiled. "Flynn, you wanna get the little ones in the car for us?"

Flynn hunkered down into a crouch, where the younger six pups were milling around their mother's feet, opened his arms and made a strange noise deep in his chest. One by one, the wriggling pups climbed onto the tigerkin, draping bodies of various sizes over long arms and bony shoulders and, in the case of a particularly enthusiastic Juliet, on top of his head. With the children clinging to him like tiny monkeys, tails wagging in delight, Flynn stood and jogged out of the barn.

"What the fuck," Jaxon breathed, and Tobias found himself nodding in agreement.

Sarah pressed a hand to her heart. "Is he -"

"You can trust Flynn," Aislinn said quickly. "He'd give his life for children."

"I'm seriously weirded out right now but you know what? Screw it." Zeke shook his head with a laugh. "Come on Jax, Sarah - follow that tiger before he disappears."

Tobias managed to hold himself in until they'd gone, then he dragged Aislinn into the shadows of a support beam so he could examine her body inch by inch without having to look at shattered syringes and bear corpses. "You're really okay?"

"I'm really okay," she replied, but something haunted shifted behind her eyes.

"What? What is it?" Tobias leant close enough that their breath mingled. Her scent rose around him, honeysuckle with smooth vanilla overtones mingled with blood and sweat and bear. "What's wrong?"

"I'll tell you later, when we're safer," she murmured. Something must have moved in his face because she added, "I promise, Tobias. Just... not here. Please."

He ran his hands over her shoulders, pushing back thick, red-brown hair so he could trace her cheekbones with his lips. "All right."

"Thank you." She turned her face into his, brushed her lips against his own. "You can stop rubbing your scent all over me now." He froze. Aislinn gave a throaty chuckle and nipped his jaw. "Flynn's no threat to you, Tobias. Don't let him under your skin."

"You say that," He growled. "He *kissed* you."

"He's transitional too, though he has a far better handle on it than you do." Aislinn pulled back a little, her eyes tracking towards the door. "Flynn's got a tough exterior and he's half wild. His Sabre energies are the strongest ever recorded and you can see the proof of that on his body - likewise, aspects of his personality mirror that animalistic nature. He's very tactile. Very, *very* tactile; but he won't be inappropriate without invitation."

"He kissed you," Tobias repeated, feeling unusually petulant.

"And he may do it again," Aislinn said firmly. "Which is why I'm trying to explain it to you, Tobias. It's not romantic. Okay?"

Tobias wasn't sure he agreed but he nodded anyway. "I don't want him to freak you out."

"Me either, but you also have to trust me enough to let me handle it," Aislinn returned, cupping his jaw in gentle fingers. "Can you do that?"

"Of course," Tobias straightened indignantly. "I would never -"

"Don't say that, Tobias Greenwood, because a week ago you would've gladly fed me to the crocodiles," Aislinn returned. Unspoken between them was the certain knowledge that Flynn, for all his idiosyncratic tendencies, had never reacted badly to her altered scent. "Come on; we'll meet him outside."

Feeling suitably cowed, Tobias nevertheless hooked his fingers through Aislinn's as they picked their way through the debris littering the barn's floor and stepped out into the night. Flynn prowled up out of the darkness, bending to rub his head against Aislinn much like a cat would do. "They're on their way," he said, his thick accent curling through the night as though it owned the darkness.

"Good. Thanks." Aislinn stroked his satin hair with her free hand, eliciting the return of Flynn's loud, rumbling purr. "Sorry to volunteer you both for the run - I need it."

The tigerkin shrugged with curious fluidity. "I'm always good for a run. What about Olaf, though? Fucker got away."

"We can't do anything right now. The pups have to be our first priority - but once everyone's safe, we'll start making plans," Aislinn promised. Her serious face faded into a gentle smile. "Besides, I've missed you. Surely you won't deny me a drink and a hug or two?"

"Of course not." Flynn's chest rumbled with a purr, amber eyes glittering with a light that was anything but plutonic. "I've missed you, too."

In typical Aislinn style, she missed the cues completely, turning to Tobias and lifting their joined hands to nip at his fingers. "What about you? Ready for a run?"

No, Tobias thought, he was most definitely not. His body hurt, he had no clear recollection of anything that had gone on, and Flynn was watching him over the top of Aislinn's head with smug amber eyes that seemed to glow in the dark. "Sure," he said, and dragged his wolf form on like a coat.

A moment later Aislinn followed suit and then Flynn, his tiger body equally as breathtaking as his midform; pure muscle and deadly energy that towered head and shoulders over Tobias, whose wolf form was by no means small. How he was supposed to compete with a male like that, he had no idea. As though sensing the train of his thoughts, Aislinn huffed and nudged him with her nose.

Then they were off, Ash leading the way across moon-silvered grass which waved in the gentle wind. Flynn bounded along on one side with the ease of long term association and Tobias loped along on the other, doing his best to keep his aching body moving and wondering, not for the first time, if he was well and truly in over his head.

~ The End ~

Thanks for reading!

Can't wait for the next instalment?

Keep up to date with all the latest shenanigans at:
www.sliceofsammy.com

About the Author

Hi, I'm Sam!

I've been writing my whole life, scribbling stories on anything close to hand – from the shopping list to napkins to post-it notes (don't mention post-its to hubby haha).

I grew up reading fantasy of the likes of Anne McCaffrey, Terry Pratchett, and their peers. I'm also a lifelong vampire fan, along with all things spooky. In my late teens I was introduced to paranormal romance and discovered a whole new layer of storytelling with a bit of a spicy edge! Taking what I learnt from all of the above, I devoted myself to creating full-bodied characters, meaty plots, epic adventure, and a little bit of naughty sauce on the side.

I completed a Diploma of Professional Writing and Editing after high school and spent the next several years in my writing cave, working on a novel that is now in a drawer somewhere, followed by a couple of others who shared the same fate. (What can I say? I'm a recovering perfectionist.)

I came close to debuting my novel career in 2009, then ended up pregnant and took some time off to have kids. I debuted for real in 2019 with *Sorcery and Stardust* and won ARRA's Favourite Debut Romance Author for 2019, which was extremely cool!

I write speculative fiction that is a fusion of multiple sub-genres and therefore doesn't fit particularly well into any of them, but after many years and a lot of angst, I'm okay with that. I love all my characters and their stories for different reasons, but have a soft spot for an excellent villain and a tortured protagonist.

I currently live in south east Melbourne, Victoria, with my hubby, two kids, a Golden Retriever and a turtle. I volunteer with the Romance Writers of Australia, and I'm passionate about great writing, interesting characters, chai tea and happily ever afters.